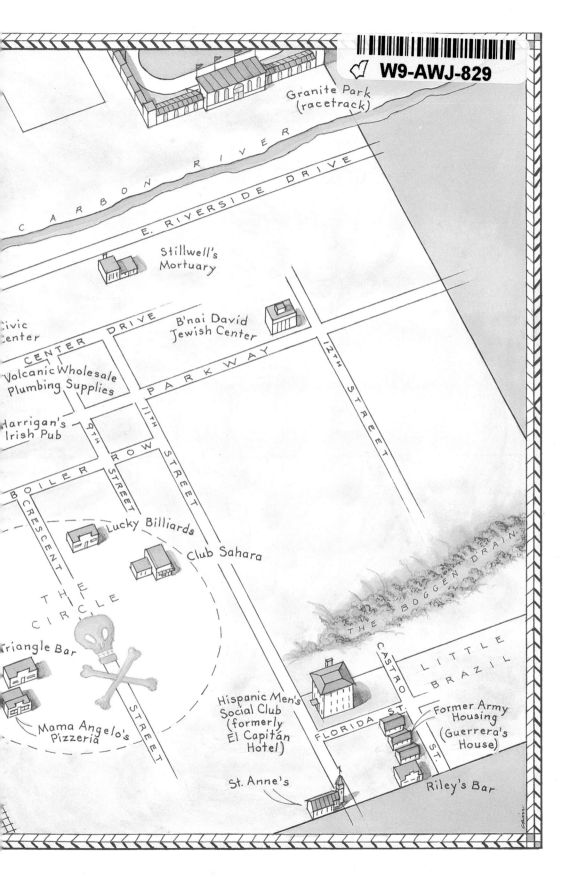

GAS CITY

BOOKS BY LOREN D. ESTLEMAN

Kill Zone
Roses Are Dead
Any Man's Death
Motor City Blue
Angel Eyes
The Midnight Man
The Glass Highway
Sugartown
Every Brilliant Eye
Lady Yesterday
Downriver
Silent Thunder
Sweet Women Lie
Never Street
The Witchfinder
The Hours of the Virgin
A Smile on the Face of the Tiger
*City of Widows**
*The High Rocks**
*Billy Gashade**
*Stamping Ground**
*Aces & Eights**
*Journey of the Dead**
*Jitterbug**
*Thunder City**
*The Rocky Mountain Moving Picture Association**
*The Master Executioner**
*Black Powder, White Smoke**
*White Desert**
Sinister Heights
*Something Borrowed, Something Black**
*Port Hazard**
*Poison Blonde**
*Retro**
*Little Black Dress**
*Nicotine Kiss**
*The Undertaker's Wife**
*The Adventures of Johnny Vermillion**
*American Detective**
*Gas City**

**A Forge Book*

GAS CITY

LOREN D. ESTLEMAN

A TOM DOHERTY ASSOCIATES BOOK
NEW YORK

GAS CITY

Copyright © 2007 by Loren D. Estleman

Edited by James Frenkel

Endpaper map by David Cain

Book design by Spring Hoteling

A Forge Book
Published by Tom Doherty Associates, LLC
175 Fifth Avenue
New York, NY 10010

www.tor-forge.com

Forge® is a registered trademark of Tom Doherty Associates, LLC.

Library of Congress Cataloging-in-Publication Data

Estleman, Loren D.
  Gas City / Loren D. Estleman.—1st ed.
    p. cm.
  "A Tom Doherty Associates book."
  ISBN-13: 978-0-7653-1956-2
  ISBN-10: 0-7653-1956-X
  1. Serial murders—Fiction.   2. Police chiefs—Fiction.   3. Mafia—Fiction.   4.
Power (Social sciences)—Fiction.   I. Title.
  PS3555.S84G37 2008
  813'.54—dc22

                                                                        2007034927

First Edition: January 2008

Printed in the United States of America

0 9 8 7 6 5 4 3 2 1

To Debi, the soul in the body of work

Pandemonium, city and proud seat
Of Lucifer.

—JOHN MILTON, *Paradise Lost*

GAS CITY

Break of Day

A couple of days before Arch Killian's seventy-eighth birthday, he mentioned to his son that he'd outlived all his old friends and no one was left to serve as his pallbearer.

His son said, "Dad, isn't that the idea?"

"Not when I was young. The idea was to go first and leave a lot of people to miss you."

"I'll miss you."

"You're just used to me."

It occurred to Arch too that he was one of the few left who had a personal memory of the original Morse McGrath. The number of those who even remembered a time when the old man was alive was small, and each new harvest of obituaries in *The Derrick* made him wonder if he was going to keel off his porch some morning and be written up in the almanac like the last passenger pigeon. Or more accurately the last gray bird who had seen one.

He remembered that encounter every morning, when his doctor-mandated three-mile walk took him to the top of Factory Hill. That was the moment the sun struck orange crucifixes off the onion-shaped storage tanks belonging to the McGrath refinery.

The play of light, crowned by the eternal flame fluttering atop the two-hundred-foot stack, painted an abstract picture of the man who had built it: fierce and florid, ablaze with a self-faith that at times licked over into fanatic, then in his final years burned there perpetually.

Arch had been twenty-six then, and had worked for Carbon Valley Surveying eighteen months. The job involved searching for buried irons and sighting along ranks of trees with ancient rusted fencing grown into the goitered trunks—in effect, reasserting property lines through archaeology. Most of the boundaries had grown over, with only the odd spent shotgun shell or calcified condom to imply the existence of civilization. He'd been bitten by stray dogs, set aflame by poison ivy, and served a feast to ticks and chiggers whose bite-scars would still be visible as high as his calves half a century later.

He'd never been happier. No straw boss crowded him, his schedule was a polite suggestion only, and his partner was loyal. Lou Pupkin was in awe of the theodolite; therefore he was in awe of Arch, and accepted his measurements like Noah.

It was like being a cowboy. He'd dressed like one, in a floppy hat, flannel shirt, leather-reinforced breeches, and stovepipe boots, and cultivated a Buffalo Bill goatee. Times were gaudy, just after a war, lots of money around, and he'd had no wife to moderate his tastes. Maybe if he had, he wouldn't have caught the old man's eye and his life would have been different.

So surveyors were an independent lot. Because they drew up the property lines there was an unspoken understanding that the lines didn't apply to them. The understanding didn't include most property owners, some of whose fathers and uncles had been tried and acquitted of burying trespassers on grounds of justifiable homicide. The law had changed its view, but the owners' sons and nephews hadn't. It wasn't unusual in the old days for surveyors to disappear, their remains and equipment showing up a year or two later, after a hard rain and deer hunters got into places no one else ever went. By then it was next to impossible to convict anyone of murder, however heavily suspicion might lie upon the owner of the property where the bones were discovered. Shotguns were as common as Bibles and the pellets weren't traceable. Arch had taken the advice of veterans and carried a broom-handled Mauser in a flap holster on his hip.

On a thick day late in June, he and Lou Pupkin were in search of the western boundary of the old railroad right-of-way along the river. The city had bought a section to develop a park. The property ran bang up against undeveloped land belonging to McGrath, but it hadn't been surveyed since before the old courthouse had burned down. The irons had long since returned to corruption and all Arch and Lou had to work from were restored plat maps and petrified stumps where the tree line had stood before clear-cutting.

Most of the way ran through swamp. Lou was afraid of snakes. It took him half an hour to walk two hundred yards, spreading the tall grass in front of him with the stakes and probing old muskrat huts before he'd plant a foot. They started at seven and by noon both men were plastered with black and green muck, lumped all over with mosquito bites, and barely speaking to each other.

"Arch."

Arch, elevating one foot of his tripod with a hunk of bark, heard the motor at the same time Lou saw the car, its pistons ticking crazily like a watch without a balance wheel. He straightened to observe the vehicle approaching across the field bordering the swamp. It was a boxy old touring car with a high center of gravity and a flat windshield that caught the sun in sheets. The body rocked independently of its suspension and the hoop wheels bucked and dipped over the cornstubs and furrows, warping and bouncing back like a car in a cartoon. Any modern vehicle would have stuck or snapped an axle. Any modern driver wouldn't have attempted the journey except in a half-track.

He'd expected it to stop on the edge of the swamp. It kept coming, dashing water out of the wiggler-infested puddles, until it hung up on a toppled elm, whose tarantula of mossy roots snagged in the undercarriage. The driver tried reverse, then forward. Gears crunched, the ticking of the motor quickened to a clatter and began to shake itself apart. The car stalled. Then damned if the maniac behind the wheel didn't try to start it again. The starter ground and ground. It grew mushy and then the battery died with a dry rattle. Steam poured as thick as lager from the radiator. The door on the driver's side popped open and Morse McGrath climbed down and plunged ahead on foot.

He looked taller and thinner than he did in photographs, an animated jackstraw in a black suit and a gray homburg with the brim square across his forehead. He was pale and clean-shaven and although he carried a cane he didn't lean on it, pumping it instead in one hand like a drive-rod and holding down his hat with the other. Whatever propelled this assembly had simply abandoned one machine for another, smaller and more agile. He hopped over snarls of weed and sank up to his knees in scum, but his line of advance never altered. His deep-set black eyes remained on Arch, fixed like a swooping owl's on a movement in the grass. It was the unbreakable stare of a madman. Arch unbuttoned the flap on his holster.

McGrath stopped; not, Arch was sure, because of the defensive gesture, but because the old man had reached the last dry patch before the grassy knob where the survey team stood. A black pool of unknown depth separated them for a distance of fifteen feet.

"You're on private land."

He spoke in the sharp nasal twang Arch had heard in newsreels. Brown and ochre mud had turned his black broadcloth into camouflage.

Arch explained they were taking a shortcut through the swamp.

"I don't want you driving no stakes on my property."

"We're not. We're just trying to get to the other side."

"Who sent you, kneelers?"

"We're surveying for the city."

"Kneelers, the bunch of them. Papists. You're not passing through, you're taking measurements. I won't have Roman idolatry on my own soil."

Arch admitted he was using the firm ground to line up a reading. The tripod's feet kept sinking into the earth on the city side.

"You a kneeler?"

He had been raised Catholic. No priest had heard his confession since the army. "With respect, Mr. McGrath, I don't see it's any of your business."

Lou sucked air through his teeth. He held his bundle of stakes on his shoulder like a rifle on parade.

"So you know who I am. Who are you, or ain't that my business neither?"

Arch told him his name.

"Shanty Irish. You're one of them, all right. What's the matter, ashamed to own up to it?"

"You've got a right to throw me off your property, Mr. Mc-Grath. You've even got the right to ask personal questions. I just don't have to answer them."

"I bought the right to throw you off. Hard cash. Your people would call that Mammon, though you didn't when you squeezed it out of Jews and atheists on the rack. You're still on my land," he added.

"We wouldn't be if you'd stop talking."

The narrow pale face went deep copper. The cane shot up over his head. "Get out! Get off my land!" He was shrieking. An acre away, a flock of startled grouse took to the sky, their wings jackhammering.

Arch looked away from McGrath for the first time, making eye contact with Lou, whose mouth hung open. Arch jerked his head and folded his tripod.

The old man's high-pitched shouting ended in a strangled rattle. The sound made Arch turn. McGrath was on the ground, apparently wrestling with himself. He was still holding the cane above his head as if he were standing, but one of his old-fashioned high-topped shoes kicked its heel on the edge of the brackish pool, splattering lichen-stained water as far as his vest. His face was magenta and he was still making the strangling noise.

"Jesus God, he's rabid." Lou crossed himself.

Arch dropped the tripod from his shoulder and plunged into the water. It was thigh deep and cold as iron. His feet sank in the muck bottom and kept sinking. He pitched forward, using his weight and momentum to free them, one at a time, then sank again and had to start over. Finally he got a sole on solid earth, grasped a clump of razor grass near the base, and hauled himself onto dry ground. McGrath was at his feet, body twisted into a braid, his knuckles yellow where he gripped the cane. His hat had fallen off. Strands of thin gray hair were pasted like seaweed to his forehead. Only the whites of his eyes showed.

"Don't let him bite you!" Lou called out.

Arch hesitated. In fact, the old man's chin was covered with lather. Then Arch unbuckled his leather tool belt and knelt astraddle the thin figure. He gripped him with his thighs and pressed one of the bony shoulders to the ground while with the other hand he grasped McGrath's jaw between thumb and forefinger. It was clenched hard; the muscles on either side stood out like doorknobs.

At last the teeth came apart a quarter-inch and Arch let go of the shoulder and jerked the wooden-handled screwdriver from its loop on the belt next to the gun holster. He inserted the steel shaft between the two rows of teeth, pressed down McGrath's tongue with the blade, and with his other hand worked a section of the tool belt into the space until it stuck out on both sides of the jaw. He pulled out the screwdriver then and let it drop to the ground. The tongue tried to retreat, but he grasped the end of the belt and with both hands jammed the edge as far back as the corners of the mouth. He held it there until he was sure the old man wouldn't spit it out and swallow his tongue. Then he turned and swung one knee back over and sat on his heels. He took off his hat and swept his sleeve across his forehead. He was panting and his shirt was soaked through with sweat, as wet as his pants.

He waited. He didn't know how long these things lasted. What if the old man died? Was he liable? He was framing his defense when McGrath opened his mouth and took in a long wheezing lungful of air. He coughed. The belt slithered out from between his teeth. His irises were back, murky but sentient. They moved from side to side and fixed on Arch.

"Get . . . off . . . my . . . land."

Saliva bubbled in his mouth. He turned his head, spat, and struggled up onto his elbows. Arch rose and stuck out his hand. The old man looked at it, then took it. His hand was slimy with sweat and dirt, but his grip was strong. It was like grasping a garden claw. Arch leaned back and McGrath came to his feet. He snatched his hand back then, looked around and found his hat, and bent to scoop it up. He staggered. Arch took a step, but the old man found his balance and slapped the hat against his hip to knock off the dirt. He was still holding the cane. He turned and made his way back toward his touring car, using the cane this time as it was intended. Arch hung back and watched him pick his way through the puddles, growing firmer and straighter with each step.

At the car he paused with one foot on the running board and put on his hat. "Get off my land."

There was some comedy when the car wouldn't start and Lou had to wade across and help Arch push it off the elm and then continue pushing, slipping and cursing, until the starter caught. McGrath nearly hung the car up again turning it around, but he punished the gears, rammed down the throttle, and jounced away over the gopher mounds and ruts.

"Well, you're welcome, you old shit," Arch said.

Lou said, "Told you he was rabid."

Arch was living in a rooming house on Boiler Row, a drafty barn with a mansard roof he would recognize years later in Charles Addams cartoons. The woman down the hall gave piano lessons to students who consistently lacked talent, and the Marxist next door saw furry green capitalists at two o'clock in the morning. Ten days after the incident with McGrath, Arch had his first visitor. He was a skinny young roughneck in riding breeches and lace-up boots and a leather aviator's jacket, a pair of goggles perched atop his tweed cap. The landlady wouldn't let him inside. His Indian motorcycle farted gray balls of smoke out of its twin pipes next to the curb.

"Mister, I'm supposed to tell you this here's the twentieth century. If you won't pop for a phone, at least get a pigeon." He handed Arch an envelope.

Arch thanked him and shut the door, feeling a burn of shame for not offering a tip. He'd sent his pay home that morning and had just enough left to buy lunch through the week. The neatly typewritten note asked Mr. Killian if he would be kind enough to stop by the McGrath refinery Friday morning at eight. It was signed by James B. Sharp, identified below his signature as Morse McGrath's personal secretary.

That was the week Arch Killian went to work for McGrath, at a starting salary double what he'd been getting from Carbon Valley. (To the penny; clearly, someone had researched it.) He stayed thirty-nine years and never met Morse McGrath again face to face.

I

The Crisis

CHAPTER ONE

He was on the telephone with Marty's sister when the nun came up and touched his arm. He pegged the receiver and went with her, moving fast.

Afterward, the nun said it often happened that way. It was as if they waited until they were alone. He'd been in the room with Marty all evening, listening to her labored but steady breathing, and had only stepped out to stretch his legs and report to his sister-in-law, who was stuck in Mexico, some little shit village whose switchboard shut down for two hours at siesta time. He'd just got back in time to hold Marty's hand while her blood pressure dropped into the basement.

The nurses asked him to wait outside for a few minutes. They called him "Mr. Russell." No one had called him mister in more than thirty years. He wondered if they knew who he was, apart from Marty's husband. It didn't seem possible that they wouldn't, but then the hospital seemed to exist entirely within its own boundaries, like the Vatican. Even the parking lot attendant peered down at you from his booth as if he were about to ask to see your passport.

He thought they'd spend the time tidying her up, but when he was allowed back into the room, all they'd done was draw the respirator from her throat and unhook the wires and tubes. She lay with her eyes and mouth gaping, damp hair smeared at her temples. Rage shot through him like an electrical charge. He hadn't reached that level of fury since he'd stopped wearing the uniform. It filled the space Marty had occupied. He wanted to break things, push in faces. People were meat. It didn't matter that this one had kept her fifth-grade perfect attendance certificate in a frame on the wall, miscarried twice, given birth finally after seven months on her back to a daughter who turned whore at fifteen and ran off with carnival scum, and then a son, dead at twenty in a minefield; that she hadn't cursed God even then, as he had. Instead she'd added Saturday Mass to her schedule from then until she couldn't get up the cathedral steps without being carried, a thing she was too Sligo-proud to permit. The nurses and the young squirt doctor had addressed her as Martha Rose because that was the name on the admissions sheet, but he knew that among themselves she was Twelve, and not even Room Twelve. He hated them with a heat that was almost pleasant.

And then the rage and heat were gone, and there was a hole through him and he had to turn so the wind wouldn't whistle through it. He'd been preparing for this moment for weeks—*years*, he corrected, from the time the results of the first tests had come back and he'd stopped arguing with them—and he'd hoped the dread of the waiting would give way to a sense of release. He'd felt it for a moment, with the last exhalation, when she took her leave of her body, a lacy apparition in a cheap religious print. But this was a new level of emptiness. What he'd thought was the bottom collapsed beneath his weight, the thinnest of crusts, and he went plummeting yet again. It was like falling in a dream. They said if you woke up before you hit, you were okay, but if you didn't, well, that was when people died in their sleep. It seemed better than this eternal falling.

He closed her eyes, a kneading sort of operation, not at all like turning down the slats in Venetian blinds, and tipped up her chin gently. It would be the last thing he did for her, after months of helping her dress and undress, trimming her nails and hair, and he wondered how he would fill the time from then on. There would be arrangements to make, calls to place, beginning with Marty's sister; after that, what? Wake, vigil, services. Friends and family and near strangers eating his food and telling him stories about his wife, half of which he'd never heard and would only remind him of the time they hadn't spent together, all those nights he'd slept at headquarters because it hadn't seemed worth going home just to turn around and come back for the morning turnout. Then they would all shake his hand and leave.

And after that, what?

When he turned from the bed, Hugh Dungannon was standing in the doorway. His suit was virgin wool, black with a sheen like polished walnut, and as always he wore a fresh clerical collar, but he managed to look rumpled just the same. He was a big man, at war with his size. He partially succeeded in shrinking in upon himself, but his clothes were not so flexible, gathering and wrinkling in the spaces he left. His hair was white and splendidly thick, but he chopped it close to his scalp, calling attention to his cauliflower ear and making his face with its prognathous lower half stick out like a shorn lion's. He had the golden-brown, unblinking eyes, and a deep dimple in his upper lip that suggested the leonine cleft. He'd been at Our Lady of Perpetual Misery for so many years even Russell had to remind himself they'd sat at adjoining desks in Sister Catherine Eustatius' English Composition class. It was the sister's powerful right hand that had given Hugh that ear.

"I'm sorry, Francis," he said. "She was in a state of grace."

"I know. One of the nuns told me you were here with your stick."

"Six hours ago, it was. I thought you might be here as well."

"I couldn't sit any longer. I went out for a quick one."

"Just one?" Dungannon smiled.

"Practically. It goes a lot farther than it used to."

"Not much else does. Remember when we tore your da's sofa apart looking for a quarter to buy beer?"

"Anyway, the time came and I knew you were here, but I didn't get off the stool. I figured if a bishop couldn't pray her across without my help, what good's the whole business?"

"Now you sound like an atheist."

"I know He exists. We had a falling out."

Dungannon changed the subject. They had had this discussion before. "I'll stand you to a cup of coffee. The cafeteria's closed, but they keep a pot on for me. I don't sleep but four hours either way."

Russell hesitated. The habit of staying with Marty had gotten its hooks in deep. His desertion that afternoon had had no precedent.

The bishop read his thoughts. "She's in good hands. You can make the arrangements tomorrow."

The hallway was quiet, as if the building itself were whispering. Dungannon's patent-leather pumps, hand-lasted to his disproportionately small feet, made soft squishing sounds on the linoleum. Russell's rubber heels squeaked. The noise mortified him. A clock suspended from the ceiling read two minutes past eleven. In an hour it would be the first morning in fifty-five years without Martha Rose Noonan.

Only one row of fluorescents glowed in the cafeteria. Russell preferred the muted effect, but hadn't the energy to protest when Dungannon palmed up the rest of the switches. He regretted agreeing to coffee, wished he'd pled exhaustion and gone home. Steel and Formica gleamed in the bright light. The floor had been waxed within the hour. It smelled like High Mass.

"Me own mug." Dungannon plocked down an oversize white vessel in front of Russell and filled it from the carafe. He socketed two cardboard cups together and poured for himself. No light showed through the stream.

Russell sipped the bitter stuff and set down the mug. "Mother of God."

"Some days I just chew the grounds." The bishop sat down and raised his container in both hands, ignoring the fold-out handles. "Who are you using?"

"Stillwell brothers."

"Good men. I baptized Dennis. They use the modern method. No formaldehyde. Does this talk upset you?"

Russell shook his head. He was only half listening. "Marty had a poem she liked. By Rossetti."

"I'll use it. Christina?"

"Dante Gabriel. From *The House of Life*. 'As when two men have loved a woman well,' is how it starts."

The leonine face smoothed out. "I didn't think she'd remember."

"She never mentioned it. Not once in thirty-seven years."

"You married a saint."

"She was a blowtop. She threw a skillet at me once."

"I'd have thought she'd be more original."

"It seemed inspired enough at the time. I earned it, I guess. I never was much in the husband department."

"She knew when you married she'd have to share you with the city."

"The city didn't get any bargain, either."

"She died, Francis. You didn't kill her."

"It ain't that. She always said a mackinaw was as warm as mink. I took it another way."

"You were a good provider. House on West Riverside, new car every two years, box at the Corinthian. I know how you feel about opera, so that counts double."

"She said she'd have been as happy with one bedroom and a bleacher at Granite Park."

"They're supposed to say that."

"I took it as criticism. She was saying I should've stayed a cop."

"What do you mean, kick in doors and shout at felons to put their hands on their head? She'd never know if you were coming home."

"She never knew as it was."

The bishop took a slug of coffee. "There's a misconception about priests, that we're not of the world and don't know its ways. But I've heard more confessions than you. Some men keep mistresses, beat their wives, perform unspeakable crimes upon their sons and daughters. You're no transgressor."

"You need good works to pass through the eye of the needle."

"Even so, it's a little late for this conversation, unless you want to put the uniform back on. Who'd run the place when you got yourself killed?"

"Who's running it now?"

Someone was operating a floor buffer in the hall, a low-grade hum. Dungannon glanced that way. This time Russell read his thoughts. You're never more than twenty feet from another pair of ears.

"You're the best chief this town ever had," Dungannon said. "There's voting citizens lived here their whole lives never knew another."

"Citizens in jail, too. Sneak thieves and dopers. I can't remember when was the last time we arrested a man wearing a necktie."

"Maybe we should start a program in the Circle. Hand them out at Christmas along with the secondhand overcoats."

"Maybe we should knock on some doors on West Riverside."

The golden-brown gaze rested on him. "You're worn out, Francis. You ought to go home and sleep."

Russell smiled. "Don't worry, Hugh. I'm talking through my hat is all."

"I know that. Not everyone does. And not everyone has had my practice at keeping secrets."

"I'll get you that book of poems. It's the ninety-first stanza. 'Lost on Both Sides.'"

"I might have it at the rectory. Father Gillespie taught poetry, remember."

"I'd rather you didn't read from a book belonging to him."

"I never knew you didn't like him."

"He committed suicide."

"He fell under the interurban."

"Threw himself."

"The cardinal investigated. He ruled it an accident."

"I investigated, too. Gillespie had cancer of the spine. Morphine wasn't enough and he started going to the Circle for heroin."

"He was in pain."

"He was a priest."

"You expect too much of people, Francis. Starting with yourself."

"That's what Marty said."

"She was a smart woman."

"She was no smarter than she wanted to be."

He left Dungannon sitting there, turning his cup between his palms. On the way out of the hospital he passed an ox-faced orderly buffing the floor. The orderly didn't look up.

CHAPTER TWO

Before the wells and the refinery—before Gas City, when brochures invited a restless population to settle in Garden Grove—the city fathers had commissioned the construction of a variety theater on the north end of Commercial Street adjoining the arboretum. The arboretum was gone, replaced by a housing project funded by the Defense Department to shelter refinery workers during wartime, but the Corinthian remained, a homely gray box stunted by the Deco and neoclassical high-rises that had sprung up around it.

The interior was more impressive. Gutted during a shabby period of reincarnation as a movie house, then restored for Grand Opera at double the cost of original construction, the lobby presented Greek pilasters, Egyptian friezes, and a soaring staircase, beyond which an auditorium done in gilded plaster and burgundy velvet seated twenty-five hundred, with an orchestra pit built to accommodate one hundred pieces. The somewhat narrow proscenium had during its history showcased talented tenors on their way east to New York and superannuated coloraturas on their way west to dinner theaters and cruise ships. Ernestine Schumann-Heink was generally con-

ceded to have expired there in the middle of a production of *The Bo-
hemian Girl.*

First in line when season boxes went on sale was Anthony Zeno,
proprietor of Volcanic Wholesale Plumbing Supplies, who also
presided over the theater's board of directors and sat on the Gas City
Cultural and Civic Improvement Commission. Slender and white-
haired, with patrician eyebrows and the nose of a Sioux chief, he
managed to appear as comfortable in full dress as he did in denims
when he tended his herb patch Sundays. He attended openings with
a copy of the score and libretto, and followed each line and lyric
with a finger, checking places where the performance departed from
the text and writing a polite letter of correction to the director the
next morning. He adored opera with the attention of a U.S.-born
Genoese, and liked to remark that lack of talent was all that had prevented him from selecting the stage as his career. "That, and Joe
Gallante wiring six sticks of dynamite to the battery of Fat Paulie
Buffo's Cadillac." More and more he liked to joke about those unla-
mented days.

Almost before Fat Paulie came down, Zeno was put on a train to
Gas City to take his place. He hadn't expected to remain long. He'd
had his eye on the Manhattan Dry Cleaners Guild, which to his
thinking was not being run efficiently, and he intended to have
arranged a number of advantageous contracts with the McGrath refinery by the time the New York slot opened so that he would be
considered favorably to fill it. Two things happened to alter that
plan. First, the plumbing supply business, purchased at a bankruptcy
sale merely to give him something to declare to the Internal Revenue Service, proved surprisingly successful in the hands of the directors with whom he'd placed it. The profits for the first year
exceeded the custodial fee his outside investors paid him to manage
their brothel and horse parlor interests in The Circle, and caused
him to consult a tax attorney to set up shelters for his legitimate
income. Second, his wife Trina died at age twenty-eight—of a con-
genital heart defect, as reported in *The Derrick.* She had dissolved
thirty-four phenobarbitol capsules in a glass of vodka and drunk it

while listening to the radio. In the course of his mourning, he discovered he'd made friends, first among them Francis X. Russell, the local chief of police, who called him every night and attended the races with him afternoons at Granite Park. In time their visits became less frequent, but they had lunch on occasion at Rinaldi's and played cards at each other's house, and almost before he knew it, Anthony Zeno had put in twenty-five years in Gas City.

He reminded himself to call Francis after the opera. Marty had never approved of their association, he knew, but neither had she objected to their spending time together. The chief had few friends—people respected him but thought him aloof, not the sort to share a pitcher with and argue about who hit harder, Sailor Bantry or the Macroom Mauler—and when her sister visited she worried about him sitting in the parlor smoking his pipe while they caught up on the sister's travels over Irish coffee in the kitchen. In her world, even the company of a hooligan was preferable to one's own. And now she was gone, and it was Francis who needed to be taken to the races.

Zeno should have called before this. They hadn't had much contact since the wedding. Three years ago, that was; he supposed he should start referring to it as his marriage. Deanne was not Trina. She was half his age, to start, and she only came with him to the Corinthian because everyone in the place knew what a season box cost and she shone whenever a pair of opera glasses were trained on her from the orchestra. People saw her that way, heard her clear, upward-canting laugh, and wondered among themselves (he'd heard them, whispers carrying as they did, farther than normal speech) what kind of pills he took to keep her interested in bed. It never occurred to them the flame had no heat. He and Deanne went out as often as they did because the silence at home was like a throbbing ache. Her ash-blonde, blue-eyed, firm-breasted energy in public, clinging to his arm and hinting broadly at the lewd goings-on under the Zeno roof, almost convinced even him they were a normal couple.

And now he'd been thinking too much and had missed most of the second act of *Fra Diavolo*. He paged through the script, drawing an arched eyebrow and a smirk from Deanne, who had adopted the attitude that his interest in anything more challenging than Greco-Roman wrestling was an affectation: Scarface Al telling the boys in the press that with him, "Grand Opera's the berries." The last time she'd said that, he'd had to restrain himself from slapping her. At that moment, her eyes had lit with a malicious glint, her point proven. And he knew she'd go on, stockpiling her ammunition and refining her tactics, until her theory became fact for everyone to see. It was women who made gangsters, with their suicides and derision.

On stage, Lorenzo was working himself up to invite Lord All-cash to a duel. Zeno found the thread and had become engrossed when Toby, seated behind him, leaned forward and whispered in his ear. He turned his head then and saw the usher standing inside the curtains. He had a call.

Zeno rose, laid the script in the big man's lap, and handed him his gold pen. "Keep track."

The receiver was dangling from the wall phone near the stairs. He picked it up and waited until the usher drifted down the steps before speaking his name into the mouthpiece.

"Mr. White will be passing through tonight," said the caller. "Can you be at home between eleven P.M. and midnight?"

He said he would, and the conversation ended. The voice was one he'd been familiar with for ten years, without being able to fix it to a face or even a nationality or gender. Coaches and vocal exercises had shorn the smooth contralto of its origins until it was as round and featureless as a river stone.

He returned to his seat, and although he resumed following the score and libretto, the company may have substituted another opera in his absence for as much of it as he retained. More than a year had passed since he had last spoken with Mr. White. Mr. White did not "pass through" Gas City unless a subject of sufficient importance had come up to detach him from his comfortable forty acres upstate. It didn't help Zeno's concentration that he was more than half certain what the subject was.

Zeno had time, after the final curtain call, to go backstage and congratulate the company on behalf of the theater, but tonight he forebore the treasured privilege. He avoided the predictable small talk with acquaintances by dispatching Toby to bring the car around to the rear of the building and left with Deanne through the fire exit. She made no comment, and when they returned home went up to her room without being asked; Zeno was not to be interrupted at the Corinthian except in cases of extreme urgency. For the three years they had shared a house, "extreme urgency" had always meant Mr. White.

The house stood at what some older citizens still considered the less fashionable end of West Riverside Drive. Zeno's predecessor and his bodyguards had occupied two floors of the Railroad Arms, a brief walk from the whorehouses and betting boards in his charge. Zeno had higher aspirations, but had been too aware of local sensibilities to plunk himself down in the middle of gentrified society. In the meantime, the refinery business had expanded, and with it the fortunes of the community. Young executives with an urge to nest had edged out the hardware stores and working-class neighborhoods that separated his two-story Tudor from the walled estates of the McGraths and their satellites, and now his thirty-five hundred square feet of brick and stone was one of the less ostentatious homes on his block. Residents who gleefully pointed it out as the lair of the notorious "Tony Z" invariably had to press hard to convince their visitors. The absence of a formidable fence, floodlights, and baleful dogs disappointed the idly curious, and caused crime buffs to demote his standing in the "organization." In truth he had few rivals for his substantial but mundane responsibilities, and considered even such protection as Toby offered a symbolic necessity at best. His bodyguard did not live on the premises, returning most nights to a small furnished apartment on Commercial Street.

Tonight, Zeno didn't dismiss Toby. Protocol demanded someone besides himself open the door to his visitor. While he waited, he poured a glass of club soda with a smudge of bourbon and sat in his small study on the second floor, drawing calm from the sight of his rows of books and record albums.

At 11:48, the doorbell rang downstairs. Zeno finished his drink, poured another—all soda this time—and measured an inch of

Napoleon into the bottom of a snifter for his guest to abandon after one sip, a criminal waste of a resource more precious than water. He didn't know if Mr. White even appreciated the difference between a premium brandy and a drugstore label. He was a little more than half convinced Mr. White enjoyed the waste more than the sip.

"Good evening, Anthony. How was the opera?"

Zeno grasped the moist hand his visitor offered as Toby drew the door shut from the hallway. The palm was hot. Mr. White had run a temperature for years that would have killed most men after three days. Early in their acquaintance, Zeno had suspected some kind of venereal disease, but he knew of no strain that remained virulent so long without destroying. After each contact he wanted to submerse his hand in alcohol.

"Not very distracting. The tenor rushed the first act. I think he had a train to catch."

Mr. White acknowledged the joke with a chuckle—he seemed to recognize humor without understanding the concept—sat down, and took his drink. Then he set the glass on the orangewood table at his elbow. This signaled the start of the meeting. A relief, because small talk with him was excruciating for all concerned.

Nicholas Bianco—who traveled under the name Mr. White— did not make himself visible to any of his people below Zeno's station; a disincentive to advance themselves, if they ever laid eyes on him. His face was puffy, with a waxen sheen, which Zeno attributed to baboon-gland injections in his forehead, cheeks, and chin. His neutral-colored hair started suspiciously low on his forehead and grew back improbably thick to the nape of his neck. He was on his fifth wife, a woman who was younger than Deanne and who still played with dolls. It was rumored that he drank his own refined urine for vitality. That was the sum total of what Zeno knew about the man, after an association of nearly forty years.

"How are things in the Circle?" Bianco asked.

"A little light this season. There was Mother's Day, and Father's Day coming up: Family time, the money stays home. School lets out next week. Business will pick up then."

"I saw your report. I mean have there been any incidents?"

"Nothing unusual. Man got in a fight with his wife in a bar and went out to his truck and blew his head through his hat with a shotgun. Woman stabbed her boyfriend in a room at the Railway Arms, didn't hit anything vital. She's out on bail. Some cars broken into."

"Just so there's no cause for energetic action."

"On our part? Not—"

"On the part of the police."

"Maybe, if any of these things happened on Magnolia or South Terrace. The agreement is to confine all such activity to the Circle."

"My information is the agreement may not hold."

"I haven't heard anything to make me think it won't."

"I'm talking about the death of Chief Russell's wife."

So he'd been right about the purpose of Mr. White's visit. Zeno was convinced he had spies in his own backyard. There were residents as near as Blacksnake Lane who were not yet aware of the chief's bereavement. "I was going to call him when I heard from you."

"That may be part of the problem. You're too close to the situation to see the hazard."

"That's a polite way of putting it."

"Don't get nettled, Anthony. Your friend Russell is in mourning. At such times it's normal to consider adjusting one's priorities. The spiritual overtakes the material, and all that. We've invested a lot of money in Gas City over the years. It isn't as if we could deduct a dead loss from our income taxes."

"Francis Russell is a man of his word. That's what got him reelected four times. If he were starting to have reservations I'd be the first one he'd tell."

"What got him reelected four times is the knowledge that anyone's wife or daughter can walk the streets of the city day or night without fear of harm, as long as she steers clear of the Circle. A tank-wiper in the McGrath plant couldn't afford to pay his taxes if he had to depend on his police force for the protection *we* pay Russell for the privilege of providing. That's what keeps our local interests in business without interference. He stays in office because everyone knows he's in your pocket."

"All the more reason to believe he'll continue to hold up his end."

"Except now he has no one to spend the money on except himself. How many suits does an aging civil servant need after he's buried his wife?"

"There's one way to settle this," Zeno said. "I'll talk to him."

"Talk is cheap."

"Exactly."

He knew he'd scored a point. For all his people feared him, Nicholas Bianco was a petty accountant at heart. He employed the finest tailors and bought the most expensive cars, but only because he preferred not to have to replace his durable goods every other year. In the little silence that followed, Mr. White actually picked up his glass a second time. But he put it back down without drinking and stood.

"You've been here a long time," he said. "That's not always good. A man forms attachments and forgets where his loyalty belongs. But I think you're too smart for that. Talk to your friend the chief."

Zeno rose, relieved. "You'll be glad you made that decision."

"I hope so. I keep thinking about a meeting I attended when I was new and very young. The Little Fellow was there, so you can appreciate how long ago that was. Someone had been subpoenaed to talk to a grand jury, and the likelihood that he'd remember who his friends were was under discussion. There were four men there besides the Little Fellow and me. Each of the four swore the man could be trusted to protect their interests. Then my turn came. Everyone was looking at me, this skinny kid from Columbus, and I can still feel the Little Fellow's eyes boring holes in my skull. I always think that what I said is the reason I'm where I am. Do you know what I said?"

" 'Why risk it?' "

Mr. White lowered his bloated lids. "I guess I told you that story. But you have to agree it's a hard point to find fault with."

"The Little Fellow's been gone a long time. The Green Point Mob was still in business, importing Mexicans and machine guns. He might have hung around longer if he'd listened to those other four a little more often."

"On that occasion he did. The man the four defended so eloquently turned state's evidence and three of them went to prison. The fourth stumbled into a sharpened toothbrush in the county jail."

"They didn't know their man as well as I know Russell."

Mr. White moved a shoulder. "Why risk it?"

Chapter Three

It had been said, by a blue-collar poet who had claimed Gas City for his home before he went to the state penitentiary on a morals charge, that no one could know health without first knowing what it is to be ill, and that no city could be great without containing something that was base and mean. Under this theory, the graceful homes along West Riverside, Magnolia, and South Terrace, the Corinthian, and even the mammoth McGrath refinery could not exist but for The Circle.

Bounded on the west by the railroad, on the east by the Boggen Drain, with its north and south perimeters defined by working-class Boiler Row and the bottom swoop of Blacksnake Lane, this relatively small area had originally been known as the Black Circle. Local lore reported that the commander of the nearby army base (now closed) drew a circle around it on a city map with a piece of black crayon in 1917, then sent in squads armed with axes and sledgehammers to dismantle it when police failed to stem the tide of crimes against enlisted men on leave. In those days its medieval streets, many of which were still paved with bricks blackened by horse manure and coal soot, had been walled with honky-tonks and picturesque bordellos whose female personnel beckoned customers from second-floor balconies. These were long gone, but the activities that had sustained them remained intact, albeit concealed behind lath-and-plaster walls and in basements where unlicensed liquor and junk were sold and consumed under tentacles of calcified pipes. All the Soldiers' Crusade had managed to do was let out the fizz, leaving behind the brackish aftertaste.

Such places serve a purpose, or the cities they live off would have found a way to get rid of them by now. In Gas City, The Circle functioned as a container for vice. It leaked prolifically, but like those lead-lined drums in which atomic waste was stored on the floor of the ocean, designed to last fifty years against a radioactive half-life of five centuries, it was considered an improvement over no stopgap at all. By agreement between Chief Russell and Anthony Zeno, the sex shops, hash dens, and craps tournaments that might otherwise have contaminated Commercial Street and the residential neighborhoods were restricted to these ten square blocks. Order was maintained by thick-bodied employees of Volcanic Wholesale Plumbing Supplies. Uniformed police were never seen except in squads once every four years, which appeared on television herding pickpockets and prostitutes into the backs of vans one week before election. The Circle boasted its own unofficial mayor in the person of Morris "Moe" Shiel, a Volcanic foreman who directed the peacekeepers and ran interference between residents and Anthony Zeno, and its own mass transit system, operated by the handful of taxi drivers who did not object to transporting passengers across Blacksnake Lane after sundown, for which they demanded and received exorbitant fares at the beginning of the journey. The only thing the area required to be considered an independent city was its own telephone exchange.

At the western edge of The Circle, separated by a narrow alley from the graffiti-snarled stone walls of the train depot, dozed the Railway Arms, home to permanents and transients. Its arched front entrance and rows of clerestory windows had been designed during the close of the nineteenth century to attract distinguished visitors from every nation, yet the hotel stood nearly alone among its contemporaries on its reputation of never having sheltered a single celebrated guest. (A cherished legend that Grover Cleveland had registered there during his whistle-stop campaign for a second term in the White House had evaporated when a local historian pointed out that ground was broken for the hotel in 1899, two years after Cleveland left office. The historian decamped for California abruptly following.) Each year, fewer trains rocked along the patched and pitted tracks, and for decades those visitors who chose modern convenience and security over historic architecture and junkies in the lobby had stayed in the convention center downtown. The income from elderly residents, dope addicts, and those guests who rented rooms by the hour was insufficient to sustain the high ceilings and fretwork of a gentler time; suspended panels had long since concealed the murals in the vaulted lobby and the brass stair rods were painted an uninspired beige. Frosted glass inserts in an octagonal counter off the registration desk still advertised cigars, cigarettes, and gum in goldpoint letters, but the space behind was dark and the loose flakes of tobacco in the humidor drawers had lain there since the Golden Age of radio comedy. The rooms, spacious once and ventilated in that ingenious fashion that predated air-conditioning, had been partitioned off into cells nine-by-twelve, their windows and transoms painted shut.

In one of them, a man named Palmer opened his eyes and meditated upon the smoke detector mounted on a wall near the ceiling. Its cover was loose and the unit dangled from its bundled wires like an eyeball hanging outside its socket. The fact it was there told him he was in room 112, 309, or 404. These were the only nonsmoking rooms in the hotel, the minimum required by the state capital. Its condition, and the murky stench of cigarettes consumed there within the past twelve hours, bore witness that some recent guest had ignored the sign on the door threatening stiff penalties for disobeying State Law HR-759. When he rotated his head on the pillow, he saw what he'd expected to see: a nightstand littered with hunch-backed butts with the name of his brand printed on them. He was the offender.

He considered turning himself in. Failure to report violations was punishable by a five-hundred-dollar fine and revocation of his hotel security license. Still considering, he sat up, felt inside his shirt pocket, found only an empty pack, and groped among the butts until he located one slightly longer than an inch. He set fire to it with a match from a book he found at the base of the lamp. A red inverted pyramid decorated the cover, with the Triangle Bar's logo scripted across it at a forty-five-degree angle. He wondered what had become of his Zippo.

He was wearing a blue shirt and the gray pleated trousers of his good suit. Both needed pressing. The nail of his right big toe poked through his argyle sock, and there was a familiar gamey smell beneath the stale tobacco that told him he hadn't changed in two days. It reminded him of deer camp. He trusted his sense of time. His nose was infallible when it came to measuring how long a particular form of corruption had been in progress. It was just his luck this least pleasant of all his detecting skills should be the last to desert him.

In the midst of this philosophizing, a key rattled in the lock and Clare Sayer came in.

She had on a knit blue sleeveless top that set off her short auburn hair, blue eyes, and the muscle tone in her upper arms. Her skin was ethereally pale, and freckled before a sunny disposition. She avoided exposure and there were no freckles visible now. Navy capri pants caught her strong calves at midpoint. She wore cork sandals and painted her toes a businesslike shade of oxblood. She had high breasts and buttocks you could bounce BBs off all day.

"It's alive," she said, when she saw he was sitting up. "I was all set to sell you to the medical school." She unstrapped her bag from her shoulder, dropped it to the floor, and changed hands on the greasy paper sack she carried.

"I hope to hell there's a bottle in there," Palmer said. The echo of his own voice cut a rusty kerf in his skull. His throat felt furrowed and his tongue seemed to be peeling.

She opened the sack under his chin. Hot grease exhaled into his face, inserted a lever under his stomach, and heaved it over.

"Jesus Christ." He pushed away the offering and clamped a hand over his nose and mouth until the spasm passed.

"Man's got to eat," she said. "That's a rule of this hotel."

"So's No Soliciting."

"You're still a fair-looking man, if I squint a little. Your hygiene needs work. Anytime I want to crawl under a dead carp, all I have to do is walk down to the Drain." As she spoke she took a cheeseburger wrapped in paper and a waxed cup with a plastic lid out of the sack and put them on the nightstand. Then she thrust the sack back at him. "Look under the fries."

Breathing through his mouth, he rooted inside. The open cardboard packet of French fries had been dumped in upside down—a drive-in regulation, he'd decided—and he groped among dry charred shoestrings until he felt the bills.

"This how they give you your change now?" He left them there and withdrew his hand.

"Some work, others sleep. I did more by nine A.M. than most people do all day. Or in your case, since Tuesday. That's your end, Rockefeller. Now you know what it's like to make money on your back."

"You didn't use this room." His stomach started another slow revolution at the thought.

"What if I did?"

"Shoot you, then myself." It surprised him that he said it without hesitating.

She watched him. He noticed the thin craquelure at the corners of her eyes. She wasn't that old. He'd known her, what, four years. When they'd met he was thirty-nine, had guessed her to be in her early twenties. It was possible he'd guessed wrong; but then four years in The Circle were like twenty most other places.

"At least take a bite of the burger," she said. "I made them do it over twice to get it the way you like it. They never believe me when I tell them to ruin it."

"They serve eggs, you know. This is breakfast for me."

"You don't like eggs."

"When did I ever say I don't like eggs?"

"I've never seen you eat one."

"You've never seen me pee, either. That doesn't mean I don't." Saying it, he became aware of another discomfort. His bladder was full to squeaking.

"Yeah, I never understood that. Most men don't care if I watch. A couple even had me hold it. They paid me twenty."

He got off the bed. His head sloshed, as if the urine had backed up that far. One leg was asleep and a thousand electric needles tattooed him from knee to ankle as he wobbled into the bathroom. Just to reinforce his principles, he locked the door and turned on the tap. His stream was better than the plumbing's, which wasn't saying much.

When he came out, he realized he was famished. He sat on the edge of the mattress and ate the cheeseburger in six bites. The Coke was heavy on syrup and light on fizz; the formula varied according to who was in charge of the fountain.

The drive-in was a woolly mammoth, one of the last of a small regional chain edged out by a franchise with headquarters in Salt Lake City. In times past there had been cute carhops on roller skates, but the current management had torn out the carports and intercoms to make room for tractor-trailer rigs to park. Now you drove up to a window and tried not to look too hard at the people who were preparing your food in the Third World kitchen.

Clare sat in the blown-out easy chair with legs crossed and watched him eat, as if he might hide most of the meal under his pillow. For some reason she'd taken on the responsibility of keeping him alive. He figured she'd made a bet with someone. Maybe there was a pool and she'd drawn a late date. She was a hooker with a heart of shit.

She didn't speak again until he was foraging for fries among the seams in the sack. "Turnbull's been asking for you. Something about one-oh-eight."

"What's the matter, somebody make off with the bedspread?"

"I didn't ask. I'd sooner make conversation with a fire bucket."

The rest of the fries were cold. Since all they ever had to recommend them was heat, he took the bills out of the bottom of the sack and crumpled it. He laid it on the nightstand, folded and stuck the bills inside his shirt pocket without counting, and bent to fish his shoes from under the bed. His head filled to bursting. He straightened to keep from blacking out.

"You ought to go back to your room and hose yourself down," Clare said. "You look like Beaver Cleaver's been at you."

"That isn't new. You need to get out more."

"Look who's talking."

A killer had been depositing pieces of his victims, prostitutes mostly, in inconvenient places throughout the city for weeks. Clever reporters for *The Derrick* had named him Beaver Cleaver. Clare knew he'd been following the case. She probably thought he wished he were back with the police. But his interest came from relief. Assembling bloody parts and interviewing winos were someone else's responsibility.

He ran the back of a hand down his cheek. It was like stroking a rusty hull. "How'd I wind up here, anyway? I usually try to pass out in a smoking room."

"You passed out in the hall. This was as far as I could drag you." She bounced her crossed leg. "You know, you're an amateur drunk. Two little snorts and you drop like a bucket of spit."

"Cheaper that way." He went through his pockets, found only his passkey. "Seen my lighter?"

"You threw it out the window when the flint wouldn't work."

He kissed her and thanked her for feeding him, gave her buttocks a polite squeeze, got one in return, and was pleasantly surprised to feel himself reacting. He had a blurry recollection that he had had some trouble in that vicinity sometime in the past forty-eight hours, which was why he hadn't quizzed her too closely about circumstances. On his way out he noted that the room was 309, and took the fire stairs down a flight to his room. He left his clothes in a heap on the bathroom floor and stood under the hot spray for five minutes, then stepped out to mow off the stubble. He felt the many planes and angles on his face for signs of bloat. His eyes were puffy, but apart from that there was no evidence of a dead carp as yet.

He put on a white shirt, gray flannel slacks that hadn't bagged too badly in the knees, his second-best argyles, the shoes he'd had on in 309, and his corduroy sport coat with suede patches on the elbows, which Clare always told him made him look like a disgraced English professor. He combed his hair, which was getting to be more salt than pepper, inspected his cheeks for broken blood vessels and found one, poured a slug from the pint of Ancient Age he kept in the medicine cabinet into the toothpaste glass, and tossed it back. The shock paralyzed his vocal cords. He waited while the tingling spread from the floor of his stomach where the cheeseburger lay to the tips of his ears, then screwed the cap back on the bottle and put it away. He'd thought about pouring another, but remembered what Clare had said about him and two little snorts. She'd been right so far as she'd gone: He was an amateur drunk, but he was a gifted amateur. And he still had a job, unless that was what Turnbull wanted to talk to him about. Whatever was going on with 108 may have been just a jumping-off point for the let-you-go speech. He brushed his teeth, rinsed his mouth with bourbon-flavored water from the glass, and went down to the lobby.

Turnbull, the day man, sat in his platform rocker behind the registration desk, reading a boating magazine with his head tilted to keep cigarette smoke out of his eyes. He'd quit smoking, but his posture hadn't gotten the message. In earlier days, Palmer thought, Turnbull had struck one match per day, when he lit up before breakfast, igniting the rest of his two-and-a-half packs off his own smoldering stubs. Now the day man was gaining weight, cheeks turning convex. Palmer felt a little more lonely than usual. The vice was the only thing they'd had in common.

"Must be payday," Turnbull said. "Getting so I don't see you any other time."

"I missed you too." Palmer unzipped a fresh pack, slid a filter into the groove in his lower lip, and lit the other end with a Triangle Bar match. "What about one-oh-eight?"

Turnbull fanned away smoke with his magazine and planted a finger on a registration card lying next to the green metal file box on the desk. "David Egler, checked in last night. Checkout was two hours ago. No answer when I knock."

"Skip?"

"Paid up front. Guerrera checked him in."

"Lose your passkey?"

He shook his head slowly. "I got a feeling."

Palmer waited.

"Feeling says, 'This is one for Palmer.' One of those things we pay you for."

The hotel detective peeled the cigarette from his lip. It always took him half a day to resume manufacturing saliva after a binge. "Let yourself in, didn't you? Didn't like what you saw."

"Just go take a look, okay?"

The room was on the ground floor. The building was half vacant, plenty of space high up, but Guerrera, the night man, had feelings too, genuine ones. He didn't care about jumpers one way or the other, but he was a good Catholic. He didn't believe in making it easy.

Palmer knocked twice, waited both times, then used his passkey. The room was directly above the old pot-type furnace in the cellar, unrentable in winter because of the relentless heat. There was a warm spell on, and the furnace was cold. The sweat of residents who could afford to rent only the unrentable rooms soaked the walls to the studs and gave off a clammy feel when the room wasn't broiling, as it wasn't now. Faith alone kept the wallpaper in place, and guests discovered the chronic damp patch in the carpet when they stepped on it in their stocking feet. The room itself seemed to be perspiring.

The double bed, centered between two hopeful windblown seascapes bolted to the wall above it, was unmade and unoccupied. A charcoal pinstripe suit coat, freshly pressed and smelling faintly of cleaning solvents, hung neatly in the closet; a pair of crisp black penny loafers lay on the carpet near the foot of the bed, arranged side by side with the toes pointed toward the door.

Palmer pushed against the bathroom door. It bumped against something and he sidled in around it. The obstruction was a foot in a ribbed black sock.

The man who belonged to the foot lay twisted onto his right shoulder in the narrow space between the toilet and the sink. His bottom half was propped on his knees and one arm hung down inside the porcelain bowl, submerged to the elbow in foul water. He had on a white dress shirt and charcoal pinstripe trousers. There was gray in his hair, which had been cut recently; a strip of untanned skin bordered the nape. Palmer leaned down and felt his neck for a pulse. The skin was cool.

Back in the bedroom, Palmer plucked a small green empty bottle off the nightstand and read the label: SECOBARBITAL. There were dosage instructions and the name of the prescribing physician, which he didn't bother to memorize. A fifth of Old Forester stood beside the reading lamp, half full, a hotel glass next to it.

He found a flat wallet in an inside breast pocket of the suit coat in the closet. It contained no photos except the one on a driver's license issued to David Andrew Egler and a Social Security card, no credit cards and not so much as a dollar in cash. He looked at the date of birth on the driver's license. Egler was forty-three.

There was no suitcase in the room. Guerrera had been right not to give him a room on a higher floor. Palmer returned the wallet, locked the door behind him, and went back to the lobby. Turnbull was still reading about boats.

"How much was in the wallet?" Palmer asked.

The desk man marked his place with a finger and looked up. "I didn't go in, I said. He blow?"

"In a manner of speaking. Some people can play Russian

roulette with booze and pills plenty of times before they hit the winning combination. Maybe that's how it was with Egler. Or maybe it was beginner's luck."

"Shit. Suicide?"

"He didn't leave a note. Or did you cop that too?"

Turnbull's face was blank, a little gray. He got up, went through the door behind the desk, was gone a minute, then came back with his oxygen rig, holding the transparent cup over his nose and mouth. Palmer pressed out his cigarette under the lip of the desk. Oxygen was worse than gasoline.

"He didn't throw up enough to do him any good," he said. "Personally, I don't care about the money. The cops probably will. They'll ask me, then Guerrera. If Guerrera saw money in that wallet after Egler paid for the room, they'll ask me again. Then I'll care too."

Turnbull turned off the nozzle and laid the tank in his chair. He took a fold of creased bills out of his shirt pocket. "Even Guerrera wouldn't know how much he had on him."

Palmer shrugged. The day man separated two bills and tossed the rest onto the desk. Palmer counted. Thirty-six dollars. He went back to the room, slid the bills into the wallet and the wallet into the suit coat, then returned to the lobby and used Turnbull's telephone. A sergeant he didn't know listened, then said he'd send a car.

"New guy?" Turnbull was sitting with the oxygen tank in his lap. His color was better.

"Turnover at the desk's a bitch. You burn out dealing with the public."

"You never told me why you left the department. I figure it was a bad break. You shot a kid with a toy gun."

"How could I shoot anyone with a toy gun?"

"I meant the kid had the toy. Jesus."

"It wasn't anything like that. Some dope walked out of the evidence room on my watch."

"No shit. You deal?"

"It was more complicated than that."

"You got framed?"

"It wasn't that complicated."

Turnbull waited, then lost interest and opened his magazine. Palmer wished he'd given him a more satisfactory answer so he wouldn't ask again. Being a busted cop was as bad as being a defrocked priest. It took practice to keep your lies straight.

CHAPTER FOUR

Francis Xavier Russell lived on West Riverside Drive near South Terrace Street, in a house built by his father, an Irish-born bricklayer in full possession of the vices and virtues of the race as celebrated in story and song. He had been a slave to the Wee Drop, albeit from sundown Friday to Sunday morning only, but he'd loved his family demonstrably, and was an uncommonly good layer of brick. The only improvements his son had seen fit to make were additions, and although he'd doubled the square footage, he had done so always to the rear, without violating the integrity of the side that faced the street. Anyone who saw it from the front would consider it a charming example of the unassuming American saltbox; it was only in late fall and winter, when the leaves were gone from the trees on either side, that a pedestrian or motorist approaching from west or east saw the sprawl behind, and the house revealed itself as a mansion. Cynics who called it the House of Graft never suspected that Marty had cleaned it herself from top to bottom, with a bandanna around her head and rubber gloves to the elbows. The couple's only serious fight had taken place the day he'd hired a twice-a-week maid. He'd paid the woman for two weeks when Marty forced him to fire her after half a day.

The house stood on the apron of Gas City's most fashionable neighborhood for no other reason than that it had survived its respectable working-class origins to rub shoulders with wealthy refugees from the state capital. Daniel Seamus Russell might have been amused to witness the elevation of the shanty Irish by sheer displacement at the hands of the African hordes upstate.

All the windows burned with light when Anthony Zeno's molten-silver town car slid into the curb in front. Toby, seated behind the wheel, rested a timberlike arm in a tailored sleeve across the back of the seat and fired a silent question at his employer. Zeno shook his head, let himself out, and walked alone to the front door. Inside a pair of cylindrical chimes gonged to his touch on the button.

The door opened immediately, as if he'd been expected. Russell's long humorous face peered out with a cigarette burning in the corner of his mouth.

"You're entertaining," said Zeno, who was sure he wasn't. "I should have called first."

"Come in."

The house was empty, as the visitor confirmed the moment he stepped inside. A lone umbrella leaned in the stand and the air smelled of a solitary brand of stale tobacco. A television murmured from the living room—*parlor*, Russell called it; his father and mother had lain in state there, and he could not be brought to refer to it by the more modern term.

Zeno reached for the hat he hadn't worn in a decade. He remembered in mid-gesture and patted down his hair. "I almost didn't know you without your pipe."

"I gave it up. Marty gave me a pouch of that apple-flavored shit every Christmas for thirty-five years. I bet I've got another two years' supply if you know anybody that smokes a pipe."

"You were the only one."

He followed Russell without hesitation to his study, an old habit to avoid Marty's enjoyment of the endless parade of sitcoms, dramas, and late-night talk shows yammering in the parlor. It had been the dining room in Daniel's time, a cramped, noisy place of funny stories, family arguments, and clattering crockery. The formal dinners where the couple had entertained political cronies and distinguished visitors belonged to the renovated section in back. Here, Russell had smoked, read paperback westerns, listened to records, and drunk Green Spot with friends, most of whom Marty couldn't stand. The original butterscotch wallpaper had turned nicotine brown and the fabric-covered chairs and sofa bore the imprints of all the familiar pairs of buttocks that had occupied them. Not one had an arm that hadn't been burned a score of times by careless sparks.

Russell opened the compartment in the phonograph cabinet where he kept the glasses and bottles, poured his guest two fat fingers of amber liquid from a square container, and set it on the low table paved with newspaper sections from days past. Nothing had changed, including the distant sound of the television, but the house was quiet with a thundering absence. Zeno, who tended to like people who liked him and to dislike those who didn't, missed Marty's presence with the pang of a surviving enemy. He leaned forward from his customary end of the sofa and lifted his glass. "Your health."

The police chief, seated primly in his armchair with his knees together, fluttered his lips rudely and drank from his squat glass. It had been half full when they entered and he topped it off afterward. Flakes floated on top; the ice made from Gas City's hard water was laced with iron and white lime, and Russell's had melted long since.

"Perpetual Misery?" Zeno asked.

Russell flinched, as if the question was too personal. Then he took another sip. "Four o'clock Saturday. Wake's at Stillwell's Friday night."

"I'd be there if I didn't think it would cause talk."

Russell smoked and said nothing.

"Charlotte coming in?"

"Nobody's heard from Charlotte in twelve years."

Zeno hesitated. "You might be a grandfather."

That was as personal as it could get, but Russell didn't react. He stubbed out his cigarette in an old-fashioned tin stand, blowing two more jets of smoke than his nonsmoking guest would have thought possible from one last drag. "I don't see Charlotte carrying any far-ther than the nearest butcher shop."

There were no pictures of Russell's runaway daughter in any of the rooms Zeno had ever been in, but plenty of young Tom: missing his front teeth in a grade-school photo, marching with the high school band, standing with his father in hunter's woolens next to a six-point buck on the tailgate of a Dodge truck, and the last one, here, in his uniform in front of the Stars and Stripes. He had his fa-ther's long jaw and his mother's eyes, small for his face and wise for youth. Zeno had always admired Marty's eyes. Deanne's were too big and too blue.

The chief seemed to have read his mind. "How's Deanne?"

"Healthy as a horse. And just as expensive to keep." There were few secrets between them.

"Marty said she had good fashion sense."

"What are your plans, Rusty?"

He was lighting a cigarette. He laughed and coughed smoke. "You're the only one still calls me Rusty. I haven't had a red hair on my head since Big Mike was in." He dropped the match in the stand. "Just now I'm planning to go ahead and finish this pack. Then maybe I'll open another, or go to bed. I'll call you when I know."

A blanket was folded neatly on the other end of the sofa with a pillow on top. It was obvious he was sleeping in here now. "I meant after the services. There's no reason to snap my head off."

"Joe Cicero calls me just about everything but Rusty. You see that cartoon on yesterday's editorial page? He's got me slopping at your trough. Good likeness."

"I get my news off TV, just like everyone else. That's why he's desperate." Zeno changed the subject from *The Derrick* and another source of his high blood pressure. "Hugh Dungannon says you're thinking of retiring."

"I never said that."

"He got the impression. He's concerned. He came to see me today at Volcanic."

"Priests don't get impressions. Diocese could save money by

putting him out to graze and sticking a slot machine in the confessional. Drop in a quarter, push the button for your sin, out pops a card telling you how many Hail Marys you owe."

"I didn't know you two fell out."

"He's the oldest friend I've got."

"I'm pretty close to next," Zeno said. "If you are thinking of hanging it up, you might tell your old friends. I'll throw you a party that'll shake Big Mike out of the ground with a glass in each hand."

"I can get drunk without help."

Out in the other room, the program had changed. Zeno recognized the jazz theme of a police drama.

"You used to be a good conversationalist, Rusty. Now it's like pitching pennies into the drain."

"My goddamn wife goddamn died. You want a limerick?" The chief's color faded as quickly as it had come up. "I don't know what I'd do if I retired. I don't fish and I hate golf."

"There's tennis. That's how I stay in shape for Deanne."

"I got a thing against games you got to take lessons to play. And I got no Deannes to stay in shape for."

"Okay, so you're not retiring." Zeno rose. "You shouldn't stay in this house alone. Where's Marty's sister?"

"Coming in from Mexico."

"Why the hell Mexico?"

"She gets together with her widow friends and they charter tours. Last fall it was Hawaii. Bunch of old prunes sitting on a beach drinking iced tea with a nail in it and slobbering all over the cabana boy."

"Doesn't sound half bad. Without the cabana boy, I mean."

"If you want me to hang it up, why don't you come out and say it?"

"I only want it if it's what you want. If it's keeping busy that worries you, I can talk to someone at the capital. They keep losing their security chiefs to the Secret Service. The change of scenery might be good."

"You afraid I'll do something stupid if I hang around here?"

"Not stupid. A man with no one to come home to can get too close to the work. He loses perspective. I'm speaking from experience."

"This wouldn't by chance have anything to do with Mr. White coming to see you last night." The chief played with his pack. The cigarette in his mouth was only half smoked. "Don't look surprised. I've had a car outside your house ever since we caught that hophead Joe Rocks throwing poisoned meat to your dog."

"Joe OD'd two years ago."

"Anyone can buy rat poison. I'm just trying to find out who this offer of employment is coming from. If it's from you it's one thing, if it's from Bianco it's another. I shook his hand once. It was like cleaning out a sink trap."

"Gas City's my responsibility. I don't take orders from Mr. White any more than I give them to you. Have I ever?"

"No. You always were the diplomat. Fat Paulie didn't know which fork to use when it came to putting out someone's eye."

Zeno's face went numb as if it had been struck. "You should get some sleep. I'll come by and see you after the wake."

Russell closed his eyes and left them shut, as if he no longer had a visitor. He seemed like a child trying to convince his parents he was asleep. Zeno let himself out.

"Home?" Toby asked, when he was back in the car.

"Harrigan's."

"Cops hang out there."

"Tell 'em to do their worst. I'm only ten lashes away from getting my own statue in Our Lady of Perpetual Misery."

When the front door thumped shut, Russell sat for another minute with his eyes closed. Then he laid his cigarette in the stand to smoke itself out, got up, and unlocked the metal cabinet where he'd kept his service weapons since his children were small. His short-snouted Police Special rested on its pegs, but he ignored it in favor of the Remington twelve-gauge, whose pistol-grip stock and cigar-shaped forepiece glistened from hand-rubbing in the course of use. He'd known men with revolvers to flinch at the last instant and miss the brain even with the muzzle in their mouths.

He sat for twenty minutes with the shotgun across his lap. He must have dozed off, because its weight perplexed him at one point and he looked down to see what was causing it.

"Nope." He got up, locked the gun back in the cabinet, and placed the keys on top above the door, out of reach of childish hands. Some habits weren't worth the trouble to break. Then he made up the sofa and stretched out on it, pulling the blanket up to his chin. From cabinet to sofa, it was the second night he'd performed the ritual. He hadn't a notion which night if any the answer would be, "Yep."

CHAPTER FIVE

The detective with most of the questions was named Prokanik. In his gray sport coat and slacks that almost matched—a valiant attempt at a suit without the bother of a fitting—he might have passed for one of the bull-shouldered Polish tank-wipers who worked for McGrath if it weren't for the dead eyes in the tired face. It was Palmer's observation that honest physical labor never choked off a man's spirit as much as daily exposure to the damp side of the rock upon which the city stood. Here, in a body five years short of forty, was a month's suspension just waiting to happen.

His partner, a woman named Boyle, seemed fresher, or at least a little better at dissembling behind a skilled application of makeup. Palmer, chauvinistic at the center, thought she might be attractive if she let her hair grow out and unfastened at least the top button of her blouse. The three spoke in low voices in the hall outside 108. Inside, the forensics team was busy with its measuring tape and glassine bags and self-developing cameras, entering more of David Andrew Egler's final few hours into the official record than the whole of his forty-three years prior.

"You were an officer?" Prokanik looked up from the fold of

newsprint he used for a notebook, a mechanical pencil in his other hand. Idly, Palmer wondered where one laid his hands upon blank newsprint these days. Maybe the city had a deal with *The Derrick* over its postpub scrap.

"Uniform division. Before your time, probably." He couldn't remember what he'd said that had revealed his past employment. Intermittent blackouts in times of relative sobriety were something new in his experience. "I've been here seven years." Thinking, *My God.* Six was a "brief sojourn." Seven might as well be ten. Ten years at the bottom rung. One step from there to the ground, and breakfast in a bottle in a paper sack.

"Sad case," Detective Boyle said.

Palmer looked at her quickly. Had he been thinking out loud? But her eyes were turned toward the half-open door to 108.

"Man makes his decision," she said, "gets his suit cleaned and pressed, puts on a fresh shirt. His shoes were polished, did you notice? You could use the reflection to pluck your eyebrows. Looking to make a good impression when Homicide comes to call. Only the barbiturates are too much for his stomach. He winds up slumped in front of the toilet, up to his elbow in his own puke."

"Maybe he had help," Prokanik said.

Palmer said, "There was no struggle. The room already looked like shit when he checked in. No bruises on his face or wrists."

The pencil stopped moving. "Gave him a good going-over, did you?"

"It's my job. In thirty days he'd have been hotel property."

"Uh-uh. He belonged to the city since about noon. Go through his wallet?"

"Just for ID. If he turned out to be the mayor's son it would've changed the order of the calls I made. I don't rob the dead, if that's what you're thinking."

"Good to know you draw the line somewhere."

"Stan," Boyle said tonelessly. She looked at Palmer. "Would you mind telling us why you left the department?"

"The hotel offered me a greater opportunity for advancement."

The whir of a motor-driven camera from inside the room ended the little silence. Prokanik twisted the lead back into the barrel of his pencil. "Sad, all right. Better we should find him in Hefty bags from here to East Riverside."

"Is that your detail?" Palmer was interested. "No kidding, Beaver Cleaver?"

Prokanik lifted a lip. "A reading man, I see. The TV stations just call him the Black Bag Killer."

"He quit," Boyle said. "Or maybe the moon's in the wrong phase. Anyway we're available for Mr. Egler." She got a card from her shoulder bag and held it out. "You can get us at this extension if you remember anything else. Can you be reached here?"

"We never close." He fingered the card. Suddenly he felt a surge of loyalty to the management. "Think you can keep the Railroad Arms off TV and out of the paper?"

"That's up to them, Mr. Palmer. Palmer's your *last* name, correct?" Boyle looked sympathetic. He'd already suspected she was the more dangerous of the pair.

"My mother called me James. I was Jimmy at school, but it didn't stick. 'Mr. Palmer' sounds weird. Palmer's always done the trick." He was jabbering, a sure sign he was sober.

"Fascinating." Detective Prokanik clipped his pencil to his notes and slid them into his breast pocket. He grasped the doorknob to 108. "We'll call you if we have more questions."

It was a dismissal, and Palmer took it down the hall. He looked at the card before putting it away. Boyle's first name was Patricia, and she was a detective third-grade. The card bore the city seal—embossed in gold for detectives, and probably still in silver for the uniform division. Some things never changed, including their tactics.

A bunch of soggy paper snakes had begun to uncoil in his stomach. He headed toward the stairs and his room, where he kept what it took to return them to hibernation.

Near the fire door he stopped to look at a flat greasy box on the floor outside 116. It was partially open, and a narrow slice of pepperoni cheese lay inside, curled at the tip like a Persian slipper. Mama Angelo's moon face beamed at him from the top of the box. There really was a Mama Angelo: a sallow-skinned crone who dressed all in black and sprayed flecks of spittle when she talked, sometimes over a pizza fresh from the oven. Her grown sons ran numbers for Tony Z. out the back of the restaurant, and that was the story on why the health inspector never came around.

Tilting his head toward the door, he heard the tinny blubber of a prime-time soap opera, but it could as easily be coming from a TV set in one of the adjoining rooms. The partitions were as thin as Mama Angelo's pepperoni cheese.

He went past the fire door and around the corner to the desk. Guerrera, the night man, was listening to the clock radio. Palmer knew enough Spanish to understand a caller was complaining about construction on the FDR Parkway.

"Fuzz finished?" Guerrera tilted back in the rocker and turned down the radio. He was a stocky thirty, very brown, with heavy black eyebrows and a hairline that began at the bridge of his nose. Strangers assumed he was an Arab until he opened his mouth.

"Not till you hear the vacuum cleaner. That's always last."

"Good. Turnbull can tell Housekeeping to skip it tomorrow."

"You got any cigarettes besides that Mexican shit?"

"They're Indian, from the reservation. No tax." He took a pack from his shirt pocket and flipped it onto the desk. It was green, with an orange totem eagle on the front. "I keep telling you I'm not Mexican."

"I didn't say you were, just your smokes. Get off your box." Palmer bummed a match, one of the old-fashioned kind with a white phosphor tip, and struck it on the nubby plaster wall, adding a new scratch to the hieroglyph. The flame burned a third of the way down the cigarette before the tobacco caught: Geronimo's revenge.

The night man looked at the clock. "I hope they're out of there before the supper crowd gets back. Rolling a rubber bag through the lobby is hard on business."

"We might lose a star in Michelin. Who's in one-sixteen?"

Guerrera rocked forward and slid over the green metal file box. Palmer intercepted it and spun it his way. The registration cards were divided by the alphabet in front and cross-referenced by numbers in back. There was nothing for 116.

"Vacant," Guerrera said.

"Vacant rooms don't eat pizza. We've got a squatter. I'll go back and throw him out." He turned away.

"Wait."

He turned back. Guerrera's expression was flat. "Wait till morning. Maybe Turnbull put the card in the wrong slot."

Palmer slid the numbered dividers and cards out of the box in a brick and started shuffling through them.

"He might of put it anywhere," Guerrera said. "Better wait and ask him in the morning."

He dropped the cards back into the box and snaked a rectangle of printed paper out of a cardboard pocket display on the desk. He turned Mama Angelo's smiling idiot's face toward the night man. "Mama lets you slide on what you owe her because you hand these out with the keys. She blacked out the phone number to cut down on prank calls, won't accept an order not placed from a permanent address. Guests have to go through the hotel switchboard. From dark to dawn that's you. Did you forget who pays the taxes on this dump?"

"Who could? What he don't own in the Circle he runs."

"When he finds out you're checking in guests under the counter and palming the cash, what do you think he'll do, fire you without references? Deport you?"

"I'm American. I was born down on Castro."

"He'll bury you there if you're lucky. Probably he'll just dump you in the river, or pave over you on the parkway, and people can call in to the radio and bitch about the orange cones on your face. He'd do that just because of the money, but he has other reasons. Compulsory hotel registration's a state law. We've got a Republican up there who stays awake nights thinking up ways to make Jerry Wilding look bad. Tony Z. spent your salary and mine just on the decorations for the mayoral ball. Just how deep are you in?"

"It ain't like that."

Palmer backed off then, but only because of Guerrera's aftershave. When he got up and leaned his thick forearms on the desk, the fumes washed forward like a chemical spill. He kept a bottle of Old Mariner in a guest mailbox and slapped it on several times a night.

"You picked one hell of a time to be a hotel detective," Guerrera said. "Why don't you stick to busting up underage parties in the Governor's Suite and confiscating their liquor? If it wasn't for them brats from the Upper West Side, you'd be drinking Listerine."

He was smiling, teeth blue-white against brown skin all the way to the molars. He was scared, all right, and of Zeno, but not because he was chiseling off the books. He was scared because of Palmer. Palmer didn't like him, or desk clerks in general, but he had a sudden vision of a kid from Castro Street in Little Brazil, sharing a flat with four generations of his family, and of how long it would take anyone to notice he wasn't reporting for work.

He lowered his voice. "Whose boy is he, Manolo? What's he cooling off from? You had to talk to him even if you came on after he checked in. He ordered pizza. It was still warm."

That last was a bald lie. He hadn't touched the slice any more than he would have eaten it when it was fresh, speckled with Mama's saliva as it would be. But Guerrera's smile drifted away. He flattened his palms on the desk and pushed himself straight.

"You want to start working, go up and rattle doorknobs. I'll call you if a bum wanders into the lobby. That's if you're listening. When's the last time you wore your pager?"

Palmer shot smoke at the wall and mashed out his cigarette in the big ceramic tray on the desk. As he turned the corner toward the stairs, the volume went up on the night man's radio.

He smelled Clare Sayers' perfume when he unlocked and opened his door; she used something citrusy with a sharp nip. She was sitting cross-legged on the bed in a pale blue bra and black panties, clipping her toenails. The knit top and capri pants she'd had on earlier were folded neatly over the back of the wooden chair he used for a valet. He admired the muscles in her calves.

"Brought you a present." She pointed with her clippers at a small grocery sack standing on top of the squat chest of drawers.

"Another cheeseburger?" He spread the top of the sack and looked down at a carton of Chesterfields and a blister pack containing four disposable butane lighters in assorted colors. "Thanks. What's the damage?"

"I said it was a present."

"I can buy my own cigarettes."

"Not if you don't go outside. I heard you had a full day."

"It started late." He undressed to his undershirt and shorts, sniffed at his shirt, and hung it in the closet with his jacket and slacks. "Taking the night off?"

"Just till eleven. It's third Wednesday."

At 11:00 P.M. on the third Wednesday of every month since the beginning of the year, Clare had gotten into a taxi cab with its service light turned off and taken it to an address on South Terrace. Palmer didn't know what address or who lived there, but when she came back three or four hours later she had a month's rent on her flat on Depot Street. He assumed what took place during those three or four hours involved something her other customers couldn't afford, but since he didn't take a cut from anything she made outside the hotel he never asked for details. In four years, he'd never seen her flat either.

He got in next to her and propped himself up with a pillow, watching her round off the nail on her little toe. She took good care of her feet. She'd told him once that most women in her work didn't, and lost business from fetishists.

"Did you forget you have cigarettes?" She blew nail-dust off the clippers.

"I can't taste anything for an hour after I smoke one of Guerrera's. What'd he tell you about one-oh-eight?"

"He didn't. Turnbull said you had a do-it-yourselfer. Cops leave?"

"Pretty soon. I knew one of the squaddies who took the call. I didn't know any of the others."

"Well, it's been years. I think you were off the last time we had a suicide."

"I mean from before."

"I keep forgetting you were a cop." She switched feet.

"Who's in one-sixteen?"

"Not another stiff, I hope. This shithole's starting to go to hell. I may have to move my business to the Wigwam."

"He was alive long enough to eat most of a medium-size pepperoni cheese."

"Just what we need. Another fucking suicide."

"He isn't registered."

She paused, then resumed clipping. "I wouldn't sweat over it. Turnbull's got to pay for his oxygen, and Guerrera's probably supporting twenty or thirty cousins."

"I don't think it's a chisel. Guerrera was too scared."

"Maybe it's one of Moe Shiel's boys. Wouldn't be the first time one of them came here hot."

"He isn't afraid of Moe. Moe leaves the Hispanics alone as long as they behave themselves outside Little Brazil. So you haven't heard anything?"

"Nobody pays me to listen. When'd you start?"

He got up and broke open the carton. He watched her lean over to lay the clippers on the chair and pick up an emery board. The long muscle in her thigh stood out like a bowline. "Egler was almost exactly my age."

"Who's Egler?"

"Stiff in one-oh-eight. I saw his driver's license. Our mothers might have passed in the hospital."

"Was he born upstate? You told me you were born upstate."

"Not the point. When I was in the blue bag, most of the suicides I worked were fifty or sixty. One old lady was seventy-five, got tired of missing her husband and put her head in the oven. Either that or they were screwed-up kids. Teenagers. Wonder why he did it?"

"Maybe he had a little dick."

"Cut it out." He stripped the cellophane off a pack.

"I wasn't kidding. A lot of guys dwell on it, believe me. Did you see it?" She smuggled a look his way.

"No. He died with his pants on."

"I bet it was little, then. If I was a guy and I had a little dick, I wouldn't take my pants off before I clocked myself."

"He did go to some trouble to spruce up. Then he died heaving in the toilet." He flicked the wheel on a new lighter. The flame shot up six inches. "Jesus."

She giggled.

"I could've singed a cornea."

"Stop making me laugh. You want me to saw off a toe?"

"Suicide's funny?"

"It is when you set yourself on fire with a ten-cent Bic. Forget Egler. You'll never do it."

"What makes you so sure?"

"You're hung like a gorilla."

He got the flame adjusted and lit his cigarette. "A lot of good it does me while you go on grooming yourself like a chimp."

She leaned back against the headboard, turning the emery board over and over in her fingers like a miniature baton. A small patch of freckles showed below her navel. "Do gorillas and chimps make out?"

"Like monkeys. What about South Terrace?"

"It's only nine-thirty, Palmer. Stop bragging."

"I had a bad dream last night about not being able to perform."

"I dreamed I was a ballerina. What's your point?"

He put out the cigarette and went over to the bed.

Afterward, she carried her clothes into the bathroom and came out a few minutes later fully dressed. She didn't mind undressing in front of him, but putting on her clothes seemed to be a private act. She had just enough time to shower and change at her flat before meeting her cab.

He sat up in bed smoking. "I wish you'd let me go with you. There's a killer out there."

"There's always one. You're bad for business."

"That's what Guerrera said about having a corpse in the hotel."

She leaned down and kissed him, softly and long. She smelled of him. "Get some sleep. I'll call you when I get back."

"I already had my forty-eight hours," he said. But she'd left.

He finished his cigarette, then used the bathroom and poured a half inch of Ancient Age into the toothpaste glass. He sipped it like cognac until it was gone. Maybe drinking slowly was the trick. If there was a trick.

He dressed in the same clothes and found his pager in the drawer under his sweaters, a primitive model that beeped and vibrated only and took regular batteries. He replaced the dead batteries with working ones from his portable razor and switched it on. A tiny green light glowed. He clipped the pager to his belt and went out to rattle doorknobs.

CHAPTER SIX

The Stillwell Brothers Mortuary occupied an Edwardian ramble on East Riverside, originally the home of one of the city's early Republican mayors. In between it had been a billiards club, a women's lodging house, and a speakeasy during Prohibition, when the flow of money and French-Canadian champagne between it and the new courthouse had eliminated the need to speak easily. Now the wide double doors that had been installed on the side facing the Carbon River facilitated the passage of cadavers and coffins, and the big, low-ceilinged kitchen-cum-distillery served as a preparation room, with all its pumps and plaster of paris and jars and jars of Lyf-Lyk Embalming Agent. The rather small foyer contained an open guest book on a stand, whence visitors passed between pocket doors into the viewing room, where the original parlor had been enlarged to accommodate a casket on a dais and rows of folding wooden chairs. There a side door led to the more casual atmosphere of a hospitality room and refreshments on a long trestle table with a blue cloth. A great stone fireplace—all that remained of the formal dining room—provided a pedestal for the long-dead mayor's painted likeness in a carved mahogany frame.

Martha Rose Russell lay surrounded by white satin in a glistening cherrywood coffin with marble grips on the gold handles. She looked small and pleasant with an elaborate wig of brown-and-silver waves covering her sparse hair, rosary beads wound around her hands clasped in white cotton gloves below her breasts. Her dress was the slate-blue one with a white collar she'd worn to services and entertaining Hugh Dungannon and lesser church officials in the Russell home. A blanket of flowers covered the closed lower half of the casket; Francis Russell thought it looked as if it had been donated by the derby winner at Granite Park.

Old Arch Killian was the first to arrive, accompanied by a younger man Russell didn't recognize. Arch was a cousin or something to the Noonans, whether by blood or marriage wasn't clear. The old man was thin and bouncy, with a shock of pale hair like a straw heap, in what looked like the same brown suit he'd worn to family reunions back when anyone still bothered to reunite with near strangers. He shook Russell's hand energetically, said something comforting while smiling with his lower teeth, and reached back to give the younger man at his side a push from behind. "This is my boy Earl."

Earl was in his late thirties or early forties, well built in a blue suit off the rack, and looked nothing like his father. Russell had a blurry flash of a scrawny kid in a white shirt and red suspenders, eating a cupcake in the kitchen on West Riverside. "It's good to see you, Chief Russell. I'm sorry about the circumstances." His grasp was strong and brief.

"Thank you."

"She was a grand girl," Arch said. "She wore a yellow dress to Betty's funeral. I've always remembered that. Yellow was Betty's favorite color."

"Marty always put thought into things." He shook hands with them both again, an old politician's trick to move the line along. "There's food and drinks in the next room. Help yourself."

"We'll just say hello to Marty first." The Killians went up the aisle between the chairs. The old man fairly skipped when he walked. He might have been on his way up to the bandstand to put in a request.

Russell's sister-in-law came in, late as usual, while he was talking with Dennis Stillwell. She wore something black and expensive that looked cheap on her dumpy frame. He could barely look at her. They'd named Charlotte after Carly, and the daughter had favored her aunt in looks, right down to the blonde hair that was by now all peroxide and the cow eyes set too far apart in the broad face. She laid a plump hand on his upper arm. "Did you eat today?"

"Toast, at breakfast." He had all he could do not to brush away the hand. Bright red nail polish seemed to him less appropriate than a yellow dress. Where did the old man get his memory? Russell couldn't recall attending his wife's funeral, and held only a dim picture of her in life.

The hand spread to close on his bicep and applied pressure to turn him toward the side door. "You need your strength tonight. No one wants to attend a double funeral. I'll send them in to you. Don't forget, I was a professional hostess."

"How could anyone? You never let them. The damn restaurant burned down twenty-five years ago."

She laughed. Carly always laughed when you insulted her to her face. "Try the puffed shrimp. I ordered it myself. The caterer wanted to put out cold cuts."

"What's wrong with cold cuts?"

She laughed again. Stillwell excused himself and left silently on crepe heels. His black suit shimmered. His brother Lee did all the embalming and restoration and drove the hearse, and only showed up when it was time to take the guest of honor to the church. Dennis was the one with the manners and the sympathetic conversation. Together they looked after most of the city's extinguished distinguished and held the contract to bury indigents in Stranger's Field.

Russell entered the hospitality room. Some people had slid in there already, to fortify themselves with finger food and nonalcoholic drinks and talk before going back out to confront the dear departed. He recognized some, was reminded by others of their

connection, and ignored those who didn't seem to know who he was;
did people crash funerals, he wondered, the way they showed up un-
invited to wedding receptions for a free meal? The long table was
crowded with cakes and crackers and slices of cheese and Carly's
magnificent, matchless puffed shrimps and a corned-beef brisket on
a big platter ringed with little round slices of rye bread like potato
chips. There were plastic forks and plastic cups and pitchers of juice
and iced tea and a stainless-steel forty-cup coffee urn with a spigot
like on one of McGrath's tanks filled with crude. Somewhere between Russell's adolescence and youth, just about the time he was
old enough to start attending them, Irish wakes had changed. What
had become of the bottles of Bushmill's and Green Spot, the kegs of
beer, the huge bowl of gin with just enough chunks of orange and
pineapple floating on top to call it fruit punch? Gone the way of the
off-color story, the political power-brokering, the brawl in the parking lot that brought out the police, and a foaming schooner for each
officer in exchange for leaving the paddy wagon behind. He'd lived
too long, and Marty too short.

"Not like the old days, eh, Francis? Your old da' would've been
six sheets to the wind by now, with knuckles all split and bloody and
mouses on both eyes."

He gave Hugh Dungannon a hand to squeeze. The bishop had
on the purple today, and the look of a fat merchant-emperor in the
closing days of Rome. His face was as red as a cardinal's hat. Russell
suspected he'd been into the good Napoleon he kept behind the
Books of the Saints in the rectory. "I was just thinking along those
same lines. Thanks for coming, Your Reverence. I didn't expect to
see you before the services."

"We're old friends, Francis; and that's a remonstrance as well as
an explanation. We've never stood on titles in the past."

"Maybe we should have. I'm more comfortable these days with
Chief than Francis. It's kind of like watching a grandmother trying
to lead a cheer."

"I'll say Chief from the pulpit and nowhere else. When you
say, 'Your Reverence,' I hear me old mum saying, 'Hugh Patrick

Dungannon, you go straight out back and cut me a switch.' Are you mad at me, then?" He looked anxious, and a bit bloodshot. Russell was sure he'd guessed right about the brandy.

"I'm just a little tired. Doesn't all this strike you as a bit of the old pagan? What's feasting to do with death?"

"Not a bit of it. It's life we're celebrating, and Marty's was an example for the rest of us. I just saw Carly. She looks grand. Brown as a nut and fat as a Christmas ham. Don't tell her I said that last part. Women have peculiar ideas about feminine beauty. If I weren't chaste, I'd prefer meat on the bone. Don't tell the archbishop I said *that*."

"I won't, Hugh. You should go home and rest. You've a requiem mass tomorrow, and you're too old and fat to cut yourself a switch."

"I will that, Francis. The books have me worn out. A diocese is a small business after all, and things can't get much smaller at Perpetual Misery without having to put up the candlesticks for auction. They've brought in a banjo player at Most Holy Trinity up in the capital; I suppose he strums 'O Susannah' to organ accompaniment. Is there anything to that, do you think?"

"It's an old people's faith. You have to bring in the young lambs or the flock will die out. Though I doubt 'O Susannah' will do it." He wanted to look around for rescue, but was afraid to break eye contact. In any case no one was likely to come forward and interrupt a conference with a bishop.

"Trouble is the young lambs don't put anything in the plate their parents don't give them for the purpose, and they split it in half for each child so we don't get any more than if they were barren. When the wee ones get old enough to contribute on their own, they move away. Even McGrath's having trouble finding warm bodies. There's talk of shutting down the midnight shift." Dungannon shook his head and dropped a heavy paw on Russell's shoulder. "Let's face it, Francis. I'll never be cardinal. Water finds its level, then recedes."

"You're as subtle as an IRA bomb, Hugh. As usual."

"Father O'Neill always said I hit the high notes with an axe." He gave the shoulder a squeeze. "Take care of yourself. Marty didn't do it all those years just to kill time." He walked away slowly, without a stumble or a sway. He was drunker than Russell had thought. He wondered if things at the church were as bad as all that, or if Dungannon had exaggerated to make his ponderous point. Their grandfathers had grown up in the shadow of that grotesque tribute to medieval architecture. He could picture the yellow flame going out on top of Factory Hill before Our Lady of Perpetual Misery fell to the wrecking ball.

After that, he was actually glad to see Moe Shiel charging his way from the other end of the room, for once without his flying squad of burly workers from the Volcanic loading dock at his back; Shiel took death threats with his morning oatmeal, but even his most determined enemies wouldn't try to slip a knife between his ribs in the police chief's presence.

" 'Evening, Chief. I'm sorry for your loss." He was a wiry five-and-a-half feet with a head squared off at the top by a steel-gray crewcut and at the bottom by a jaw shaped like a crate. Russell imagined that when he opened wide that savage slash of a mouth to bellow at his street army, the top half of his head tipped all the way back on a hinge. For this occasion he'd drawn a shabby tweed coat over his black T-shirt and green work trousers. The chief doubted he owned a necktie or a collar suitable to one.

"Thank you, Shiel. How are things in the Circle?"

He grinned his granite grin. "We had to lay some pipe down on Blacksnake Lane last night. Couple of Riverside boys got into it with some of the spics at Riley's."

"West or East?"

"Oh, East. We dumped 'em in a cab, same service we provide the kids from Magnolia, though it's plain enough they started it. If your name ain't Diego or Jesus, you don't ask a señorita to dance. Couple of Little Brazil boys checked into County General with headaches and a broken arm. We shut down the place and sent the rest home. It wasn't nothing worth the city's finest getting their blouses all bloody."

"Thank the Lord for that. We should never have let Riley's

reopen after the last election. It's been a rotten spot since the Irish moved uptown."

"They'd just go over to the El Capitan or hang out at Mama Angelo's and make trouble there. Anyway, Riley's was a rough enough cob when Riley was above ground. My old man called it the Tub of Guts."

"I've forgotten who your father was."

"No reason you'd remember. He was a tail gunner on a beer truck, but that's all crap down the river. He helped Big Mike get in the first time. The old lady said he was always starting the stove with Republican posters."

"Big Mike didn't believe in letting hands go idle. Anything else?"

Shiel met the change of subject with a shrug. "Just that Dutch job at the Railroad Arms day before yesterday, but you know all about that."

"No scandal there. Insurance claims adjuster with North American Life and Liability. His wife divorced him. Apparently he wanted to make sure she didn't collect on his policy. At least he had the good taste not to check into the convention center."

"That's how I'd do it: Blow the stake on the presidential suite, order a sirloin blood-rare and a bottle of twenty-four-year-old Scotch from room service, and take a header off the terrace. That's if the other side was in," he added, rapping thrice-broken knuckles on the trestle table. "I wouldn't cause no trouble for you and Mayor Wilding."

"Well, that's white of you, Shiel, and an incentive to stay in office. Judging by how long it's been since the other side was in, you might see one hundred." Russell stuck out his hand.

The little man from Volcanic Wholesale Plumbing Supplies knew a gesture of dismissal. He gave him the grip usually reserved for a pipe wrench. "Thank you kindly, Chief. Wisht I could of said the same for your missus." He marched off, pumping his arms and thumping the floor straight through the padded carpet with his hobnails. On the way he scooped up a handful of shrimp and crammed them into his mouth like peanuts.

Russell watched his retreat with a mixture of relief and resentment. Shiel was The Circle's unsworn chief of police as well as its unelected mayor, and his band of thugs prevented the necessity of exposing officers in uniform to ambush in a part of the city that had no love for authority. The sworn chief was grateful for that, but disliked the little hoodlum personally and chafed at his familiar attitude. He reported directly to Anthony Zeno (who if he had an office at Volcanic seldom sat in it), and so seemed to consider himself Russell's equal. It wasn't that he was a Jew, although Russell had his full measure of distrust for that tribe inherited from earlier generations; the man had a yellow streak as broad as his personal escort, and he was socially uncouth, which in a way was worse. You could ignore a man's lack of courage, as you did a missing limb, but when he picked his teeth with his thumbnail just before shaking hands with someone to whom polite custom demanded you introduce him, there it was out in the open, and it reflected on you.

But the ordeal was less than half over. For the next hour, Russell accepted condolences from a parade of lieutenants, sergeants, and officers, uniformed and in plainclothes, who passed before him in an unbroken line as if they had all arrived on the same bus. He conducted police business briefly with some of them, and at greater length with detectives Prokanik and Boyle, who acknowledged that the suicide at the Railway Arms was a closed case and that nothing new had developed in their investigation of the Black Bag murders, as local TV reporters had christened them; their Standards and Practices consultants had banned the use of Beaver Cleaver on the grounds of decency, and their legal advisers had agreed, but for a different reason: Joe Cicero, publisher of *The Derrick*, had copyrighted the nickname.

"Has he quit, then?" the chief asked Prokanik, automatically deferring to the masculine half of the partnership.

"We don't know enough about him to say he has, sir." The detective's upper lip was moist, and he'd cut himself deeply shaving; collodion glistened in a two-inch laceration on his chin.

"He's been at it since February. How much *do* we know about him?"

"Zero so far, Chief." Boyle spoke up. She was a good-looking short-haired woman who appeared to use no more cosmetics than allowed by the manual of dress for female officers. "None of our street sources knows anything. This kind of criminal doesn't operate in the same society as the professionals."

"Read up on the subject, have you?"

She colored slightly. "No, sir. I spoke with Dr. Aguilar. That is to say, we did."

Russell kept his expression even. Feliz Aguilar was the department psychiatrist, and a reform installed by Mayor Wilding upon his succession to the office so long held by his late father, Michael. The chief had acquiesced, but in nearly four years, not one member of the force had consulted with Aguilar voluntarily. The doctor filled his time writing papers for medical journals and evaluating officers involved in shootings, a regulation also suggested by the mayor. This situation had less to do with Russell's opinions about head-shrinkers in general than with a police tradition, as old as the Cohorts of imperial Rome, of keeping one's own counsel.

He wasn't taken in by Boyle's clumsy attempt to ring Prokanik in on the decision to meet with Aguilar. What was less obvious was whether she was trying to cover a break with partner protocol or share the blame in case the chief disapproved of the consultation. He decided to throw her a curve.

"Well, I'm happy to see the taxpayers are getting a bit of their money's worth from his salary. What do they say in the capital?"

"The capital?" Comically, both detectives spoke at once.

"I know we don't usually confide in the state police, but they have experience with this kind of case. They broke that string of child rapes upstate two years ago. Call up Captain Keynes. Share information, but don't ask him in. We're after insight, not rescue."

"Yes, sir," Prokanik said. "Thank you. Once again, sir, please accept our sympathy."

They withdrew swiftly, eager for a telephone. A precedent had broken with a sharp crack.

Conversation quickened, as in an auditorium one minute before the lights went down and the curtain rose. Jerry Wilding was in the building.

He came in three minutes later, and Russell knew he'd paused in the other room to bend his knees and cross himself at the coffin. He'd had the good taste to leave his army of photographers in the parking lot with the official car and vans, but his personal bodyguard of four men as big as himself in blue serge with earpieces swept in behind him. His enemies were more determined than Moe Shiel's.

"I'm sorry, Francis. Martha Rose was a grand lady."

"Thanks for coming, Your Honor." Jerry's father, he was certain, would have known to call her Marty, even if he'd had to pay someone to tell him. There was little enough of him in his son, apart from the uncanny physical resemblance: the truck driver's build in the thousand-dollar suit, the big, barber-shaven face, the ridge of black hair that glistened like a phonograph record. It even had the grooves. Russell broke free of the two-handed grip with as much delicacy as he could summon.

He lowered his voice. The chatter, which had dipped in awe upon the mayor's entrance, had climbed to a fresh level of excitement, but there were ears all around. "Is it true McGrath's thinking of closing down the graveyard shift?"

The mild sympathetic smile remained in place. "Where'd you hear that?"

"It's a wake. People can only talk so much about what an artist Lee Stillwell is." He knew now Hugh Dungannon had spoken out of turn. He'd lost the art of hearing confessions.

"You've been here all night. I bet you could use a smoke."

The crowd slid apart to let them through. Out on the rear porch with its view of the river, the mayor produced one of his little cigars, another break with Big Mike and his fat Havanas. He looked around for a telephoto lens, then bent to the gold lighter in a bodyguard's hand. The antitobacco lobby in the city was small but loud. "No pipe?" He watched Russell light a cigarette from the same flame. The bodyguard stepped back and became part of the architecture with the others.

"Gave it up. Too much to carry around."

"What did you hear about McGrath?"

"Just that he's having trouble hiring new workers."

"That isn't the reason. This is between us, Francis."

Russell nodded without rolling his eyes.

"The big companies are shipping their oil to refineries in Mexico and Central America. Junior can't compete with dollar-an-hour wages. The orders he has won't support a third shift."

Junior was Morse McGrath II, the octagenarian son of the original Morse. He'd come out of retirement after *his* son, Morse III, died at age forty-seven of coronary thrombosis. And he wouldn't have thanked Jerry Wilding for calling him Junior.

"What are we going to do, go back to growing flowers?"

"No danger of that. I'm setting up a meeting with his board. We're going to offer tax concessions and push hard for higher tariffs on reimporting fossil fuel. I'll make the announcement two weeks before the election."

"I guess I was busy making funeral arrangements while you were getting tight with the governor."

"I'm not saying it won't be like swallowing a porcupine for him, but he campaigned on jobs, and McGrath's the biggest private employer in the state. He's up for reelection in two years. He'll swallow it all right."

"You're not worried about Rice-Hippert in November?"

Wilding waved his cigar. It looked like a brown twig between his thick fingers. "She had her four years after Big Mike died, and a fine mess she made of them. Sitting that one out was the smartest thing I ever did. Come January she'll be back in private practice, scrambling to make up for the time she wasted. But that's *her* porcupine. I want to talk to you about some changes I'm planning next term."

Russell listened. Only the smoke from his cigarette moved.

"I want to reorganize some city services, starting with the police department. Nothing's changed there in thirty years, but crime has. I'm talking about this series of fiendish murders. I doubt we've seen the last of them, or of others not connected to the traditional motives of greed and grievance. I'm proposing a police commission to supervise the department's day-to-day operations, and I want you to serve as commissioner."

"Who'll be police chief?"

"I'm eliminating the position. It means rewriting the charter, but I have the support of the council, and I'm confident I can swing the vote in an off-year election. You'll be paid more, of course, and you won't have to worry about campaigning for office ever again. It's an appointed position."

"Meaning I can be fired by one man instead of thousands."

"The city would have to buy out your contract, same as a major league coach. The income inducement is substantial."

"How does the city benefit?"

"By not placing the burden of multiple investigations on a single pair of shoulders. At present, you're a cop as well as a CEO. As police commissioner, your duties will be strictly administrative. Let others play Sherlock Holmes. It's their turn in the grinder."

"Mmm." He took a drag. "How long have you been cooking this up?"

"Oh, for some time. Since I got elected, actually. I wasn't sure this was the time to spring it, but it occurred to me you might welcome the distraction."

"When do you need an answer?"

"Before September, when the race heats up. I won't have much time for anything else after that." He flipped his cigar stub over the porch railing. "You've too good a brain to waste poring over police reports, Francis. The team needs you."

After the mayor left, the party—for that's what it was—began to flicker. Russell shook a few more dozen hands, said "Thank you" a hundred more times, declined Carly's halfhearted offer to stay with him and see the thing through, and finally found himself alone in the building with Marty, Dennis Stillwell finishing paperwork in his little office off the foyer, and the caterers, who were cleaning up. The saltines, cakes, and cheese had sustained heavy damage, and the corned beef looked as if it had taken a direct hit from a mortar. Only

Carly's puffed shrimps were untouched except by Moe Shiel's decidedly non-Kosher hand. Marty would have considered it a successful blowout.

He took some satisfaction from the ghastly evening. Not from the tributes to his wife, some of which were genuine, many of which were politics, and mostly all of which were self-serving. Certainly not from Jerry Wilding's proposition, which was just another version of Dungannon's and Zeno's hints at retirement, albeit a hideously more costly alternative to the taxpayers. The mayor might not have been Zeno's man the way Russell was, but he'd dined on Big Mike's experience his entire life and knew you didn't fuck with the balance in Gas City.

No, the moment he'd take home to put himself to sleep on his sofa was the surprise on the faces of detectives Prokanik and Boyle when he'd told them to consult with the state police on the Black Bag murders, shattering a long tradition of independence from the Republican authorities in the capital. He bet that got back to Zeno before Wilding and Dungannon caught wind of it.

In the viewing room he looked down at Marty, her face arranged in more restful sleep than he'd ever been responsible for. He bent over the casket, peeled one of the cotton gloves down from her wrist, and kissed the rubbery flesh. "I'm sorry to leave you, old girl. The work won't do itself."

II

THE CRACKDOWN

CHAPTER SEVEN

The shot heard round the city came from the four-inch barrel of a Police Bulldog .38 Special, Serial No. DX98104613, registered to Sergeant Linus "Fathead" Wilson, a fifteen-year veteran with the Uniform Division, attached to Vice. It shattered a lighted display of bottles behind the bar of the Hispanic Men's Social Club (formerly the El Capitan Hotel) on the corner of Florida and Castro streets in Little Brazil and created a sensation.

El Capitan had opened six months before Pearl Harbor, with a ballroom on the ground floor decorated with palms and bullfight posters and live parrots in huge cages suspended from the ceiling. Xavier Cugat and his orchestra had played there to a capacity crowd in 1946, but the Spanish-speaking population that had swarmed into the neighborhood to work at the McGrath refinery during the war continued to grow, and the Irish residents and visitors from uptown had found the Latin American flavor less than romantic and fled. City services had declined locally, the hotel had changed hands several times. One of its current owners had worked there as a bellboy in his youth.

His was not a Horatio Alger story. The only reason the Hispanic Men's Social Club survived was it opened after hours, when Riley's

Bar swept out its customers and they migrated up Castro to drink and shoot craps and entertain women upstairs. Nothing about the place was legal, including its observance of the fire code. The emergency exits were chained and padlocked to discourage invasions by street gangs and presumably inspectors. In the case of the inspectors, at least, the precaution was unnecessary; no one representing City Hall or the police department had crossed the club's threshold in more than a decade. Hence the reaction when Sergeant Wilson's bullet destroyed the liquor display.

Although he'd fired on orders from his lieutenant, the choice of targets was his, and he'd made it with cold reason. The spectacle of showering glass and spilled spirits both announced his squad's seriousness of purpose and froze the bartender in the middle of reaching for the sawed-off shotgun he kept on the same shelf with the cash box. He threw up his hands. In the immediate echo of the blast, the frantic salsa chattering out of the vintage Wurlitzer was the only sound in the room. Then the officers went to work.

Shouting and shoving, using their batons as prods, they herded customers across the room by their arms and collars and flung them against the bar, where they kicked their feet apart, forcing them to clutch at the bar for balance, and groped them from neck to ankles for contraband, which they deposited onto a table. The pile of pistols, pills, switchblades, syringes, brass knuckles, box cutters, and Baggies of cocaine, heroin, and marijuana grew quickly. A latecomer, apprehended trying to squeeze a thirty-eight-inch waist through the twenty-inch window in the toilet, was dragged, kicking and screaming the names of the saints, across the floor with batons lashing him from all angles, and handcuffed to the brass foot rail at the base of the bar.

"Chew on that, Chico." For this remark, Wilson was suspended for two weeks with pay pending an investigation of a complaint filed by an eyewitness. The man in handcuffs remained on the security floor of the Carbon County General Hospital for another ten days for treatment of lacerations and internal injuries and was released into police custody.

Those officers who weren't busy with customers assaulted the craps tables and slot machines with axes and leaded batons, and coins and multicolored chips joined the glittering carpet of glass on the floor. The jukebox was seized and tipped over in a splinter of neon tubes and smashed 45s. The Latin beat stopped. Six cases of Gordon's gin disappeared from a storage room in back.

When the noise receded, Detective Lieutenant William Casey, a plainclothesman eight years younger than Sergeant Wilson, paced up and down the length of the line of men at the bar, chanting their rights as provided by the U.S. Constitution and smacking his palm with his leather sap to keep time.

Not all of those who'd been in the club when the raid took place were captured.

Just after the shot, a sixteen-year-old juvie named Ramon, known to most of his acquaintances as Eel, had cleared the narrow window in the toilet with an inch to spare, hit the alley behind the building running, and easily outdistanced the two bulky officers who had been stationed in back to seal off retreat. He ran a jagged race for several blocks, hurdling barricades and ducking through holes in fences. When he was sure the police were no longer in pursuit, he broke the window in the back door of a neighborhood market on the edge of the Boggen Drain and let himself in. He used the telephone behind the counter to call Moe Shiel, who'd been in bed for several hours after paying his respects to Chief Russell's wife at Stillwell's Mortuary.

At about the time Shiel was stirring himself to answer the bell, Joseph Cicero came to the final paragraph of the letter his managing editor had handed him:

> Shame on you, Mr. Wynant, for drawing that vile filth. And shame on you, editors of *The Derrick*, for publishing it. Whatever shortcomings our Chief Russell may suffer from (and I do not for one moment agree he has any, as our *decent* citizens can travel most of the streets of our city without fear or offense), only someone who is himself *morally impoverished*

would point them out so insultingly in the very hour of his bereavement. "Let him who is without sin," etc.!

Yours sincerely,
Mary Catherine O'Connell

"Well, at least she's sincere. I had no doubt of it." He laid the sheet of pale green vellum on the desk. Just looking at the careful old-fashioned loops, no *i*'s left undotted, made the back of his hand smart, as if Sister Margaret Matthew had just swept through class, wielding her straight-edge like an Old Testament sword. "She certainly is possessive: '*our* Chief Russell,' '*our* decent citizens,' '*our* city.' I wonder when was the last time she took a stroll through *our* Circle. Is this the last of them?"

The publisher of *The Derrick* looked youthful at sixty, as he had at eighteen, at thirty, and at forty-five, and would undoubtedly at eighty in the unlikely event the paper didn't kill him before then; it was the superstructure that was eating away, like a house with fresh paint and termites. His round, deceptively genial face was unlined, broken only by the heavy black frame of his bifocals, and he had always been a towhead. At what point his hair had turned from pale, pale yellow to white—if it had—was a matter of depth perception.

Burton, the managing editor, answered his question with a grave nod. He was incapable of any other kind. He approached everything in life, including the birth of his daughter, whom he adored, like an old dog expecting to be beaten. His long sad features looked like one of those Old English caricatures made up entirely of funeral wreaths and weeping angels. Sour image, Cicero thought; just then he was disposed to hate doodlers of every era and nationality, and Andy Wynant most of all. The very editorial page in question lay folded to Wynant's cartoon on a vacant desk outside the glass partition separating Burton's office from the city room: a porcine Francis X. Russell kneeling over a trough stenciled VOLCANIC WHOLESALE PLUMBING SUPPLY CO., ANTHONY ZENO, PROP. It was a particularly vicious likeness, emphasizing the police chief's long nose, large ears, and bramble-bush eyebrows, with slop dripping off his chin. The execution was old-fashioned, more Thomas Nast-y than Gary Trudeau clever, and the issue had outsold both the local *Morning Light* and all the national papers at city newsstands. Cicero had okayed it with his own initials five days ago. What the hell was it doing still sitting on someone's desk? He reminded himself to ask Burton who sat there during the day. Probably whoever it was had meant to torment him. Everyone on the staff knew publisher and manager frequently met there hours after dayside had gone home. His own office was too isolated at night, a frozen marble chamber on the top floor.

A police scanner on a shelf beneath a row of framed front pages crackled and spat the details of a routine call. Both dispatcher and reporting officer sounded bored and sleepy. Burton turned his attention from them. "There'll be more letters tomorrow. Some of the older readers take a few days getting mad enough to hunt up an envelope and stamp."

"Older readers are all we have. Everyone under forty turns on the idiot box and laps up everything those Eyewitness News hyenas dish out, straight from City Hall."

"Maybe Wynant should have put *them* in front of the trough."

"Maybe he should go to work for Disney. He can turn Donald Duck into a pederast." This was not a suggestion. Cicero always left hiring and firing decisions to his manager. As a twenty-year-old cub reporter, he'd worked for a newspaper where the opposite was true, and watched it crumble from the top.

"It's not his fault," Burton said. "We told him what we wanted, and we signed off on what he delivered. It isn't our fault either. Who knew Russell's wife was terminal? We were told she was having her gallbladder removed."

"Then we're as bad as the competition for not asking more questions. Are we a newspaper or a guide to the lonely heart?"

This was a long-standing source of contention. Meaghan Cuddy, who wrote the column "Dear Aunt Meg," had been senile for years. Her responses to troubled readers who wrote in for advice had grown steadily more looney, and members of the staff had sometimes been forced to draft more reasonable answers for publication. Miss Cuddy, apparently, was lucid enough to recognize the counterfeits when they appeared in print, and invariably called Cicero on his private line to threaten legal action. The publisher wanted to drop the feature, but Burton had pointed out that her contract had another year to run, and Cicero refused to buy it out. The budget was too tight to pay good money for blank space.

"We wouldn't be getting so many angry letters if we had put Wilding on his knees next to Russell," the editor said. "It looks like we're picking on the chief."

"That was the strategy: Apply pressure to Wilding to dump Russell. He won't, of course, any more than Big Mike would have, and we could hang Russell around his neck and hammer at them both clear through to the election. Cut free, he might float, but he'd sink under the extra weight."

"I'm not clear on why we're supporting Rice-Hippert. We practically hounded her out of office last time."

"We did hound her out of office. That was because the *Morning Light* threw in with her, and we were always able to lick the *Light*. Now that we have a joint operating agreement, there's just TV to worry about, and it's kicking our ass. *That's* why we're supporting Rice-Hippert. Or rather, going after Jerry Wilding. Someone has to."

Here was a subject worthy of Burton's perpetual suit of gloom, and it was big enough for both men to fit into. Acting upon dark prognostications shared by their sales departments, Gas City's two remaining daily newspapers had hired teams of lawyers to hammer out an agreement by which both publications would share advertising revenue that would otherwise be lost to thirty-second commercial spots on television, their hated mutual rival. They'd saved further costs by banding together to issue a joint Sunday edition, *The Derrick-Morning Light*, pooling their staffs, which months before had been locked in cutthroat competition for every breaking story in the greater metropolitan area. At the stroke of a pen, fifty years of fierce combat, some of it violent, involving bombed-out newsstands and delivery boys kidnapped and beaten, had vanished as if it had never existed. The ghostly howling of half a dozen slain competitors—*The Truth, The Chronicle, The Daily Drum, The Standard, The Republican and Democrat* (a short-lived merger), and *The Evening Star*—had disturbed Cicero's sleep for weeks during the negotiations. The result had been a brighter economic picture for both publications and a decidedly more tepid reading experience for their subscribers. Reporters from *The Derrick* and the *Light* seemed to spend more time trying not to step on one another's toes than they did getting the story. What they missed, the TV crews gobbled up and vomited out undigested into living rooms throughout their viewing area.

"Someone has to," Burton echoed. "Especially if it boosts circulation. Nothing like a good old-fashioned scrap for selling papers." His expression looked like the right half of the masks of Comedy and Tragedy.

"We're a business, Sid. I'm not saying we're the Chamber of Commerce—they don't need us leading the cheers as long as they've got the broadcast stations to do it for them. But we have to pay for the paper and ink."

"Journalism One-Oh-One. I haven't heard that argument since I got my BA from State."

"They're actually teaching business now? I thought it was all Ben Franklin and Horace Greeley."

"It is again, for all I know. That was a long time ago." The editor cocked his head toward the scanner: disturbance at El Capitan. Last night it was Riley's Bar. They took turns. "Anyway, we'd better lay off Russell for a couple of weeks. I know how you feel about printing retractions."

"I'm all for it—just as soon as we find out he built that bowling alley onto his house with glue and old pay stubs."

"I think it was just a rec room. Couple of weeks, that's all. Long enough for them to forget he was ever married. We'll use the time to take another swipe at Zeno. No one writes letters on his behalf."

"Fat Paulie Buffo's widow can vouch for that. I disagree. Not about Zeno. He's a thug, but he's too smart to take us on like a goon from the East Side. I know where we can get scabs if he hits us with a labor strike. No, what we need to do is turn the heat up on Russell, not down. We can uncover enough to convince them it was him they were mad at all along."

"We're bound to lose subscribers."

"We've lost Mary Catherine for sure." Cicero thumped the letter with his finger. "We'll pick up others. It's like you said: nothing like an old-fashioned scrap. In any case, we can't afford to look like we're letting our readers dictate policy. The TV boys would swoop in for the kill."

"I think you're wrong, Joe."

"About those faggots in their perms? They'll rip the guts out of a straggler faster than you can say *National Geographic*."

"Not about them. About you assuming they even know we're still here."

They were silent for a moment. The scanner crackled, trying to communicate something outside its range.

Cicero stirred then. "See if you can find something else for Wynant. A strip, maybe. Every cartoonist dreams of landing a strip."

"That's because there's never an opening. They have to wait for someone to die, or get too old and sick to lift a pencil. *Alley Oop* started out as a contemporary commentary on the Mesozoic. We're tied up with the syndicates for five years minimum."

"*Make* an opening. Why should the Chicago papers be the only ones to get in on the ground floor? Copyright whatever he comes up with in *The Derrick*'s name. Maybe it'll go big and pull us out of purgatory."

"Where do you suggest we put it? We're barely selling enough advertising for the pages we have, and they're chock full. Last month we had to cut the President's speech to a paragraph."

"You should have cut that, too. They can get the whole thing on television. Dump the bridge column. Have you ever actually met anyone who plays?"

"My wife and I and Phil and Gladys Cooper, our neighbors. We get together every Sunday afternoon."

"No kidding. I always pictured you curled up with a fat book Sundays. One of those sad sack Russians."

"I've hated every rotten 'four, no trump' for five years," Burton said. "But Amy would divorce me if I dumped the column."

"Promote him to contest editor, then. When's the last time—"

Burton cut him short with a hiss. He reached up and turned the volume up on the scanner. Here was a new voice, taut with excitement. It was barreling all over the dispatcher's questions.

"That's Casey," Burton said.

"Who's Casey?"

"Lieutenant with Vice. The city cops just hit one of Zeno's joints in Little Brazil."

CHAPTER EIGHT

C alm down, Moe. Take a deep breath and tell it from the beginning."

Unlike Moe Shiel, Zeno had not been awakened by the telephone ringing in the small hours of Saturday morning. He'd had a chain of disturbing dreams—nothing specific, just a lingering sensation of anxiety—and had turned over in bed to nestle closer to Deanne, for no other reason than to redirect the course of his unconscious thoughts. Jarred awake by the contact, she'd raised and twisted her head to give him a poisonous look, as if he'd disturbed her sleep for something else.

There was no use trying to sleep after that. He'd thrown on a robe over his silk pajamas and gone down to his study, where he sat at his desk and called California to track the opening-night figures on two films in which Volcanic had an interest. Hollywood was a useful source of declarable income, and more often of deductible tax losses. He'd attempted more than once to lure its bookkeepers east, but apparently the racketeers who ran the studios offered more benefits. Someone else had crooked the world before he was born.

His hand was still on the receiver when Shiel called. In his panic, the little mug had reverted to his Boiler Row childhood: Every other word was Yiddish. Now, exhaling, he proceeded more slowly to describe what had taken place at the Hispanic Men's Social Club minutes after the legitimate bars had closed that morning. Zeno sipped bourbon and soda and listened without interrupting.

"Who'd you get it from?" he asked when the other stopped again to draw breath. He was puffing like a quarterhorse, but his agitation was passing.

"Skinny little squirt they call Eel. I slip the *chamacos* a ten-spot now and then to keep their eyes and ears open. My boys stay out of Little Brazil. He was in the dump when it got hit. I made a couple of calls downtown, just in case he smoked it all up on reefers. No soap, boss. It was Bill Casey's squeal."

Zeno swore, too softly for the receiver to pick up. Casey was a senior lieutenant, a squad leader. He'd hoped it was some rogue elephant of a sergeant with a personal beef. "Where'd they take them?"

"Third precinct, on Eleventh. They got a big Holding, natch. Two blocks down it crosses Florida."

"Okay, Moe, go to bed. You were right to call me right away."

The last of Shiel's fears evaporated from the line. "I'd of handled it myself if it was just some cops from the Third. Casey hangs his hat at headquarters. Jesus Christ, boss, is Russell off his nut? He seemed okay at Stillwell's. They wasn't serving nothing stronger than some shrimps that had me on the can for an hour."

Zeno broke the connection without replying and called Caleb Young at home. Young headed up the legal firm he retained. Without apologizing for waking him, Zeno told the lawyer what he wanted. Young expressed no surprise at the curious turn of events, but then nothing had seemed to stir the smooth surface of his voice and features in the twenty years of their association. No jury had ever been able to measure the strength of his case based on his demeanor. He said he'd call when the job was done.

On a hunch, Zeno dialed Sal Tahiti's private line at the Club

Sahara, his cash cow on Crescent Street, and get George Mi-calakopoulos on the pay phone at the Triangle Bar on Depot, where the horse action in back was the major draw. Both men reported nothing unusual. He gave them an abbreviated version of what had happened in Little Brazil and warned them to be on their guard. They promised to comply, but expressed no great concern over anything that took place outside The Circle.

For the next few minutes Zeno sipped his drink and regarded the first editions shelved on the east wall, trying to peer through toward Eleventh Street South and the Third precinct. Felipe "Flip" Bedondo, his junior partner in El Capitan (and the one whose name appeared on the papers), would be muttering to himself already; he'd never made his peace with the occupational hazards of operating an unlawful enterprise. Getting him out of the tank on the double was the better part of valor, and the price of doing business with a member of an excitable race. He preferred working with northern Italians, and Greeks most of all. He had many such prejudices hardwired into him, and his experiences so far had done nothing to weaken the connection.

The Irish he'd learned to take on a case-by-case basis.

He lifted the receiver again and plucked out a number he didn't have to think about. The purring over the wire seemed to come from the other side of the world, instead of just the other side of Factory Hill, where West Riverside began its gentle ascent to the McGrath estate. You didn't realize you were rising until you saw the stone pillars flanking the shining wet drive, and knew you could go no higher. The sound was like leaves rattling on a dead limb. He was about to hang up when it stopped with a hollow plop. "Yes."

"Francis?"

"Hello, Anthony." There were no nicknames now. The names themselves merely acknowledged each other's existence.

"You're sober?"

"I am."

He sounded surprised. The good humor in his tone would have encouraged Zeno if he didn't know it for a dangerous sign. He was certain Russell had not been asleep, despite the delay in answering.

"Well, you've had your adventure," Zeno said. "I suppose I should be grateful you didn't aim higher."

"It was a potluck affair. Not much time to plan." Here was the mocking Russell of the campaign trail. It had destroyed many a contender for his office almost before the contest had begun.

"No doubt Marty would have approved. She never liked me."

"She never said anything about you one way or the other."

"That says plenty."

"I wouldn't make book on it. I never did know where she stood on anything until she told me. I surprised her once with a party at Harrigan's for our anniversary. The twenty-fourth, it was. All our friends came. I even invited Carly."

"I wasn't there, of course."

"Of course. All that evening you'd have thought I got the Pope to mention her at Easter. I never saw her shine so. I only found out when we drove home I'd crapped on the altar. She didn't say a word to me for a week. I figured out she'd intended to spend the day with me only, but then the next year she wanted to go back to the old country. We never had a day to ourselves that whole trip. She watched me dance a jig with my cousin Phin and laughed like a girl."

"A trip to Ireland's a bit different from a roomful of drunks at Harrigan's."

"Not so much as you'd think. The point is I got my first clue when she kissed me or hit me with a skillet."

"I know how you feel."

There was a little silence. He thought he heard the TV murmuring in the background on Russell's end. The chief never watched at home, although Marty had. Maybe it had been on since before she went to the hospital.

"Who'd you give it to, Young?" Russell asked.

"Yeah. He specializes in criminal work. Rasmussen handles the business side. You know how it is with Flip." This was a unique conversation.

"I've known Flip almost as long as I've known you. He's older than he looks. Before that I knew his sheet. You'd think he'd be used to tight spaces by now. I told Casey to go ahead and lean on him. He might crack if Young takes an extra minute or two putting on his cuff links."

"He doesn't wear French cuffs. What do you want, Francis? You wouldn't give a shit what goes on at El Capitan if they were fucking donkeys there."

"I would if the donkeys were underage. You couldn't top what Jerry Wilding offered me tonight. Last night. He wants to make me police commissioner."

"We don't have a police commissioner."

"He intends to fix that. The job comes with a raise and probably a corner office opposite his at City Hall. You know the one I've got leaks."

"If I thought that's all you cared about I'd send over a team of roofers." His thumb found a chip on his glass, annoying him beyond reason. "Obviously you didn't take the job. If you had, you and I wouldn't be sitting here talking before the birdies started singing in the trees. Old men need their rest."

"I didn't give him an answer. If I take it, I won't be a cop anymore. It's all signing requisitions and going to lunch with movie producers who want to shoot in our fair city. Somebody else will keep the peace."

The peace being what they'd had until that morning. Zeno saw it all now, as clearly as if he'd been inside the cluttered warehouse that was the mayor's head. "You know this didn't come from me," he said. "I don't tell Jerry what to do any more than I did Big Mike."

"Mike would've stomped on your foot if you'd tried. He was a hooligan himself. But you never had to tell him a thing. He knew better than to fix what ain't broke and so does the boy. It's Hugh Dungannon, spreading gossip like the old Nelly he is. He's scared the Vatican's going to turn Perpetual Misery into a pinball arcade and ship him out to Arizona."

"On the level?" Zeno set down his drink.

"He as much as told me so last night. He said Junior's getting set to lay off the third shift at McGrath."

"That sounds like this year's version of the time he threatened to pull up stakes and move out of state. Then Big Mike condemned the old Hinch Building and expanded the employee parking lot."

"It's working this year too. Jerry promised him the governor, all tied up with a big bow like a bottle of Stewart's. Oops," he said. "That was confidential." Zeno wondered if he'd been drinking after all.

"There's a lot of that going around. Is Hugh going soft in the brain or what?" He was glad he'd stopped going to confession.

"I told you he's scared. He wants to stuff all the candy back into the piñata and slap on a Band-Aid."

"You could help with that. Little Brazil's just action on the side, which is the reason you decided to stick your toe in there in the first place. We can say you jumped the gun a little on the election." He could sell that to Mr. White. Paddy wagons were a staple in The Circle every fourth October.

"I don't know if I can help you there, Anthony."

"Help *me*? I'm trying to save your ass, you mick bastard. You've got it stuck out a mile."

"Maybe so. It felt good making the call."

He took a long steady draft, swallowed, and waited for the burn. It was slow in coming and quick to recede. He'd put in too much soda.

"If you want to be a cop all of a sudden, you should start with Beaver Cleaver. That kind of case is rotten business for everyone. People think twice before they go out, even in good neighborhoods. No one wants to set up shop in a graveyard. You can't let a nut killer run around breaking all the rules."

"Maybe no one's taken the trouble to explain them to him. It isn't as if we post them at the city limits." A match cracked next to the receiver. Zeno listened as he drew in the smoke. "I've stuck a toe in there as well. I hate to tell you, you're not the worst thing in this town. I'd not even put you in the top five. What I really ought to do is draw a black crayon clear around the Circle and send in the wreckers, just like in nineteen-seventeen. They didn't do things by halves in the old horse cavalry."

Here finally was a bit of the old Francis, casting jokes like javelins at targets he knew were outside his range. The Circle was the Ottoman Empire, Soviet Russia, and the Middle East bloc all rolled into one. You couldn't batter it down from outside, and no one inside was going to lend a hand. The place would go on drawing its venomous breath long after the Stillwell brothers had buried them both. God save the population from turning into miniature versions of old Morse McGrath. Zeno felt some of the tension going out of his shoulders. It may have been the bourbon taking effect at last.

"You had a busy day and a busier night," he said. "How long has it been since you took personal time? You must have six months built up. Go back to Ireland and dance another jig with your cousin. I'll make you a present of a first-class ticket. Consider it belated congratulations on your twenty-fourth anniversary."

"Things are looking up. A few days ago everyone wanted me to retire. Now I'm getting job offers and free trips. There may be a pony in it if I hold out long enough."

"There may be a lot more if you don't take me up on this one."

Russell chuckled a little, coughing; his den must have been foggy with smoke by then. "I've been wondering just when the gangster would come out."

"That wasn't a threat. Not from me. You don't need to be afraid of me, Francis. Not me."

"God help you if that's true."

Zeno said nothing. He could only repeat himself from here.

"Thank you for calling. I missed talking to you. I have to turn in now. I've a funeral this afternoon."

He listened to the dial tone, then cradled the receiver. Upstairs, the shower was running. He remembered Deanne was flying to New York for the weekend, just in case she'd missed something at Saks and Bloomingdale's last time.

He wasn't the least bit sleepy, and the prospect of sitting around alone waiting for Caleb Young to call had no appeal. He thought maybe he'd go in to Volcanic and sell some toilets.

CHAPTER NINE

He saw no more pizza boxes in front of 116, but he knew the room was still occupied.

On four occasions during the past three days, Palmer had used his passkey to let himself into 114, which was vacant, and put his ear to the flimsy partition that separated the rooms. He'd heard a throat clearing, the rustle of a newspaper, springs sighing under shifting weight; a substantial amount of weight, to go with the deep clearing of the throat. It was a man. The hotel detective had half hoped that George Micalakopoulos, proprietor of the Triangle Bar, was once again stashing a woman in the Railroad Arms, unknown to his wife. But that wouldn't explain Guerrera's nervousness whenever 116 was mentioned. No one feared the fat little Greek, just the service he employed to collect gambling debts.

That brought him back around to the theory that the man was in hiding. He never seemed to go out, and although Palmer had failed so far to intercept anyone bringing food to the room, he doubted he was fasting. A hot plate, a supply of canned goods, and the infrequent call to Mama Angelo's to break up the monotony could keep him inside for weeks.

Maybe it already had. There was no telling how many times Palmer had swum past the room in an alcoholic stew, oblivious to signs. Oblivion had been his permanent address for so long his skin had begun to jump from the exposure.

"So let him lay," Clare Sayer advised. "Mrs. Washington in four-ten has a Coleman stove, and the little creep on the top rear grills knackwursts in the bathroom. That's the fire marshal's headache."

"Their names are in the register. And they go out from time to time."

"I still don't get why it matters."

"Apart from the fact it's a state violation that could shut down the hotel and put me out on the street, I'm responsible for the safety of the guests. This guy could be Beaver Cleaver, did you ever think of that?"

"Those guys don't hang out in hotels. They live at home and take baths with their mothers." She was sitting in the tub, in fact, reading *The Confider*, while he sat on the edge with his shirtsleeve rolled up, stroking her back with a sponge. Another cluster of freckles was hiding out under her left shoulder blade.

"You read too many tabloids," he said.

"You don't read anything."

"I read the register."

"So I hear. It's all I've been hearing for days. If you're so god-damn curious, why don't you knock on the door?"

"Because if this guy pushed in a bank, he might answer it with bullets."

"Now he's a bank robber?"

"Some kind of robber, maybe. Probably not. It might be enough to spook Guerrera, but not Turnbull. He doesn't show it as much, but every time I bring it up he takes a fresh hit of oxygen. If I'm right about the other thing, it would explain why this character hasn't chopped anyone up in a while. He's been here the whole time."

"Call the cops. Constanza in Housekeeping says that Polack detective the other day was cute."

"He's about two ticks shy of a burnout. The woman's the sharp one. I don't want either one on my case if this turns out to be some schlub hiding from his wife."

"Speaking of schlubs, I owe you money for several days. I had a good week despite the suicide. It's in my bag."

"Buy yourself a subscription to *The Confider*. This pimp's retired."

She folded the paper. "When did this happen?"

"Tuesday. You can lay them in the lobby if you want. Turnbull and Guerrera might squawk, but I won't."

"Boo-hoo, Palmer. The guy was your age. So what? His wife dumped him, so he clocked himself to make her sorry. What's the odds it didn't work? You're just going through a jag."

"I hope it lasts a while. I'm starting to get used to it."

She twisted and raised herself to fish the pack out of his shirt pocket. She really had fantastic breasts. "Match me, big boy. Mother's hands are soapy."

He lit her cigarette with one of the butane lighters she'd bought him. "Next time you call yourself Mother I'll set your hair on fire. I'm a sex fiend, not a mass murderer."

"They aren't mutually exclusive. Not that I've seen any evidence lately. If it weren't for my job I'd have no sex life at all."

"I've been busy."

"Busy looking through keyholes."

"That's *my* job."

"Which you didn't bother to do the first seven years."

"I was pretty conscientious the first three. Then I met you."

"I am a distraction." She blew a plume at a crack in the ceiling. "Trust me, respect is for the dead. The living need cash."

"The hotel pays me, and they throw in a bed and a roof. I can live with the cheap plaster. What've I got to spend it on except Chesterfields and Ancient Age? By the way, I haven't had a drop for two days. Does AA have a chip for that?"

"Just a coaster. Don't get me wrong, Jim." He knew she was seriously pissed when she used his Christian name. "I'm behind you all the way, right up until Tony Z.'s boys blow in the door. Then I don't know you. I don't have another paycheck to fall back on."

"I know that, Clare. If I thought you had a heart of gold I'd never have asked you for anything but my cut." He drew a dry cigarette out of the sudsy pack and lit it. He was on his second lighter. His tobacco consumption had risen in inverse proportion to his drinking.

She let drift a mouthful of smoke. She never inhaled. It seemed to him a waste of seven varieties of poisonous chemicals. "I've got a four o'clock. I could push it back an hour. This guy thinks a blow job is God's gift to the married man."

"Can't do it, Clare. I'm on the clock."

"You have a clock?"

"Since Tuesday. Think of it this way: You may be saving a marriage."

"I've saved a hundred for every one I've broken up. Keep your pity for the girls on Blacksnake Lane. They'd do anything for twenty bucks except diagram a sentence."

He knew something irrevocable had happened. He also knew he'd done nothing wrong, in the greater scheme of things, to bring it about. He wondered, with a jolt, if he'd outgrown Clare Sayer. The thought did nothing to make him feel good about the turn of events that had led to this pass. From this point on, he felt, anything he could do for her would fall squarely under the heading of charitable services.

He suppressed a cynical chuckle, knowing she'd draw the wrong conclusion from it. That shoe had been on the other foot for so long, and his rehabilitation—if he could call it that, at this early stage—was so new and fragile they could swap places at any time.

"So what now?" She snatched up the sponge from the edge of the tub and went to work on her elbows. "You could sneak in and lift his fingerprints. Even Jack the Ripper had to fall asleep sometime."

"Maybe later. I left my Boston Blackie kit in my folks' house upstate."

She hooked a leg, slick with lather, over the side of the tub. Making things easy had never been her long suit. "You had parents?"

"Still do. Did you think I burst from a pod?"

"I never gave it much thought. So what now?" she repeated.

"What else? Talk to whoever brought him his pizza."

She shuddered, without affectation. "Mama Angelo. *There's* a candidate for mother of a mass murderer."

"I think her sons are too busy running numbers to hack people up."

"Bring back some bread sticks, will you? The regular kind, not the cheese. I'm watching my weight."

"Me too. Yours, that is."

"Don't start anything you can't finish, Palmer." She spread her toes and threaded a washcloth between them.

On his way down Depot Street, the sun pierced the overcast of several days, smirking at the piles of rotting railroad ties and clumps of marigold growing between the tracks of the Columbus Central. Trains rarely paused at the gaunt defaced building next to the hotel, strung with arches and crowned California style by a red tile roof covered with soot. Where the street crossed Boiler Row and became Commercial, the trains ducked underground and stopped to take on and let off passengers in the polished white ceramic surroundings of the station beneath the convention center. Palmer heard them hooting at night, blowing raspberries as they rocketed past the Railroad Arms.

The break in the clouds had healed over when he reached Mama Angelo's Pizzeria, or maybe the little square former neighborhood market existed under a perennial smudge of smoke from its brick chimney. He entered the tiny, surprisingly clean take-out area next to the little collection of booths, and was relieved not to see the old lady behind the cash register. He knew she took off one day per week, but had hardly hoped it would be Saturday. In her place, an olive-skinned brute of thirty, with a low forehead and a scrub pad of thick black hair, hung up a wall phone and pegged a rectangle of scribbled paper onto a revolving rack above his head.

"Sausage and mushroom, right?" He seemed to recognize the hotel detective, which was more than Palmer could say for him.

Mama's boys weren't twins, but they looked enough alike to confuse anyone who didn't see them every day. He knew they were only half-Sicilian. Their mother was Albanian.

"Which one are you?" Palmer asked.

"Gino."

"I work at the Railroad Arms. I guess you knew that."

"I see you there."

"You made a delivery there Tuesday, room one-sixteen. Pizza, not a payoff. I know what goes on in back."

"You want to order or what? This a busy day."

Palmer guessed his English was better than that. Both boys had been born at County General. "I'm not a cop, just security. It was pepperoni cheese." He held up a twenty.

"You know how many of those we sell?"

"You might remember this delivery. Guest down the hall squiffed himself the same day. The cops were in and out and there was a lot of traffic."

The telephone rang. Gino snatched the receiver off the hook. "Mama Angelo's."

Palmer took out another twenty and fanned them out like opera tickets.

"We're busy. Call back." Gino hung up. His gaze flicked from the bills to his shoulder. The other deliberately misinterpreted the backward glance.

"Maybe Nick dropped it off. He in back?" He took in his breath to call out.

A fist carpeted with wiry black hair closed on the bills. Palmer held on. Gino frowned with his whole face. "I dropped it off."

"How'd he pay?"

"Cash. All singles."

He'd thought a credit card was too much to hope for. "Tall, short, old, fat, skinny, black, white?"

"Middle-aged, like you. Taller, a little. Not so wide. His shoulders kind of fell off, you know? I think he was white." Gino tugged. Palmer held on.

"You *think*?"

"The light was behind him. You don't spend any more on them bulbs in the hallway than you have to."

"What else?"

"Had on kind of a shirt and pants."

"Kind of?" Jesus.

"Hey, I've had 'em come to the door in a jockstrap. Don't ask me did he wear glasses or an eyepatch, or had hair or not. All I was looking at was the money. He had a roll big as a coconut, all singles."

"A roll of ones?"

"I got a good look when he peeled 'em off. Not even a twenty wrapped around the outside for looks. Put that in your pocket, you limp like a punk with a two-foot hard-on. Maybe that's why he sent out."

"He tip you?"

"How much you think?"

Palmer grinned. There wasn't any more to get. At least Gino's English had improved. He let go of the bills. Gino stuck them in his apron pocket. The fictional version of Mama beamed out from the bib. "What'd he do, skip out on the bill?"

"Yeah. I'm the collection agency."

I think he was white, he thought, on the street. You could malign the race of your choice anywhere in the Circle and someone would take it personally and beat the shit out of you. He was halfway back to the hotel when he remembered Clare's bread sticks.

He didn't turn around. If Gino's brother Nick—or much worse, Mama—had overheard the conversation, he didn't want to take the chance of walking in on a domestic disturbance. He'd worn the black band on his shield for too many fellow officers who'd done just that.

A roll as big as a coconut. Even allowing for exaggeration, that was a lot of singles. You needed that show twenty for a proper Gas City Bankroll, that badge of four-flushers from Granite Park to Riley's Bar. Maybe the guy had stuck up a Dollar Store.

Back on native soil, he did turn around at the stairs. One-sixteen was two down from the fire door, as blank as the face behind it.

"Scotch tape? Yeah." Turnbull got up from his rocker, found the plastic dispenser, and slapped it on the desk. "Redecorating?"

"Homemade roach trap." He took an envelope off a stack of stationery on the desk and put it in his side pocket with the tape.

Outside 116 he knelt, laid out his tools on the runner, and examined the doorknob all around in the light of a butane flame. What he found looked promising—if someone from Housekeeping hadn't grasped the knob last. He tore off a strip of cellophane tape, smoothed it over the smudge, and peeled it off carefully, using both hands to keep it from curling back on itself.

After that he worked fast. He didn't have a story ready in case Johnny Dollar heard something and opened the door on him kneeling in the hall. He spread the envelope on the floor, laid the tape sticky side down on the inside of the flap, preserving the smudge, folded it over, and got up, pocketing the envelope along with the dispenser and lighter as he swung open the fire door.

On the second floor landing he got the envelope back out, lifted the flap, and held it up so that the twenty-five-watt bulb in the ceiling shone through. The loops and whorls were unsmeared, and the print itself was too big to belong to the thumb of any of the maids. He grinned when he thought what Clare would say when he told her he'd decided to take her advice and fingerprint the nameless guest. She might even forgive him for forgetting the bread sticks.

Now all he needed was a police lab and access to the FBI database.

CHAPTER TEN

Sylvia Cicero introduced herself, to the appropriate company, as "Joe's misdemeanor."

This wasn't quite accurate. When they began dating, she'd been his assistant for months, and asking out pretty secretaries was as much a part of the business day as Manhattans for lunch and cigars in the boardroom. By the time society and statute condemned romance in the workplace, she and Joe had been married ten years.

Plump by design ("Fat doesn't wrinkle"), she was a pleasant-looking forty, twenty years younger than her husband. The difference wasn't conspicuous. She wore her brown hair in waves with an aggressive streak of silver in front and dressed older than her age in pearl necklaces and coral-pink sweaters buttoned at her throat and draped across her shoulders like a cape. Many who knew her on short acquaintance thought her sweet and rather vacant. Members of the Carbon Valley Historical Society, of which she was president and founder, knew her for a political savant who removed obstacles from among her constituency with the cold skill of a surgeon slicing out a malignant tumor. Joseph Cicero sought her advice on every subject from which color necktie to wear for lunch with an astronaut to which candidates to endorse for public office. Sylvia was *The Derrick*'s policy in every way that counted.

They were having tea one Sunday in the sunroom of their house on North Terrace.

"I need to patch things with Angela Rice-Hippert," he said. "Any suggestions?"

She nibbled at a ginger snap. "You're backing her campaign for mayor. How big a patch do you need?"

"I went after her pretty hard throughout her term. I don't want her thinking I switched sides just because I'm mad at Wilding and Russell."

"That *is* the reason, isn't it? Aside from building circulation."

"Yes, but she can't know it. If she gets in, and she's still got a grudge, we could lose the contract to post city business. That pays the rent."

"You'll still get a piece of it if it goes to the *Light*."

"I'm not interested in helping Arthur Townower pay *his* rent."

"I see. Honeymoon's over." She stopped there in the interest of peace. His decision to enter into a joint operating agreement with the publisher of *The Morning Light* had led to chilly relations in the Cicero household for a month.

"Anyway," he said, steering the conversation in a safer direction, "she might stiff us both and take it to a supermarket shopper. All the charter says is the information has to be posted in print. It doesn't say where."

"If Wilding is reelected, you'll be in the same leaky boat."

"He's too much politician to do anything so direct. Reporters from *The Derrick* will find it a little more difficult to get access to officials and city employees for interviews and statements, the brand of liquid soap in the washrooms down at the office will be found by inspectors to be in violation of the health ordinances, the cops in Stationary Traffic will start enforcing the two-hour slots in front of the building. That sort of thing. We can put up with that until he gets bored with it. Rice-Hippert is a vindictive bee eye tee see aitch." He seldom swore in public and never in Sylvia's presence.

"You could write a series of editorials praising her to the saints, but I'm sure you're already planning to do that."

"It starts next month. Sid Burton's ghosted a humdinger to kick it off." He smiled in his proprietary way. He was as proud of his managing editor's skill with words as he was unsatisfied with his own. He considered selecting the right man to forge his signature a form of authorship.

"Invite her to dinner."

"I considered that, but wouldn't it be too obvious? She's no dummy."

"She's also a woman, and women enjoy being paid court, even if it's for selfish reasons. She'll see it as a sincere effort to suck up."

His face brightened, then clouded over. "I suppose we'll have to invite that brown mouse she's married to."

"If you can think of a way to tell her to leave him home, I've got a job for you with the historical society. Invite Sid and Amy Burton. We'll make it a dinner party."

"Sid's a browner mouse than Hippert. We might as well hang crepe in the dining room."

"Amy's chirpy enough for both of them, and I'm not the worst hostess in the city."

"The First Lady's a hermit next to you." He drummed his fingers on his cup. "You're not planning to cook, are you?"

"I wouldn't dream of poisoning our next mayor before she's taken the oath. We'll cater. Is Rinaldi's still advertising?"

"They just bought a full page for St. Patrick's Day. Corned beef, cabbage, and veal *piccata*."

"Some of Mrs. Rice-Hippert's supporters might object to veal. I'm thinking stuffed squab. Even vegetarians won't protest a few less pigeons in Roosevelt Park."

He spilled tea on his hand. Fortunately, he hated tea and had let it grow cold. "Gosh, Sylvia. Promise me you won't repeat that joke at dinner."

"Gosh, Joe." She mocked him. "Promise me if you call the guest of honor a bitch to her face you won't spell it."

The invitation was accepted for a week from Saturday. In the meantime, Chief Francis X. Russell's wife died, and the funeral was scheduled the same day. In her office at Waterman & Rice, the legal firm she'd helped establish twenty-three years ago, the mayoral candidate laid aside the notes for a speech she was composing to wrestle once again with the decision whether to cancel with Cicero. The service at Our Lady of Perpetual Misery (Good God, did these people never let up on themselves?) would be over by then, but sitting down that same evening with the man who was doing his best to skewer the widower in public might hurt her with Catholic voters. Their faith was not hers—in fact, when she'd defeated the late Michael Wilding's weak sister of a deputy mayor, she'd been Gas City's first Protestant chief executive since a Republican had held that position, back when old Morse McGrath the First was still old Morse McGrath the Only—but there were sensibilities to consider. She couldn't afford to write off the people who returned Russell to office year after year. Especially now that he actually seemed to be doing what they'd put him there to do.

Within hours of the raid on Little Brazil, a reporter with one of the local TV stations had called her at home for her reaction. It was her first hint of the thing and she'd reserved comment. Later that morning, after a strategy session with her campaign manager, she'd issued a cautious statement, congratulating the Gas City Police Department on its initiative, and expressing her confidence that all the parties under detention would be accorded their constitutional rights. The second part was a warning, a message of support for the Hispanic community, and a reminder that such had not always been the case. It was a strictly defensive move.

She wasn't sure where the chief was going, and it irritated her. Half of every penny pissed away gambling and drinking after hours went to one end of West Riverside, and a little less than half of that went to the other. Anyone running for office could take comfort from that statistic—particularly the reform candidate for mayor.

In open court, you never asked questions you didn't already

know the answers to. The political arena was the largest courtroom in the world, where one miscalculation could get you laughed out of it by the gallery. Nothing in her experience explained satisfactorily why a corrupt public servant would reverse a twenty-year pattern of behavior overnight. True, Russell was in mourning. It was reasonable to expect a man to reexamine his life in such circumstances. But she'd toiled too long in filthy trenches to place any faith in a sudden and permanent conversion without some tangible prize in sight. If it *was* a tick of conscience, a raid on a fairly unimportant target would probably be the beginning and end of it. More likely the old sot had gotten drunk on grief and Irish whisky and mixed up his dates. October was crackdown season in an election year.

Well, that was Wait and See. She had a team to do that and then advise a course of action if the problem, if that was what it was, didn't go away by itself. Whether to dine with Joseph and Sylvia Cicero was hers alone. To be a leader, you had to lead. During her first campaign, her opponent had depended on his people to tell him what to do at every turn in the trail. The custom of delayed response had sent a message of indecision and malaise; hardly the sort of thing one expected of a crony of Big Mike's. She had won handily, but that powder-puff contest had done nothing to prepare her for the savage onslaught by Mike's son Jerry after four years of garbage and transportation strikes—Anthony Zeno, laying aside his usually subtle manipulation of the labor unions for a more direct role—and a skyrocketing budget. Where did they think the money came from to privatize those services while new contracts were being negotiated? The race this time had been closer, but the Wilding dynasty was established by a comfortable plurality.

She'd returned to private practice, where it took her some little time to reflect and realize she'd been set up to fail. Jerry had remained *hors de combat* from the first election after his father's passing in order to give voters a taste of life without the machine in place, and to learn to miss the good old days when the grease was spread around and the gears turned smoothly. Any outrage that might have been directed at the backslapping and deal-making at City Hall quickly turned another way when the trash was rotting in eight-foot piles on the street and you had to walk clear from the north end of Commercial to West FDR because the buses and taxis were idle. Four years of that, went the reasoning, and any candidate who campaigned on a reform ticket would be dead for another twenty. It was as slick a shell game as had ever been played, and she was the pea.

Now she was wised-up, rested, and filled with resolution born of cold anger. And she knew how to run a dirty campaign as well as anyone, post–Big Mike.

Angela Rice-Hippert was forty-eight, but looked ten years younger, thanks to a combination of heredity, good cosmetics, and eight hours a week spent walking a treadmill and lifting hand weights. A light wash kept her hair a crisp silver blonde, cut short on the sides and in back and worn in an awning over her high forehead. She was slim, two inches under six feet, and always appeared in public in a skirt and blazer and heels that complemented her height rather than drew attention from it. She'd modeled for magazines to pay her tuition through law school—nothing salacious, although a monochrome shot of her posing in a chaste white nightgown had made the rounds eight years ago. That was the deputy mayor's idea of a smear, and she hadn't responded to it. She was convinced the picture's circulation had increased her profile among young male voters.

Now, sitting cross-legged on the Queen Anne bench in the consultation area of her office, surrounded by rows of law books bound in cream-colored leather, she made a decision. She knew Douglas wouldn't object. Her husband heeled her like a poodle whenever etiquette required a male escort, and he never passed up a chance to talk to someone new about his collection of pocket watches. He was useless for just about anything else, but he was loyal, and he belonged to a good family.

Let Jerry and his snipers do what they wanted when the details of her day came to light. She understood something that possibly even Joe Cicero did not. Obsolete though they were, unable to compete for speed with even a low-budget station on cable, newspapers provided a greater service than just cheap packing material on the day after publication. People never believed a thing they'd seen with their own eyes until it showed up in print. Any modern politician who thought he could ignore newspapers in favor of the live press conference and ten-second sound bite was dancing on a platform built of brittle glass tubes. She got up and used the intercom on her desk to tell her assistant to confirm with Joe and Sylvia Cicero.

The publisher's home, designed on the Wright principle but with practical ceilings and a roof that didn't leak, took up three thousand square feet—modest according to South Terrace standards, but still dominating its tract north of the river. A woman came in to clean twice a week and a Micronesian gardener tended the hedge and square lawn. Sylvia had decorated the rooms in such taste that even frequent visitors found it difficult to describe any feature beyond the seating in the dining and living rooms, still as comfortable after three hours of food and discussion as when the evening began. The music that played on the stereo was bland and housebroken. Nothing, in fact, competed with the startling frankness of the hosts' conversation.

The Rice-Hipperts arrived behind Sid Burton, Cicero's dour managing editor, and his wife Amy, who looked like a tiny canary in a bright yellow cocktail dress and cap of shiny black hair, and punctuated her sentences with squeaks the way some tribal Africans used tongue-clicks; you never knew when one was coming, and the effect was surprisingly charming—surprising, at any rate, for anyone who knew of them only at second hand. The former mayor shook hands and introduced her husband. Douglas towered over everyone at four inches above six feet, with rounded shoulders, boyish features, and brown hair receding before the eyes, falling like pine needles to the shoulders of his blue suit. She wore blue as well, a simple sleeveless dress she'd changed into from the dark suit she'd worn to church.

The squab was excellent, served with asparagus in garlic butter and fresh rolls, with Boston cream pie for dessert. After the dishes were cleared, Cicero brought out a bottle of wine he'd been hoarding in his cellar. That gave him the opportunity to talk about his twenty-year-old Bordeaux, and Douglas to gas on about his hundred-year-old Hamiltons. It was as lively as he became throughout the evening.

Coffee was served in the open pale living room. There, the publisher unbuttoned his jacket and asked about the funeral of Chief Russell's wife, and by this compass set his course toward the subject of politics.

"Bishop Dungannon's eulogy was moving, I must admit," Rice-Hippert said. "He read a poem Mrs. Russell herself had requested."

"How was the chief?" asked Cicero.

"Like a wooden Indian. We might have been attending the opening of a new wing at the jail."

"You can never tell how he feels about something in his press conferences," chirped Amy Burton. "The Irish are so stoic, don't you think?"

Her husband inclined his grave head. "They don't tear their chests and throw themselves across the box. To see that, you have to go to St. Anne's on Florida."

"Speaking of Florida Street." Cicero lifted his eyebrows above the black rims of his glasses.

Mrs. Rice-Hippert drank coffee, making no face over the weak brew, which was evidently Sylvia's own contribution to the menu. "The same old tired election-year ploy. They'll be drinking and shaking dice again in El Capitan by tomorrow night."

"A bit early," the publisher said. "The raid, not the grand re-opening, which I agree will be soon. Come election day, everyone in town will have forgotten it was ever closed."

"Only the male voters. The women will have seen through it." Amy slung three sugar cubes into her cup. "You have my vote, Madame Mayor. There are entirely too many toilet seats left standing in City Hall."

"Oh, Amy!" Sylvia laughed.

The candidate smiled. "I'm delighted to have your support, and I'm grateful for the honorary title. It seems just yesterday Mr. Cicero referred to me as 'the night-mayor of Gas City.'"

"That wasn't personal." Burton seemed inclined to elaborate, but was prevented from doing so by his employer, who set down his cup and saucer on the nearest transparent glass surface and remained leaning forward from his seat.

"I'm in business, not public service. I can't afford the luxury of an unpopular stance. You remember what the situation was four years ago. Had we come out for you and against Jerry Wilding, they'd be selling chintz furniture in the office of *The Derrick* today. It takes time to educate readers that what they really want to hear is the truth."

"Four years," she said, "to be precise."

"A bit more. But we're making progress. Have you read us lately?"

"I have a subscription, as I'm sure you know. The letters column has been entertaining."

"Can you hazard a guess as to the writers' average age?"

"What *is* the truth?" asked Douglas Hippert, before his wife could respond.

Everyone looked at him. His expression was genuinely curious.

"Just because the trains run on time is no excuse to leave the crooks in charge," Cicero said. "We've gotten used to the situation because the trash gets collected and you never see a hooker west of Depot Street or south of Blacksnake Lane. Tony Z.'s benevolent as gangsters go, but he's not young, and whoever takes his place might not be so easy to get along with. We may be a lot less comfortable for a while after we tip over the table—there are sure to be strikes and a crime wave on the west side—but we'll be better off in the long run. At least we'll have a less successful form of corruption in place," he added, sitting back.

"That little speech could put us all out of a job," said Rice-Hippert.

"Not if it's aimed at the right audience. We've got a whole new generation of voters coming up who barely remember Big Mike Wilding, and who watch television and know there's a world outside this city. And then we've got Beaver Cleaver."

Amy Burton squeaked. The noise spun down through a vacuum

of silence. Satisfied with his effect, Cicero touched the bridge of his heavy glasses, winding himself up like one of Douglas Hippert's antique watches.

"This maniac's dumped body parts on Factory Hill, in Roosevelt Park, in a Goodwill box on Crescent, and in the Boggen Drain. Either he doesn't know he's supposed to confine his butchering to the Circle and maybe Little Brazil, or he doesn't care about Chief Russell's understanding with Zeno and Moe Shiel. Crazed killers make poor collaborators. It's a basic flaw in an otherwise tidy system. And we'll keep hammering at it until we bring Jerry Wilding tumbling down from the top."

"You're saying you want to go after Chief Russell because the Black Bag murders are still unsolved." Rice-Hippert chose the sanitized TV nickname for the case. "What if he catches the killer?"

"No, we're going to go after him as Zeno's tame cop, as we've been doing right along. Beaver Cleaver's a type. There will be others, and whether the police nail him, or another garbage bag shows up in front of the convention center, or he flat out stops—which I find even more disturbing—we'll scare the hell out of voters with editorials reminding them you can't just throw a fence around crime, dust off your hands, and walk away. It'll climb right over the top and attack your family."

"And I suppose I'm to help by taking the same line in my speeches and statements."

"That's up to you, counselor. But it would present you as a solution to the problem."

"What if Wilding dumps Russell?"

"Well, he can't fire another elected official, but he can distance himself. Big Mike wouldn't, but he had tenure. Jerry's only a one-term mayor at this point. If he does step back, he'll appear weak. Either way your polls go up and his take a dive."

She set aside her cup. She leaned forward, distending her nostrils and pulling taut the skin over her cheekbones. It was a debate, and she was on the offensive. "What if Russell doesn't cooperate? What if he follows up on El Capitan with a raid in the Circle? Just for the sake of argument, what if he's actually decided to clean up his act and make good on his oath?"

Her listeners, even Amy and Douglas, settled back, chuckling; all except Burton. A quizzical look had crept onto his somber face.

"You state that as an impossibility," he said.

"Anything is possible. Hypothetically, the Black Bag Killer will turn suddenly sane and surrender himself to the police."

"I started out as a police reporter. If you'll excuse my saying so, I'm the only one here who has experience with the criminal personality."

"Not quite." Cicero was dry. "I've spent a lot of time at City Hall."

"Joe." His wife reached over and touched his wrist. He patted her hand and subsided into a listening posture.

"I'm not talking about the simply corrupt, or for that matter a loose screw like our cleaver killer." The managing editor counted off his points on his fingers. "I mean the convenience-store thief who slips a clerk fifty to leave the back door open, the underboss who bribes the judge to throw out a search warrant, Anthony Zeno financing improvements to Francis Russell's house. Underworld types always worry that the graft won't take, that someone will double-cross them and go straight. It's a twisted form of faith in the basic honesty of men that we, who consider ourselves honest, don't share, and it keeps them up nights. With them it's a worst-case scenario."

"With us, too," Rice-Hippert said. "We're counting on Russell to lapse back into corruption."

"Assuming Zeno gives him that chance," put in Cicero. "If he gets nervous and terminates our chief of police, we've spent all this time and ink crucifying a martyr. We can't come back from that."

Sylvia Cicero smoothed her skirt.

"I wish I had my gavel," she said. "This forum has taken a sinister turn."

The host retrieved his cup. "Fortunately, we're discussing science fiction. An old leopard like Russell doesn't change his spots just because he lost his wife."

"You say that so no one will think you're naïve," Burton said. "In Tony Z.'s crowd, it's the opposite."

"Possibly. It's an interesting moral paradox. You're a student of political science, counselor. How's your history?"

"Try me." She locked gazes with Cicero.

"In nineteen fourteen, Franz Ferdinand, the Austrian imperial heir, was shot and killed by a Serbian nationalist in Sarajevo. Do you know the motive behind the act?"

"It was in retaliation for the subjugation of the Serbs in Austria."

"It was not. Franz Ferdinand had stated his intention to introduce reforms favorable to the Serbs in his empire. Had he survived to ascend the throne, he would have made a revolution unnecessary. In plain terms, he was killed because he was going to give the rebels what they were shouting for. They needed a despot in the palace in order to seize it."

"What's good for reform is bad for the reformers." Rice-Hippert allowed herself a nod. "I hope we're not so cynical as that, in spite of what Mr. Burton says."

"We're agreed on that," Cicero said. "That bullet plunged the world into war and killed ten million people."

CHAPTER ELEVEN

After the Great Fire of 1834, the city fathers—refugees, some of them, from the French Restoration—had rebuilt the city with an angry vertical line separating Church and State. They named it Commercial Street. Our Lady of Perpetual Misery loomed three blocks to the west, shaped like a tombstone, and the buildings of government began a block to the east. This was where Cathedral Street became Civic Center Drive.

The center was triangulated by the county courthouse, police headquarters, and the Municipal Building—City Hall. The last had had pretensions to grandeur until the clock tower was demolished because of structural problems, leaving behind a plain brick box that resembled a high school, and more lately a flea market. The new courthouse, sixty as of last spring, stood on its predecessor's stone foundation and looked like a prison. All its windows were barred and a chain-link fence surrounded the asphalt lot in back where the jail vans parked, with razor wire unspooled across the top.

The police station alone fulfilled all expectations for buildings of its function. Gypsy film crews sometimes obtained permission to shoot it for period features, with vintage black sedans deposited in front for atmosphere. Neoclassical arches framed its windows, stacked five stories above the crackled-marble steps that led to its entrance with a lighted porcelain globe the size of a jack-o'-lantern mounted on either side. This was where the officers gathered to drag on their cigarettes, and if you had business inside, you had to pardon your way past them and track in smoke. After passing through the sharkjaw bower of a metal detector, you spoke to a sergeant, jacked up like a pharmacist behind a paneled desk on a raised platform, and if he thought you were upper-floor material he handed you a pass and pointed you toward the elevator. The car pulled itself up the cable hand over hand and smelled like the inside of an old leather suitcase.

If, heaven forbid, your business involved Homicide, you found it on Four, in a thirty-by-thirty-foot room separated from Vice by lath and plaster, with a connecting door to encourage intramural cooperation. Too many desks were arranged in rows, like a schoolroom, and you touched them for balance as you passed down the aisles, as if you were walking on a moving train, because the boards were warped beneath the linoleum and walking on them made you a little carsick. Light came down from fluorescent bars and through the arched windows looking out on the downtown convention center, and several blocks north of it the river, flashing like the silver backs of the fish that used to swim in it, back when Gas City was called Garden Grove and McGrath was just a village in Scotland. You were fifty feet above the street and five million miles from home.

"Mooning over your black captain?"

"What?" Patsy Boyle turned to face her partner, hunkered behind the slag of bloated case files in the middle of the huge block of golden-oak desk with drawers on both sides, which if anyone ever tried to move it would snatch up four square patches of linoleum, exposing the tarry mess underneath.

"If you are, turn around. State police headquarters is that way." He pointed at the partition behind her, lined with framed photos of dead officers no one had looked at in years.

"Make sense," she said.

"You've got a case on that black captain. Admit it."

"You're a redneck, Stan, you know it?"

Detective Prokanik's brows lifted, simple hydraulics in the tired face. "I'm a Polack, not a hillbilly."

"Well, you talk like one. Black captain. How many colors of captain did we talk to lately? Just say captain if you can't remember his name."

Which was Roger Keynes, who'd had the weekend watch when they'd driven up to the capital on Chief Russell's orders to show him the file on the Black Bag homicides and poke around in his brain for a trick they hadn't tried. He was a still man in an office as still as a reflecting pool, with a view of the rotunda; a smooth, brown, polished-looking career cop in a uniform broke to his whip-saw frame. He might have been thirty-six or sixty-three, with no gray in the light stubble where he shaved his head. It gleamed like a walnut pistol grip.

"Anyway, you can stop slobbering over him. He's got pictures of his wife and kids all over his desk."

"I don't fantasize about cops," she told her partner. "I was thinking about Beaver Cleaver."

"Better not let them hear you calling him that upstairs."

"He needs a name. The Black Bag sounds like an archvillain in a comic book, whereas this guy's just a jerkoff with a box of Hefties."

Portrait of a jerkoff:

"White male, aged eighteen to twenty-four; same demographic as *Playboy*," Keynes had said, tapping the file flayed out on the black volcanic-glass top of his desk. "That's boilerplate. Random violent felons are rarely black or Asian or Hispanic, almost exclusively men, seldom younger than voting age, and if your guy's older than twenty-four, he'd have started before this and you'd have known about him. Late bloomers don't rate high enough to make the scale. There's also physical strength to consider, and that falls off after forty."

"What if he's new in town?" Boyle asked. "He might've started somewhere else."

"I got on the mainframe after you called. The MO doesn't

match any in this hemisphere going back two years. I could dig deeper, but that's one hell of a long dry spell for this kind of animal."

"Anything else? Peg leg, parrot, talks with a lisp?" Throughout the interview, Prokanik had leaned back in his chair, hands in his pockets, occasionally jangling his keys and change; doing his best to be irritating and succeeding, at least with his partner.

The captain didn't react to his tone. "He's right-handed—from the angle of the cuts. The fact he uses a surgeon's bone saw doesn't necessarily mean he belongs to the medical community. You can get one from any surgical supply catalogue, or pick it up in a junk shop for ten bucks. Makes his cuts at the joints. Butchers learn how to do that first day on the job. He's a brute, clubs them from behind with his forearm and probably starts cutting while they're unconscious. Whatever he uses for a workshop wouldn't make *House and Garden* when he's done."

"You broke a string of rapes, right?" Prokanik asked.

"The department did, yes. Child rapes."

"If no one was killed, how do you know about bone saws and if the vics were still alive when he started cutting and what he hit them with? Why not a hacksaw and a baseball bat?"

"All that's here in the medical examiner's report." He held up a pink sheaf stapled on one corner. "Have you looked at the file?"

Prokanik flushed deep cherry and pressed his lips tight as stacked timbers.

Boyle took pity on him and changed the subject. "Most of his victims were working girls. What's he got against prostitutes?"

"Maybe nothing. These timetables say he hunts at night, and they're in greater supply after dark. He may not even have issues with women. He killed two men, including a female impersonator on his way home from the last show at the Club Sahara. Both were under average size. A bigger man in good health isn't so easy to knock cold with a forearm slam. Our child rapist wasn't a pedophile, the shrink said. He's a puny squirt, afraid to take on a full-grown woman. They have to stick a phone book under him to sodomize him up at the Gray Bar Hilton." He'd smiled his quiet smile and handed back the folder. "That's all I can tell you without painting the barn. Wish I could be more help."

All the way back down the interstate, Boyle had talked about the state police captain's take on the evidence. It had all seemed so obvious when he explained things, you wondered why you hadn't seen it right away. But it was like someone describing a theater set when the curtain was still down, then ringing it up so you could look at the details. Prokanik, in the passenger's seat, had watched the silos and Citgos pass and replied in single syllables. That must have been when he got the idea she had a case on Keynes. He was convinced his wife was sleeping around and had sex on the brain. She decided to forgive him for that, if not for his lambent racism.

"We've got to go along with the chief on this one," she said now. "We're at least six weeks ahead of the investigation on five bucks' worth of gas."

"Let's swear out a warrant on every guy in the greater metropolitan area that reads *Playboy* and wipes his ass with his right hand." He slid a folder off the pile and smacked it open on his side of the desk.

Boyle gave up on him and sipped her Coke. They were reviewing old arrest files, isolating suspects in assault cases who fit the profile Keynes had given them, but the one she had spread in front of her wasn't holding her interest. She was a strong-boned brunette who cut her hair short herself so all she had to do was run her fingers through it after a shower. It had the effect, unintended, of calling attention to her large eyes and away from her too-small nose. She spent all the time she saved powdering the hell out of the circles under her big dumb cow eyes, so useful in interrogations and so much of a pain in the ass when it came to being taken seriously by her colleagues and superiors. They were as bad as big breasts. She had those, too, although you could tone them down with athletic bras and dark blazers. Glasses only made her eyes look bigger, and shades were for lieutenants and better. Without going to lesbian extremes, which would be a career dead end in that department, she had to live with the fact that she looked like a pretty TV actress researching a role in a police drama.

"Oh, boo-hoo, Patricia," was her mother's response whenever she forgot herself and complained about it in the maternal presence. "You ought to get down on your knees and thank God you take after your father's side of the family. The only reason I had a boyfriend in high school was I looked old enough to buy beer." She was already convinced her daughter was a lesbian, and had chosen to show her support by inviting an ugly single girl to every holiday dinner and trying to fix them up.

But she could avoid her mother, apart from the duty calls. Work was another thing. She suspected she owed her gold shield to the two years and three months she'd spent married to Billy Boyle, and the bureaucratic inconvenience involved in resuming her maiden name after the divorce; she'd just decided to keep it. When Rice-Hippert was in office, Chief Russell had responded to the mayor's push to promote female members of the department to positions of responsibility by pulling half a dozen personnel files and green-lighting the Dugans and Callahans. Had he bothered to read past the top three lines and found out Patricia Lydia Boyle was French and German on both sides going back to the Hundred-Year War, she'd still be in the blue bag, taking down lists of items missing in burglaries and going out for pizza and coffee. So she'd let that prejudice work for her, and it was the only thing she ever got from Billy that she couldn't hock for twenty bucks or less.

That was when everyone had started calling her Patsy. If pretending she was a beer-bellied Son of Erin was what they needed to keep their cocks from shriveling up into their guts, she could stand it, as long as she got to work cases.

"Who's this alley cat? Lynch must be setting out milk again."

She looked up from the report she'd been staring at and saw the cast of Prokanik's eyes, still thirty-five years old in a face that seemed to be pulling away from the skull. She followed it to the hall door. There was always a moment of suspense, when it struggled against the senescent pressure of the aged pneumatic closer, when it looked as if the rite of passage had been granted at last, and the door would remain open, the new champion; but as always the closer came out ahead on points. The door settled into the frame, to rest up and train for the rematch. But for the first time in a long while, Boyle was less interested in the fight than in who had promoted it.

He *was* like an alley cat, she decided; Prokanik's snap judgments were as sound as a poet's, visually. The man making his way toward them looked scruffy enough in the same cheap corduroy coat with patches and saggy flannels, like a professor who'd been expelled for getting drunk and lecturing on Creationism in Biology 101, and he moved like a cat, loose in the limbs and awkward as hell except when he spooked something, or something spooked him, and he leaped a fence three times his height, did a triple axel, and landed on the edge with his toes clamped, easy as licking his ass. He could do with a brushing, and something on his ribs besides sour mash and nicotine; but she thought he might make a fine mouser, and something to crouch on its haunches in the window waiting for the hum of a familiar motor.

She snapped shut the folder, a savage movement that gusted out a front-and-profile mug of a sex offender. It drifted right and left on the current of air, mocking her, and settled on the linoleum with a soft-shoe shuffle. She was suddenly prepared to repel this invader from The Circle.

"Detective Boyle?" He held her card out at arm's length, the printed side turned toward him, as if it were a scribbled set of directions and he'd followed it into a ditch.

"Yes." She smiled, tight as a corset. "Mr. Porter, right? From the Railroad Arms."

"Palmer." His smile was as loose as his joints, and she knew she'd lost the round, as surely as the door to the broken-down closer. He knew she knew his name. "Thanks for keeping us out of it. We only got one mention, in the early editions of *The Derrick* and the *Light*. The TV stations didn't cover it at all."

"That's too bad. They ought to run it with the number of the suicide hotline."

"That isn't their job. They need the space for the box scores."

"The hotel dick." Prokanik smiled his granite smile. He half rose and stuck out his hand. "You used to be a cop."

Boyle watched the hands. This was one male ritual she found riveting, like watching a *National Geographic* special or a cockfight on Castro.

It disappointed. Palmer withdrew his and shook blood back into the fingertips. Prokanik sat back, fanning his feathers.

"The old place never changes," Palmer said. "Not that I spent much time on Four. I got an extra five minutes' sleep not having to figure out which tie to wear."

"You beat slobs had it made," Prokanik agreed. "All the lasagna you could scarf down at Rinaldi's for nada, including the spit."

"The old place never changes. Not even the paint and Polacks."

Prokanik's chair croaked back. He wasn't as tall as Palmer, but when he rose on the balls of his feet their chins were in line.

"Simmer down, detective. My stepmother's Polish. I grew up on oom-pah-pah and Kreplach."

"You don't look like you're eating so good lately. Whores holding out on you?"

Palmer grinned. The strong, tobacco-stained teeth in the lean face made him look wolfish. Boyle had seen men try to bluff it out with Prokanik, smiling at him when he bunched those big immigrant muscles, but showing too much molar with the effort not to shrink back. Palmer wasn't one of those. Last week, when they were plugging away at him about the suicide in the hotel, she'd sized him up quickly as a professional drunk and probably a pimp, hanging on to his job by the nail of his left little finger. Probably he still was all those things, but she didn't know, if she were meeting him today for the first time, if she'd have formed the conclusion so fast. Maybe he was at his best Mondays.

"Back off, boys," she said. "Between muscle and reach, I wouldn't know which way to bet."

"I'm going to the can." Prokanik walked around the other man, as if he were a chair or a potted palm, and out the hall door. It caught halfway, then let the closer have another round and latched with a click.

"He needs to take off a week before the city gives him a month," Palmer said.

"He's a good cop." She took a pull at her Coke. It had gone flat, which was what Coke did when you forgot you were drinking it. She staked her territory with half-empty cans. "You know we've got no drag with the TV and papers. You didn't come up here to thank us for that."

He rested a hand on the back of Prokanik's chair.

She nodded. "You've got ten minutes before he comes back and throws you out of it. Stan camps out in the john."

"That explains a lot." He sat down and took a folded envelope out of a pocket. "I've got a bashful guest down at the Arms. Never leaves his room. You've seen our rooms."

"Another Egler?"

"No, this one's moving around." He had his elbows on the desk and the envelope in both hands. "He isn't registered and the day man and the night man at the desk aren't talking."

"The law says they have to register. That's state's jurisdiction. You need to call the capital."

"I'm not here to turn in the hotel. I think the guy's hiding out from something. It must be pretty bad or Turnbull and Guerrera wouldn't clam up so tight."

"What's in the envelope?"

He blushed. He couldn't have surprised her more if he'd jumped up and dropped his pants to his ankles. "Jiminy Cricket G-man." He passed it to her over the heap of file folders.

She spread it open and lifted the flap. There was nothing inside.

"Look on the flap."

All she saw at first was a three-inch strip of Scotch tape with a smudge on it. She turned the envelope at an angle and saw the loops and whorls. She made a noise in her throat. "How'd you get this if he never leaves his room?"

"Off the outside doorknob. I'm not even sure it's his, but none of the maids has that big of a thumb and I'm the only man who goes around rattling doorknobs."

"Maybe it's yours."

"I only just got back in the habit."

"We're not a personal service," she said. "We don't run prints and probably get the FBI involved for just anyone. Not even an ex-cop."

"You've pulled my file by now, so you know what that's worth."

"I pulled it. Raw deal."

"Bullshit. I dealt it all by myself. I'm not asking a favor. It occurred to me you and your friend with the slow bowels might be interested in a nameless faceless stranger hanging out in a half-empty hotel in the Circle in a room that's supposed to be vacant. Especially now."

"You know how many tips we get that the Black Bag killer's living next door or working behind a counter or picking up the trash?"

"Not a clue. But I know you run 'em all down."

She tapped the desk with a corner of the envelope.

"It's not as if you don't have a thumb to compare it with," Palmer said. "Plastic bags pick up prints like sixty. I'll bet you got a dozen samples on file."

"You didn't see that on TV or read it in the papers."

"I was a lousy cop, but I was a cop. Some guys just don't care how many leads they spray around. Nut killers usually start out without a record. If he's never been arrested or worked for the government or applied for a permit to own a firearm, his prints aren't in the database."

"It's tainted evidence. No warrant or chain of possession."

"I shouldn't have to keep reminding you I'm not a police officer. I don't need a warrant. It's probable cause. You don't need to trace it back to knock on a door."

"What's your end, Palmer? There's no reward posted, and if you think this will get you reinstated—"

"I'm hotel security, detective. I draw a paycheck. Sometimes I take off the big plush hat with the feather in the band and earn it. If there's a maniac holed up on the first floor, or just some guy who pushed in an armored car upstate, and it gets out, and I sat on my hands, I'm going to have to start pimping full time. I'm not comfortable wearing hats."

"You could wind up wearing one anyway, if the state yanks the hotel's license."

"If I thought you cared about the state's business, I wouldn't be here."

"Scotch tape." She touched a corner that had come loose. "The print could still be yours, if you were clumsy about it."

"It isn't, but you can check it against my file. I left two complete sets; when I came on the job and when I was arrested."

"You're lucky that didn't go to the DA. There's a law in this state against hiring convicted felons for security work."

"It was a misdemeanor, but there you go with the state again. Maybe they don't give you enough to keep you busy." When she didn't respond, he sat back. Prokanik's chair made a little complaint, like a frog with a slipped disk. "The guy's my height, narrower in the shoulders. Carries a big roll of cash. All singles."

"You got all that off a doorknob?"

"I got that off a guy that brought him a pizza. Even a cannibal craves carbohydrates."

"This guy's got you by the short hairs. Are you sure you're not leaving something out? Maybe he's prancing around with your girlfriend."

"She'd prance around with a kangaroo if he had a roll in his pocket. No singles, though. This is all on the level."

She tapped the envelope twice more, then opened a drawer, dropped it inside, and pushed the drawer shut. It sounded like a freight car door sliding in its track.

"Does anything ever come back out of there?" Palmer asked.

"Sometimes. This could be one of those times. Like you said, we don't have enough to do: just chase homicidal maniacs and run down suicides and do a little investigating on the side for house dicks who really don't have enough to keep them busy."

"What'll it cost to make this one of those times?"

The huge eyes went dark, as if a steely cloud had passed between them and her brain. "You're out of practice asking for a hand. Get off the elevator before it goes to the basement. That's where we store the rubber hoses."

The grin this time was different. "In my day it was potatoes."

"Potatoes." She thought it was a euphemism for something.

"Spuds. You put them in a burlap sack till they get soft, then go to work on the kidneys without taking them out of the sack. If you do it right, you don't leave bruises. But, lady, nothing stinks like a rotten potato. I don't guess it smells like roses down there yet."

She hesitated. "I thought that was a dead rat."

"A bad potato, on its best day, *wishes* it smelled like a dead rat. Especially when it's been used on a child molester."

"A lot's changed since Big Mike," she said.

"Okay." He shoved back and stood up. "Thanks. I'll call later in the week to find out what you found out."

"If there's anything to find out, we'll call you."

"No soap. I don't have a phone and you can't trust either of the desk men with the message."

This time the door held out a little longer. The odds seemed to have shifted.

CHAPTER TWELVE

Francis X. Russell ate a big breakfast.

If he were Pope, and had been in the hospital in a coma, with the College of Cardinals meeting and laying a fire in the chimney and trying on the miter in private just to see how it looked in the mirror, his eating a big breakfast would have been a major story; and it was big enough for him, even if no one else knew that for weeks now he'd started his day with strong coffee with a nail in it and maybe a slice of dry toast if he'd forgotten supper the night before.

Not that the chief's lean belly had ever contained more than just the minimum of staples required to nourish his sinewy old heart. He had a natural disdain for food, and preferred it boiled down to the consistency of wet mortar to absorb the corrosion of his motor functions by alcohol so that he might drink more without falling off his hands and knees. But of late even that practical purpose had lost its appeal, as well as its necessity. He was drinking more without effect, an alarming development. It was the same as if the bacteria in his body had built up an immunity to antibiotics, leaving him wide open to disease, or in this case sobriety. God knew he didn't drink the stuff for the taste.

His own cooking was scarcely incentive to feed himself anything more substantial than clear liquid siphoned from old grain, then colored with a bit of caramel to make it glitter in the glass. All he knew about cooking was it involved the application of heat and salt, with plenty of pepper to anesthetize the taste buds against what was coming. He lacked a Marty Russell to draw him out of his gamey Gaelic cave with pancakes made of butter and air and sausage links that popped when you bit into them and potatoes sliced thin as snowflakes and fried in oil and fresh basil.

Francis X. Russell ate a big breakfast. And it was his second in a row.

He'd made the first on the Sunday morning after the funeral: bacon and scrambled eggs, plenty of both fried in the same skillet, with the eggshells tossed into the coffee basket to sand off the raspy edge, the way he'd learned to do when he was a police cadet. He'd been hungry that morning, all right, but mostly he'd wanted to postpone in delicious anticipation the moment when he sat down and opened the combined Sunday edition of *The Derrick-Morning Light*, fat as a brisket and heavy as fresh flounder, with Dagwood and Dick Tracy and Charlie Brown and Mary Worth wrapped around the outside in all the colors of the state flag, and read the constipated little item on Page Three reporting the police raid on the Hispanic Men's Social Club on the corner of Florida and Castro.

Joe Cicero and that pallbearing editor of his had sandwiched the two paragraphs between city business and the death notices, a sea change from the friendly old days when they'd have slathered the account across the front page with a trowel, under a headline in Armageddon type, with a jump to the City section, and photographs of the detainees hiding their faces behind their hats and under their coats. But it must have galled the publisher to run it at all. Russell could see the curried white head bent over that jewelry-store counter he used for a desk, gleaming like a poured mirror in his top-floor office done all in glass and marble like a bank or the lobby of a movie theater, supporting himself on his hands and fighting the old fight between Joseph Pulitzer and the little man in the green eyeshade in

the accounting department, and coming up at last with two paragraphs sandwiched between city business and the death notices. The
two paragraphs told Russell less than he got from thirty seconds talking to Bill Casey over the phone on the wall: The Vice Squad lieutenant had released Flip Bedondo, Zeno's front man at El Capitan,
and a few others not being held on dope or weapons charges on a writ
signed by Judge Hollander. Only a lawyer as smooth and gentle-
spoken as Caleb Young could have gotten that dyspeptic old Dutch
Calvinist out of bed without Hollander convening court there and
then in his nightshirt and slapping him in jail for contempt. Young
was the velvet glove on Zeno's iron fist, the drop of honey in the
paregoric, the blanket on the back of the slatty old mule, without
which you never knew when Hollander would stay bought. The
judge had developed the bad habit, after seventy, of slipping in and
out of gear when he was running for reelection. In his dotage he
thought his seat on the bench had something to do with ballots.

The TV stations had played the story up bigger, being TV and
not knowing just how big a story it was and that you had to chain
and beat and underfeed it to keep it from straying out of the backyard. Monday morning they ran footage of some poor slobs in
county jumpsuits being arraigned in Hollander's court, with no one
to plead for them but public defenders. That day—today—there was
no anticipation involved; Russell was just plain hungry.

He loaded up his plate at the six-burner range Marty had found
waiting for her with a big green bow tied around it when they'd
come home from church one Sunday, almost four years ago. It was a
gift from Zeno on the occasion of Russell's fourth term of office,
but the chief had let her think it came from him, at Zeno's suggestion. Marty had loved to cook. She could stand for hours in front of
the stove, stirring gravy and tasting sauces and tuning the burners
like strings on a violin, humming "I'll Get By" with her forehead
glistening. Russell had given her tools and space, knocking down the
wall that had separated his mother's old kitchen from the pantry, ex-
tending the counters, installing a stainless-steel double sink and
garbage disposal, a refrigerator that opened out in two halves like

Kingdom's gates, an island with a butcher-block top—worn hollow now from all the chops and chickens she'd cut up there—and a full set of shiny copper-bottomed pots and pans hanging from a halo suspended from the ceiling.

She always sang "I'll Get By" when she was happy and involved, about not caring when there's rain and darkness because I'll get by as long as I have you, and the only times she didn't sing while cooking were when she was upset with him, a clue, if he'd been on the ball, to when he was out of favor. He'd thought about asking Hugh Dungannon to play the song at her service, but changed his mind because the melody had always lifted his mood and he didn't want to associate it any time he happened to hear it with saying good-bye to Marty.

The poem she'd asked him to have Hugh read was something else. He sure wouldn't ever read it himself, and it wasn't likely he'd ever overhear anyone else reciting it by chance, not at headquarters or in Harrigan's or sitting on the sundeck there on West Riverside. It wasn't a town for poets, only limericks. *There once was a Gas City chief/Who hooked himself up with a thief. . . .*

He sat at the white-and-red enamel table, a survivor from his childhood, every chip as familiar and comforting as a bead in a rosary, munching and sipping and remembering the kitchen as it had been when the table was new and unblemished: never quite light enough, with its single north window, overhead bowl fixture, walls painted dark green, and the tough linoleum floor that had started out red with a pretty pattern, but which several tons of ground-in dirt and ten generations of scrub brushes had turned a sullen shade of brick to match the outside, and the surface as wavy as galvanized iron. Despite that and the cramped space, that was the room where friends and family had gathered most of the time, all the sun-boiled brick-layers and masons, sweaty beat cops, streetcar drivers with their left arms burned dark as hickory up to the pale creamy line where their rolled shirtsleeves crept up when they raised the brown bottle or the tall tumbler, and their wives, small and sharp-featured or big and freckled, with their red chapped hands; smoking, drinking Green

Spot and Schlitz, and sampling what was on the stove—risking a swat on the back of the hand from Katy Russell's spatula—while kids thundered in and out, the girls with their cotton summer dresses soaked and plastered to their boyish chests, the boys half-naked in their cut-down old church pants hanging off their cracks, water-logged from the big iron lawn sprinkler sputtering outside. There was always plenty of gab and spills and smoke, and the radio in the big tiger-maple cabinet in the parlor was always blasting out dance band music loud enough to rattle the tubes; or if it was a planned af-fair, Donald O'Connor sang on the phonograph, asking who threw the overalls in Mrs. Murphy's chowder, with Danny Russell weaving in from time to time to start it over again or put on a new record when the needle popped and scratched in the no-man's-land next to the label. There was always music even in the intervals, for there never was an Irishman born who didn't think he could wring tears from a printer's stone with his "Mother Machree." It was just about the loudest room ever devoted to anything except bowling, and sometimes the neighbors called the cops, and no wonder another couple of generations were required before the factory houses came down and the first of the walled estates rose like second-growth shade oaks between there and Magnolia Street. It took that long for the last drunken booming laugh to fade to a weak cackle.

That was the room where, wearing long pants at last, no longer hanging off his crack, with a white shirt and a Glen plaid coat and a machine-tied bow tie, Russell had introduced Martha Rose Noonan to his parents; not because they wouldn't recognize her as one of those waterlogged kids thundering in and out, but because this time he was presenting her to them as his bride-to-be. He'd bloodied Hugh Dun-gannon's nose for the privilege, putting the first twist in that hunk of drainpipe he breathed through and shattering that triangle for good, or at least until Marty made him promise to have Hugh read a poem at her funeral, about two men having loved a woman well.

The results were as expected. Katy Russell had cried, but then she'd cried when the health department closed down Kogan's Kor-ner Market, forcing her to walk two blocks over and three down to order a leg of lamb. Danny Russell had swiped his nose with his battering-ram forearm, corded all over with thick veins like cargo netting, and squeezed Francis' hand with the one he used to knock a brick in half with one swipe of his trowel. He'd never shaken hands with his son before, and Russell still felt it in his knuckles whenever rain or snow threatened.

The wedding reception was as lavish as a bricklayer could afford, and as he was known as an uncommonly fine layer of brick, it was lavish by most immigrant standards. A tenor sang at the affair in the Knights of Columbus Hall. The bar was open, the air was so thickly larded with the stink of corned beef and cabbage even the angel food tasted of it. When the toque-hatted chef wheeled the cake through the doorway, the room cringed, anticipating the decapitation of the wax figures of the bride and groom. Father Gillespie officiated at the ceremony in Our Lady of Perpetual Misery. He was dead in a year, some said by his own hand, and his likeness was removed from the wedding album bound in white leather trimmed in gold leaf. The empty black corners remained permanently in mourning.

Six months later, Marty was pregnant the first time, Hugh Dungannon was in the seminary, and Russell took an oath to serve and protect the citizens of Gas City. When his name was called, he'd gone up to get his diploma for having finished twelve weeks of training and stand still while the mayor—Big Mike, serving his first term—pinned his shield to his blouse. The silver ingot, fashioned in the shape of the city seal, had lain on his breast like a pocket Bible. Russell had seen no difference then between Holy Scripture and the elaborate phrases he'd repeated with right hand raised, inserting his name in the blank. He'd been that young. With the city seal—a brace of griffins rampant abreast the motto *Ides calendrum est* in a scroll—replicated in gilt on a blue velvet banner swagged behind Big Mike's huge head, there in the same varnished-maple gymnasium where Russell had learned jujitsu and the Japanese art of stick-fighting, he'd been thoroughly under the spell of the graven image. It was First Communion, with starchy new uniforms instead of baptismal robes and regulation sidearms in place of votive candles. The

Rapture had still been on him when he'd mounted Marty that night, straight as a Billy and sweating like Samson in the pagan temple. (He'd always blamed himself, despite assurances by her doctor, that his ardor that night was responsible for her miscarriage. Father Gillespie, two months shy of his fatal appointment with the interurban, had agreed with the medical opinion, but gave him five Hail Marys as a balm to his conscience.)

Seven miscarriages later, with Tom on the way at last and his wife confined to her bed, Francis had accepted another shield, this one in gold, laid out like a gold watch in a pigskin folder, from Knucks Carnahan, the chief of detectives. He put away his uniform, to be brought out again only for official funerals and the St. Patrick's Day Parade, and bought a gray suit and a blue suit off the rack. Knucks was gone ten weeks later, driven out by a series of scandals that tore a hole in the department hiearchy and started Russell, and every other officer too new to have failed a fitness record, on his rise: detective third-grade to sergeant, sergeant to lieutenant, and after some tough cases and some good breaks that played out well in print, chief of detectives, the highest appointed rank in the police department. That was the happy time, with Tom starting school and Charlotte on the suck, and Katy Russell, fresh out of black weeds, getting the best there was to get out of being a grandmother. When she died, at age sixty of emphysema, Russell and Marty gave up their apartment on Commercial Street and moved into the house on West Riverside. The children had rooms of their own and a big backyard with an iron sprinkler to plaster Charlotte's cotton summer dress to her boyish chest and hang Tom's cut-down old church pants off his crack.

Next came the gamble of running for police chief, and many late nights spent in conference in the bedroom with Marty, who thought Francis too good for politics, but refused to be one of Those Wives who stood in their husband's way just because they were jealous of the time he spent at the office. She gave her consent—and put a match to a candle at Perpetual Misery the next day for the immortal souls of Francis X. Russell, his wife, Martha Rose, and their children, Thomas Aquinas and Charlotte Cathleen, clinging like cockleburs to her full skirt. She told Francis about that, as she did about everything, and he felt doubly safe, because God listened to Marty, and he wasn't sure He was paying attention when Francis himself prayed.

The gamble was no gamble at all, not when Mike Wilding stood next to you on the platform. Scandals shriveled away in the high beam of that big grin, broke in the steel-reinforced grip of the mayoral handshake, flattened under the fat tires of the big square black-and-chromium battlewagon he rode in from rallies in Roosevelt Park to the black-oak clubroom of his office at City Hall (with the built-in bar and double bed in the room behind it, that Gracie Wilding didn't know about), and from there to the barn the taxpayers provided for his relaxation west of the gaunt Scottish castle haunted by Morse McGrath II and the ghosts of the father whose example Junior could not duplicate and the son he had harried into an early grave. The two houses were of the same vintage, and there wasn't a villa in Rome or a moldy fortress in Spain that could boast of more phantasms per square foot.

More elections followed, each with its own distinct personality, but none as suspenseful as the first. The city liked its shoes white between Easter and Labor Day and its Wildings and Russells with their left hands on the Holy Bible every fourth January. The suits in Russell's closet multiplied, not off the rack now but made to his order by the same swish Belgian on Seventh Street who cut Big Mike's trademark striped double-breasteds to his massive frame. Along the way, Tom had taken perfect-attendance certificates at William Jennings Bryan Elementary, just like his mother, punched holes in the opposing line on the football field at Gas City High, and been shot through the head by a sniper in a tree while taking his mess in a jungle in Southeast Asia. Charlotte was gone by then, run off with a troubleshooter for a supermarket chain based in New York City, a man two and a half times her age, not to be heard from again. At least Tom had a marker and a flag. Charlotte was empty air. Neither Francis nor Marty had been able to remember the last words that had passed between them and their daughter before they found her

closet empty and traced her and a man who answered the troubleshooter's description to the Greyhound station downtown, and a
ticket through to Port Authority Bus Terminal in New York.
Whether they got off there was a case beyond the ability of the police chief of Gas City to solve; the troubleshooter never reported
back to work, and his landlady packed up his effects and put them in
the basement when his rent went unpaid for three months. That was
what had become of Charlotte Cathleen Russell.

And Francis X. Russell, meanwhile, had put an end to street
crime outside The Circle through a simple arrangement with the one
man who had the determination and backing to zone it off and make
the plan stick. That was what had become of Francis X. Russell.

The arrangement had come before the friendship. You knew it
was a good arrangement, because business conducted between
friends was always open to suspicion, whereas business conducted in
the cold light of logic, with no personalities involved, was fully as
sound as the benefits that came from it. No one in his right mind
would vote against safe streets, and when it came down to it and
times were hard and family was all that counted, no one would take
time off work to stand in line for two hours and vote against gambling and prostitution, especially when it took place in a neighborhood God had abandoned decades before you were born, and which
you would no sooner visit than the Black Hole of Calcutta or the
Las Vegas Strip, unless your wife was out of town, or Sarah Jane at
Beauty From the Beast, where you got your highlights, had reservations for Ladies Night at the Club Sahara.

The friendship came overnight. One day you were business acquaintances, exchanging the occasional courtesy call when something had gotten out of hand outside The Circle but was being taken
care of, or arrests were going to be made in the back room at Harrigan's, and the next day Trina Zeno had committed suicide, and because the anniversary of Tom's death was coming up you made a
different kind of call and shared a bench on the river, saying nothing, just watching the current and smelling the fish that no longer
swam in it and the arsenite of lead that lay on the surface like the

skin that formed on a bowlful of soup and something deeper, the flat
dank stench of vegetable decay and the decomposing flesh of eight-
ton lizards in the Primordial Ooze. You went from there to Granite
Park to watch the quarterhorses run, steroids in their feed to make
them go and tampons stuffed in their nostrils to make them stop,
and you didn't say anything about anything there except the horses,
but when you split off at the end of the day you did so as friends.
Nothing was simpler, except love between a man and a woman, and
there were no words complicated enough to explain it.

Marty was gone, Tom and Charlotte, too. Big Mike was dead of
good living, and Father Gillespie was roasting in hell for the sin of
self-murder. The parade of gabbing, smoking, drinking, sampling,
singing adults had marched all the way from the kitchen to the
grave, and not a few of the sprinkler-soaked kids, those who hadn't
drifted on when Gas City became as cramped as that old kitchen and
disappeared beyond the horizon. Only Hugh Dungannon was left,
fretting over the impermanency of his position in that disintegrating
hulk at the end of Cathedral Street, and Russell, eating a mess of bacon and eggs and drinking coffee here in the same kitchen, that
wasn't the same kitchen at all, not by a big fat long shot.

He hadn't had the shotgun out in days. The last time he'd taken it
out just long enough to unload it and lock the shells in his desk to
make the process less convenient. But he hadn't needed to do that.
The whole business was melodramatic, and Russell wasn't the type
who could sit through that kind of thing even when it was on a stage;
even Zeno had known better than to invite him to the opera when
Deanne was away, boosting the consumer confidence index in New
York. Russell thought of Father Gillespie and the grease trail he'd left
all the way from the Civic Center to Boiler Row, and felt no compul-
sion to require Carly or whoever she hired to peel his scalp off the
ceiling of his study and sponge away the gray matter and pieces of
skull like the shards of eggshell in the coffee basket. He'd found a
tidier and more sporting way to accomplish the same thing. You didn't
sit in a chair night after night with Anthony Zeno across your lap.

You were young, you were young for such a long time, and then you were old without ever having been middle-aged. No one called you middle-aged when you qualified, except as a joke, told usually by yourself. No one ever means it, because the middle of something is nothing. One day, all unprepared, you went to the post office, and someone who didn't know who you were held the door for you when you were still ten paces away, as if pulling open a door was too much for anyone to expect of someone in your condition, or you overheard someone downtown who was too new to realize an old building spreads secrets like a six-party line called you the old man, and you re-alized by the way he said it the words weren't capitalized, and that it was a description and not a title or a term of simple respect. You were old, your friends were old, and some of them were dead, and most of your enemies were dead, and what was the point of going on once you'd buried the last of the bastards? So you turned on your friends.

He skipped the police pages in the Monday *Morning Light*, which would have nothing to add to what had been reported Sunday, and read the Entertainment section, where the Club Sahara adver-tised Amateur Stripper Night in a two-column rectangle, with a car-toon of a leering camel in the corner.

CHAPTER THIRTEEN

The six-foot black barmaid put a fresh napkin with a cartoon camel on it on the bar and set a thick glass of beer on top of it with a handle. Moe Shiel scooped up the foam with two fingers, flicked it to the floor, said, "Ah!" and thumped down the glass half-drained. "Veronica, why don't let's get married and I take you out from behind them taps?"

"Suppose I like it behind the taps?" she asked.

"Then I'll put a wet bar in the basement."

She wasn't pretty except when she smiled; then the whole bottom half of her face turned into teeth. She wore her abundance of hair teased back and sprayed, a tumbleweed effect, and sneakers that didn't go with her uniform of green vest, white shirt, black leatherette bow tie, and satin-striped tuxedo trousers. Stiletto heels during her stripping days had raised corns like walnuts on her toes. "Who's Sal going to find to replace me?"

Shiel turned on his stool to look at the fat man with the Rice Krispies face dumped into his corner booth counting bills into neat stacks of singles, fives, tens, twenties, and fifties. It was a mark of the Club Sahara's security that its manager felt no need to lock himself in a back room to fondle cash. A tiny white *X* painted two feet inside the leather-upholstered front door identified the spot where the only thief who had ever tried to make off with the receipts had fallen with two slugs in his back. Sal Tahiti belonged to the police reserve and hung his concealed weapons permit in a frame next to his state liquor license. The permit, an archaic-looking document with a gold seal and rusty calligraphy, was signed by Chief Russell.

Shiel turned back. "He won't starve for months."

"You better not come back in here if we elope. Sal never made his peace with the obstetrician who whacked him on the ass."

"He don't scare me. I bet I talked to a thousand guys that said they was here the night he popped that guy. They must of been stacked up like tires. If you ask me, Sal painted that *X* himself. Paint's cheaper than ammo."

"Why should I ask you? Ask Sal. I'll pay up your tab if you do. Things have been slow around here lately."

"Accept my proposal and I'll go right over and ask."

She went to the other end of the bar to deliver a beer and pour bourbon from a bottle with a spout for a customer in a blue work shirt and jeans rubbed white at the knees. He might as well have had McGRATH GASWORKS stamped on his bunched forehead.

Veronica came back and folded her arms on the bar. "There's one thing wrong with your plan. You've already got one wife on Boiler Row."

"We're separated."

"By a wall."

"The apartment next door was vacant when I left."

"When she threw you out. What bartender did you ask to marry you that time?"

The little tough shook his head sadly. "You got me all wrong. I'm a one-woman man."

"One at a time. What's your secret, Moe? You're a rat with bad teeth. I'll bet that tab of yours you never used a toilet and a sink on the same trip to the bathroom in your life. Except the bet's no good, because your tab would pay the mortgage on this joint and no one ever asks you to pay up. Not even Sal. I didn't just come in on the blackbird boat; I know where your juice comes from. How that makes you think you're Don Juan is what I want to know."

"It's my cologne," he said after a moment's thought. "*Eau de Moe.*"

She blew air through her nostrils like a horse, picked up her bar rag, and started polishing.

Outside, the sun was still shining, but inside the club it was always 3:00 AM, with stars glittering on the indigo ceiling and the colored strobes mounted along the runway on the other side of the room flicking on and off in sequence like traffic lights at a deserted crossing. The dancer there was down to her pumps and needle tracks, and the scatter of men seated within arm's reach waited with their fistfuls of singles for the opportunity to tuck them into whatever orifice or fissure presented itself. The music whickered and thumped tinnily, dragging a little where the tape stretched thin over the reels, and Veronica refilled Shiel's glass from the tap and replaced the gas worker's boilermaker and got fresh fruit out of the little lighted refrigerator to make pitchers of exotic drinks for the after-supper crowd and kicked shut the door with a sneaker. It was all show, a bone to throw to the family vote in late autumn with busts for possession in the restrooms and a couple of strippers tossed into the tank for taking their business out into the parking lot, and Shiel, who had a gambling problem ("Not enough cash, that's the problem"), was avoiding the back room this week.

It was a hardship, and not just because he liked to win, and even enjoyed himself when he lost, which he did on such a regular basis he'd come to believe some cosmic plan was in the works to keep him in cotton drawers and make him go on buying his cigarettes from the black market to beat the tax. He missed the whirl and click of the little round marble as it slid along the edge of the wheel and dropped into place between the frets—never on his number—the washing-machine surge and rattle of the balls shifting in the keno cage as it spun on its axis, the merry little chimes made by the one-armed bandits and the almost orgasmic clunk of a handful of silver dollars dropping into the tray, a kind of premature ejaculation, but better than none at all, and enough to make him feed the coins back into the slot until they were gone. He liked to watch the finishes light up on the electronic board at the end of every race at Granite Park, and he was old enough to remember the blackboard that had preceded it, and the squeak of the chalk when the results came in over the fleet of telephones that were always ringing; the chalk tended to break when a long shot finished in the money, from the strain behind it. It all made for a clashing wall of noise when the man at the door, corked on both sides to deaden the sound, recognized you and let you in, like an orchestra tuning up for the best concert of your life. You wanted to smuggle in a tape recorder so you could play it back as you lay in bed with your hands behind your head and knew you'd never have another bad dream.

But a tape recorder would only get him in trouble with Sal Tahiti, who even if he hadn't really put a man down on that white X with two slugs from his big square .45 auto, knew someone who could. It didn't matter that Tahiti and Shiel worked for the same man. Sal took care of business on-site and hardly ever called uptown for a second opinion. Shiel would no sooner steal away his best attraction behind the bar than he would run off with Veronica at all. He loved his wife, even if they couldn't live together without letting blood over some little thing. Veronica had called his bluff. He couldn't get one over at the poker table in back either.

Luck had smiled on Morris Shiel only once in his life, and he was still getting by on that. He'd been Tony Z.'s foreman on the loading dock behind Volcanic Wholesale Plumbing Supplies for two years when the Lennox brothers broke the padlock on the back door and made off with the register and the safe where they kept the petty cash. A squad car team had discovered the damage, and when Zeno and the shop manager were unavailable had called Shiel, whose number was third on the list. Everyone knew the Lennoxes were responsible, because they never went anywhere without a crowbar in the trunk and because they were the only B-and-E artists in town whose brains were cooked enough on hop to target Zeno. Shiel had shown his appreciation to the squad car team by letting them put a

Lo-Flo Whisp-R-Flush toilet, still in the box, and a sixty-dollar tap-and-die set in the backseat of the black-and-white; Volcanic's insurance covered it, and everyone on the staff had instructions to cooperate with Chief Russell's officers. Zeno had nodded his approval when Shiel reported.

Trouble was, Bronco Bob Burnett, commander of the Eighth Precinct, had been put up by the opposition in Mike Wilding's party to run against Russell in the forthcoming election, and when he read the blotter he did the local arithmetic and had Shiel picked up and taken to a room in the Railroad Arms where in those days the police department conducted its unofficial interrogations. Shiel had spent two days there with a pair of burly third-graders who took shifts beating the living shit out of him, trying to get him to sign a statement implicating two officers from headquarters with looting and accepting a bribe from Anthony Zeno on the chief's behalf. Shiel had refused, lost some teeth and part of the vision in his left eye, had his jaw broken in three places, and wound up with a face that would make a dog gag until it healed and the stitches came out. But he knew it would heal, and that if he signed his name he'd never walk out of the hotel, but would wind up in the Boggen and be reported as a flight case, leaving behind a sworn statement with no witness to challenge it in court. After they gave up and dumped him in front of his Boiler Row apartment house, Zeno had him put in a private room in Carbon County General, where doctors sutured him up and wired his jaw and let him recover while Bronco Bob got written up on charges of falsifying reports to improve the record of law enforcement in the Eighth Precinct. The charges were dismissed after Burnett withdrew from the race in order to spend more time with his family. Russell ran unopposed, and a duck hunter stumbled on what was left of Frankie Lennox in the Boggen Drain the following spring. No one ever knew what became of his brother Jackie.

When they wheeled Moe Shiel out of the hospital, a man he'd never seen before, in blue serge and a matching yellow tie and handkerchief, got out of a town car and helped him from the chair into the backseat. Moe was still too giddy from his last morphine drip to care if the man was friend or foe. He laid his head against the leather, gray as smoke and just as soft, and let the car lift him to West Riverside and Tony Z.'s house in the greensward. There'd been truffle soup, brandy so mellow you could snort it up through your nostrils, and cigars that burned for an hour like lox smoking, and when the driver collected him again and took him to his apartment, he had a new job and twenty men under him, with the responsibility of enforcing the arrangement between Zeno and Chief Russell in the Circle.

He never saw the driver again, although he knew his name was Toby and that he was closer to Zeno than his wife. But he never had to work another day in the slobbering heat of summer or bone-freezing cold of winter on the loading dock at Volcanic. Without having to make a single speech or shake more than one hand, Moe Shiel had been elected the mayor and chief of police of The Circle, on the stength of one man's vote.

It had been a challenge. Even Russell's regulars seldom crossed the Columbus Central tracks, and then usually in herds, to bust up a brawl at the Triangle Bar or sweep the hookers and junkies off Blacksnake Lane when Big Mike needed ink and a photo op. A radio run to a disturbance anywhere inside those ten square blocks needed clearance from the top, because the motor pool at police headquarters was backed up with patrol cars needing windshields and body work from the downpour of bricks and bottles that broke loose every time they parked in front of a tenement. The sight of one or two cops inspired no fear in that neighborhood. It was a country unto itself, even more than Little Brazil.

Shiel had started with a show of force at an institution nearly as sacred as Our Lady of Perpetual Misery. For three generations, cars stolen throughout the metropolitan area had gone to Apache Auto Salvage on South Crescent, where they were chopped up and their parts were reshuffled, reassembled, and sold through legitimate used-car dealerships across the state with fresh paperwork: Joe John Binder, who owned Apache along with his three grown sons, Beau, Lee, and Nathan Bedford, was known popularly as John the Baptist, and the family collectively as the Born-Again Binders, for their success in washing tainted vehicles in the Blood of the Lamb and returning them purged of all sin to the street. They were independent operators who did business with independents, and grandfathered in since before Zeno. He ignored them so long as their clients spread their thefts evenly around and no violence was involved. In truth, he may have been a little afraid of them, or at least of the unpredictable element they represented, as the Binders were bullies who picked fights drunk and sober and intimidated their victims and the victims' families to keep them from filing complaints with the police.

Moe Shiel didn't go to his employer with his plan. Instead, he loaded his men into the back of a Volcanic tractor-trailer rig and drove it through the front of Apache Auto Salvage, reducing the glazed-brick building to rubble, crushing several vehicles in various stages of assembly, and pinning Lee Binder between the bumper of the tractor and a hydraulic hoist, shattering his pelvis and pulverizing his ribs. When the debris stopped falling, Shiel's men poured out of the trailer with axes and sledgehammers to finish the job on the fixtures and equipment and repel a counterattack by the rest of the Binders and their paid help. Nathan Bedford's skull was fractured and two mechanics joined him and Lee in County General with broken limbs and internal damage.

The assault stunned inhabitants of The Circle, who could think of nothing to compare it with since the U.S. Army took the neighborhood apart block by block in 1917. The effect was even more chilling when Joe John, raging against Shiel and Zeno to a rapt audience in Riley's Bar, interrupted his litany of planned reprisals to take a telephone call from his wife: A tractor-trailer rig with VOLCANIC WHOLESALE PLUMBING SUPPLIES lettered on the side was parked in the driveway of their home, its motor rumbling.

The truck was gone by the time Joe John got there with Beau Binder in tow, but the message was clear. When Lee, who took the longest to recover from his injuries, was released from the hospital eight weeks later, the family moved to the capital, where they became Nicholas Bianco's headache. After that, Moe Shiel's authority to maintain the peace between Depot Street and the Boggen Drain was never seriously questioned.

The stunt in front of Joe John Binder's house was the only bluff that had ever paid off for Shiel. He'd been alone in the truck, with no backup in case the Binders and their friends came out in force to haul him out from under the wheel and stomp on him. There would be no more such demonstrations; for that day he'd spent taking blows from two detectives at the Railroad Arms had turned him into a physical coward. The experience had sapped the color from his hair, turning it gray overnight, and his liver white. Courage was not a renewable resource. He'd used up most of his on that one occasion, and the rest to keep himself from wetting the driver's seat of the truck waiting for Joe John's wife to take notice of it and call her husband. From that day forward, with the exception of Chief Russell's wife's wake, he never went anywhere without four of his best men along for protection. His detractors smirked and said he was imitating Mike Wilding (and later Jerry, Mike's son), whose four highly trained plainclothesmen stood like corner posts on the platforms where he spoke and closed around him like a steel curtain when he walked. Shiel let them say it, because it was less humiliating than the truth.

"Hit you again?" Veronica asked.

He jumped, startled out of his cave, and saw her holding his empty glass by its handle, her other hand resting on the beer tap. He shook his head and slid off the stool, jerking his chin at his escort, who put down their seltzers and ginger ale and got up from their tables to accompany him down the narrow hall to the restrooms in back: two in front and two behind, just like with the mayor.

"Stay back, Moe!" shouted one of the men in front, who had stepped out ahead of his partner to push open the door of the men's room.

Shiel's first reaction was annoyance. He couldn't get any of his boys to call him Boss, as he did Zeno. Then he realized the man had unshipped the big plated magnum from under his left arm and was pointing it with both hands at something on the floor inside the room, with his foot holding the door open. Shiel's heart bumped then and the blood slid from his face in a cold sheet. The other three men pressed close around him, unholstering their weapons with a noise like squeaky shoes, and he thought, *This is it*, bracing himself for the volley.

After a long time, the man standing in the men's room doorway took one hand off his gun and leaned forward from the waist. The edge of the door kept Shiel from seeing what he was doing. Something rustled.

"Jesus!" He reeled back, retracting his foot across the threshold to keep from falling. The door sighed shut.

"Jelly, what the fuck?" The other front man, gun still in hand, stepped past him and shoved open the door. There was a beat, and then he said something that might have been "Jesus," too, except Shiel couldn't tell for sure because he gagged it.

Curiosity got the better of his fear then. He took a step, hesitated when one of the men behind him grabbed at his shoulder, then shrugged off the hand and went past the two men leaning white-faced on opposite walls with their guns dangling and caught the door that was closing again and looked down at the black plastic garbage bag that was heaped on the tile floor and at what was seeping out.

III

THE CRUSADE

Chapter Fourteen

Clare yawned and stretched and arched her back, crackling her bones in that way that set Palmer's teeth on edge, like chewing tinfoil. She started to climb over him to get out of bed, disregarding the sixteen inches of clearance she had between her side and the wall, pretended to be clumsy and rubbed him from breast to thigh until he growled and lifted her by her muscular buttocks and prepared to enter her. But she squirmed out of his grasp and slid down his body, her red head vanishing under the bedspread, and he decided to let her.

Afterward, when she'd showered and brushed her teeth and dressed, she leaned over the bed to kiss him, and he thought he still tasted himself on her lips. He wondered—with purely clinical interest—if different men tasted differently, and if some women were connoisseurs, like those people who talked and talked about wines, and if they classified them according to region and environment and age and whether they traveled well. If there were women like that, Clare would qualify.

But that wasn't what he asked. What he asked was how many men she had slept with.

Her face, still inches from his, pulled into a frown. She appeared to be thinking about it. "One, actually," she said. "You're the only man I've ever slept with."

"How many did you fuck?"

"How many women have you fucked?"

"Six."

"Counting me?"

"Sure, counting you. Why would I leave you out?"

"Well, it's like when you ask someone on a corner for directions and they say turn left at the third stoplight, but you don't know if they're counting the first one right in front of you."

"Well, you weren't the first."

"I wasn't guessing I was. That was just an example. Wow. You're practically a virgin."

"Six women doesn't mean six times. You're my witness to that. You didn't answer the question."

"More than six."

"Seven?"

"Seven for sure." She straightened, striking a pose as characteristic as it was unconscious, shooting one hip with an arm across her body below her breasts and her other elbow resting on it, the back of that hand supporting her chin. She wore a green sleeveless top and a black suede skirt that came to her knees and buttoned up the side. It was a cover shot except for the homely walking shoes on her feet. She always carried heels in her handbag. "Could you live with seventy?"

"I didn't say anything about living with anything."

"What about seven hundred?"

He was silent.

She said, "I didn't think it was possible to shock you."

"I wasn't shocked. I was figuring the math. If you averaged fifteen minutes per man, that's ten thousand five hundred minutes. There are ten thousand and something minutes in a year. Spread that out over, say, ten years—"

"Fifteen. I bloomed early. Where you going with this?"

"I was just wondering when you ate."

"Your base number's off. Some guys finish in three minutes."

"I figured that in," he said. "I balanced it out against you and me and spread it around. There's a wide margin of error, but that's still a lot of time in the sack."

"It isn't seven hundred. I don't keep a running score, but it isn't anywhere near that. What if it was? A girl has to eat. I'm too short to model and I didn't finish high school. If that's what this is about, let's talk about you. How many dirty twenties did you pocket before they busted you out of the department?"

"More than six."

She watched him light a cigarette, then plucked it out of his hand, took two puffs, and gave it back. Smoke never got as far as her nostrils before she blew it out. "So what the hell." It was a question, but it didn't sound like one.

"I was just wondering how I measured up."

"Christ, Jim," she said after a moment. "I thought you were pumping yourself up to throw me out."

"I'll never throw you out, Clare. You can walk out when you're ready. You might want to run."

"Run from what, you? I'd break your arm if you so much as raised a hand."

"I seem to remember doing more than that at least once. You didn't break it. Or was that a dream?"

"You were drunk. I can always duck a drunk. They telegraph their punches."

"You can't duck me sober. Not that I'd swing on you then. Whatever agreement we had, I want you to know you're not stuck with it. I'm not the guy whose head you held to keep him from drowning in the toilet. That was somebody else."

"If it was, you're half of a set of twins."

He was silent again. This time he wasn't doing math.

"Don't go Holy Joe on me, Palmer. This is just a binge in reverse. Those never last. Tomorrow you'll go out for a beer and wake up on Castro, celebrating your first anniversary with your fat wife and a little brown baby."

"Are you betting on that, or hoping? I mean, without the fat wife and little Julio."

She looked at the watch strapped to the underside of her pale wrist, a little silver hexagon with hands shaped like apostrophes. "I got to go."

"At least you're not mad at me anymore."

"Who says I'm not?"

"You called me Palmer."

"Christ." She went to the door.

"You didn't answer the question," he said.

She opened the door. "You're full of questions today. Which the hell was it?"

"You know which."

She looked at him, or at his reflection in the mirror on the closet door; or so he thought. He could see hers from his angle, but not his own, and their gazes seemed to connect. Mirrors were tricky.

"You measure up okay," she said. "It ain't how you swing, it's how far you hit the ball."

He took a drag, exhaled slowly. "Keep on throwing those spitters."

She made a sound in her throat and pulled the hall door shut behind her.

He grinned and smoked, and watched the smoke float toward the ceiling and then break for the cold-air vent high on the wall opposite the door to the bathroom, and his grin with it. The muscles of his face relaxed into no expression. She hadn't said a word about the man in room 116 since he'd told her about lifting the thumb print from the doorknob. He wondered how wide the thing went.

The mouthpiece of the telephone on the street smelled like sauerkraut. The plywood stand on the corner where dogs and kraut could be bought had been boarded up for years. In Gas City, the half-life of a stench seemed to be twice as long as everywhere else. Waiting for the switchboard to connect him, Palmer held the mouthpiece away from his face and stroked the ball of his thumb over a telephone number someone had scratched with a pocketknife inside the metal hood that sheltered the instrument. The zero and two had been done with jagged angles like a Latin motto engraved in marble.

"Boyle."

"For how long?" He grinned at a potty little post office van shuttling down the street.

"Okay, comic." Air stirred on the other end. She was hanging up.

"It's Palmer," he said. "Checking back like I said."

She came back on. "Something broke last night. Not on your thing, but I've got news. Where can I call you back?"

"You know Harrigan's?"

"I'd be a lousy cop if I didn't."

"I wasn't sure they still hung out there. Did you eat? They used to make a mean burger, I mean mean. But the chicken salad's safe. They just open a can."

"Hang on." Something cupped the mouthpiece on her end. "Okay, I'll see you there in ten. I won't have time to eat."

He had to leg it up Commercial to be there in ten minutes, but he was too impatient to wait for a bus and the first cab came into view only when he was two blocks away from his destination. The companies kept their fleets away from The Circle, and the wildcats were scattered, and too nervous and well-armed for his comfort. At the bar, Palmer hung back to let two big police officers in uniform trundle out, caught the heavy leaded-glass door before it swung shut, and let himself into Harrigan's Irish Pub.

Long before Palmer's time, back when the men who ran the city all spoke in brogues and pinned their ties to their shirts with diamonds, the place had been just Harrigan's, with prints of bare-knuckle prizefighters and gaunt ballplayers hanging crooked behind the bar and rats in tight coats with derbies on the side of their heads swaggering in and out of the curtained private rooms picking their teeth; even "Bar" had been left off the sign on the shaded front window as an unnecessary expenditure of paint. Now it was a watering hole for cops and businessmen, and if anything the theme was more aggressively Old Country. Caricatures of local and visiting Irish celebrities formed a frieze around the walls and the bartenders and waitresses wore green-and-white-striped aprons and nameplates shaped like shamrocks, serving officers in uniform and plainclothes and junior executives seated on the stools and in booths separated by stained-glass partitions. The effect was emphatic, and puzzling only to native Dubliners who had never seen a slab of corned beef or heard of leprechauns until they landed in America. But the old mulch of beer and stale grease and cigarettes remained.

Palmer hovered ten steps inside the door, waiting for his pupils to catch up, caught sight of a hand waving from halfway down the line of booths to his right, and headed that way. He slid along naughhyde and sat back smiling at Detective Patricia Boyle, looking a little less official today with her blazer unbuttoned behind a bottle of Corona with a wedge of lime floating inside.

He pointed at it. "I didn't know you could get that here."

"You can get whatever you like," she said, "except anything authentically Irish. You look like you ran all the way. Don't you own a car?"

"I got drunk one night two years ago and forgot where I parked it. Coke," he told the waitress, who wrote it down anyway, glanced at the level in Boyle's bottle, and went away without asking her if she wanted anything.

"I guess she thinks you're on duty."

She fluttered her lips and swigged from the bottle. "I thought you were going to have the chicken salad."

"I never eat alone in a joint."

"On the wagon, I see."

"Friend of mine calls it a binge in reverse. What broke last night?"

"New Black Bag murder. Don't you watch TV or listen to the radio?"

"I slept in. Where?"

"Club Sahara. That's where he dumped it, anyway. He broke the hasp on the back door and lugged it in and dropped it off, just like the guy who fills the paper-towel dispenser. Moe Shiel found it. Or one of his bodyguards did."

"I bet he's still heaving. Unless you think he did it."

"Not little Moe. This character works with his bare hands."

"Man or woman? The vic, I mean."

She smiled crookedly. "Like the taxidermist said when the guy brought in a trout he shot with a twelve-gauge: 'Which way you want me to go, fish or fowl?'"

"No head, I'm guessing. No torso either."

"Nor pelvis, which would be conclusive. Just a bag of arms and legs, and none too fresh. If the prints don't light up the board, we'll have to wait till he dumps off the rest and reassemble it." She swigged again. "It was a woman. Probably. The hands and feet were small, and there were flakes of polish on the nails. One of the early cases was a transvestite, so we're not jumping to conclusions. Does this talk bother you?"

He got out a cigarette, made a gesture with it.

"Because you look a little pasty," she went on. "You were red as a lobster when you came in."

"I told you I have a girlfriend. A woman friend. It's not her, I saw her only an hour ago. But you think about it."

"This character works at night. Just don't let her go out alone after dark."

"That would come under restraint of trade."

"Ah. Business acquaintance?"

His Coke came. He got rid of the straw and took out his butane lighter, which sparked twice but didn't ignite. It was empty. The waitress was gone by then. "What about my thumbprint?"

"It wasn't yours."

"I didn't mean *mine* mine. I thought you said you didn't have much time." He slid a matchbook out of a shallow glass ashtray. The cover had a merry elfin face on it in a green top hat.

"Sorry. I didn't get to sleep in." She had a handbag next to her on the seat, glossy black vinyl with a brass clasp. Out of it she took a four-by-six sheet of stiff paper and laid it in front of him.

He looked at the crossgrain features printed in full face and profile above ten oval smudges in parallel horizontal grids. Uncombed dark hair receding away from a sharp widow's peak, lines that might have been carved with a router, a strong porous nose, hastily scooped-out cheeks, eyes that might have been any color but reproduced pale and didn't quite line up, a full lower lip with the upper fastened to it as if with a snap. Resignation in the tilt of the head. An everyday sort of face, not unlike his own.

"They ought to tone those lights down at Receiving," he said. "They'd take the eyebrows off an ape."

"Know him?"

He inserted a fingertip under one corner and flipped it over. The name was printed on the back, to prevent eyewitnesses from reading it and making any connections not strictly visual, with a description: Vernon Albert Goshawk, 37 (from the birthdate), eyes and hair brown, height . . .

"No." He turned it back over fast, as if he might catch Goshawk making a face. The patient expression was the same.

"Why'd you look at the back?"

"I wanted to see if it was Hallmark." Palmer lit his cigarette and sat back against the stiff upholstery. "I never saw him. I don't even know if it's him. He local?"

"No priors here. He did a nickel bit in Attica for assault GBH less than murder. Got out ten years ago. Since then he's been picked up for questioning in six states. All violent crimes, including two homicides; no bills of indictment. I had this overnighted from Washington as soon as that thumbprint lit up their computer. I wanted it as clear as possible."

"You're still wanting. I could Xerox my butt and do a better job than this."

"It's close enough for government work." She tapped the picture. "This is a professional pattern, all hits and runs. Cleveland PD picked him up on a statement by an informant. The snitch said he always insists on being paid in singles. They're not worth counterfeiting, and even if anyone took the trouble to mark ten or twenty thousand bills, what store clerk would take the trouble to check even three or four? That's why he carries around a bankroll that could choke a whale. He's probably got plenty more in a suitcase."

"The snitch didn't talk to a grand jury?"

"He couldn't."

He blew smoke out his nose. "Good going, Cleveland."

"Well, you can't wipe their ass every time. I doubt Goshawk's lived anywhere long enough to apply for a driver's license, and he never fishes the same hole twice. He isn't Beaver Cleaver. You can rest easy on that."

"I will, thanks. Here I was afraid we had Charlie Starkweather staying at the hotel, and all the time he was just Pittsburgh Phil. What kind of name's Goshawk?"

"English. It's not an alias. He probably had a falconer or something way back on his father's side. The hunting instinct is sometimes inherited, Dr. Aguilar says."

"Does he. Who's he?"

"Department shrink. He was talking about Beaver Cleaver, but I think it applies. They're both stalkers. The difference is Beaver's in it for the rush, whereas Goshawk's a worker bee. We needed this, we really did. We're not getting enough shit from the papers and TV."

"Hey, sorry. Next time I get a hard-on to do my job I'll take a cold shower and curl up with Perry Mason." He tamped out his cigarette. The smoke was scraping his throat. *Maybe that's how it starts*, he thought. He didn't know if he should quit smoking while he was quitting drinking and pimping. It seemed like a lot all at once.

Boyle was staring at him. "What were you thinking just then?"

He smiled at her. "A man would never ask that question."

"He would if he was a detective."

"I wouldn't know. When the detectives came on, I knew my work was finished."

"You're sure acting like a detective now."

"It's in the title. Hotel detective."

"Yeah, and a custodian doesn't have custody of dick and an apartment manager manages the puke in the lobby. You drag winos out by their armpits and pound on the door when the radio's loud. You don't scurry around with a magnifying glass and Scotch tape."

"I didn't use a magnifying glass." He sipped his Coke for the first time and stuck a hand in his pants pocket and left it there, a distracted gesture. "You're not the only one giving me flak. I'm starting to feel like the guy that joined a gym and went on a diet and lost a hundred pounds and all his friends keep telling him they liked him better fat."

"My mother has an answer for speeches like that," she said. "'Boo-hoo.'"

"You're lucky she didn't put arsenic in your milk."

She swirled her beer. The lime wedge sailed a couple of laps. "Go to AA and leave the job to the journeymen. You couldn't make it in the blue bag. What makes you think you can work cases just because you stopped pissing yourself in public?"

He chewed the inside of a cheek. Then he took his hand out of his pocket and rested it on the table. The palm was empty.

"My fingers are as sticky as anybody's on the fourth floor at headquarters."

The bottle struck the table with a bang. The surf of conversation that had been surging at the nearby tables died down. She waited until it came back up and heads drifted the other way. Vivid streaks stained the tops of her cheekbones.

"There are no wants or warrants out on Goshawk," she said, "but no one ever comes here for a vacation. We need to find out who's his target, and bust him on a Sullivan if he's dumb enough to get caught with a gun. When that doesn't work we'll give him the old get-out-of-Dodge. You can help by clearing the rest of the floor, in case he comes up shooting. Tell 'em it's a fire drill or something, and try not to shout it at the top of your lungs. Then go back to your doors and winos."

"Waste of time," Palmer said.

"Well, it's paid for. You paid for it."

"I mean he left."

She looked up from her bottle. "Left the room?"

"The hotel. He didn't forget his toothbrush. Unless he was in there with nothing to play with but himself, in my opinion as a man who pounds on doors he's gone."

"When?"

"Just before I went out to call you. I let myself into the empty next door; I do that sometimes, for the kick. He's quiet, but no one's *that* quiet. You can hear an ant fart through those walls. When none did I went in and searched the room."

"What about the wastebaskets?"

"Wastebasket; singular. We're not the Waldorf. There wasn't even a gum wrapper. Same story inside the drawers and under them and in back of them and down in the well inside the dresser and under the mattress and box springs. Whatever he had in there he took with him or flushed down the toilet."

"And when were you planning to tell me this?"

"I'm telling you now."

She picked up the bottle, set it down without drinking, drummed her fingers on the side. "We'll sweat the desk men. I forgot their names."

"Turnbull and Guerrera. Another waste of time. All you've got on them is failure to register a guest—a misdemeanor—and without the guest you haven't even got that. Anyway they're scareder of Goshawk than they are of you, and scareder yet of whoever paid him those singles. They know what happens to snitches in and out of Cleveland."

"You're scared too. If we pump them, they'll know where the tip came from."

"You bet I'm scared. I'm just now getting to the point where I've got something worth being scared about." He took another sip, just to wet the inside of his mouth, and pushed away the glass of what now looked like sewing-machine oil. "But I'll take what's coming. I have to run these things out same as you."

"Then you won't mind letting us into one-sixteen. Just in case your sticky fingers missed something."

"I already hung out the Do Not Disturb sign for the maids."

"Wait there for us." Boyle scooped the mug shot into her bag, put money on the table, and got up. She was shorter than Clare, barely the department minimum, with larger breasts under the blazer, but she reminded him of her just the same. "Your soda pop's on the city. You want to save. From the looks of the place they pay you in cash and don't take out for unemployment."

After she left, Palmer reached inside his pants pocket again and this time fished out a small triangle of torn paper and stretched it between his thumbs and forefingers like a fortune from a cookie. It was still damp at the edges. There wasn't a toilet in the hotel you didn't have to flush twice to get the job done. Goshawk must have known that, but he'd been in a hurry.

CHAPTER FIFTEEN

For a generation, the Garden Grove Athletic Club had been open to women by order of the state, but few women belonged to it. Almost no concessions had been made to them by its directors, continuing a rigid tradition that went back to its refusal to change the club's name when the city had changed its own. The cafeteria served buffalo and wild boar, the bar scorned cocktails for domestic beer and premium liquors served straight up or with ice, and although there were separate shower and sanitary facilities for men and women, both featured the same glaring white tile, planed wooden benches, and hideous green lockers, with no doors on the toilet stalls. Angela Rice-Hippert made a point of being photographed jogging around the indoor track, but apart from her and a few campaign volunteers, the only female regularly on hand was Delores, the cheerful two-hundred-pounder who replaced the big glass jugs in the watercoolers. Male nudity was a commonplace even when she was around, for she was as much a part of the scenery as the wooden racquets on the walls and the trophies in the glass display cases. "I seen more pricks than a Chinese doctor," she told her friends over a glass of beer in Riley's.

The building stood adjacent to Granite Park, with a view of the backstretch through the picture windows in the top-floor gymnasium. Wind and rain had rounded the edges of the sandstone, and it lay on its square lot like a giant bar of soap.

Anthony Zeno, after his tennis lesson, swam a lap around the regulation-size pool and walked naked down the puddled hall to the showers with his towel draped around his neck, carrying his racquet and sweaty workout clothes in one hand. The devoted Toby glided silently behind him, paying no overt attention to the narrow pale bare buttocks it was his job to protect with his life. The bodyguard affected his employer's gray tailoring and benchmade shoes, and resembled him in a squashed-down way, like a younger, mildly distorted reflection in a flawed mirror; but the effect did not extend to the complete lack of expression in his face. It was something more than machinelike, but less than human, and it never changed. After an adolescent scrape with the law, he'd been diagnosed as autistic by the psychiatrist who had examined him, but that was before he'd learned to drive and shoot. Automobiles responded to him as if they shared the same circulatory system, especially at high speed, and he regularly outqualified the officers who competed with him on the police range. Like Sal Tahiti, he had a concealed weapons permit signed by Chief Russell, but unlike the manager of the Club Sahara he kept it on his person and out of sight until needed, like the heavy plated magnum he carried in a spring-steel clip under his left arm. His suit coats would not fit him properly without it.

Zeno's hairless belly sagged a bit in response to the same forces that had turned his hair white and thickened the high arch of his eyebrows, but he was in excellent shape for a man approaching sixty. His hours at the club saw to that, and if he were ever tempted to skip a session on the court, the high breasts and burnished features of a wife less than half his age came to mind and he overcame the temptation. Once in a very blue moon, Deanne called upon him to prove himself worthy of the gift, and he was determined to meet the challenge.

Conservative in behavior, and carefully schooled in the manners and deportment expected of an executive in a major corporation,

Zeno was without physical modesty. Bathing suits were redundant at the YMCA where he'd spent time as a boy, and he often conducted conferences in the buff in the steamroom. But today, when he toweled off after his shower and padded back to his locker and saw the man seated on the bench in front of it, he halted suddenly and brought his towel around in front of him. Something about the heavy solid figure in the fine black suit and white-on-white clerical collar put him back in parochial school, trying to avoid the Arctic blue eye of Father Kowalski; even when the suit was rumpled and came with that coarse, battered, comical face, close-cropped head, and ridiculous cauliflower ear. Even when it came with Hugh Dungannon.

Zeno shot a look at Toby, standing as always with his hands loose at his sides in a position that gave him a view of the showers and the door to the locker room. He got nothing back.

"Don't blame the boy, Anthony," Dungannon said. "He knows we old fellows can't be made to stand outside doors. What if we develop a blood clot and it goes straight to the brain? He'd never forgive himself, even if the Lord did."

The bishop's brogue, faint in his American-born youth, had become more pronounced over the years. Heard from the pulpit, it sounded like song.

"Your Reverence." Zeno tied the towel around his waist.

"Everyone wants to give me the rank these days, even Francis, who popped me in the nose when we were both eighteen. Have we drifted so far, then?"

"I haven't seen you in a while. I haven't been to church lately."

"Four years, to be exact. Before Trina was buried outside the faith."

"You made that decision. I didn't."

"I had no choice in the matter. The doctor who signed the certificate was not as cooperative as the reporter from *The Derrick*. It went into the record as a deliberate overdose. A man needs to go to confession."

"A man needs to know how many people he's confessing to when he does." He spun the combination dial and opened his locker. His suit and shirt hung from individual wooden hangers. There were cedar trees in his shoes.

"Now, who might have put that thought in your head? Francis, perhaps?"

"The city isn't that big. News gets around." Awkwardly, he stepped into his silk boxers and pulled them up under the towel. He took the towel off then and flung it on the floor. He thrust his fists into his shirtsleeves and fumbled with the links.

"I had a touch of the Creature before Marty's wake and dropped a stitch or two when I was giving Francis my condolences. It packs more wallop than it once did. I said nothing I heard in the booth, but even so I was indiscreet. I'm getting on, there's no use denying it. Then again, what did I say that was so secret? Everyone knows McGrath's in a tight, and the city with it. They share a lung and a liver. All the more reason not to go off half-cocked and do anything we'll live to regret."

Zeno cast a glance around. Dungannon saw it. "We're safe as houses here," he said. "You can depend on the boy for that. I asked him to make sure the door stays shut."

"He knows enough to do that without being asked. But your voice carries. You're not in vestments at the moment."

"It's the slow time here, so who's to eavesdrop?" But he lowered his voice a decibel. "That's one of the advantages of being the man in charge of the shop, isn't it? You can take off work in the middle of the day and there's none to dock you a penny."

Zeno buckled his belt and sat down on the end of the bench to put on his socks and shoes. "I'm not so worried about anyone overhearing this conversation as I am about where it goes from here."

"There's no worry there if the conversation goes the way I'd prefer."

"Make yourself plain."

"Those Spanish boys spend entirely too much time and money at El Capitan. It will do them good to have something in their pockets for the collection plate at St. Anne's."

"I thought that was it. I've already had this conversation, with

Russell. A man has a right to make one mistake, especially when he's suffered a loss. I'm a businessman, regardless of what you might think. There's never been a business in the history of the world that made anything of itself on the policy of one mistake and you're out."

"I disagree. Because we're talking about the business you happen to be in."

Zeno made a precise operation out of tying his shoelace. The bows came out as even as if they'd been shaped by a machine. "I'm not Al Capone. I have an MBA and I insist on being audited annually by the IRS."

"That's admirable, Anthony. A man who protects his flanks has nowhere to go but straight ahead. Let me ask you this: Does Francis agree the raid on El Capitan was a mistake?"

"You know the answer to that or you wouldn't ask."

"One always hopes it will be different."

Zeno watched him out of the tail of his eye. The big shorn head was sunk between the boulderlike shoulders, as if to deflect a blow that had already been struck. The man clung stubbornly to his faith in the unfathomable ability of God to compromise with the Devil for the greater good. He was corrupt on a level that Zeno himself could not contemplate.

"And what of your friends?" the bishop asked. "Do they see what happened as a lapse in judgment, not to be repeated?"

Zeno stood and combed his hair before the mirror inside the door of the locker. "What did you come up here for? Not this catechism."

"They'll murder him, Anthony."

A drop fell from a shower nozzle and struck tile with a splash. It was loud in the cavernous room.

"You've been reading magazine articles about the Cosa Nostra." He put on his tie and leveled the knot carefully. "That isn't how things are done now."

"All things come back in style. A year ago that necktie was too wide."

"That's a clumsy comparison for a man who reads poetry at funerals."

"I didn't see you there."

"I told you the city isn't that big."

"You could prevent it," Dungannon said. "You could offer Francis a job in the private sector, where he can do the work he's paid to do and not the work he's paid not to. A real job, with real responsibilities. He's a proud man. It's his one great sin."

"What would he do, sling drinks at the Triangle?"

"I was thinking you might give him Morris Shiel's job."

Zeno was putting on his coat. He turned with his hands still on the lapels and laughed at the earnest expression on the big man's face. "Loading dock foreman at Volcanic? He might not see it as a step up."

"I doubt Shiel's set foot on the dock in years. I know how things are done in the Circle and who does them. They could stand improvement. It would be a grand move for you both, Anthony. Francis could crack heads all day and you would gain respectability. Shiel's a hooligan."

Zeno turned back and smoothed his lapels. "He gets things done."

"He's a yellow rat and a disgrace to the children of Israel. He won't even go to the toilet without protection."

"Neither will the Pope."

"That's close to blasphemy even for you."

"Do I tell you how to run your church?" He adjusted his display handkerchief.

"It's the only thing. Francis won't retire. I've given up trying to persuade him."

"Jerry Wilding already offered him a new job. He won't take it."

"Some paper-shuffling position, no doubt. Jerry thinks everyone wants a soft seat. His father was a better judge of men."

"He didn't take it for the same reason he wouldn't take one from me. You don't get far with Russell treating him like an idiot."

"That's true, that's true. It's his sin, as I said." The bishop breathed out slowly, like a pressure cooker letting off steam. "Perhaps you can disgrace him."

Zeno started, jerking the handkerchief out of his pocket. He refolded it and tucked it back in. "I didn't quite hear that."

"It shouldn't be difficult. I don't know the details of your understanding, but I assume there is a delivery system in place. You could arrange to have someone witness it."

Another drop crashed down in the silence.

"Surely you have someone in your organization you can sacrifice," Dungannon continued. "He'd have to go inside for perjury if the case against Francis—and against yourself, of course—is to collapse, sometime after the election. Joe Cicero would cooperate in the meantime, and Jerry Wilding would be only too happy for the excuse to withdraw his support. You could reap the benefit for years."

"I thought you were Russell's friend."

"His very best. Who but a best friend would destroy your reputation to save your life?"

Zeno slammed the door on the locker and turned to look down at the man seated on the bench. "You'd save his life, all right, if it didn't get in the way of how you live yours. You'd save your church, too, if your skin depended on it, but you're not doing it for even that reason. You're too fat and lazy to start over again somewhere else if the city falls apart and Perpetual Misery closes. You're also a goddamn fool. Russell lost his wife. How long do you think he'll want to live after you take away his good name?"

"Francis would never take his own life."

"Why, because he's a good Catholic?"

"There's none better, and I include myself. He never forgave Father Gillespie for killing himself almost forty years ago. He mentioned it just last week."

"A week before that, Marty was alive. El Capitan was bouncing right along and Russell's best friend wasn't trying to get me to frame him for bribery. A lot can happen in a week."

"It wouldn't be a frame, now, would it? We're none of us guiltless."

"I'm feeling a step closer than I was a little while ago."

Dungannon rose, dwarfing Zeno with his height and bulk. His

breath was sour, and the whites of his eyes looked as if the wine was backing up into them. Toby, who had not stirred when the locker boomed shut, rose on the balls of his feet.

"Francis would never take his own life," the bishop repeated. "That's why he's depending on you to do it for him."

He left then, a big man light on his feet, with the crouching gait of a boxer. Toby relaxed as much as he ever did.

His employer zipped his leather gym bag and they went out. The parking spaces in front of the club were reserved for members and guests, but the gray town car was in the side lot where the staff parked. Toby, who was too young to remember Fat Paulie Buffo but knew of his fate, never left the car unattended in view of any public street. He started the motor, drove up to the side entrance, and got out to hold the back door open. Zeno threw his gym bag and cased racquet onto the seat and slid in next to them. His tennis lessons usually left him tired but exhilarated. Today he just felt drained. He didn't blame all of it on Dungannon. He had an appointment upstate.

The bishop was coming down the front steps when they circled the end of the building. He paused as a taxi rolled to a stop at the base of the steps, then leaned down to open the door for the woman seated behind the driver. He smiled at her and said something. She responded, hauling the strap of her shoulder bag up her slender bare arm. She was a redhead, with a nice figure in a green top and gray suede skirt. They seemed to know each other, and Zeno realized he knew her from somewhere as well. He asked Toby if he could place her.

The man behind the wheel turned his head a quarter-inch as they slid past. In the side mirror his features were immobile beneath his rimless dark glasses. "Club Sahara." He had an odd, toneless voice, like a computer recording. "She works the bar sometimes. Got a customer here, I guess."

Zeno knew about the private rooms in the back of the Garden Grove Athletic Club. They paid for the constant improvements to the facilities.

"I wonder what those two have to talk about," he said.

Toby said nothing. He never speculated more than once per conversation, and he never took part in one unless he was addressed directly.

"Take the interstate. We're getting a late start."

Toby bypassed the old state road and swung onto the entrance ramp. The car seemed to lift off as they swept up the long curve. They were doing eighty when Toby inserted the car into a space between a twelve-passenger van and a flatbed truck accelerating to make the hill, as smoothly as if he were chambering a round. The driver of the truck tugged on his air horn. Toby didn't react.

The four-lane slab ran parallel to the state road, past dead diners, chalky farmhouses, and board-and-batten buildings looking as insubstantial as houses of cards, with empty serving windows and signs weathered into word-puzzles with letters left out. A rust-striped semi trailer stood up to its hubs in weeds, advertising a rock museum that had gone out of business six months after the governor had cut through the yellow ribbon to open the interstate. Mike Wilding, who had helped elect that particular governor, had fattened his campaign chest by tipping off local real estate developers which properties to buy along the route and sell back to the state at a steep profit. The old road, broken now in many places with crabgrass growing through the cracks, was one long drive past a graveyard of failed businesses. An hour before Zeno got to where he was going, it bent off into rural countryside.

Nicholas Bianco had bought a fine old twelve-acre horse farm upstate, bulldozed the white colonial two-story house and two barns, one erected of native fieldstone 150 years before, torn down two miles of white fence, and built seven thousand square feet of brick house with an eight-foot wall around it. Fourteen mature apple trees had been cut down and replaced by aluminum towers with floodlights on top operated by motion sensors that slammed them on every time a squirrel scaled the wall after dark. This made it easy for the four Rottweilers that prowled the grounds at night to catch the squirrel and tear it to pieces. Bianco called the estate Peace Park.

Toby stopped before the electric gate, tapped the horn twice, posed for a camera perched on one of the posts, and drove on through when the gate drifted open. He stayed with the car in front of the porch while Zeno went up and rang the bell.

Bianco—for he was not Mr. White at home—answered it himself in loose slacks, cordovan loafers, and an old blue silk shirt buttoned to his throat. His hot, moist hand enveloped his visitor's, and he laid his other palm on Zeno's back to steer him inside. Zeno could feel the heat of it, in a precise palm-shaped patch, minutes after it was withdrawn. The waxen sheen of his host's face was even more pronounced under the ambient lighting that illuminated every room from behind ceiling soffits. There didn't seem to be a lamp of any kind in the place, which may have explained the complete absence of books and other reading material, at least anywhere in sight in the open plan of the ground floor. As far as Zeno knew, no one had ever been invited upstairs. This was a situation he had no cause to regret.

They stepped down into a conversation pit carpeted in silver pile, with chairs and sectional sofas upholstered in the same color all around. A squat bottle of cheap rum with a parrot on the label shared a Lucite-block coffee table with cut-glass tumblers and a steel bowl filled with ice cubes. It was characteristic of Zeno's superior that he drank expensive brandy served in his lieutenant's homes—wasting all but one investigatory sip—and returned the favor by pouring them swill in his own.

Zeno hadn't much time to reflect on that shabby truth, for he realized belatedly they weren't alone. Part of a chair in one corner separated itself and stood up, and it turned out to be a man wearing a suit the same dark-silver shade of the chair and carpet. He was tall and thin and slope-shouldered, in his middle or late thirties, with a face of such arresting ordinariness that it faded in the bland even light that fell on everything with the same quality. He did not smile; he did not offer a hand. Both hung at his sides with the fingers bent slightly in a way that reminded Zeno of gunfighters in westerns. He'd met men before whose fingers curled like that, and it usually meant the same thing it did on the screen.

Bianco filled a glass with rum and ice without asking Zeno if he wanted a drink and stuck it out at him. He had no choice but to take it.

"Anthony Zeno, this is Vernon Goshawk. He's new to our state, and I thought it might save a lot of explanation if he sat in on our talk."

CHAPTER SIXTEEN

The triangular strip of paper was not quite two inches long, half an inch wide at the broad end, torn horizontally from ordinary white twenty-pound typewriter stock, and furred all around. Obviously it had been ripped up by hand and not shredded by a machine. It was one of three irregularly sized bits Palmer had found floating in the old white porcelain toilet in the bathroom of 116, and the only one that contained legible writing. One had been blank, probably torn from a margin, and another had borne only a medium-black curve that might have been part of an *o* or uppercase *D* and possibly a dot belonging to a lowercase *i*.

Those letters, and the more rewarding legend on the third piece, had been typed or printed, and blurred where the ink had run when they were immersed in water. The legend read:

> very Tues. at 2

The tip of what might have been the bottom swoop of a lowercase *e* stained the paper left of the *v*, and part of the numeral *2* was missing at top right. The phrase "every Tuesday at 2" (2:00? 2:15? AM?

PM?) had set off no alarms and hardly seemed scandalous enough for the toilet's venerable flush mechanism to have rejected it.

After rescuing the third piece and reconsigning the rest to the city's wastewater treatment system, Palmer had placed it on the edge of the sink and watched it dry. He'd had an inkling then that the detective business was not all it was made out to be on television.

Now, knowing what he had learned of the man who had tried to dispose of the piece from Detective Boyle, he was pretty sure of the nature of the document, if not its significance.

After Boyle left him at Harrigan's, taking with her Vernon Albert Goshawk's mug with fingerprints and vital statistics, Palmer strolled down Commercial, encountering less resistance from pedestrian traffic as the street jogged into Depot. He paused to let a team of movers load a truck blocking the sidewalk with broken-winded furniture from an apartment building, then entered the Railroad Arms through the brick portal that matched the arches in the imitation hacienda construction of the train station across the alley. Dust hung suspended in a bar of sunlight above the black-and-white floor tiles in the lobby; not even the motion of the revolving door disturbed it. In the light of Palmer's recent awakening it all looked like a hand-tinted picture postcard in a wire rack, static and curling at the edges.

Turnbull sat in his rocker behind the desk, reading another boating magazine with his oxygen tank perched on a shelf at his elbow. He was one with the dust in the sunlight.

Palmer tore a match out of the book from Harrigan's and struck it on the scratcher. "Do you even own a boat?"

The day man pushed the oxygen tank farther away from the tiny flame, an automatic movement. He didn't look up. "If I did, I'd be out sailing it down the river instead of reading about it."

"Which river? Not ours. I tried skipping a penny across it once. It turned into green foam halfway across." He lit the Chesterfield between his lips.

"You had a penny and you threw it away?"

"I was drunk. Clare back yet?"

"What am I, her social secretary? Hey!" He snatched the oxygen tank into his lap. Palmer had snapped his dead match at it, bouncing it off the aluminum tube with a *tink*. "You want to blow us up?"

"Sorry. I overshot the ashtray." Palmer held the matchbook open with his thumb. "When did one-sixteen take a powder?"

Turnbull laid the tank across his thighs and returned to his magazine. "One-sixteen, one-sixteen. You got one-sixteen on the brain. There ain't anyone in one-sixteen."

"I know. I'm asking since when."

"Since the radiator went to hell last winter. We're on the waiting list for a fix. We fired the regular man for drinking on the job. As I recall he was drinking with you."

"I don't remember him. I was drinking then."

"You were easier to get along with then."

"Everyone says that. I'm thinking of taking it up again, just as a hobby this time."

"I'll buy the first one."

Palmer rested his other hand inside the matchbook. "You sure it was the radiator and not the toilet?"

"Radiator." Turnbull turned the page and stared at a glossy advertisement of a bilge pump.

"I'm only asking because I was in there this morning. The toilet didn't flush so good."

The desk man said nothing. Palmer tore out another match, struck it, let the flame steady down, and flipped it toward Turnbull's lap. Turnbull jumped up and brushed it to the floor along with the magazine. He cradled the oxygen tank against his chest. "You think I'm kidding? This stuff's as bad as gasoline."

"Who told you to book Goshawk into the hotel?"

"Who the fuck's Goshawk?"

Palmer lit a third match and bounced it off Turnbull's shoulder. Turnbull leapt back, caught the backs of his knees against the seat of the rocking chair, and fell into it. The wall behind him prevented him from tipping all the way over. His eyes were all white in the cigarette-ash face.

"I can do this all afternoon. It's a new book." Palmer tore out another.

"Jesus, don't!" Turnbull sat hunched forward, hugging the tank. "I didn't know his name, honest to Christ. Guerrera booked him. It was his shift. I never even saw him."

"You didn't ask Guerrera about it?"

"Sure I did. He went as white as those boys ever get. You think I was going to ask him anything after that?"

He lit the match. The desk man hunched tighter, trying to curl his whole body around every exposed inch of tank. Palmer held the match for a moment, then blew it out. A question mark of smoke detached itself from the head and drifted toward the ceiling, where it hung as motionless as the dust in the sunlight. He closed the book and put it in a pocket. "Pull Guerrera's personnel file. I want his address."

Turnbull uncurled himself. He was wheezing. He placed the plastic cup at the end of the hose against his nose and mouth, turned the valve, and inhaled deeply. Pink bled slowly into his gray face. After a minute he turned the valve the other way, reached back to set the tank on the floor behind the rocker, and twisted in the seat to pull out the top drawer of a two-drawer file cabinet. He spread a folder without taking it out and looked at the top sheet.

"Twelve forty-eight Castro."

"What apartment?"

"No apartment. Army housing, little shit places." He shoved the drawer back in.

Distractedly, Palmer fished out his matchbook. Turnbull threw himself back in the chair to block the tank with his body.

"You forgot to tell me when Goshawk left," Palmer said.

"I didn't know he was gone till you told me you went into the room. Ask Guerrera." He watched him with animal suspicion.

Palmer flipped the book onto the desk and squashed out his cigarette in the ashtray. "I'm quitting smoking. These fuckers will kill you."

He was on the street when he realized he'd forgotten to tell

Turnbull the police were coming to search 116. He decided not to go back: Let the man have his rest.

He caught a gypsy cab driven by a Middle Easterner with no chauffeur's license on display. A tasseled rug hung over the front seat and the car smelled like cabbage.

Eleventh Street marked the border between Little Brazil and the mixed working-class neighborhood east of The Circle. On one side, the first generation of postwar tract houses stretched unbroken to north and south, with basketball hoops above the garage doors and bikes on the front lawns, and on the other, Edwardian brownstones continued their stately decomposition next to the stacked blank yellow-brick boxes of the projects. The signs on the takeout restaurants and corner markets turned Spanish. Pickup trucks outnumbered cars two to one, and convertibles hung two inches above the pavement with their tires sticking out like doorknobs and teenage boys riding four to a seat with their arms stretched out across the back, Marlboro boxes rolled up inside their shirtsleeves and hair built up into skyscrapers. The air was deep-fried and quivered visibly with each downstroke that blasted from car radios and portable boxes and the jukes glowing like radioactive material back in the hollowed-out tunnels of the bars. It was all too rich, like a movie set. Someone had pushed all of Mexico and Central and South America through a funnel and deposited it in an area a man could walk across in seven minutes.

The cab turned left onto Florida Street. The Hispanic Men's Social Club was dark and padlocked, with birds nesting in the once-stainless-steel letters of EL CAPITAN standing on the roof. A lost soul slumped in the doorway smoked and watched the cab turn down Castro.

Here were the houses built by the army for the married enlisted men and their wives before the base closed: one-story units assembled on-site from walls shipped in stacks with doors and windows already installed and siding attached. They'd started out uniform, each on its own square lot, but the current residents had painted them all colors and tricked out the lawns with plaster rabbits and miniature windmills and woodpeckers made of plywood and paint. The grass was clipped short and most of the driveways had been hosed down recently, the blacktop shining under family sedans with mismatched fenders and doors and virile little two-seaters with red-lacquer finishes, beautifully restored, and square plumbers' trucks with paneled compartments like old-time chuck wagons. A tractor-trailer rig took up one entire driveway, towering over the house to which it belonged. The neighborhood smelled like sizzling meat, with the sting of fried onions. It was suppertime from one end of the street to the other.

The fire department had been through on a public-relations jag, fixing each place up with a reflective green address sign that pegged in the grass or attached to the mailbox post. The tax proposition to update the aging hook-and-ladder fleet had failed anyway, but the fire chief had been a good sport about it and hadn't taken back the signs. In front of 1248, Palmer gave his driver five dollars to wait and went up the front walk to a door with a religious medal nailed above it for good luck like a horseshoe.

The door swung away from his knuckles and he looked down into the black bottomless eyes of a stout young woman holding a baby. A little girl hung on to the woman's stained white apron with a thumb in her mouth and a boy close to the same age peered out from behind her other hip with a finger in his nose; not quite a matched set, but intended to be displayed side by side. The woman, who had a pretty face and beautiful skin, resembled Guerrera slightly. Palmer guessed a sister or a cousin. The night man seemed too young for a wife and stability.

The cooking smells were thick here. Now he heard the sizzling, coming from back in the house. "I'm sorry to disturb you so close to dinner. I'm looking for, uh, Manuel." He'd had to pause to remember Guerrera's Christian name.

The pretty face tightened when she heard *Manuel,* and she let loose a torrent of dialect that was taught in no course on language. It sounded like a combination of Portuguese and the kind of Spanish spoken on soundtracks by villains who had gold teeth and accessorized their costumes with ammo.

"English?" He tossed the word into the rush of vowels and consonants like a paper airplane into a fan. "*Inglés?*"

The blades stopped whirling abruptly. "*Inglés*," she said to one child, then "*Inglés*" again, to the other. "Eugenio!"

This sounded like someone's name, and it had the effect of a trumpet call. The children spun away from her and bolted deeper into the interior of the house. At the same time a vise clamped down on Palmer's forearm and he had no choice but to allow himself to be dragged across the threshold by the hand that was not involved in holding the baby. He wondered if the woman stunned what she cooked.

The living room was clean, but cluttered with toys, and under the cooking odors there was a smell of the kind of disinfectant that came with diaper pails. There was cheap furniture and a TV set on a rolling cart and an electric fireplace with one of those winking Jesuses hung above it in a plastic frame and a crucifix on every wall. A very old woman wearing a faded flowered housedress and blue deck shoes with her big toes worrying through the canvas sat in a platform rocker with her hands crabbed on the arms, not rocking, staring at the TV screen, which was all snow with the speaker crackling. Palmer pictured her on a long adobe porch, grinding corn in a stoneware bowl. There seemed to be children all over, and a boy of about fourteen in an undershirt and baggy fatigue pants, who folded the clasp knife he was using to clean his nails and got up from the sofa and went out past Palmer without looking at him. You needed a kind of Whitman's Sampler just to sort out the relationships.

The little boy and girl did not emerge from the kitchen. Instead they hung back inside the arch, peering around it, as a boy of nine or ten came out, looking at the stranger with a grave expression on his round face. He had very thick black hair that started just above his strong eyebrows and had on a white shirt, black slacks, and new black running shoes with thick soles. He was three feet inside the living room when the woman let go of Palmer's arm, bent down to seize one of the boy's, and said something at him in a breakneck pace with *Manuel* in it twice. The boy nodded and looked up at Palmer.

Palmer said, "*Inglés?*"

"Yes, I speak it very good. I am Eugenio." His voice was surprisingly deep, and Palmer wondered if he was a year or two older than he looked.

"My name is Palmer. I work with Manuel at the Railroad Arms."

The woman stared at him as if she were trying to read his lips. When he stopped, she looked at Eugenio, who said something in which Palmer heard his own name and the word *hotel*. She started talking before he finished. He nodded again.

"My mother wants to know if you know where Manuel is."

"I was going to ask you the same thing. I wanted to ask him something."

There was another exchange between the boy and his mother. The woman moaned and let go of his arm. She turned away, bouncing the baby.

"Manuel is not here," Eugenio said. "He does not come home from work."

"When did you see him last?"

"Last night, when he went to the hotel."

"Is he your father?"

"My uncle. My mother is his sister. He never does not come home from work."

Palmer hesitated, then put a hand on the boy's shoulder. He had no practice at it. The boy shied back. Probably he'd been warned against male strangers with affectionate hands. He let his drop. "Maybe he ran into an old friend or something." He couldn't remember if that had ever happened to him.

"All of Manuel's friends live on this street."

"Did you call the police?"

This was a word the woman knew. She turned back, pale under the natural pigment.

"They can help." Palmer looked at her as he said it. "They do a lot of other things besides arrest people."

"Will you look for Manuel?"

He looked down at Eugenio. "I'll ask around. But you should call the police. Also the hospital. He might have been in an accident."

"This is the first thing my mother asks me to do. I call. He is not there."

"I'll ask around," he said again. He tried smiling. "Maybe he met a girl."

The boy considered this. He shook his head. "Manuel does not like girls."

"He told you that?"

"No, but it is a small house."

The information surprised him, although he wasn't sure why. He knew next to nothing about the people he'd been working with for years. He couldn't get the names of the maids straight, and one or two of them had been there when he came.

"You know the number of the hotel?" he asked.

"Yes."

"Why didn't you call there?"

"I did. The man who answered said he left at the usual time."

He wondered why Turnbull hadn't mentioned that.

"Will you call me there when he comes home? Palmer."

"I remember. I will call if he comes home."

He left, wondering again about Eugenio's age. That was a very grown up *if*.

The driver was listening to an Arabic station. He turned it down when Palmer told him to take him back to the hotel. The neighborhood looked less foreign on the way out, but he didn't pay it close attention.

Guerrera had booked Goshawk into 116. Someone had told Guerrera to do it. Guerrera was missing.

He thought about the snitch who had turned Goshawk in to the police in Cleveland. The suspect had walked, because the snitch didn't talk to a grand jury. He couldn't. Corpses don't talk.

Palmer got out a cigarette, groped in his pocket, and remembered he'd left the matchbook on the hotel desk. That reminded him of the decision he'd made there. He poked the cigarette out through the window crack and sat back against the scratchy upholstery. A fine detective's grasp of details he had. He couldn't even remember he didn't smoke. That put all his suspicions in a different light.

Maybe Guerrera had met a guy instead of a girl. Maybe the two of them were sitting cross-legged on the floor of a loft on East Riverside, reading poetry and listening to Lena Horne. The night man didn't have to be dead at the bottom of the Boggen Drain. Most people didn't wind up there, even in Gas City.

CHAPTER SEVENTEEN

Francis X. Russell approved of his office on the top floor of police headquarters. It was a corner room, not as large as the mayor's in the building next door, but it was big enough to contain his desk and old horsehair swivel, armchairs and sofa covered in the same stiff tufted leather, and a worktable that could accommodate plenty of paperwork and large-scale maps of the city and county, with plenty of room left for pacing. Big windows shaped like fans—the tops of the arches that ran around the building—looked out from the west and south walls on three-quarters of the city, with views of the gasworks, Perpetual Misery, and City Hall (now called the Michael J. Wilding Municipal Building): Father, Son, and Holy Ghost, with the scarlet-and-absinthe neon of Anthony Zeno's pocket duchy discreetly tucked out of sight behind the monstrosity of the courthouse. Russell's academy class hung in a plain wood frame behind his desk, four rows of uncreased, largely deceased faces in quaint ovals with the patent-leather visors of their service-station attendants' caps squared across their brows. The walls were painted green above the high wainscoting and supported more pictures, a shadow-box display of discontinued badges going back to the city marshal's, suspended by two tiny silver chains from a scroll containing the *Ides est Calundrum* motto, and an early nineteenth-century steelpoint engraving of the river and landing and wooden buildings of the original settlement. A portrait taken of Marty at age fifty and Tom's service photo shared a folding silver frame on the desk.

The office, in fact, balanced solidly between official and personal, and was a model of its type. Even the water-stained ceiling met the approval of a man who'd walked a beat for years with nothing between him and the summer monsoons but a rubber poncho and a cap wrapped in cellophane. Big Mike himself had admired the room, and quietly had his own private gymnasium across the courtyard done over in imitation, but without changing the mahogany bar he'd used to entertain visiting dignitaries and city contractors. Russell considered the place home, and it was a good job he did, because he'd spent most of his time there for five terms.

Tonight, he poured Green Spot into a glass from the bottle in the deep drawer, filled it the rest of the way with water from his private bathroom, and sat sipping and watching the sky sag to the western suburbs, pressing the last molten bar of light into a thin sheet, until even that was gone and the street lamps sprang on. Then there were just the cars crawling along the illuminated strips behind their pencil beams and the traffic signals checking through their order and the stacks of lighted windows in the tired skyscrapers and ailing department stores and the yellow pennant of flame flapping atop the stack at McGrath. In the open parking garage next to *The Derrick*, cars spiraled down like gumballs. He felt like a model-train buff playing God over his tabletop layout, contemplating moving this billboard from one side of town to the other and plucking up that molded-plastic traffic cop from the intersection of Commercial and FDR Parkway and setting him down at the corner of Crescent and Blacksnake Lane. He'd done something similar as a boy, scooping black ants into a jar and dumping them out on a red-ant heap, just to watch them fight.

He stirred himself then, placing his glass in its ring on the blotter and studying the piano keyboard of his telephone, a modern electronic marvel with a direct line to every captain and squad lieutenant in the department, with a glowing green key that connected him to the mayor's private number. (He had an Irishman's prejudice for the color, and against the arrogant red of the Union Jack.) He pressed one, waited through the series of clicks and bright musical scales that followed, and gave his greetings to Lieutenant William Casey, who'd been waiting for his call. They spoke for three seconds, and then Russell cradled the receiver and finished his drink. He thought of mixing another, then decided to put it off as a reward for later. He swallowed the rusty last of it—the city water was hard, laced with lime and iron and a bit of arsenic from the McGrath plant, but he was a native son and preferred his water with character—then thumped down the glass and dialed a number he knew by heart, but which professional discretion had prevented him from entering onto the official keyboard.

"Hello." Deanne Zeno's voice: a bit of varsity squad cheerleader, a touch of gin-and-tonic, and that overlay of tired cynicism that set one's teeth on edge when it wasn't accompanied by the years it took to earn it. Mostly it was the way she said, "Hello," without the customary question mark at the end, as if she knew damn well who was calling and that whatever information he had to impart had already appeared on the six o'clock news. He hadn't the patience to take on Deanne in a knockdown-dragout. It took all the energy he had to ignore the challenge.

"Deanne, this is Francis Russell. Is he at home?"

She breathed in and out, that quick little two-beat note that made him want to haul her out to the woodshed by her earlobe. "He's at the office. Try there."

"Volcanic?" He steeled himself for the response.

"Well, yeah. How many offices has he got? He's there all the time now. I'm a toilet widow."

"Well, people need toilets. I'll try him there, then." He aimed his finger at the plunger.

"I wouldn't count on him being there. Maybe he's got something on the side."

He couldn't resist. "Deanne, dear, that doesn't feature. *You're* the kind of woman men keep on the side." He rang off then, and looked up Volcanic Wholesale Plumbing Supplies in the Yellow Pages he kept in the belly drawer. The number had dropped out of his memory, if it had ever been there in the first place. Volcanic was just something for Anthony to tell his accountant to put on his 1040.

Zeno answered. It was after closing. "Volcanic."

"Anthony, this is Francis. I've developed a leak."

There was a blip of silence. "Call back during regular business hours. I don't know one end of a pipe wrench from the other."

"That's not what Moe Shiel says. He says you taught him everything he knows."

"Come to the point, Francis. I've been upstate and back. It's been a long day."

"My condolences. I hear Mr. White leaves a great deal to be desired when it comes to the responsibilities of a host."

"What's this about, Francis?"

"Consider it a courtesy call. You might want to notify Caleb Young before he goes to bed that his services are required at the Third Precinct."

Air stirred on the other end. Volcanic was an old building that breathed heavily in and out.

"Are you there?" Russell asked.

"I'm waiting for details."

"You'll want to inform Caleb that in addition to the usual charges he'll be representing Salvatore Tahiti in the matter of carrying a concealed weapon. I canceled his permit this afternoon."

"Did you make a courtesy call to him as well?"

"It slipped my mind. I asked Billy Casey to be particularly thorough. I doubt the Club Sahara will be reopening any time soon."

"Oh, Francis."

"You sound as if I just gave you bad news about the condition of my health."

"As a matter of fact, you did. I spent all afternoon pleading your case upstate. I was eloquent and convincing. I got you a stay."

"Well, I thank you for that, but I didn't ask you to put yourself out on my behalf."

"It's out of my hands now," Zeno said. "You think you're kicking in a strip club, but you're knocking down everything from Blacksnake Lane to Riverside Drive. Not that you'll live to see it."

"Are you threatening me, Anthony?"

"I'm returning the courtesy call. I'm asking you to reconsider that vacation in Ireland. You may want to apply for a visa and stay several months. As a matter of fact, you ought to put in for citizenship."

Russell was touched. "I consider that the advice of a friend."

"Do you plan to follow it?"

"Not for a while. I've a lot to clear from my desk just now." He ran a fingertip around the rim of his empty glass. It was good crystal and gave up a high clear hum. "I almost forgot. I asked Casey to go round the long way past the Triangle Bar. I'm not certain the Third will hold them all, so Caleb may be in for a trip up here to head-quarters. I won't be here then, so tell him hello and ask him to pass along my regards to Judge Hollander when he calls."

Something creaked; Zeno slumping back into his chair. "God-damn it."

"Good-bye, Anthony. You might think about taking time off yourself. See Naples and live."

After he hung up he felt a little bad about that last part. Zeno had sounded more concerned about Russell than about his enter-prises. He dialed the number again to apologize. The line was busy.

Next he pressed the green key, and had the treat of seeing Irene Garvey turn from her Sherman-tank typewriter and pick up the re-ceiver in her office across the courtyard. Whenever the light went out in her window and he could no longer see her steel-gray head and heavy horn-rims, it was past time for everyone to be home. She'd been Mike Wilding's private secretary since his first campaign, when he'd hired her out from under the superintendent of schools, and Jerry had coaxed her out of retirement when he'd succeeded An-gela Rice-Hippert. It was heavily rumored that she'd had a rubber stamp made with Big Mike's signature and had gone on signing con-

struction contracts and okaying city ordinances (antedating the sig-
natures) following the stroke that had eventually killed him. If true,
she'd been the unofficial chief executive for nearly two weeks. The
rumors had helped defeat Acting Mayor Keegan's bid for a term on
his own. Not only did she know where the bodies were buried, she
was the only one at City Hall who knew which forms had to be rec-
quisitioned and filled out in order to disinter them. A number of fortunes had failed to be made because someone had neglected to pay
her the court due the high priestess of the cult of Michael Jerome
and Jerome Michael. Although she was a year past mandatory retirement, Russell doubted even Jerry had the courage to suggest she
start training a successor.

"Mayor's office."

"Good night, Irene. I've always wanted to say that."

"It seems to me you already have. What is it, Chief?" She regarded small talk on the office line as a theft of city services. Even at
the best of times a man could strike sparks off the flint in her voice.

"I don't suppose his honor is burning the midnight tonight."

"He's addressing the Rotary Club."

"Will he be checking in, do you know? I've a message for him."

"Can't it wait till tomorrow?"

"I've an idea he'll be too busy to take the call then."

"What is it?" she said again. She made no move to draw a pencil
from the steel cup on her desk. She had a formidable memory, for
dictation and just about everything else.

"Please tell him I said to thank him for the offer, but I won't be
taking the job."

"Is that it?"

"That's the lot."

"Good night, Chief." She cradled the handset and returned to
her typing.

Russell tried Zeno again at Volcanic. No one answered. He decided against trying him at home in case Deanne picked up again;
the woman was a worse chore than Irene Garvey, whose thorniness
at least had the virtue of experience. He looked at his empty glass,

but he'd lost his taste for whisky that night. He opened and closed drawers, found one of his old briers and a box of wooden matches, blew through the stem, and filled the bowl from the tooled-leather humidor on the desk. He tamped it down with his thumb, applied flame, and puffed, caving in his parchment cheeks, until it caught. If Irene bothered to look his way before she drew the cover over her machine and put out the light, she saw Francis X. Russell canted precariously far back in his chair, argyles crossed on a drawleaf and his head wreathed in blue smoke from his first pipe in a month.

The double-barreled raid on the Club Sahara and the Triangle Bar required reinforcements, and Lieutenant William Casey had no farther to look for them than fifth-floor Narcotics, which had split off from Vice to form an independent unit about the time the junkies on Crescent Street found themselves in competition with young executives on Riverside for their daily supply. Following a brief discussion over who had seniority—Casey edged out Lieutenant Oscar Brown of Narcotics by three days—plainclothesmen attached to both squads signed out shotguns and extra rounds and drafted most of the second-floor Uniform Division into service, leaving behind a skeleton crew to answer the telephones. They stopped at the Third and Eighth precincts to collect more officers and continued on their way in a procession of black-and-whites, unmarked sedans, and jail vans with bulletproof mesh on their radiators, sirens and flashers off, an eerily silent sight, and new in the experience of all who witnessed it. The man- and firepower far outweighed Moe Shiel's attack on Apache Auto Salvage and may have surpassed even the army assault on The Black Circle during the last days of the horse cavalry.

The results were ironic. The mission's primary target, the Club Sahara—the tawdry gem of Anthony Zeno's operation, whose profits financed much of Nicholas Bianco's organization throughout the state—fell almost without resistance, while the Triangle Bar, a Russell afterthought, put another face on the wall of slain officers on the fourth floor of police headquarters. Several patrons attempting to escape arrest by way of the Sahara's side door were beaten back by

Casey's men stationed in the alley, a croupier in the gaming room was shot in the arm when he was slow to drop the long-handled rake he used to gather in the house winnings from the roulette table, and a stripper managed to bite through Sergeant Linus "Fathead" Wilson's left earlobe before he clubbed her down with his baton; but these casualties fell far short of the risk involved in an operation of that size. Sal Tahiti was cooperative, and allowed himself to be spread-eagled, searched, and relieved of the .45 semiautomatic pistol he'd carried legally for years, making no protest even when his handling seemed rougher than necessary for the charge of illegal gambling. He was flung against the table where he counted the receipts and the officer conducting the search tore his pockets and the lining of his suit coat. But Tahiti could not know what had taken place on Depot Street twenty minutes before.

A bartender at the Triangle, alarmed by shouts and breaking glass, mistook the first plainclothesman he saw charging his way with a shotgun for a bandit or a rebel from the ranks, snatched up a pearl-handled revolver from behind the bar, and fired, missing the bulletproof vest the man wore under his shirt and drilling him through the neck. Other raiders returned fire, and the bartender slammed against the shelves of bottles on the back wall, riddled through with slugs and double-O buckshot. He was killed instantly; the officer he'd shot bled to death minutes later. George Micalakopoulos, the Triangle's manager, six employees, and eight customers were rounded up in the horse parlor in the back room and taken into custody. Micalakopoulos, in addition to violation of the gambling laws, was charged as an accomplice in the murder of a police officer, and with manslaughter in connection with the death of the bartender. Sergeant Wilson, already facing suspension for calling a suspect "Chico" during the raid on the Hispanic Men's Social Club, and still bleeding profusely from his torn earlobe, was especially infuriated by the loss of the officer, and nearly tore off a detainee's jaw with his fist before his colleagues managed to wrestle him out of the van where he'd cornered the man. The police review board read the reports and questioned eyewitnesses and exonerated the sergeant from a charge of brutality but let the suspension stand on the earlier infraction.

Radio silence was strictly observed, and not a whisper of the raids reached Joseph Cicero through the scanner in Sid Burton's office, where the publisher of *The Derrick* sat reading Meaghan Cuddy's advice column for tomorrow's issue, which had just come in over the wire.

Dear Aunt Meg,

I suspect my husband is having an affair. For twenty years he's been quite happy with his potbelly, and I have to sneak into his dresser drawer, throw out his underwear, and buy him replacements to get him to make the change.

Lately, however, I've caught him doing calisthenics in the bathroom, and I was shocked to discover six new pairs of jockey shorts in assorted colors in his drawer. He says that he's begun to take an interest in his appearance to please me, but whenever I try to show my thanks with a little affection, he says he's too tired.

Should we see a marriage counselor, or do you think I'm merely being paranoid?

—Worried Sick in Toledo

Dear Worried Sick,

Where there's smoke, there's fire, and your potbellied prince is dipping his wick in it. Buy a gross of G-strings for *your* underwear drawer, use them to reel in a young stud, and give the old goat back a bit of his own!

—Meg

"The old bat's getting worse," Cicero muttered.

He scratched a big X through Aunt Meg's reply with a red pencil, scribbled "A.W." in the margin, and laid the long sheet on top of

the stack in his managing editor's out-box. He'd found a job for
Andy Wynant at last after taking away his drawing pencils in the
wake of the flap over his cartoon ridiculing Chief Russell in his time
of grief: drafting more conventional responses to run in place of the
columnist's steadily more demented counsel. He prepared himself
for another round of indignant telephone calls from the old lady upstate, threatening to take him to court for violating the terms of her
syndication contract.

The telephone rang on Burton's desk. It was the line for the city
room and he let the night man take it, at his desk on the other side of
the glass partition. Burton, who'd stopped at the desk for a brief conference, waited while the man answered, frowned a moment later
when the receiver was thrust toward him, and lifted it carefully to his
ear, as if it might explode. Cicero, watching, saw the editor's sad face
fade from its usual unhealthy gray to watery white. He returned the
receiver to the night man and loped toward his office. The man on
the telephone was writing furiously.

The door flew open. "What?" demanded the publisher. He was
half out of his chair.

"Line three." Burton hung on the doorknob, panting as if he'd
run up three flights. "One of our stringers, calling from a drugstore
across from the Club Sahara."

Cicero sat back down, picked up the handset, and pressed the
button. The man at the city desk kept telling the young man on the
other end to slow down. Cicero listened for half a minute, then
hung up gently.

"Jesus." He crossed himself for the blasphemy.

"We can't play this down," Burton said. "It isn't like El Capitan."

"No. Front page banner. Bump the weather to Section C. Who's
covering Wilding at the Rotary Club?"

"Jackson. He's got Maxwell with him."

"Maxwell shoots speeches and people presenting checks to each
other. We need an action man. Pull Jackson and tell him to hightail
it down to Crescent Street. Who shot that warehouse fire on East
Riverside?"

"O'Meara. He's a maniac. Accounting wants us to cancel his in-surance."

"Get him. This whole thing's maniac from the chief on down."

"What do you suppose Russell's up to?"

"I don't know, but we'd better get Maxwell and a reporter over to his place right away if we're going to run him in Section A instead of on the obituary page."

CHAPTER EIGHTEEN

On the advice of her campaign manager, Angela Rice-Hippert held a press conference in the Abraham Lincoln Room at the convention center. All the public rooms were named after U.S. presidents, and all the Democrats were taken that day. She'd rejected the Warren G. Harding Room on the theory that some of her constituents were old enough to remember Teapot Dome. For the occasion, she wore a dove-colored suit that brought out the gray in her eyes. Someone had written somewhere that the great leaders of history all had eyes of gray or blue, and some of her constituents might have read it.

"Mrs. Rice-Hippert, what's your reaction to last night's police raids in the Circle?" The question came from Dave McCormick, a part-time anchorman whose stand-ups taped in front of buildings in the civic center were a nightly staple on WGAS, the older of the city's two broadcast stations. In person his brown hair, blocked and varnished, resembled a piece of furniture.

She directed her response at the camera on a tripod to Mc-Cormick's right, mounted on a swivel so reporter and subject could share equal airtime. The sound man leaned in with his Popsicle on a stick. "Dave, I'll make you a present of the first thought that crossed my mind: What took them so long?"

The throat of the crowd rumbled. Many of the spectators stood with the backs of their legs pressing against the seats of the folding metal chairs that had been provided for their comfort. Questions flew up from all over like flushed birds. She pointed at a familiar rumpled face above a familiar rumpled Harris tweed jacket.

"Philip Jackson, *The Derrick*," he said. "How—"

"You don't have to introduce yourself, Phil. We're practically common-law."

Jackson reddened at a fresh rumble of laughter from his colleagues. After ten years on the City Hall beat he had still to develop a sense of humor. "You've been giving Chief Russell a hard time for weeks about the way he does his job. How will what happened last night affect your campaign strategy?"

"How will it affect yours?"

Jackson frowned. "I'm not running for office."

"You could have fooled me, you and your paper. You've been hitting Russell from the right while I've been plugging away at him from the left. Don't get me wrong, I'm grateful for the help. But neither of us has ever complained about the way the chief does his job. The problem has always been he wasn't doing it at all. Not until last night."

More questions broke. She held up a palm and lifted her voice above them. "I'm not going to stand here and criticize the chief for becoming conscientious in his old age. I'm just wondering why he didn't go in there twenty years ago. If he had, perhaps that brave young man who gave his life last night would be home with his family right now, watching this press conference on TV. For Officer Randolph Fletcher it was too little, too late."

She knew then she'd had her sound bite, but the conference had just begun. She selected an ash-blonde in heavy eye makeup who photographed much less emaciated on WCRV, the upstart station on the extreme western edge of town. Her crew consisted of a woman loaded down with sound equipment and an ape in a tank top with a camera on his shoulder. "Yes, Karen."

Karen Spendlove raised her beautiful contralto. "Mrs. Rice-Hippert, our viewers would like to know if you intend to debate Mayor Wilding on the matter of this new police policy."

"You mean the policy to police?" She let the tide go out on that one and work its way back. The more reporters gathered in one place, the longer it took a clever remark to sink in. Then it would be misquoted or presented out of context. She blamed her lack of patience with the entire process as much as anything else for her defeat four years before. She suffered from it still, but had learned to dissemble, and at that point completed her journey toward the pure politician. "Seriously," she said, "that will be an issue for debate, if Jerry Wilding agrees to a debate. I'm still waiting for him to ask me how to spell RSVP."

"Matt Shaw, *Morning Light*." The bearded young man in camouflage fatigues stepped on the punch line. "Will you be attending Officer Fletcher's services?"

"I will. In the meantime I'm asking everyone on my campaign team to contribute to the fund the department is collecting to give to Randolph Fletcher's wife and children. They're evidence, if any was ever needed, that you don't have to live in the Circle to become a victim of the crimes that take place there."

"What about George Micalakopoulos?" Back to Phil Jackson of *The Derrick*, who at least knew how the name was pronounced. "Do you agree he should be prosecuted for Fletcher's death and the death of the bartender who shot him?"

"The law is clear on that point. It's not my place to agree or disagree. I'm an officer of the court."

"Don't you think he's a scapegoat, to distract attention from a mission gone wrong, resulting in two unnecessary killings?"

She let a little silence go, as if she were considering the question. What she heard was Joe Cicero's voice, speaking like God through His prophet, and knew the line his newspaper intended to take. It was the only line it *could* take, having committed itself to the demonization of

Francis X. Russell. But it was a stack of sweaty dynamite. If it blew up, the worst that could happen to *The Derrick* was a drop in circulation, and columns of letters from indignant readers. She, however, faced four more dreary years at Waterman & Rice, twice a public failure, and heavy hints from Alec Waterman to sell out her partnership and take away the onus with her. She steered wide of the question. "I haven't that luxury, Phil. This campaign will not make political hay out of the sacrifice made by a defender of this city and its citizens."

That made two sound bites in one day, and she knew her manager would say it was worse than none, because they'd cancel each other out and it would be as if she'd had nothing to say on either subject. She certainly could expect no help from *The Derrick*, whose policy was locked in the chase in favor of crucifying Russell for the sin of changing his stripes; and Arthur Townower's *Morning Light*, once a clarion voice for reform, had fallen into harmony with Joe Cicero, who if anything was more reactionary than ever, only this time against the Wilding-Russell ticket instead of for it. The enemy of her enemy was her enemy indeed, and served only to present a second front. She took a few more questions from out-of-town reporters and left with flashguns pouncing.

"Wriggle, wriggle, wriggle. Politicians. I'm glad I'm just your garden-variety whore." Clare Sayer got off the bed and killed the TV. The screen folded up Angela Rice-Hippert's face and smuggled it back into the tube. "How tall is she, do you think?"

"Seven feet. If she wins, they'll have to cut a hole in the limousine roof for her head to stick through. I understand she's still growing." Palmer was sitting in the cracked-vinyl armchair in his room with a can of Coke from the machine in the lobby. His shirt was open, exposing his undershirt and two silver hairs among the others curling over the top of the scoop neck.

"I'm serious. I bet she's six-one in heels."

"What's the difference? She's too old to model."

"It's blasphemous is what it is. God gave her a gift and she traded it for votes."

"I think the law came first. He must've given her something else too, or she'd be a PD at the courthouse, making less than the janitor at McGrath." He drank and belched quietly. "Anyway, when's the last time you went to church?"

"What's God got to do with church?" She scrambled back onto the bed and scooted up to the pillow. She wore Palmer's faded purple bathrobe and a towel around her head like a turban and her feet were bare. He thought she looked like an albino Nubian princess. She used his shower more often than the one in her flat, which she said knocked like an angry neighbor and slobbered rusty water.

"So much for politics and religion," he said. "What about sex?"

"Too hot. Anyway I just took a shower."

False summer had hit Gas City like a flatiron, drawing coils of heat from the asphalt with a sweetish odor of anticoagulating tar and sealing it beneath the canopy of smoke from Factory Hill. The window on the railroad side was open, propped up with the sawed-off baseball bat Palmer kept for protection, with an electric fan on the sill, a museum piece with a cast iron base and brass blades that feathered and exchanged the heat in the room for the heat from the cinderbed.

"I wasn't suggesting we *have* sex. I was asking do you want to talk about it?"

"What's wrong with it?"

"Not a damn thing from my side."

"Well, then, what the hell do you want to talk about it for?"

"We covered everything else except money, and there's no sense talking about something you haven't got."

"I've got money. You stopped taking it from me. You want to go back to the way it was?"

"I meant real money, like your customer on South Terrace."

"Who says he's got real money?"

"Didn't I mention South Terrace?"

"I said we meet there. I never said he lived there."

"He pays your rent."

"*I* pay my rent, with the money I earn, same as that stork on TV.

I buy my own liquor and groceries and balance my own checkbook and pay the bills. Nobody keeps me."

"Sorry. I didn't know it was a sore point."

"It's the truth. What's this real money jag, anyway? You want to own a racing stable?"

"It seems to me I dumped enough at Granite Park when I was drinking to buy two or three. Hell, no, I don't want anything like that. I was just making conversation. That's what real people talk about: politics, religion, money, and sex."

"We're not real?"

"Uh-uh. We're scenery." He leaned his head back and shook the last drops out of the can and down his throat.

"Still thinking about Guerrera?"

"He's still missing. Turnbull's training his replacement."

"He probably hopped a boat to Colombia or wherever it was he came from. Anyplace has got to be better than Little Brazil."

"Except here."

"Here's not so bad. They don't have it so good on the west side as you think."

"Guerrera didn't have it so bad on Castro: clean, comfortable house, a sister to give a shit when he didn't come home. I bet he played with the kids sometimes."

She turned on her side, propping herself up on her elbow. "You went down there?"

"I wanted to ask him something." He got off that subject. "It all seemed okay for too many people in one little place. A teenage cousin or something that might be trouble, but they were all there in the middle of the day so I've got to think Guerrera was supporting them all."

"Maybe that's why he took off. Get out from under."

"Maybe."

"What did you want to ask him?"

He fumbled in his shirt pocket. "Look how wrinkled this pack is. I've been carrying it around for two days. That's how you know you're licking it." He found a matchbook in the same pocket. It was as limp as a handkerchief. He reached over and put it and the pack of cigarettes on the nightstand without taking one out.

"You still dicking around with the guy in one-sixteen? You said he left."

He breathed in, held the sodden air like smoke, let it out. It wasn't the same. "His name's Goshawk. He's a heavyweight, a free-lance hitter."

She said nothing, looking like Lady Sphinx under the terry headdress. Silence was her most effective weapon and his greatest weakness. He told her the rest then, starting with the thumbprint on the doorknob of 116 and what Detective Boyle had told him. Clare had been out when the police came to check out the room, and so had Palmer, who'd sworn Turnbull to silence when he'd learned of the visit. The day man had been too upset with Guerrera for not showing up and making him pull a double shift to argue about it, or give the hotel detective a hard time for going to the police.

"Why didn't you tell me Guerrera's nephew called here looking for him when I asked you for his address?" Palmer had asked him.

"You was trying to blow us both to hell. I guess it slipped my mind." He'd reached behind his chair to make sure the oxygen tank was safe from flying matches.

"What do you think Goshawk's going to do if he thinks you know more than you're saying?"

"I never even heard of him before today."

"You better hope he thinks so. He cleans as he goes. Guerrera may not be the only one that misses his shift."

Palmer told Clare about that conversation as well, and when he got to the piece of paper he'd found floating in the toilet in 116—the one even Patsy Boyle didn't know about—she snatched the towel off her head and flung it at the wall. Her hair, freshly washed, flared out all around like a brushfire.

"Goddamn it, you're not a cop! Even the cops in this place aren't safe. Did you know the one that got it in the neck at the Triangle?"

"He was after my time. I know the risks, Clare. I wore the dress blue to my share of funerals."

"And what, wanted to be guest of honor? What if this character Goshawk finds out you're dicking around? You told Turnbull he cleans as he goes."

"I was all set to show Boyle that piece of paper when she told me to run along and go back to peeking over transoms. She could piss off a priest."

"Priests piss off as easy as anyone else. You don't know what you're talking about. And you don't know a fucking thing about being a detective except how to get yourself killed pretending to be one. She was right: Peeking over transoms is your job. What the hell do you care what Goshawk did after he left the hotel?"

He was quiet for a minute. He hadn't really thought about it. "I guess I just don't like someone thinking he can park his pet killer here at the Arms because the security man's too much of a drunk to notice."

"It's true, isn't it?"

"Sure it's true. That's an even better reason."

"If you're in first grade. Jesus, Palmer. I knew you were a sot, but I never didn't think you were a full-grown man."

He reached across the arm of the chair and scooped up the half-empty pack, slid a cigarette between his lips just to feel it bob up and down when he spoke. "Well, it's finished now. All I've got is 'every Tuesday at two.' I don't even know if it's two or two-thirty. I doubt Boyle could do anything with it. It's information on a target, where to find him when, but who's the target? I don't know the where, and I don't know if that's the when Goshawk'll pick. It'd be one hell of a coincidence if it is. Toilets aren't usually that discriminating."

"Who says he's even got a target? It might have been his personal to-do list."

"Well, for one thing it was typed, not written out. Who does that?"

"You'd be surprised. I had a customer that inventoried his sock drawer every week, typewritten with two carbons. Everything isn't a clue."

"If it wasn't, he wasted a lot of time tearing it up into little bits and flushing them down the john. I figure what he was doing the whole time he was in the room was studying surveillance reports, memorizing everything, and destroying it instead of leaving it behind or getting caught with it on his person."

"So what if you're right? It's the same thing as reading about a murder in the papers. You can't do anything about it after it's happened, and you don't know enough to do anything about it now. Maybe it *has* happened. I don't see why you're still sweating it."

"I can't help thinking about Guerrera."

"You never thought about him when he was around. Does somebody have to die or drop out of sight to become your best friend?"

"I don't like him any more now than when I saw him at the desk. If something happened to him or he got spooked and split, maybe it's my fault for getting nosy. Look at this cop Fletcher. For all anyone knows he was a deadbeat and smacked his wife around. Now he gets the full press up at Mount Ararat with black bands and eighteen guns. Everyone feels guilty it wasn't them."

The electric fan had a loose bearing and a dog-eared blade that clipped the edge of the cage every time it came around. The whurl-whurl-*ting*! took center stage in the pause. It sounded like a drumroll broken now and then by a tap on the cymbal.

"I think you should have a drink and a smoke and forget all about the cop and Guerrera. A three-day bat's as good as an ocean cruise."

"No, I'm done with that."

"I said the same thing once. About hooking."

He took the cigarette out of his mouth. "I always thought hooking was your choice."

"It is now. Somebody gave me a chance to try something else, and I did. Worst choice I ever made."

"Who was the guy?"

"Uh-uh. I've got my ethics."

"Well, there's nothing wrong with raising your sights."

"There's everything wrong with it. It puts you square in somebody else's. Down's the only safe direction. No one wants to bump you off when you're at the bottom."

"Would I know him?"

"Not a chance."

"Before my time?"

She nodded. "After, too. I'm still seeing him."

CHAPTER NINETEEN

Randolph Fletcher had been with the department four years, the last sixteen months as a detective assigned to Narcotics. He'd come close to being shot once before, when a contact tried to hijack a briefcase of heroin from him during an undercover sting, but the contact had been high at the time and couldn't get the safety off. Fletcher had never fired his sidearm anywhere but on the police range.

His funeral mass was held at Our Lady of Perpetual Misery with Bishop Hugh Dungannon presiding. A soprano sang "He Is Knocking at the Door," and Police Chief Francis X. Russell, in crisp dress blue with gold braid, spoke of the officer's service and sacrifice and read "I Have a Rendezvous with Death," which appeared on the first page of the department manual of arms. Following the ceremony, six officers in uniform carried the flag-draped casket on their shoulders down the cathedral steps and out to the hearse, and every black-and-white not assigned to other duties joined the official cars and the limousine bearing the family from Cathedral Street to Commercial and east on Riverside Drive, crawling through a succession of changing traffic lights with police cruisers parked at the intersections stuttering their flashers: It was a daytime reconstruction of what had taken place thirty blocks south three nights before.

At Mount Ararat Cemetery, the damp from the river beaded on the grass and on the awning erected above the open grave. Six officers wearing Sam Browne belts and white cotton gloves stood at attention throughout the Lord's Prayer, then shouldered belt-action rifles and fired three times into the overcast, rattling the bolts in between rounds. All the spent shells that could be recovered from the grass were presented to Gloria Fletcher, the widow, who accepted also the flag from the casket, folded into a triangle with only the blue field showing, from Chief Russell, who saluted her. She was a chubby young woman in a black dress too heavy for the heat and a thick veil and her hands shook when she took the offerings. A small boy in a navy suit and a girl a little older in a gray dress and a straw hat sat close to their mother on folding chairs. TV cameras and motor-driven Canons recorded the details from a discreet distance.

When hydraulics drew the casket into the ground, the reporters broke cover to pursue the dignitaries making their way to their automobiles. Mayor Wilding, racked inside his quartet of bodyguards, ignored them, striding uninterrupted to his slab-sided black Cadillac with its red inside headlamps and assortment of sirens and enviable black box on the dash that changed red lights to green. Angela Rice-Hippert, protected less obtrusively by her campaign manager and various aides, waved aside questions with a hand in a glove that buttoned below the palm and concentrated on not snagging a heel in the soft turf. Chief Russell, more amiable but no less impregnable, maintained his pace, towing reporters and equipment in his wake and saying, "Now, fellows and ladies, let's have some respect for the occasion." He slid under the wheel of the plain unmarked unit he used for an official car and drove away. Lieutenant William Casey and a group of officers escorted the widow and children to their limousine. No attempt was made by the press to penetrate this cordon. Editors at WGAS and WCRV shortened the footage to eliminate the push for a quote, and *The Derrick* featured a full-length shot of Rice-Hippert descending the church steps on the front page, with a smaller picture of Wilding in the middle of his security below the fold. *The Morning Light* ran a photo of the procession with head-lamps lit under a piece about the president's visit to Mexico. Officially, Arthur Townower was still straddling the fence on whom to support in November.

Forty-eight hours earlier, Sheldon Purlman, the bartender shot to death by Fletcher's fellow officers in the Triangle Bar, had been lain to rest in the cemetery adjoining the B'Nai David Temple on Twelfth Street, north of the Boggen Drain. Purlman was a veteran, and would rate a flag on his marker, but no eighteen-gun salute (it would have been questionable taste even had he been entitled) and a much smaller crowd. Reporters did not attend, and the dozen or so mourners included Purlman's grown daughter, his eighty-year-old blind mother, a few friends, and Moe Shiel and his bodyguards. Shiel had not known the bartender well, but he considered his presence a duty of his unacknowledged office as the Circle's keeper of the peace; for however long that lasted now that the elected police chief had invaded his jurisdiction. He chanted the familiar prayers with Rabbi Firestein, but he was more concerned about his own immediate future than the memory of the deceased. In addition he was still suffering from shock over his grisly discovery in the men's room at the Club Sahara, before the raid. He had no experience with criminals like Beaver Cleaver. You couldn't scare them off by parking a truck in their driveway, even if you could find it, and you couldn't bash in their skulls with a pipe wrench if you didn't know what they looked like or where they hung out. The law of the jungle had been repealed, and he had no training in any other. He was too old to return to the loading dock at Volcanic.

"Mr. Shiel?"

The service finished, he'd turned to leave. He turned back toward the little tented area, and had to wait for his bodyguards to separate to see that Ellen Purlman, the daughter, was hailing him from her seat. She had a nice little figure in a charcoal dress and her head was bare, which was too bad because she had spiky hair cooked white to the roots with peroxide and one of those crinkled brown faces that spent too much time on beaches and in tanning beds. Her grandmother sat next to her in the coarse black of the perennial Eastern European widow, staring glassily ahead of her with her sightless eyes. He went over there, trailing his four shadows.

"Thanks for coming. Dad would have appreciated it."

"He was a good bartender. He always remembered what I drank and came back to check when I was empty." He wondered if he ought to take off his yarmulka. He was rusty in the faith.

Her hand rested on her grandmother's folded in her lap, but she didn't introduce her. The old lady didn't seem to be aware of the hand or of where she was. Shiel, who was getting on enough to have some compassion for the elderly, hoped that wherever she thought she was she found it entertaining, and he hoped that if God ever decided to take his eyes He'd addle his brain at the same time.

They were alone now. The rabbi was picking his way down the steep slope to the driveway, holding his black hem up off the ground with a bunch of material clutched in one fist.

"Were you there?"

The daughter's question startled Shiel. "No, I was home at the time. I only heard about it on the news, and then I didn't know which bartender it was till morning. I sure was sorry to hear it. Purly was—" He'd started to say, "a good bartender" again. He substituted a shrug. Truth was, if he'd run into him anywhere but in the bar he wouldn't have known the man from Pharaoh.

"Do you think it's true what they said in the paper? That the police went in there spoiling for a fight instead of just to close the club?"

"I don't know. I don't set much store by what I see in the papers or on TV. Every time it's about something I was there for, it didn't sound like anything I was part of."

"I wish it was Chief Russell first through that door."

He started again, not so much at the words as at the poison in her tone. Her baked brown face was a vicious mask.

"Smmmite."

He looked at the old woman, who had begun to rock forward

and back gently from the waist; davening, as if she'd just realized she was at a religious service. Her weather-checked lips stuck together on the labials so that she seemed to pause to hum, then parted with a snap, like a typewriter key coming unstuck from the page.

"For I will mmmpass through the land of Egypt this night, and will smmmite all the firstmmmborn in the land of Egypt, mmmboth mmmman and mmmbeast; and against all the gods of Egypt I will execute judgmmment: I ammm the Lord."

Ellen patted her grandmother's hand, a thing of papier-mâché with a thin gold band sunken into the third finger. The rocking grew more shallow and finally stopped, although the winding down was so gradual Shiel could not have said just when it did. It was like watching a pendulum swing to rest. She resumed staring glassily across the rows of stone markers and bronze Stars of David.

"She taught herself English with the Talmud in one hand and King James in the other," Ellen said. Her smile was arid. "She knows the Old Testament by heart. She's forgotten everything else except Yiddish. She spouts off at the most inappropriate times."

She ain't so out of it as you think. Aloud he said, "Do you have a ride home?"

"A friend's picking us up on her lunch hour. She couldn't get the day off. Thanks again for coming." She raised her hand. When he took it, she strengthened her grip. He could see the red nimbus around the whites of her eyes. "How do you work? Do they pay you up front or after?"

"Pay?" His hand was a captive. He couldn't free it without snatching it away, and his bodyguards were pressed in close. He didn't want them to react the wrong way. "I get a check every Friday, from Volcanic. I'm a foreman there."

"I mean for what you do in the Circle. I imagine it's cash. Dad had a policy, and I have some money saved up. What would you charge for Russell?"

He snatched his hand back then, and bumped into a guard standing behind him. Clothing rustled; their hands were on their pistol grips.

"Somebody's been lying to you," Shiel said. "My work ain't nothing like that."

"You work for Zeno, don't you? What about all these gunmen?"

"They're licensed. You want a crook, but forget it. Take your grandmother home and stay with her. Your old man ran into tough luck. He could of been crossing with the light and a car ran the red and smacked into him from the side. It shouldn't of run the red, but that's what cars do sometimes. It's just tough luck."

The red nimbus was still there. "I guess it's true what I heard about you," she said.

"Sorry for your loss." He jerked his head. The four men lowered their hands and turned to encircle him on the way down the slope. Behind him, the old woman said, "Smmmite."

Russell left the unmarked car he'd driven to and from Fletcher's funeral in his driveway. The garage his father had built, and which Russell had connected to the house by way of a dog walk, contained his personal car and was barely wide enough for that, having been designed to accommodate a Model A Ford. Marty had never learned to drive an automobile; her knowledge of the daily bus schedules had been encyclopedic. He went in through the front door, changed from his uniform into loose slacks, an old dress shirt softened from much laundering, and the pair of moosehide slippers Marty had ordered him for Christmas four years ago and that refused to wear out. They were as supple as socks and provided support for his old tired cop's arches. Their mellow gleam reminded him of an old leather chair.

When he woke up from his nap, sitting in the sprung armchair, not leather, in his den, it was dark in the room. He switched on a lamp and shuffled out to the kitchen to search the cupboards, still well-stocked by Marty from before she began to lose strength. She'd prided herself as a gatherer, taking advantage of sales and laying in supplies against the snowstorms of her girlhood in the farm country upstate, which stranded households for days. He wasn't exactly hungry, and drink had lost much of its pleasure; but Marty's pantry had seldom failed to provide a solution to the mystery of his infrequent cravings.

He seized upon a tin of cocoa, browsed further until he found a can of condensed milk, and mixed the contents with water in a pan, stirring it as it heated on the stove. The repetitive movement and necessity for attention to prevent scorching appealed to the same instincts that had led him into his profession before he'd gotten ambitious and climbed one rung too high. The warm walnutty smell made him think of Christmas and roaring games of euchre with visiting uncles and cousins in the parlor. The old folding card table had grown bowed in the legs from Danny Russell's bricklayer hand smacking cards down on the top.

He wished he could remember ever having met Detective Randolph Fletcher. He must have at one time, because he'd taken over the job of pinning shields to cadets after Big Mike's death and hadn't surrendered it even when Jerry followed Angela Rice-Hippert into the office; but all those faces were the same until life and the job altered them to the character of their owners, the way a suet gut or bony elbows reconfigured the stiff shape of a new suit. Probably he'd seen him around headquarters, but he tended to remember people more for what he knew of them than how they looked, particularly police officers. Whenever he described someone he'd seen almost daily for years to someone who hadn't met him, he was always surprised to learn later from the second party that he'd gotten everything wrong, even build and hair color. Fletcher's pictures meant nothing to him. He'd been just another of the many who drifted through the middle, calling attention to themselves by behavior neither terrible nor significantly above the average. The bullet fired by that poor son-of-a-bitch Jew bartender might have stopped the heart of a good husband and family man (he didn't know this for a certainty, because no policeman who'd ever been killed in the performance of his job had been remembered as a two-timing prick who beat his kids with an iron), but it hadn't interrupted a stellar career. In twenty years' time, if Fletcher stayed out of trouble, he might have taken home a sergeant's pension, with a couple of good-conduct certificates in his jacket, and supplemented his monthly check watching the monitors in one of the convention center hotels.

Russell didn't suppose history would have been affected one way or the other.

George Micalakopoulos was a different kind of animal, an unfaithful husband but a quiet-spoken innkeeper and operator of a discreet gambling emporium who gave to the local charities and refused publicity. He'd probably get ten years for the crime of not being able to predict the future when he'd hired Sheldon Purlman and told him where the legally registered revolver was kept in case someone came in and threatened the customers and help. Caleb Young had stood up for him at his arraignment, and Zeno had posted bail through a bond company, but the amount was a million dollars, which meant the courthouse wasn't bargaining this season. Russell would have traded three officers like Fletcher for one public enemy like Micalakopoulos, but sacrifices had to be made considering the lateness of the hour. *What took them so long?* That sly cow Rice-Hippert had nailed it square on the head. She hadn't set her foot wrong a single time since she'd loped into the ring.

The cocoa was bubbling, big translucent brown blisters that erupted from the bottom and burst with a sound like a motorboat. He turned off the burner and set it aside to cool while he reached down a thick yellow mug from the cupboard above the sink. As he did, he caught a glimpse of his long comical face in the window that came down to the backsplash. He took a step to the side to pour cocoa into the pan. A bow tie–shaped piece of glass fell from the pane and landed on the stove with a clank.

He heard the report at the same time, but in his memory the two noises were distinct and separate. His reflexes weren't slow so much as held in reserve; he'd been in scrapes, a long time ago, and had learned that most of those who came through held their ground and picked their targets. He was still standing there holding the pan at a slight tilt when a motor soared to a shrill note ending in a cry of rubber and pounded away.

After a search of a few minutes he found where the slug had burrowed into the drywall opposite the window. It left a bright yellow nick on the corner of a china shelf as it had clipped it at an angle.

Russell used a fruit knife with a curved serrated blade to dig out the slug and placed it on a square figured napkin on the counter, like a wedding ring on a satin pillow. Then he used the wall telephone to call downtown. A skin formed on his cocoa as he waited for the captain of the watch to pick up.

"Halloway."

"Mark, this is Francis Russell. I think it's time we knocked on some doors on West Riverside."

CHAPTER TWENTY

N o, Mrs. Cuddy, I'm not denying I told a member of the staff to change your column. I have a responsibility to provide my subscribers with accurate information and considered opinion. Somehow I can't reconcile that with telling a distraught reader to step out on her husband just because he bought new underpants."

Aunt Meg told Joe Cicero to go fuck himself and hung up.

The publisher let out a lungful of air, lowered the receiver into its cradle, and pressed a key on the intercom. "Lillian, call Herb Abbott in Legal and tell him to expect a letter from Meaghan Cuddy's attorney."

"Someone should have put her in a home by now," his assistant replied.

"Tell that to her syndicate."

She didn't ring off. Lillian, who had taken over the outer office after Sylvia left to marry Cicero, considered herself a member of the editorial staff, with a place in every discussion. She typed 120 words per minute and couldn't construct an undictated sentence with a crane. "She hasn't a case, has she?"

"Oh, but she has. In our court system, a lunatic can sue the sun for neglect if it doesn't shine on his garden party. Assuming the papers could be served."

"I think we should run her column unedited next time she jumps the track. It might shut her up."

"Then we'd have a half-dozen suits on our hands instead of just one. That fellow with the underpants would name *The Derrick* as a corespondent in his divorce." He clicked off before she could offer another suggestion.

Cicero was in his office on the top floor of the *Derrick* building, a stumpy piece of architecture that visitors to the city drove past without being aware it was there. The room was no larger than Lillian's adjoining, but decorated lavishly in gray marble and black obsidian, rubbed to a gleam so deep it seemed a man could stare through it all the way down to the presses in the basement. His own reflection bounced all around him. He felt as if he were being watched constantly by other disapproving versions of himself. He hated the place, and missed the reassuring oak and brown leather of its previous incarnation. Sylvia had declared it stodgy, and swept in with her swatches and color chips and female interior designer in a crew cut and double-breasted suit to turn it into a cross between the bridge of an aircraft carrier and a room at the Vatican. It felt cold even in summer, with watery sunlight trickling through the window to the north and the curtains drawn over the one to the west, which looked directly into the windows of the community recreation center across the street, which of course looked back into his. A paranoiac would feel quite smug sitting in that office. At night it was worse. He avoided it then like a dark alley in the center of the city.

In winter he found it uninhabitable, and spent more time in Sid Burton's goldfish bowl downstairs, where he felt less exposed. He doubted even Hugh Dungannon felt more judged and cut off from friendly contact in his crumbling pile on Cathedral Street.

The publisher found no comfort in the images stirring silently on the big square television set perched on its pedestal opposite the desk. Throughout the morning, both local stations had featured the same scene, taped at different angles, at every commercial break in the parade of AM talk shows, soap-opera teasers, and pitches for vaginal lubricants: Anthony Zeno, accompanied by his bald, tropically tanned attorney, Police Chief Russell, and a man and woman in plainclothes, trotting up the steps of police headquarters. The story had broken early that the chief had been shot at last night in his own home, and word had gotten out that Zeno was surrendering himself for questioning that morning, so that a crowd had gathered on the sidewalk. Police had acted quickly to set up a secure perimeter with sawhorses and yellow tape and a cordon of the kind of swollen-bellied, vermilion-faced officers you used to see stealing apples from street vendors and doing tricks with their batons on streetcorners, but which now sat in cruisers getting faster than ever on drive-in greaseburgers; but you still didn't choose them out, because now they might have a fatal heart attack while they were kicking in your ribs and their widows' attorneys would be waiting to serve you when you got out of the hospital. They held back the onlookers, stiff-arming would-be mountaineers who tried to scramble over the barricades, just as if it were a parade for a ballplayer or an astronaut. Every four-second clip ended with a reporter doing stand-up, promising details at noon.

It had started out interesting, with an excited early-morning call from *The Derrick*'s night editor, who'd gotten it from his man in the cophouse, and a discussion of whom to assign to the story. (Cicero decided on Phil Jackson and Quentin O'Meara, the stuffed-shirt City Hall correspondent and the maniac photographer of fires and riots, over the police-beat regulars on the strength of their work on the Club Sahara raid.) But the repetition of the visuals on a constant loop had sapped all the drama from the real event: Russell and Zeno, the evil twins who directed the fates of three-quarters of a million citizens as if they were a dozen green plastic army men on the floor of a playroom, together on city property for the first time. It was the stuff of allegory, and it came as no surprise that the tapeheads had missed it.

He'd been gratified, at least, to see that O'Meara had snatched himself a prime shooting stand, straddling one of the stone bannisters flanking the front steps, where not even the editors back at the stations could cut him out entirely from the footage, snapping shot after shot of the principals at whisker range. Whatever he'd paid the cop in charge of crowd control for the spot would show up on his expense sheet, and Cicero would okay it with his initials writ large. He couldn't wait to see the proofs. All they had of Zeno in the file were some tele-photo frames taken across the street from his house and Volcanic and a front-and-profile from an early arrest, of a teenager with eruptions all over his face and a long jaw designed to saw at a wad of gum.

But it all felt as if it had passed Cicero by. Even the extra edition he'd ordered directly from his bed would hit the streets an hour after the idiots had vomited everything into living rooms and kitchens throughout the metropolitan area, including inaccuracies and pompous speculation, also inaccurate. Subscribers would glance at the headline, graze the lead, jump to the photo spread on page three, and go directly from there to the box scores. The magnitude of the situation—a corrupt chief sweeping decades of cobwebs off the public trust, an untouchable crime lord squirming on the hook, a slippery mayor stuck square in the middle with nothing to hide behind but his thousand-candlepower grin—would elude them because they thought they'd seen it all over lunch.

It was a lonely thought, and made him feel like some unappreci-ated prophet out of classical literature. Cassandra, at least, was heard, even if her prophecies were ignored. No one even knew he was there.

He leapt at a buzz from the intercom like a castaway at a bottle in the surf. Even a conference with Lillian on newspaper policy seemed preferable to his perch on this wind-slashed rock.

"Sid Burton's here."

"Yes."

The managing editor entered in shirtsleeves. He never went out on a cloudy day without an umbrella or rode up in the elevator with-out his coat on. That he'd forgotten today pointed out just how big the story was. Cicero felt a little less alone then. He made room on the oyster-slick slab of desk for Burton to rest the huge black portfolio he carried. Burton lifted the cover just enough to slip out an eight-by-ten envelope that tied with a string. It took up just a fifth of the carrier. His employer predicted a formal unveiling of the rest of the contents later.

"O'Meara swung up to Russell's house after the circus," Burton said, untying the string. "Cops chased him off the first time, but he snuck back in from South Terrace through someone's backyard and shot part of a roll before they ran him off again. This is something that TV gang doesn't have." He laid a contact sheet on top of the portfolio.

Cicero leaned in close to peer at the images printed directly onto the glossy stock from 35-millimeter frames: a progressive series beginning with the house, approaching the windows on that side, and ending with close-ups of a pane of glass with a butterfly-shaped hole punched through it.

He sat back. "Do we know the caliber?"

"Jackson's pumping a source in the city attorney's office. I'm leaving a box open in case he calls it in five minutes before we go to press."

As he spoke, Burton dealt eight-by-ten proofs onto the portfolio. He'd arranged them in order, and the illusion was of watching an old-time nickelodeon. Russell, Zeno, Zeno's lawyer, Caleb Young, and the man-and-woman plainclothes team marched directly toward the publisher in high-definition black-and-white. Cicero snatched up one taken at little more than arm's length. "Page one, next to the bullet hole. I've seen these detectives before."

"Stan Prokanik and Patricia Boyle. They're working Beaver Cleaver."

"Tell Jackson to get an interview with both of them for the evening edition. Profiles, the works. One of them may be the next chief."

"What about the current chief?"

Cicero tapped the picture of the broken pane. "How sure are we this is Zeno's work and not some kids with an air rifle?"

"Even setting aside the size of the hole, I'd say pretty damn sure. Coincidence is for Features, not City."

"Well, unless Russell exposes himself to a troupe of Brownies visiting the station on a field trip, he's going to be with us for at least the next four years. We'll have to go after Wilding from another direction. You know and I know he's going nuts right now: The Circle's come to West Riverside. Let's make it his fault, for his sins and the sins of the father. All those years of neglect."

"Why?"

Cicero stared at him. In twenty-plus years, he'd never heard his manager ask the question.

Burton set another precedent—three in five minutes, including leaving his coat downstairs—by not waiting for an answer. His tragic face was animated. "I think we're failing to see the forest. Wasn't the whole point of this crusade against the administration to build circ?"

"If I were speaking to the Press Club, I'd say good citizenship, but I wouldn't be selling them either. Come to the point, Sid."

"I'm getting there; you know me. I'm not a religious man, but I'd say God gets plenty sore when He hands you a gift and you don't open it. The broadcast boobs are dropping the ball. They've never even acknowledged the city's on the crook: Both their general managers belong to the Chamber of Commerce. I think we can expect them not to recognize Russell's come around a hundred and eighty degrees. We haven't had a certifiable hometown hero since Miss Garden Grove went to the state finals, and we didn't have the scoop then." He pointed to the litter on the desk. "If we play this right, we'll have people gathering on street corners waiting for the trucks to drop off the next edition, like they used to do for Dick Tracy."

"Three days ago, we were burying Russell for getting a cop killed. How would you suggest we go about rolling away the rock?"

"He gave it the first push. All we have to do is send O'Meara down to photograph the resurrection."

"This conversation is starting to sound like it should be taking place at Perpetual Misery." The publisher drummed his fingers on the portfolio. He felt warm in that office for the first time since before the renovation. "All right, Sid, you've brought your Easter basket. Go ahead and open it."

"I thought you'd never ask. I was prepared to take it away sight unseen." Burton shunted the proofs back into the envelope, tucked it under one arm, and spread the portfolio. He stood up a sheet of sixteen-by-twenty drawing paper with a tissue protector attached by a spring clip to a piece of stiff foam board and folded back the tissue, holding it like an easel. "I thought it was time we took Andy Wynant off the Aunt Meg detail."

Cicero rolled back his chair for a wider view. Wynant's bold pencil strokes had duplicated the scene of Francis X. Russell kneeling over a trough labeled VOLCANIC WHOLESALE PLUMBING SUPPLIES, with an alteration: Russell was standing, wiping the slop off his lips with one hand and kicking over the trough with a foot in a huge hobnailed boot. The artist had signed his name ostentatiously in big bulbous cartoon letters.

"Egotistical little twerp." Cicero's tone sounded awed even to him.

"For starters, we'll get back all the subscribers who dumped us," Burton said. "Then we'll go after *The Morning Light*'s."

"That's no way to talk about our partner. Do we know how Townower's playing it?"

"Straight reportage. I've got a man in his press room. He's not even putting out an extra."

"Arthur's slipping. I remember when he had balls."

"We skirted plenty close to the farmer's knife ourselves when we backed Rice-Hippert."

"I'm glad we decided to hold off a formal endorsement until October. Did we get a statement from her?"

"I called her personally. 'We're all concerned for Francis Russell's safety. When the chief of police needs protection, we're past due for a change at the top.'"

"So much for not politicizing the sacrifices of others. Run it in a box with a file photo. Last page of City. She threw us over publicly after the Club Sahara, so she can take her chances along with the Socialist candidate. It's going to feel good running a newspaper again."

"So it's a go?"

"Page three center. Bump the photo spread to five. I want this to sock them in the eye when they turn the page, with an editorial. Make me sound like Churchill: 'We will fight them on the beaches,' etcetera, only make it local. Taking back our town. Run 'em both again tonight, with an update. Zeno'll be back on the street by then. You always have an alibi when you pay someone else to pull the trigger. Who wrote that think piece last summer on the early history of the Circle?"

"Rynearson. He's got a Ph.D. in history from State." Burton folded the tissue back over the cartoon, returned it and the envelope full of proofs to the portfolio, and tied the ribbon.

"I want a detailed chronology on organized crime in Gas City, going back before Fat Paulie Buffo: Ten thousand words, to start. We'll serialize it starting Sunday and run through to September."

"Short notice, but he's a quick study. Stopping where?"

"Stopping with Tony Z. getting the needle up at state prison. He won't, of course; nobody higher than Pittsburgh Phil's been executed since Lepke, but that shouldn't stop us from pushing for it. We need a new Satan if we're going to promote Russell to Christ Almighty. What do you think happened, Sid? Is all this just because his wife died?"

"Search me. People change their minds for all sorts of reasons. That's as good as any. Better than most. If I lost Amy—"

"You wouldn't have to play bridge anymore." Cicero used his sleeve to rub a sweaty palm print off the desktop. He promised himself a more congenial decor if circulation bumped up. Sylvia couldn't give him any more hell over it than she had over the joint operating agreement with *The Morning Light*. He felt a prick of remorse over the shock he was about to hand to Arthur Townower. It wasn't a full-blown stab; he'd never liked the Puritan so-and-so, who wore sock garters and avoided red meat as if it had maggots. Then he turned dour. "Let's hope Russell doesn't fall in love sometime in the next few months and turn himself back around."

Palmer's morning was no less frantic than Joseph Cicero's. Madison, the new night man Turnbull had trained to replace Guerrera, was a fast man with a pager, and instead of threatening to call the cops to vag out Rudy, the neighborhood bum, had turned to Palmer to throw the poor little schizo out of the lobby five times since 3:00 A.M.; each of his multiple personalities had no memory of the recent experiences of any of the others, and he'd come back as a lost three-year-old girl named Henrietta, a belligerant trucker named Tug who'd misplaced his rig, a mysterious millionaire philanthropist who refused to divulge his identity (the hotel detective had met this particular individual before, and received an uncashable check for a hundred thousand as a tip), and a fourth party he suspected was plain old Rudy. He'd just ejected him the last time when Madison told him to check on room 435, whose Do Not Disturb sign had been out for twenty-four hours, and whose telephone didn't answer. The new man figured it was a skip-out.

Palmer didn't resent the buck-passing so much as the assumption he was Palmer's immediate supervisor. A reformed man, he held off smacking Madison's curdled-looking face into the desk for the time being—it was his first week, and one made allowances for the probationary period—and went up to knock on the door. All he got in response was the early-bird sermon on WCRV. He knocked again, and this time used his passkey without waiting for an answer.

It was empty, of course. The hangers in the closet were bare, and since there were only three it was easy to figure out where the others had gone, along with the towels, the telephone directory, and even the Gideon Bible, which brought twenty-five cents to vendors on the street, whose profits were close to a hundred percent because all their inventory was stolen. Razor tracks on the bathroom sink left two thin white lines that gave him a half-second buzz when he scooped them up with a finger and took a taste. The Railroad Arms' fortunes seemed to be on the rise: It was usually heroin, and Mexican Brown at that, stepped on down in Little Brazil more times than the Mexican Hat Dance. Nose sugar was strictly West Riverside.

Some McGrath board director's progeny had had himself a party, and in his exuberance had forgotten to settle his bill. If this kept up, the hotel could soon afford to fix the toilets—if it managed to collect. He hoped that job wouldn't fall to him. Next to teaching their children manners, the rich hated paying their debts more than anything. The kids swiped the Yellow Pages, for chrissake.

When he came out of the bathroom, the TV station had broken for a commercial. Palmer was about to switch off the set when he recognized Patsy Boyle, looking uncomfortable as she and her partner escorted someone whose features he recognized vaguely up the steps Palmer had recently climbed to police headquarters. On camera, she looked better than she did in person, like one of those actresses who seemed to spring to life only when the lights came on and money was being spent. He saw Francis Russell, his deadpan-comic's face aged considerably since he'd seen him last in person, holding the door for the party.

". . . not known at this time whether Zeno is a suspect in the attempt on Chief Russell's life or has come forward with his attorney to provide information. Back to you, Ron."

It was a recent report, time-stamped ten minutes before, and clumsily edited. The camera cut away from the bag-of-bones female reporter on the sidewalk, swiping the faces of the crowd gathered behind the barricades.

Quickly, Palmer switched channels. WGAS was covering the same story, but from a different angle. The technicians broke back to the studio directly from the chief without a shot of the spectators.

He watched enough to find out what had happened at Russell's house last night, then turned off the set and stuck a cigarette in his mouth. What he'd seen was ten minutes old; he had time, and needed the tobacco to kill the urge to drink. Then he spotted a smoke detector mounted on the ceiling outside the bathroom. He must still have been drunk when 435 went nonsmoking. He put the cigarette back in the wrinkled pack and picked up the telephone.

It was still connected; the cokehead hadn't officially checked out. He dialed outside and called Patsy Boyle's extension uptown. He got her partner.

"The hotel dick. Find any footprints on the ceiling?"

Palmer felt the corners of his mouth tighten in irritation. He didn't mind the pair laughing at his amateur detective work so much as being called a dick. "Boyle in?"

"She's in the can. We got a busy day, Palmer. You got anything new, you might want to call the radio hotline. Maybe they'll give you a T-shirt."

"I don't listen to the radio, Prokanik. I watch TV. When Boyle comes back tell her I just saw her boy Vernon Goshawk there, right outside your front door. I figure that puts him at Russell's house last night."

IV

THE CRIME

Chapter Twenty-one

S ome two weeks after Anthony Zeno was questioned and released in the investigation of the attempted murder of Chief Russell, Morse McGrath II died quite unexpectedly in the spring of his ninetieth year.

For years, the board chairman and principal stockholder in Mc-Grath Industries International had observed a strict, self-imposed diet: unsweetened oatmeal for breakfast, a hard-boiled egg and lettuce leaf at noon, and for supper a skinless chicken breast and boiled potato, with mineral water served at all three meals. He had the arteries of a man half his age and his heartbeat was so strong and steady the technicians who gave him his annual EKG swore they could stand a quarter on edge on top of the machine during the examination. He had inherited his long-dead father's invulnerable mental faculties and spare angular body, but not the epilepsy that had tormented the patriarch in his later years. No one could remember when he'd suffered so much as a case of the sniffles. Acquaintances of his youth and middle age had fallen one by one, but Death had seemed to look the other way whenever McGrath entered the room.

One afternoon he checked into a private suite in the Morse

McGrath III Memorial Wing of Carbon Valley General Hospital with no complaints other than hardness of hearing, chronic impatience with the younger members of his board, and a persistent headache. He was in a coma in intensive care the next morning.

A routine CAT scan discovered signs of internal hemorrhaging in his brain and he was diagnosed with a ruptured vessel due to an aneurysm. The cranial surgeon, a leader in his field, cracked the skull, suctioned out the blood, oversewed the rupture, and closed, declaring the operation a success. McGrath did not awaken. When no brain activity was determined, the staff attempted to contact the patient's middle-aged granddaughter in California to decide whether to disconnect his breathing apparatus, only to learn she'd moved without leaving a forwarding address; it was notorious that she was estranged from the old man, whom she blamed for hounding her father into an early grave through interference in the way he'd run Morse II's company.

It was at this point that the son of the refinery's legendary founder stopped his own heart. No other construction could be placed upon the event.

That week, *The Derrick*, *The Morning Light*, and the two local television stations moved their reporting on the Russell case to the second tier. Charles Rynearson suspended work on his series of articles about the history of organized crime in Gas City to write a lengthy biographical piece about McGrath, which Joseph Cicero published in three succeeding editions, with photographs of the old industrialist shaking hands with three presidents, actor Spencer Tracy (who was to play a role based on Morse McGrath I until the Catholic Decency League pressured the studio to shelve the project), and Benito Mussolini, his host during a seminar in Rome to discuss Italy's oil explorations in Ethiopia. The current U.S. president praised McGrath during a press conference as a model of the American entrepreneurial spirit and sent a cabinet minister to the funeral. No one but hospital staff had been present at his death, but every corporation on the New York Stock Exchange, the governors of seven states, and Fidel Castro dispatched people to attend his memorial service in the First Presbyterian Church and join the two-mile-long procession to his burial in Monument Park, a piece of land originally owned by Morse I and donated to the church nearly three generations ago, after his fabled run-in with Arch Killian, an employee of Carbon County Surveying. (Morse II, it developed, had arranged a loan to Castro to purchase Ernest Hemingway's yacht for the Republic of Cuba; the loan was still outstanding.)

Arch Killian, who now considered himself the only living resident of the city who had had personal contact with the original Morse, took part in the services, leaning a bit on his son's arm during the trek to the grave and not bouncing, as when he'd paid his respects to Martha Rose Russell; although the old man remained faithful to his daily constitutional, it took a little more out of him each day than it had the day before. On this occasion, he remarked to his son that it might save everyone time and inconvenience if he left him at the cemetery.

"Dad, you're Catholic." Earl Killian sounded worried.

"Honestly," Arch said, "Do you think the worms give a shit?"

The McGrath granddaughter, wherever she was, inherited nothing, and the percentage of shares she held was insubstantial. As per sealed instructions left with Morse's attorney, his general manager was proposed for chairmanship of the board and the directors voted unanimously in his favor. To this individual fell the company's fortunes as well as its problems, including the loss of government and private contracts to foreign interests and protracted negotiations with Mayor Wilding and the governor of the state to secure tax concessions and prevent extensive employee layoffs. Speculation shared columns and airtime with the criminal investigation in the city and other events of interest:

—On the Saturday night following the shooting incident at Russell's house, the Vice and Narcotics squads, acting separately but in communication, made thirty-seven arrests in The Circle and Little Brazil on charges ranging from unlawful gambling to felony possession for sale of controlled substances, including thirteen counts of solicitation for prostitution. Gino and Nick Angelo were removed in handcuffs from Mama Angelo's Pizzeria to the eighth police precinct for running numbers in back of the establishment, and Mama was detained briefly for assaulting police officers with a wooden paddle; she was cited for interfering with the police in the performance of their duty and released. Lucky Eight Billiards on North Crescent Street was raided for accepting bets as high as a hundred dollars a ball on pool tournaments, police battered in the door of a Ninth Street rooming house and took six people into custody for processing and selling heroin and cocaine, a sting operation swept Blacksnake Lane of hookers and customers, whose vehicles were confiscated, and Felipe Bedondo spent four hours at the Third Precinct for reopening the Hispanic Men's Social Club after it had been closed by police; a haggard-looking Caleb Young secured his release on a writ of habeas corpus, then hurried to the Eighth with ten more in his briefcase.

—Both newspapers and both television stations featured photographs of Vernon Albert Goshawk in front and profile, which had been given them by the police. On a tip by an unidentified informant, Goshawk, a subject of numerous investigations, with suspected ties to organized crime, was being sought for questioning in the Russell case. Over and over, WGAS ran a half-second clip of a man believed to be Goshawk standing in the crowd at police headquarters the morning after the shooting incident, and froze on the grainy image. On-screen and in print, Zeno appeared often, entering headquarters that morning and in his teenage mug photo, a memento of his only serious brush with the law.

—Three houses on West Riverside Drive were broken into in one night by thieves who made off with more than fifty thousand dollars in cash, jewelry, firearms, and electronic equipment. The same gang was suspected in all three burglaries, the first of any consequence to take place in that part of the city in more than fifteen years.

—A late-model Cadillac was stolen in mid-afternoon from the driveway of a house on Magnolia Street and recovered six hours later from the Boggen Drain, stripped of its radio and stereo. No one could remember a car theft in that neighborhood.

—The bloated, partially decomposed body of a young male was found snagged in floating debris on the north bank of the Carbon River by a hiker a half mile outside the eastern city limits. Until the sex was established, the press questioned whether the victim was Beaver Cleaver's first not to have been dismembered, and continued to speculate based on the fact that he had slain two men previously, but the story ran its course shortly after a young woman from Little Brazil, who had filed a missing persons report on her brother some days earlier, identified the remains as those of Manuel Garcia Guerrera, who'd shared her address and had been employed as a night clerk at the Railroad Arms on Depot Street. The bullet that had killed him had grazed his heart, deflected off a rib, shattered, and pierced his liver, stomach, and spleen. Its caliber could not be determined until all the pieces had been recovered and weighed.

—After a brief hearing, a grand jury handed down a bill of indictment for George Micalakopoulos on a charge of manslaughter in the death of Detective Randolph Fletcher at the Triangle Bar. Trial was set for September in Judge Hollander's court, and the defendant was ordered to surrender his passport to minimize the flight risk. Caleb Young represented him at the proceeding.

—Beaver Cleaver did resurface a few days after Manuel Guerrera's corpse appeared, when a sanitation worker discovered a black plastic bag containing the severed head of a young woman in a Dumpster on Boiler Row. A canvass of dentists throughout the greater metropolitan area uncovered X-ray records identifying the victim as Pearl Elizabeth Arno, who'd been arrested three times for solicitation in four years and served thirty days in the women's workhouse upstate the third time. Pathologists determined that the head belonged to the limbs that had been found by Moe Shiel and one of his bodyguards in the men's room of the Club Sahara, and prints lifted from the hands in that bag confirmed it.

Once again, Chief Russell's incursions in The Circle slipped below the front-page fold and out of the precommercial teasers. Profilers throughout the state postulated that the killer kept the butchered body parts in a cool basement or similarly primitive storage area and doled them out at his leisure. The fact that date of death could not be narrowed down within less than two or three days of the actual event prevented police specialists from establishing a cycle or pattern in the frequency of the murders. Although Beaver Cleaver seemed to prefer slender women between the ages of twenty and thirty-five, of medium height or shorter, with fair complexions, the experts did not agree on whether he targeted prostitutes consciously or simply found them convenient during the hours of darkness; all were in accord that he could not have gone unapprehended this long if he did his hunting in the day, or drove all over the city with a trunk full of bloody members during business hours, looking for a place to dispose of them.

"Black Bag is what those who specialize in studying the criminally insane refer to as a 'double dip,'" remarked Dr. Feliz Aguilar, the police psychiatrist, to Karen Spendlove, who visited with him in his office with a camera and sound crew from WCRV. "He gets his initial rush by committing the act, then again when the body parts are discovered and he sees the reaction in the media."

The consulting room, on the second floor of police headquarters, was contemporary in the extreme, an abrupt contrast to the age and architecture of the building that contained it. A white wool rug with a nongeometric pattern that assumed the shapes of faces, animals, coffeepots, and genitalia more distinctly the longer one stared at it covered the rippled narrow oak floorboards to within six inches of the horsehair-plaster walls, which were sponge-painted a delirious apple green. All the objects in the room except for the Rorschach rug were in bright uncomplicated colors, even the desk, a candy-corn orange, with no place to rest the weary eye but on the rug and wonder what a chimpanzee clapping its hands said about one's emotional state. The low-backed red and blue and yellow and purple chairs in the conversation area, where the interview was conducted, looked as if they had come from a nursery. In fact, plastic building blocks littered the round coffee table, where presumably officers involved in shootings sat cross-legged on the floor assembling castles and boats and discussing their masturbation fantasies.

Aguilar himself, slim and brown and unsweating in a coral shirt-and-tie set and mauve tropical worsted, with black hair that fringed over his collar and a fine-line moustache, looked more like a Latin dance instructor than a mental-health professional. His nails were slightly long but rounded, and when he gestured with the right he showed a semicircle of dimples on the heel of the palm that might have been tattooed; he explained, off the record, that he'd been bitten by a patient early in his practice and had nearly died of tetanus. "If you must be bitten," he'd said, "make sure it's an animal. A latrine in Cambodia is cleaner than the human mouth."

Opposite him sat Spendlove, the station's highest-profile on-the-spot reporter, graduated to a sit-down interview at last. In person she was skeletal, with concave cheeks and shins like razors, but she photographed like a runway model in one-piece monochrome dresses—never slacks or suits—and her voice was low and pleasant, even if all the words that came out in it were scripted. She appeared to scribble notes in her long spiral pad: She was marking off her prepared questions as she asked them to avoid repeating any, as she did not always listen to herself. She placed the point of her pen beside the next line and looked up quickly, widening her eyes as if inspiration had just struck. "Describe Black Bag," she said.

"He's strong, as you know, because he stuns his victims with one forearm blow, without weapons. That doesn't necessarily make him a giant you'd notice on the street. Wrestlers and boxers are trained to make the most of what they have through leverage and maneuver. I'd say he's built like a truck driver. His physical skill suggests some years of experience. He may be middle-aged, which would make him aware of himself and adept at dissembling his true nature. His conversation would be quite normal, even dull. He's learned the art of camouflage."

"State Police Captain Keynes says he's a young man, aged eighteen to twenty-four."

"That's textbook dogma, straight out of *The Field Guide to North American Mass Murderers*. It's past due for an update." He smiled briefly, showing his beautiful teeth. "I know Captain Keynes, and

I know his department's psychiatrist even better. Their only professional experience with amateur recidivists is a series of child rapes, so naturally they're obsessed with the sexual angle, hence the emphasis on youth. But old men can be pretty frisky. Also, my colleague up at the capital, whom Keynes consults, is a Freudian. I don't have to tell you those people check under their beds for phallic symbols every night."

He touched his moustache, which was wispy enough to flutter away when he became animated, and went on. "Black Bag is driven by rage and resentment and fear, not lust. You'll find the first three much more developed past forty, particularly if life has dealt him a sufficient series of low blows, climaxing in a recent traumatic shift in circumstances—say, unemployment or the threat of it. At an impressionable age he suffered some slight or loss that affected him deeply, and the pain and humiliation has built with each new setback. He was brought up in an environment of shame—a stern parent, perhaps, or a strict institution—which compounds his complex with deep self-loathing, and periodic attempts to quit, or at least modify his behavior."

She glanced down, then back up; when the one-camera setup was reversed and her questions repeated (and reactions manufactured) for insertion during the telecast, her eyes would remain earnest and steady on the lens. "Would you care to make a public appeal to Black Bag to give himself up?"

He smiled again, smoothed his tie carefully to avoid dislodging the microphone the size and shape of a pen cap clipped to his lapel. "Let's depart from the text for a little, shall we? I'm just getting warmed up."

"Uh, okay." Her face tightened at the point of fracture.

"I analyzed his motives earlier in regard to dissecting his cadavers and depositing them throughout the city. He enjoys replaying the event when he sees the story on television and reads them in the paper. In a way, just talking about him here makes us enablers, but there's no getting around that. The public has a right to know, and the press the responsibility to report. He's willing to accept the risk of being caught, which increases in direct ratio to the amount of time he spends in possession of the remains and the number of trips he makes to dispose of them piecemeal, because it prolongs the enjoyment. Otherwise we'd have many more victims on our hands."

"Why is that?" For the first time, Spendlove seemed to have forgotten the pad in her lap.

"If he didn't restrain himself by drawing out the pleasure, he'd have to kill much more often, to maintain the buzz. Pearl Arno's head was in an advanced stage of decomposition, indicating he'd held on to it longer than any part of the previous victims. Other parts of her are still missing, including the torso, so he's struggling hard to hold on to this one. That explains why so much more time passed since the last discovery. My theory is he's trying to cut down, like a smoker or an alcoholic tapering off his intake until he's beaten the addiction."

"Will he succeed?"

Aguilar touched his moustache again. "No one ever has."

CHAPTER TWENTY-TWO

When the police released the body of Manuel Guerrera, it was signed for by a representative of Sparro and Sons Mortuary, who took it to the establishment on South Eleventh Street in Little Brazil for embalming. The casket remained closed before and during the ceremony at St. Anne's on Florida; days of immersion in the river had done too much damage to the tissues for restoration. Father Rojas, the assistant pastor at St. Anne's, presided, conducting the Mass in English and Spanish, two languages Palmer knew just enough about to know the priest was proficient in neither. What the church lacked in the melancholic grandeur of Our Lady of Perpetual Misery, it made up for in the almost festive appearance of the crude hand-carved icons standing six feet tall in the alcoves and Christ spread-eagled behind the altar, which were painted turquoise and teal and dusky red; they resembled piñatas.

Palmer sat eight rows behind two pews reserved with black satin bows for family. Guerrera's sister was there, dressed in rusty-looking weeds with a heavy veil probably inherited from generations of mourners; in her culture, the women put down black crepe between sheets of tissue in the same chest with Great-Grandmother's wedding dress, with the black on top, because one married but once and grieved often. The sister (Isabel, he now knew, from the pocket-sized program he'd been handed by an usher at the door) had shuffled in on the arm of grave little Eugenio, attired as before in black slacks and running shoes and white shirt, this time with a necktie, also black and also most likely preserved for the occasion. His mother was bent, and had they not met before, Palmer would have taken her for a woman of sixty. Days of worry, shock, and then loss had translated into decades, and he knew she would be middle-aged from now until she became elderly. He hadn't attempted to speak to her, and he would not be attending the graveside service. Her brother might yet be alive if Palmer hadn't become so curious about the guest in 116. If Goshawk was the pro that Detective Boyle and now TV and the papers built him up to be, he would have picked up on the fact he was being asked about. That was why he'd left the hotel, and why he'd killed the night man and dumped his body in the river, to eliminate the only connection between the killer and whoever had made arrangements to put him up without registering. A man couldn't lug around a burden like that and mouth the conventional phrases of condolence.

Turnbull had been right. Palmer should have stayed drunk. He'd awakened from the sleep of years with a reverse Midas Touch: Everything and everyone he came in contact with turned to ashes. He was like one of those electric linemen who touched the wrong wire or got struck by lightning up on the pole and survived, only to notice their own body polarity had turned around and they couldn't strap on a battery wristwatch without making it run backwards.

Behind Isabel had trooped the matched set of little boy and girl, with the ancient woman Palmer had seen staring uncomprehendingly at the TV set in the house on Castro walking between them and a step behind, with a hand on the shoulder of each. Her black dress was of an older design than the sister's, with hooks and tiny black buttons up the back that glittered like bats' eyes. She, too, was bent a little, but she would have had to bend to rest her hands on the children's shoulders, and Palmer sensed she was doing so more to keep them from splitting away and running about the church than for support; her fingertips were yellow with pressure, and her grip made gathers of material of shirt and dress. She would be the matriarch, a grandmother at the inside. Whatever the condition of her faculties when at rest, they focused with the hardness of light refracting through a diamond when the family fabric began to unravel. She had probably been baking since before dawn, covering every square inch of heirloom ivory lace tablecloth with cakes and pies and brownies and dark bread that crumbled like old mortar when the famished bereaved tried to break off a piece and butter it.

More family still behind them: a young woman or old girl Palmer hadn't seen before, flat-chested with lank hair and thumbprints under her eyes, carrying a blanket-wrapped baby that might have been the one he'd seen Isabel holding at the house; the reedy, teenage tough from the sofa, wearing a baggy camouflage T-shirt over dirty khakis with pockets with button flaps, handy for carrying cigarettes and a lighter and possibly a crack pipe and one of those little pistols no larger than a woman's compact—or was Palmer jumping to racist conclusions based on nothing more significant than the trademark slump of sullen youth, with his hands deep in his slash pockets? Then came a flock of other Hispanics aged thirty to fifty, including couples with children, one a pretty girl of about the youth's age with black hair hanging straight down her back throwing off blue halos and a bow on the back of her pink dress, an odd choice for a funeral but just as oddly appropriate on some level Palmer associated with the country of origin. They kept coming like passengers boarding an airliner, filing up the center aisle and filling the first two rows on both sides. He couldn't tell where the relatives left off and the friends and friends of friends began, but as the electric organ groaned on they continued to gusher in until every seat was filled and the latecomers stood three deep at the back, just as Father Rojas entered through a side door in his white cassock and vestments of scarlet and green and gold and mounted the step behind the altar.

Palmer felt a sense of loss then for the first time, unrelated to guilt. A young man he'd dismissed for years as part of the architecture of the Railroad Arms had lived a life outside the lobby, been loved and liked to a degree he himself had never known, and he'd been too drunk to notice, and even when he was sober had been too caught up in holding his spidery perch to guess at it. Probably he wouldn't have liked him any more if he had, but that door was closed, and he hadn't earned the right even to lean against it and weep. He felt as empty as a bottle.

When the choir sang—boys in white gowns, as fresh as produce, with voices like silver on crystal—Clare gripped his forearm tight. She sat beside him in a gray dress he'd never seen, with a hat to match made of some feltlike material that sat on her auburn hair with the serene unconscious balance of a squirrel resting on a twig. When he'd asked her why she'd wanted to come, she'd stared at him a long time and said, "A boy I knew died."

"I didn't think you knew him that well."

"We grunted at each other when I came in and went out. If you asked me to describe him so you'd recognize him on the street, I couldn't. But I knew him and he died. I go to all the funerals of people I know. I'll go to yours."

"Don't keep any dates open for a while. This is an interesting conversation, considering you couldn't understand why I cared when Guerrera went missing."

"I thought he was alive then."

"You're a Catholic," he'd said then. It wasn't a question.

"I was. Still am, I guess. I mean, the Pope hasn't excommunicated me or anything, that I know. I didn't check my messages today. But I haven't spent Sunday in church since the last funeral I went to, and he was a Methodist."

As she'd spoken, she'd hooked herself into a vestigial white bra he'd never seen before. Dressing in front of him was new; he felt they'd crossed some invisible barrier of intimacy. She dressed from the bottom up, starting with her stockings, the way most women undressed. He found it highly erotic.

"Did you lose faith?" he'd asked.

"I got bored. For one thing I don't like wearing hats." She'd taken it from her overnight bag and pinned it in place before the mirror in his room.

"I thought they changed that."

"They did. I don't have to stop wearing white shoes after Labor Day anymore either, but it feels like I'm out in public with cowshit on my heels. What about you?"

"I've never owned a pair of white shoes in my life."

"I *meant*, are you a Catholic?"

"I know what you meant. I was introducing lively banter to lighten the occasion. My stepmother used to take me with her to Mass, but I never got Communion. First time we went to confession I broke and ran. Did you ever see a kid do that to avoid climbing up on Santa's lap?"

"Most kids grow out of it. Zip me."

He'd fished the tab out of the *V* in the back of her dress and slid it up over the splash of freckles under her left shoulder blade. "Kids grow out of it when they stop believing in Santa."

Her eyes had caught his in the mirror. "You're an atheist?"

"I hope not. All the atheists I know are fanatics. They meet once a week and light candles to Madelyn Murray O'Hair."

"Are you an agnostic?"

He'd grinned. "I don't know."

"Well, you can't keep your options open forever."

"Just for a little while longer. I'm not used to having any."

Now the service ended. Palmer and Clare stood with the others while the pallbearers, six men who had sat in the front row, carried the casket down the aisle toward the double doors. It was red cedar, with brass-plated handles, and trailed a scent that reminded Palmer of watching his mother folding away flannels and woolens in the chest in his parents' bedroom. It was one of his earliest memories, and his memories of her were few. She'd been coughing even then. Cedar smelled like death.

The front pews emptied in order. Isabel, still leaning on Eugenio, passed him without turning her head, a silhouette cut from construction paper behind the thick veil, but the boy saw him. Palmer watched

puzzlement and then recognition rise in his eyes like lifting fog. Pale
taut streaks appeared at the corners of his mouth. His gaze slid forward
and he continued without slowing, with his mother's hand clenched
high on his upper arm. There would be bruises there for weeks.

Palmer and Clare stood aside from pedestrian traffic on the top
of the church steps, watching the attendants pass down the line of
cars gathered at the curb, placing magnetic flags on top of fenders
and stopping to lean down and answer questions put to them from
open windows. The unseasonable heat of earlier in the month had
fled before a series of snotlike rains, with the threat of snow flurries
for the weekend; the meteorologists were referring to the balmy period as the Spring Pause. A dank gust slapped at the couple and he
put an arm around Clare's shoulders. She was shivering.

"Let's go back to my place and boil a pot of coffee," he said.
"You can put a nail in yours. That bottle of Ancient Age is dusty on
top. I'll run a bath. You can have the end without the faucet."

"How gallant. Rain check. This is the third Wednesday of the
month."

He'd forgotten all about her standing arrangement with the
party she met on South Terrace.

"Why don't you send him a bottle of twenty-four-year-old on
me? I'll match his price tonight."

"Just because you're dry doesn't mean the country's gone on the
whiskey standard. Anyway, if it had, I'd be worth a whole case. You
can't afford me. You're my charity."

"You'd be surprised how much you can save up doing most of
your drinking at home for four years. I'm sick of having to move it
around every time I dust."

"You never dust. What about the next time? If I cancel now, he
might take his business someplace else. There's a bunch of out-of-
work whores on Blacksnake Lane right now." She dropped her voice
on the last part; Father Rojas was passing. He was a young man with
long, curling eyelashes and looked a little like both Manuel Guerrera and his sister. Palmer wondered if he was related, along with
half of Little Brazil.

The church had cleared out, the procession was sliding away from the curb. It extended around the corner and made him think of one of those slow-moving freight trains that always seemed to drift to a stop while you were waiting to cross, then began to back up. Cars not participating had formed a phalanx of their own in the parking lot next to the church, trapped for the moment by those who couldn't get enough of mourning.

"No getting a cab for a while," Palmer said. "We can go to Castro and pick one up there, if you don't mind the hacks that go past Riley's. They look like they're headed for the junkyard, but those Spanish boys turn everything they make back under the hood. They could hold their own at Indy."

"Let's walk. I've got a little time. You can drop me at my place."

He took off his coat and draped it across her shoulders.

"You'll freeze your nuts off," she said.

"I had them winterized."

As they walked up Eleventh, she laced her arm under his. "I didn't mean it as pissy as it sounded before. I think you *are* gallant."

He didn't know what to say to that, except something that would sound pissy. He treated himself to a cigarette. He'd been treating himself to a lot lately, after having cut back to a quarter of a pack a day. Smoking was a lot harder to give up than drinking and pimpery.

"Why don't I take care of you?" he said then. "It'd be a switch."

"Is that a proposal or a proposition?"

"I don't know. The idea just came. Throw the dice."

"Either way it'll come up craps. I don't want to get married, and I won't be a mistress, yours or anyone else's. I already did that."

"That's the something else you tried with the guy you won't tell me who he was?"

"Yeah. I make my budget and I pay my own bills."

"Mistress is an old-fart word. It's something a fat French minister keeps on the Left Bank. You spend more time at my place than yours. You could give up yours and we can be each other's mistress. Or I could give up mine. The roaches will miss me, but they're fickle. I won't get any argument from Turnbull. He can rent it out and pocket the rate and let the owners go on thinking I'm still living there. If they ever did come to town it must've been before my time, or when I was drunk."

"I like my place. I like just me in it. It's just right for one and when I put something down I know it'll still be there when I go to pick it up."

"I won't move anything. I don't even dust. And I don't take up much space."

She patted his arm and said nothing. They walked slowly, the way couples do when they're hip to hip, to avoid stumbling. Beside them the line of cars crept at the same pace, hardly fast enough to stir the flags on their fenders with FUNERAL blocked out in orange on the black Swiss crosses. At the corner they waited for the procession to pass, then crossed west and followed the lower swoop of Blacksnake Lane, which by daylight was nothing more than a squalid stretch of frame-and-brick two-stories erected under McKinley, with common walls separating massage parlor from tattoo emporium and Christian Science book store from sex shop, and which at night was something less than that. The street ran a jagged broken-field around trees and rocks long since dead or dug up. Natives said its name had come from a nineteenth-century bounty on blacksnakes, and from the men in rubber boots carrying long sticks with wire nooses on the ends who tramped along that route to the Boggen Drain to collect. Pamphlets issued by the Garden Grove Historical Society pointed out that there never was a bounty on nonpoisonous reptiles, and attributed the name to the cattle pens that had once proliferated in the neighborhood, and harness shops where leatherwrights cut and braided cowhide to make blacksnake whips; on ripe days in deep summer, the stench of tanner-ies and ancient manure came back to drift across the city's lower end, foul as vampires' breath.

The sidewalk, craquelured like a dry riverbed, was hauntingly empty of women in brief shorts and halter tops. The crackdown was still in force, and the cost of advertising on the street was no longer just two hours in the tank and a two-hundred-dollar fine, but a month in the women's workhouse, and for the customers their names in *The*

Derrick and confiscation of their automobiles. In the end, even the city prosecutor had shaken himself out of hibernation and fallen in with Chief Russell. It was like watching a line of toppled dominoes setting themselves back up in order, each one levering the next upright. The whole place seemed to have been struck by lightning and all the clocks and watches were running backwards.

When they reached Depot Street and Clare's apartment building, a gingerbread box separated like the middle third of conjoined triplets from its Edwardian neighbors by demolition on either side, she turned into him, went up on her toes, and kissed him, softly and with warmth. "If you're still up for that bath, my tub doesn't have any faucet in the way."

Surprised, he gripped her arms tight. She'd never asked him to her flat. She gasped and he loosened his grip. "Sorry. I thought there wasn't time."

"We've got till eleven. I said that because I wanted the rest of the day to myself."

"Now you don't."

"Now I don't. The place is a mess. I tried to get a maid to moonlight from the Arms but they all think they'll go to hell if they cross the threshold."

"Hell's worse than the Railroad Arms?" He held out his palm. After a second she scooped her keys out of her purse and placed them on it.

The flat was a second-floor walk-up, twice as big as his room at the hotel but still one room, with a bath and a kitchenette just big enough for the refrigerator and sink and a two-burner stove. The bed was a single, hence her use of the hotel for her customers, neatly made with a blue satin coverlet. There was a love seat with a reading lamp beside it, a table with one chair for paying bills and eating, and a new-looking dresser with a mirror and hair brushes and cosmetic paraphernalia on top, the makeup brushes standing bristles-up like an artist's in a coffee mug. A print of an extinct Paris done in watercolors, the only ornament in the room, hung on the wall above the love seat. Magazines and paperbacks and odd articles of clothing littered the rug, an

Oriental type with rust-colored borders and a fringe. The only window looked out over the roof of the Triangle Bar and streetwise pigeons picking through their own splatter for morsels.

"Nice view."

Clare pulled a cord, closing green curtains over the window. "I'm a hooker, not a three-hundred-a-pop call girl. Can't you pay a lady an insincere compliment?"

He hesitated. "Anything I said after that would land me at the bar, straight through the Triangle roof."

"Try anyway."

He folded his arms around her and kissed her hard. "You're the best-looking thing in the Circle."

"You've seen the competition. Try again."

"You're the best thing I know."

"Same answer. One more strike and out the window you go."

"I love you."

"Too far the other way." She ducked out of his arms and went toward the bathroom, shrugging his coat off onto the floor. "I won't be a minute. That means I'll be fifteen. There's beer in the refrigerator, or will that corrupt you?"

"I can handle a beer fine. The rest of the case handles me. How's the water from your tap?"

"Tastes like gas, just like every other tap in town. Have a beer. I'll make you forget all about the rest of the case."

"Planning to fuck my brains out?"

In the bathroom she paused and looked back at him before shutting the door. "I'm going to do my best to fuck them back in. Open one for me too."

"You want it waiting?"

"I want you to bring it in." She closed the door. A moment later he heard water whirring.

The tub was a paleocrystic clawfoot, probably original to the building, and when he stripped and lowered himself into it he realized that bathroom technology had taken a wrong turn with the invention of the modern porcelain box. The curve fit his long back and narrow buttocks like a well-broken-in easy chair, and the cast iron, jacketed in smooth white enamel, acted as a Thermos to keep the water warm. The hot and cold faucets were attached to a pair of copper pipes that came up the outside, sparing both their backs. He'd set their beer bottles on the floor inside their reach, and they sat back with the steam rising, drinking cold brew with a pleasantly bitter bite, their legs arranged with a foot aside each other's hip and their thighs touching; halfway through the bath, Clare rearranged hers to use her toes, which were dextrous enough to pick up a dime from waxed linoleum. He was as stiff as a rail when they got out and they left their beers half-drunk and went straight to bed without toweling off. When they finished the first time, panting like horses with their pulses rattling, they were slick with each other's lather and the bed was soaked. They couldn't stop laughing.

CHAPTER TWENTY-THREE

I'm glad you agreed to ride in with me this morning," Jerry Wilding said. "If you don't object, I'll issue a press release announcing the mayor and chief of police have begun car pooling until this Mc-Grath business irons itself out. Setting a good example always sets a good example."

"Just so long as no one expects it every day. I get a lot of thinking done driving myself." Francis X. Russell curled his fingers around the padded door handle to avoid sinking all the way through the suede upholstery into the trunk. The Cadillac's interior always reminded him of the inside of a humidor. It smelled of full-grain leather and spearmint and good cigars and rolled as smoothly as on casters. The springs were designed for a truck, to support an additional ton of concealed steel plates and thick bulletproof glass. Behind it traveled a smaller car of the same make, containing the mayor's personal security, four city police officers who were rotated from headquarters as often as tires to prevent them from becoming sleepy and complacent, and Wilding's driver carried a short-nosed .45 and had training in evasive driving tactics; he piloted the big unwieldy piece of machinery with the skill of a U-boat commander.

The mayor himself wore an armor mesh undervest in public, fitted to his large frame, as had his father before him, since the day Big Mike was shot on his way up the steps of the Elks Hall during his first reelection campaign. He'd gone ahead and delivered his speech, then had himself driven to County General to have a .25-caliber slug the size of a pencil eraser removed from his upper right thorax. (Legend said he was spared more serious penetration by either a thick folded sheaf of pages in his breast pocket containing the text of his address or a steel flask, but Michael J. Wilding drank only from a glass and never spoke from notes. It was his own freakish constitution that had saved him; that, and the conviction that he had not been born east of the Boggen to die north of the river.)

Big Mike's assailant, a file clerk in the basement of the city hall on suspension for an altercation with his fellow employees, fled the scene, but police traced him to his mother's house in the old German section, where he shot himself when the first cruiser swung into the driveway. That was the official account, anyway, and when the file clerk died the next day at General without having regained consciousness, it became part of the permanent record. Mayoral protection up to that time had been minimal—Big Mike liked to walk out in front during the St. Patrick's Day parade and dash into the crowds on the sidewalk to shake hands—but afterward everyone above the office of treasurer withdrew behind a barricade of Kevlar and Plexiglas and well-trained muscle.

Jerry Wilding told his driver to run up the dark-tinted window between the front and back seats, cracked the window on his side, lit one of his toy cigars, and sat back while the blue smoke found its way out of the car. "I trust Carl with my life but not with the way I run the city," he said. "I had the devil's own time finding the leak when the McGrath tax deal broke in *The Derrick*. I damn near fired Irene; *Irene!* It was her who found the son of a bitch, an independent contractor I hired to rewire the mansion. He's snipped his last bit of wire in this state."

"You talked about the tax deal in front of your bodyguards at Marty's wake."

"They're your men, Francis. If you can't trust the police . . ." He made a gesture with the cigar as if he were throwing it away. "I had them checked out too. It'd be a bitch to have to have them step out every time I talk government. That's why the city pays them damn near what it pays you. A poor man's easier to corrupt."

"I don't know about that. I've never considered myself poor."

"Hate yourself on your time, not the taxpayers'." Wilding spoke with his father's Londonderry lilt whenever he dressed someone down. It was the rattle before the strike, the humming in the transformer before it blew. "I've not had the chance to speak with you in private since you took down the Sahara and the Triangle Bar. I was doubly sad that night. We lost a police officer, a good family man, and I lost my best choice for commissioner."

"You'll find someone better. I don't work well with committees. Marty said I was like a lone old badger with a toothache, looking for a porch to crawl under and groan."

"We all wind up being what our wives say we are. That's why it's important to choose the right one. I'm offering you the job again, Francis, and I'm advising you as a friend to accept it before you get out of this car."

"If I say no, will you have Carl run it up to seventy and throw me out?"

"There'd be no satisfaction, except for you. You've been standing on a ledge ever since you became a widower, calling people inside names and trying to get them to open a window and push you off. I'm inviting you to come back inside."

"Thank you, Your Honor. That's a pretty way to put it."

"Call me Jerry, goddamnit. I know you're trying to give everyone around you the stiff arm, but I don't like even strangers calling me 'Your Honor.' It sounds like I sell used cars. Don't thank me, either. Right now you're the most popular man in town since the fellow who burned down the old courthouse with all the foreclosures in the files. People like to see greed punished, especially when fire's involved or things smashed up with sledgehammers. You've even got *The Derrick* back in our camp, and anyone who can persuade Joe

Cicero to change his mind after he's already changed it once ought to have a statue erected to him and filled with malt whisky. It wouldn't exactly harm my chances for a second term if I gave you a raise and a promotion."

He poked the cigar into the slipstream and rolled up the window. Then he parked one of his oxenbrace shoulders in the corner, facing Russell. "Tell me, Francis, what you ever did that hurt this city. Don't tell me how much you raked off from Tony Z.—which by the way diverted criminal funds from enterprises far worse. I'm not Hugh Dungannon. I don't listen to confessions, and if I did I wouldn't hear them, because I promised the old man I'd never lie whenever someone asked me what I knew. Whatever your reasons, the city benefited from the arrangement more than you ever did. We've kept vice in the Circle where it belongs and serious crime out of the residential neighborhoods."

"All except mine. I bet I'm the only police chief in the country with a squad car assigned to his own protection twenty-four hours a day."

"You wouldn't if you hadn't tampered with a good system. The same goes for those break-ins and thefts on West Riverside and Magnolia. All right, we've got a nut killer running around slicing up women, but these days you have to have one of those for anyone to take you seriously. It's been four years since we had a strike in public services. *Time* magazine called last week. They're about to list Gas City among the top ten safest places to live in the U.S. That's how bad a police chief you've been."

"I didn't do it alone. Our strike record would go back twenty years if Zeno hadn't declared war on Mayor Rice-Hippert. They ought to name him Man of the Year."

"Politics is compromise, as if you didn't know. Your predecessor didn't, and he couldn't make any headway with Paul Buffo. They were natural enemies from the start and they went down together."

"Not together. Fat Paulie took a little longer hitting the ground. I don't know where they got the dynamite. I filled out all the forms and couldn't get enough to blast the boulder in my backyard when I put in the rec room."

"That's what I'm saying. They smeared the grease here and there and then there wasn't enough left in the pot to turn the wheels. It was lubrication that kept Rome going for a thousand years, until the emperors got religion and the barbarians muscled them out."

"I always thought it was the Roman Army that kept it going."

"Only as long as it got the grease. When it didn't, the centurions butchered the emperor worse than Beaver Cleaver." Wilding smiled, the reassuring grin that appeared on billboards and city buses. It was too wide for indoors. "I'm not just handing you a cap and a whistle and letting you cut the tape on the new softball diamond in Roosevelt Park. As commissioner you'll direct the greater operations of the department and lecture at the academy. You've got a lot to teach the cadets they won't learn from the manual of arms."

"Thank you again, Mayor. I'm not just ready to be put to stud."

"Next term I'm ramming through a bond issue to knock down that parochial school where you work and build a new police headquarters. Modern lab, electronic firing range, a garage to house the fleet, training facilities all on the premises instead of farming them out all over and up at the capital. You'll be in charge of the project, from the first stroke on the blueprints to the last screw in the hinge of the last stall in the ladies' toilet. I'm going to name it the Martha Rose Russell Memorial Building."

"That trumps Tony Z. All he ever gave her was a stove."

At that moment they passed Anthony Zeno's house, serene in its greensward, and turned south on Commercial, passing Rinaldi's Restaurant, a legitimate Zeno enterprise with grapevines as thick as a man's wrist twining up the front, imported all the way from Florence. Russell turned away from the window. "You know what I want, Jerry. Throw in direct supervision of all criminal investigations and you've got yourself a police commissioner."

"No. It's too much for one man. After the election I'll ask the council to appoint Bill Casey to finish out your term. When the chief's position is phased out I'll seat him on the commission, and he can succeed you when you decide to retire."

"That's a jump for a lieutenant."

"I considered precinct commanders, but they're all too hide-bound. That feudal system of yours works at the neighborhood level, but it's hell on flexibility in a sensitive position. They're like the nuns that taught me geography: great backhands, but you couldn't convince them the world was round with a picture taken from the moon. Casey's been getting nearly as much ink as you lately, and he photographs well with an axe in his hands."

"He's good at taking orders. You'll get on just fine."

"Take the job, Francis."

"Not if it means not being a cop, which is what you want."

The mayor's grin folded in on itself. He rearranged his bulk again and looked out at the blue glass towers of the convention center, clouds reflected on the top floors as if they were passing clear through the construction. "How are your investments? I hope you didn't put everything into the house."

"I've got some McGrath stock and a little in municipal bonds, like a good public servant. I sponsored a Little League team when Tom was a boy, but they kept hitting balls into the Boggen. I suppose you could say I've got a lot invested in the Drain."

"Reason I ask, you won't collect Social Security for ten years, and it doesn't look well for a former police chief of this city to list the Salvation Army shelter on Boiler Row as his place of residence."

Russell smiled. The older he got the less he enjoyed shooting pool with a stick of butter.

"Well, it's good work if you can manage it. You can't fire an elected official except by recall, and I can't picture you buttonholing customers outside the Stop 'n' Go asking them to sigh the petition."

"I'm not going to fire you or have you recalled. You're going to resign."

"I'm just starting to like the job."

"You won't when Joe Cicero and Arthur Townower and Ken and

Barbie on TV start reporting the details of your association with Zeno."

"No one knows those but he and I, and we're not calling any press conferences."

"They'll fill in the blanks once your net worth comes to light. All it takes is a bank examiner, a property assessor, and twenty years' worth of pay stubs that don't begin to cover what you've put into the house. I don't even need a court order. As a public servant you're not protected by the privacy laws. As a matter of fact, you're required to disclose your finances, and it's safe to say you haven't been thorough about that in the past. That's another penny on the left side of the scale. Which is what you may have left after the IRS gets involved."

"I take it you're planning this for after the election?"

"Thanks to you I haven't that luxury. You'll be sending Casey to bust up Volcanic Wholesale Plumbing Supplies next, if Zeno doesn't kill you first, and I'll have to rebuild the system from the basement. That means no new police headquarters, shootings on West Riverside, and sanitation and transportation going out on strike. I'll do what damage control I can, appointing a civilian task force to investigate the inner workings of the department and asking the FBI to step in. If I lose anyway, I can always run for governor next year. It'll be my picture on the cover of *Time* with an axe in my hands."

Russell tugged at one of his big earlobes. "You're a bold one, Jerry, I've known that since you were a boy. I doubt even Big Mike beat you for balls on his best day. Well, here's Our Lady of the Weeping Widow, and you have my answer." They'd slowed to fifteen on Civic Center Drive and coasted to a stop in front of police headquarters. He opened the door.

"This will come back on Marty, too, you know," Wilding said. "The stove, and the full-time nurses you hired when she got sick. People will say she was too good to go to the hospital like everyone else."

"Go to hell, you black Protestant bastard."

The mayor leaned over and caught the door before Russell could slam it behind him. "You're upset, of course. Think about it over the weekend and let me know Monday. I like the ferrets to be fresh when they start digging."

CHAPTER TWENTY-FOUR

There was a new leak somewhere in Our Lady of Perpetual Misery.

Hugh Dungannon, who had an ear for the groan of every sagging timber and clatter of rust in the pipes, all the gasps and sighs and delicate belches of a woman long enough past her prime to have forgotten what it was like not to wake up every morning with a fresh complaint, heard the slap-slap-slap in the echo chamber of the cathedral like a conductor detecting the twang of an untuned string in a forty-piece orchestra. It had rained briefly during the night, the water had formed a reservoir somewhere among the groins and spires, and had found its way in through some new crack. Sitting in the rectory nursing a hangover with a shallow tot of Napoleon, the bishop listened to the slapping for an intense moment before locating it in a front pew. Water splashed on tile and tapped on stone, but when it struck oak it made a smacking noise like a Navajo woman beating her wet undies against a rock. It was inevitable that it would pick out one of the seats where the big contributors sat.

He had a theory about church roofs, developed over forty years of never having been in one that wasn't collecting for a new roof, in the process of building a new roof, or thanking the congregation for helping to complete the new roof. Prayers were very hard on material things, and two hundred people firing pleas upward every Sunday were like an invading army catapulting flaming projectiles onto the roof from outside. Either that, or the contractors were infidels, recycling boards and shingles from other projects, pocketing the difference, and not much concerned about where they spent eternity. He liked the other theory better.

He'd been up late, and there were holes in his memory of the night before into which he'd poured brandy, which cuffed you down and picked you back up by turns, the way it's possible for a fighter to knock out his opponent and then knock him back awake with the next punch. Boxing was a comfortable metaphor in Dungannon's utterances public and private; he'd boxed at the seminary and been pretty good, although not nearly good enough to take it up as a profession had he ever lost the Call. His nose had been broken more times than he could count, starting with a blow from that wiry rascal Francis X. Russell over Marty's affections when they were all eighteen, and he didn't hear so well out of the ear Sister Catherine Eustatius had cauliflowered for him when he'd acted out in English Composition. He looked like an old pug, and on mornings like this he felt as if he'd taken a pummeling.

His favorite sermon was the one he'd written about a grudge match between a priest and the devil, with God acting as referee. The priest was at a disadvantage: He couldn't cheat because the Almighty hated a forfeit, but Lucifer had nothing to lose by hitting below the belt and weighting down his gloves with brimstone. It ended, of course, with the priest ahead on points and the devil snarling about a rematch. The sermon was popular with his sporting parishioners, who asked him to repeat it every time some Fight of the Century was scheduled in Las Vegas.

Whenever he thought of that old shot to the nose, he felt the same anger he'd experienced at the time, but it was no longer directed at Francis. He'd never been able to absolve Marty for providing the cause, and the poem she'd made him read at her services proved she hadn't forgotten she'd allowed herself to be pursued by two men at the same time; moreover, it proved she was unrepentant. But he'd kept his composure and read it. He'd had a problem with anger when he was young. It was partially to its credit that he'd joined the priesthood. Keeping up your dukes is difficult when you're wearing vestments, and you learned to control your volume when every syllable rang in the rafters of a barn like Perpetual Misery. In any case he didn't regret the choice. The Church had given him a position and a home that wasn't frequently offered a kid from Boiler Row with a chip on his shoulder the size of Jericho. He loved the old place he'd been assigned to at last, here back home after all those assistant pastorships elsewhere. He and Our Lady were like a broken-down old couple with no pretensions between them and no need to communicate beyond fragments. But this new leak reminded him that nothing is permanent under heaven. If they took him away from her, to some modern church that looked like a service station on the turnpike, he'd shrivel away like a widower evicted from his home of many years into a sterile senior center.

He took a deep breath, let it out, and had another sip, but that was the off one that made him sleepy again and he pushed the glass across the huge ugly carved mahogany desk where Father Gillespie had sat on a morning much like this one, then gotten up and gone out and hurled himself under the interurban railway. The orthodox version of the event was he'd slipped and fallen, but Gillespie had been a man with issues, most of them not for public consumption, and it didn't do to bury a priest in unconsecrated ground. God would take up the slack on His end.

He picked up the telephone, a sleek flat one he'd brought in to replace Gillespie's ornate white French rotary that had made him feel as if he were speaking into a trumpet, and tried to call Francis in his office, but was told the chief was late that morning. He was grateful to hear the stranger's voice regardless. There were times, alone in that great Gothic ruin in the center of a buzzing city, when he felt as if he were in a cave on a rock hill in a country emptied by plague. A man had to have human contact or become odd, like the

Jesuit fathers at the seminary, scurrying down the corridors with their bony shoulders up around their ears, muttering to themselves as if jabber was what they ran on. He had nothing in particular to talk to Francis about; the man never changed his mind, not about marrying Marty out from under his old friend, and not about his mad plan to tear down everything he'd built over the past twenty years. But Dungannon needed to talk to someone, even if all the someone said was no.

He remembered then that the mayor had asked him to deliver the benediction when he spoke at the Knights of Columbus Hall next week. That would give him an excuse to call, to discuss the procedure. Jerry was a positive force, spinning a bright lariat around you when he spoke, and you couldn't come away from conversation with him without a lighter heart.

"Mayor's office."

"Irene, my dear, it's good to hear your voice. This is Hugh Dungannon. Is himself available?"

"No, Bishop, he's late." Irene Garvey always addressed people directly by their titles: no "reverences" or "honors," and the titles themselves might have been no more than names the way she used them. If Dungannon had given the matter any thought he'd suppose she was an atheist as well as a small *d* democrat, except she never tried to convert anyone.

"There seems to be a bit of that going around this morning. Please tell him I called."

After hanging up he drummed his thick fingers on the receiver, then looked up the number for Volcanic Wholesale Plumbing Supplies and dialed it. He needed to hear a familiar voice that wasn't all business. The voice he got was made of galvanized iron. Its owner told him Mr. Zeno wasn't in. Dungannon worked the plunger and called Zeno's home number quickly, before he could change his mind in case Deanne answered. He didn't care for the child. She answered. He closed his eyes and identified himself and asked for Anthony. She said he was with his lawyer. He thanked her and broke the connection before she could say something annoying.

None of the crepuscular habits of the leaders of the community was in place today. The world had slipped off its axis. He felt anxious and dragged his glass back across the desk. But the brandy had begun to taste like kerosene. He set it down and got up to see what he could do about the leak.

He checked the storeroom, a jumble of broken plaster statuary, bent and tarnished candelabra, and dusty cartons filled with stacks of *Publish or Parish*, the magazine for clergy and laity that Father Gillespie had edited, printed, and distributed throughout the diocese with the cooperation of Joe Cicero and *The Derrick*, and which Dungannon had considered a stumbling block on the path to wisdom, filled with windy essays, tame cartoons lifted from the popular press, and jokes of the Pat-and-Mike variety, ostensibly intended to market the Church like any other product, but really a vanity project on the part of a frustrated writer who'd spent ten years trying to sell a six-hundred-page sequel to *Ben-Hur*. In addition to being a moral failure, an inefficient administrator, and a bad priest, he was a lousy writer. Dungannon's first act upon assuming the pastorship was to cancel publication, and he'd been rewarded in his conviction by receiving only one letter of complaint, about the loss of the bimonthly crossword puzzle.

All the buckets were in use, collecting drips in the rectory, the church entrance, and the old parochial classroom, which was still used to teach catechism. He hadn't the stomach to search the basement, an attraction to rats that always stank of putrid flesh. It really was high time to press for donations, although he'd have preferred to wait until the crisis was settled at the McGrath plant and the parishioners were less concerned about their savings. He broke open a new box of trash bags, traced the new leak to the place where he'd expected it, soaked up the puddle that had accumulated in the curve of the seat with a towel, and fashioned a hammock from the bag with thumbtacks to catch the water. It was coming slower now, but more rain was predicted, and hundred-year-old oak was expensive enough to maintain without bringing in the refinishers. The plastic hung in gathers like black crepe and reminded him of a shroud.

————

Palmer awoke hungry for the first time, it seemed, in adult life and went out for breakfast in the pancake house next to Mama Angelo's Pizzeria, which was shut up still with an official notice tacked on the door. That created a hardship for the locals, who might survive without their pizza fix but now had to tramp all the way down to Riley's to play their numbers.

The restaurant's last incarnation had been as a Chinese takeout, and the renovation had run out of money short of the pagoda facade. Unfazed, the new owner had christened his enterprise Shangri-Larry's. Palmer ordered waffles and a cheese omelet and sat at the counter to watch the cook work his miracle. The hotel detective was capable of burning a salad. People who could turn groceries into a meal fascinated him, and he preferred to eat in places where he could witness the transformation close up. When his plate arrived with the cheese still bubbling, he laid immediate siege and drank half a pot of coffee that was so strong the stream swallowed the light that tried to pass through it, like a black hole.

He sipped his third cupful more slowly and thought erotic thoughts. Considering the intensity of last night, he was pleasantly surprised to find himself equal to the challenge of raising an erection at the memory. He'd still been warm from the bath, and overheated from Clare, at 11:00 P.M., and would have seen her in his shirtsleeves to the taxi sent by her third-Wednesday customer if she hadn't practically screamed at him to put on his sport coat; an icy rain was falling, and she said she'd nurse him through a hangover, but not the flu. She had an occupational horror of any kind of sickness.

He'd put on the coat to keep her from going out without him. It seemed more important than ever now that Beaver Cleaver was back on the job not to let her appear on the street alone after dark. It seemed more important than ever now in any case. He'd fed a stray cat once, taken it in, and let it out in the morning, and hadn't thought much about it while it was gone. When it had kept coming back, he'd decided to adopt it, and paid a veterinarian seventy dollars to give it all its shots, and having made the investment had fretted all the next day when he'd let the cat out again. He guessed this new anxiety was something like that, although he hadn't mentioned it to Clare.

The cab was a gypsy, an old maroon Chevy the owner had glued all over with yellow reflectors in some kind of style statement, or possibly to draw attention from the fact the body had been repainted using several dozen spray cans that had not all come from the same color lot. As it pulled away, the light from the corner street lamp had stuttered across the amber lenses like an animated neon sign. He'd seen her waving through the back window and lifted a hand and wobbled it in response. They'd never done that before that he could remember.

He was almost back to the hotel when he realized he hadn't had his morning cigarette. He took out the pack between two fingers, rattled the two Chesterfields inside, then crumpled it in his fist and poked it through the swinging gate of the green metal trash can next to the entrance. He'd grown used to having only one addiction at a time.

Turnbull stirred behind the desk. His eyes seemed to be swimming in rusty water. "Where the hell was you all night? I had to throw Schizo Rudy out of the lobby eight times."

"I forgot my umbrella, so I stayed at a friend's place. Where was Madison?"

"He showed up giggling an hour late and I canned him. Son of a bitch floated out the door."

"I thought he was a little nervous with the pager. I didn't think he was cokey. What time did Clare roll in this morning?" She always came to Palmer's room to sleep on third Thursdays. Whatever happened with Mr. South Terrace always left her as wrung out as a bar rag.

"She didn't."

"Sure you weren't asleep?"

"See for yourself."

Palmer looked at the rows of brass hooks on the wall behind the day man's head. His spare key hung in its spot. Clare never carried it with her.

He looked at his watch. It was past nine. "Ring me when she gets in."

"Ring down and ask." Turnbull hoisted the city directory off its shelf. "I'm calling a temp. This one can show up on fire for all I give a shit."

In his room, Palmer got an outside line and tried Clare's apartment. He gave up after seven rings. He wondered if she'd come straight back home while he was at breakfast and taken a sleeping pill; he'd seen an over-the-counter brand in her medicine cabinet. All day with Palmer and all night with Third Wednesday could turn anyone into a hermit. He decided to shower and change and try again later.

Under the spray, he felt himself reviving yet again, then flagging when he thought about not being able to get in touch with Clare. He couldn't believe he'd imagined he was outgrowing her. And he couldn't think for the life of him what had become of that cat.

Caleb Young was one of those bald men no one could picture looking better with hair. His tanned head was perfectly round except where the temples beveled back from the broad plane of his brow, like something from the terra cotta army of China. He wore suits with natural shoulders and bow ties he tied himself and met with clients at the end of the long cypress table in his conference room, seated sideways in his deep tweed swivel with a leg hooked over one arm. He'd been bald since thirty, which fitted the precocious pattern of his life. He'd graduated from high school at fifteen, passed the bar at twenty-one, and at fifty had headed up his own law firm for twenty years. The half-century mark had released him at last from the pun of his surname.

"It's an election year, Anthony," he said. "That makes you a turkey in November. You ought to be used to it by now."

"The point is it *isn't* November." Zeno measured the carpet with his Italian loafers. "The voters in this town have the attention span of a bubble. Russell never puts the screws on more than six weeks before the polls open, and then he only hits a few soft targets in the Circle. I've lived here longer than you, and I was never brought in for questioning before last month." Catching sight of his reflection in the polished zebrawood panels on the wall opposite, he pulled out a chair around the corner from Young and sat. He'd looked too much like a convict pacing his cell.

"It'll die down. All they have is a stray bullet Russell dug out of his wall and a known street soldier who may or may not have been caught on tape outside police headquarters. I've watched the tape a dozen times, an inch at a time, and I wouldn't sign an affidavit to it."

"That doesn't keep them from running it over and over again at six and eleven o'clock, with me under police escort, or that old police photo off the front page every Sunday. I spent forty minutes in custody on that old charge. They dropped it. It was the only time I was ever arrested, but they never say that in the caption. All my contacts are starting to treat me like the Grand Wizard of the Ku Klux Klan."

"Did you do it?"

"Someone in a gang I was in boosted a brand-new Mercury off a lot. He looked a little like me. They kicked me when his old man brought him in to confess."

"I'm not talking about something that happened when you were eighteen. Did you hire Goshawk to take a shot at Russell?"

"No. You asked that before."

"Sometimes the answer changes." Young swung his foot. "Personally I don't care. I don't know the chief well, and I get more upset when a little girl catches a bullet in the head playing in her room in Little Brazil than when it happens to someone who's paid to take the risk. But if you did set it up, there's more evidence out there, and I need to be ready to respond to it when it surfaces."

"*I* didn't hire him."

The lawyer had a golden ear for tone quality; the emphasis on the pronoun didn't get past him. "If you know who did, I suggest you get them to call him off. Russell's done his damage. You don't know what war is until you've killed a high-ranking police official. Look at the spot George Micalakopoulos is in. The victim was a detective third grade, and George only happened to employ the bartender who killed him, but I'll be lucky to swap the city attorney down to man two and a request for deportation back to Greece.

Turns out George forgot to mention he'd worked for the military junta when he applied for citizenship."

"You want me to get them to call Goshawk off. How long can the city keep my places closed?"

"I'm working on a court order requiring it to show cause why they shouldn't reopen. Are we changing the subject?"

"No." Zeno's face tightened along the bone. "I was warned more than a month ago I'd be in this situation, and I vouched for an old friend. Until I go back to paying my own freight, I can't get them to return my calls, let alone cancel the contract on Francis Russell."

CHAPTER TWENTY-FIVE

"What's this?" Stan Prokanik paused with his thumb on the UP button and looked at the lint-gray interoffice envelope in his other hand.

The civilian department employee lifted a shoulder and let it drop. He was a retired officer with an empty sleeve pinned above the elbow. "You're the detective."

"I hate that phrase." Prokanik pressed the button and stood back to let Patsy Boyle enter the elevator ahead of him. "Ladies first."

"Fuck you." She pushed Four. The car shuddered up its cable. "What is it?"

He had the flap open and had drawn out a smudged form photocopied on dirty-pink onionskin. "Ballistics. They weighed all the pieces of that slug the ME dug out of the hotel clerk. It's a forty-four, same as the one the chief found in his kitchen wall."

"Striations?"

"It had 'em, it says here. Matching 'em's another thing when none of the pieces is any bigger than Fred Hutzel's cock." Hutzel was the orthodontist Prokanik was sure was sleeping with his wife.

"So, nothing." The car stopped with a clunk, shook itself, and opened its doors on a track lined with grit and cigarette cellophane. Boyle held down the DOOR OPEN button stubbornly until her partner exited first. He did so without appearing to notice the gesture. He was still looking at the report.

"Nothing but a thumbprint the dick at the Railroad Arms found that gave us Goshawk's name and the night clerk at the same hotel wearing the same size bullet someone fired at the chief. I like this case. Man who kills for cash you can relate to."

They entered Homicide, which at that hour of the morning smelled more of floor wax and the dust stirred up by the vacuum cleaners of the building service than the perspiration and Juicy Fruit of later in the day. Boyle said, "I can't. Those guys ghost in and out from no address at all, and even when you nail them, some mob lawyer swoops down with a deal to snitch for the FBI, and you're the mayor of Chump City. I'd rather crack Black Bag."

"Put that in your progress report. Russell hasn't busted anyone since Fathead Wilson opened his big mouth at El Capitan and called somebody Chico."

"Russell's a cop. I think he'd agree."

"So write it up."

"So go take a flying leap."

Someone had started a fresh pot of coffee. The maker stood grunting on a yellow oak elementary-school table, struggling to squeeze water heavy with lime and iron through the coarse grounds in the basket. The liquid surged to a dribble going into the carafe, stopped, and surged again. Prokanik said that reminded him to make an appointment to check his prostate. He tossed a quarter into the Maxwell House can on the table, waited for the dripping to stop, then filled Boyle's waxed-cardboard cup first. This time she said nothing about the order. He poured into the brown ceramic mug with his name on it and followed her to the desk they shared.

They'd finished processing the files of violent felons with pro-files similar to Beaver Cleaver's, and spent two hours on the tele-phone trying to track down two who had failed to report to their parole officers and a sex offender who'd left his last address and hadn't registered elsewhere. They spent most of the time talking to elderly mothers, then called Dispatch to send cars around to their addresses, and the courthouse to request search warrants for when the mothers turned the uniforms away at the door. The last time they'd traced a skip, a sergeant had found him stuck in a crawl space and had broken through drywall to get him out. Boyle and Prokanik had finished the pot and started on another when Boyle's telephone rang. She took a gulp, burned her tongue, and spoke her name thickly into the mouthpiece.

"Boyle?" echoed the voice on the other end. "You got a cold?"

"No, a hot. Who's this?" She brushed at the coffee she'd spilled on her blazer.

"Palmer. I'm making a missing-person report."

"Wrong division. You want extension four-seven-seven. Ask for Odum."

"He'd tell me to wait twenty-four hours. She went out late last night and never came back. I've called all the places she might be, including bars and County General, in case she was in an accident. No one's seen her. She's always back hours before this."

"This the girlfriend?"

"She's a little more than that, but okay."

"Did you try her at work?"

"I said I called all the bars."

"Uh-huh. Well, my thought is she'll come wandering in by and by. They always do."

"I can think of several that didn't." The voice was granite.

"I can give it to Missing Persons, but they'll tell me the same thing they would you. They get a lot of complaints and they have to weed out the ones they'd just be wasting their time investigating. Most no-shows turn up inside twenty-four hours."

"You can issue a BOLO on the cab she left in. You've got officers patrolling all over. They can look out the window from time to time. If they spot the cab, they can pull it over and find out where the hack dropped her off. It's a small enough thing, Detective, considering I'm the one who gave you Vernon Goshawk. Twice."

"That's good citizenship."

There was a beat of silence. "I'd really appreciate the favor."

She blew air and dragged over a pad. Prokanik finished his call to an elderly mother and looked a question at her as she wrote. When Palmer finished talking she wrote his name at the bottom of the pad and turned it around with Clare Sayer's description on it and a description of the gypsy cab she'd taken to an unknown location on South Terrace. Prokanik made a face and sat back. His telephone rang. He picked up.

"No more favors, Palmer," Boyle said. "We can't go running after your girls every time they work late."

"I'm retired from that. I only had one anyway. This is personal. I'd hire a private cop, but they can't do anything I can't do myself. You can, so I called you first. If you turn anything, call the hotel. They'll page me wherever I am."

"Are you playing detective again?"

"It gets in your blood. I can see why you do it."

"I do it because they pay me to," she said. "I took another look at your personnel file. You had commendations, and you scored eighty-six on the sergeant's exam. You'd have been the real article by now if you didn't have a soft spot for hookers."

There was a throaty crackle on the line. "Actually, it was a hard spot."

"Yeah, and all the blood flowed into it from your brain. There are better places than the backseat of a squad car on Commercial Street."

"During the day shift, no less. Look at those commendations again, Detective: Nothing from anyone higher than captain of the watch. I was a mediocre success, but I'm a spectacular failure."

She only half heard him. Prokanik was sitting straight now, dragging his mechanical pencil across a square of newsprint as fast as she'd ever seen him write. "I'll give it to Dispatch, Palmer," she said. "No promises." She hung up on his response. Prokanik banged down his receiver at the same time. The corners of his mouth were drawn back in a rictus. For a moment Boyle wondered if someone had caught his wife with the orthodontist. "What?"

"That was Guzman at the desk. What was the name of Black Bag's last vic?"

"Pearl Arno." Something bumped in her throat.

"Her torso just turned up, along with some other assorted parts. At least it's probably hers. It's ripe enough. This guy must buy his garbage bags on a roll the size of a telephone spool."

"Where?"

"Southeast corner of the police lot."

"*Downstairs?*"

"Half the morning shift came in right past it. It was the uniform who checks the license plates who found it. I don't think he's going to lunch."

She was up before him. They went out, leaving Boyle's pad on the desk with Prokanik's coffee mug parked on top.

Palmer realized he was speaking into a dead line. He jiggled the plunger and called the next cab company in the directory spread out on the mattress. The dispatchers he'd talked to ranged from indifferent to hostile, with an occasional sympathetic party in between. None of the drivers within earshot of the conversations was familiar with an independent who drove a maroon heap pasted all over with yellow reflectors.

He was in the vacant room across from his own, one with a telephone. He'd conned Turnbull's temporary replacement into connecting it.

"Hollywood Taxi, you're the star." The voice was a female baritone, a little humorous.

He told the woman what he needed. He was barely listening to himself. As he spoke he drew a line through the listing with a stub of orange pencil. There were only two left in the book.

"Hang on."

He waited. The dispatcher's cage must have been on the same floor with the cabs; he heard tires chirping, the gush of engines, frames banging as they bottomed out on a ramp.

The woman's voice made him jump. "I had to clear it with the general manager. North Star's always trying to hire our drivers out from under us. You said a Chevy?"

Palmer started to describe it again. She interrupted him. "That's Borodino's rig. He fills in here when we're short on cabs. Crazy-ass Russky thinks them reflectors protect him from Cossacks. But his driving record's clean and he don't chisel so much off the company it shows at the end of the shift."

He scrambled to find a piece of paper, snatched the Gideon Bible from the nightstand drawer, and scribbled *Borodino* on a blank endsheet. "Was he working for you last night?"

She told him to hang on again. This time the wait was less than ten seconds. "Nope, fleet was up last night. If you rode with him it was on his clock. Leave something behind?"

"Something I can't replace. What's his number?"

"He don't have one. Calls in a couple times a week from a pay phone to see if we need him and his rig."

"Where's he live?"

"Can't help you there neither. We only got addresses on our regulars."

He tightened his grip on the receiver. "Do you expect him to call in today?"

"Could be. Listen, mister, I got to go. I don't play at this job and McGrath ain't hiring."

"When he does, will you have him call me?" Palmer gave her his name and the hotel and room numbers. "Tell him there's a reward just for calling."

"It better be big enough to split. Answering services ain't cheap."

"It will be."

He tried Clare's flat again and hung up after five rings. He'd been down there once, gotten no answer to his knock, and had the manager let him in, saying he was from Vice. The old man, whose hip replacement creaked when he climbed stairs, must have been accustomed to such visits to his tenants, because he didn't ask to see a badge and didn't wait while Palmer searched the place for a memorandum or something that might tell him who Clare's third Wednesday was or where he lived. But she was too much of a professional to have written anything down for a real vice cop to find. The bed was still damp from last night and the suds in the tub had dried to a briny crust on the bottom. He'd locked the door behind him and gone back to the hotel to make his calls.

Now his skin stood on edge in the old familiar way that told him he'd gone too long without a cigarette. The need was like malaria; you never really beat it, just put it off until it came back twice as strong. He went back to his room, leaving both hall doors open in case the phone rang, and rummaged the bureau and the drawer of the nightstand for a pack he might have overlooked, without success. The ashtray was empty and he'd dumped his trash into the hall chute that morning to kill time between attempts to raise Clare. On the off chance he'd stuck an old pack in the medicine cabinet when he was drunk he checked that, stared at the bottle of Ancient Age for ten seconds, then slammed the door on it. Last night's half bottle of beer seemed to purr in his stomach.

He chewed the inside of his mouth until it tore. He tasted salt and iodine. He needed that smoke, but he didn't want to go out. Now that he had a slim line on Clare he didn't trust Turnbull's temp to page him in case Borodino called. He got down on the floor and looked under the bed. Butts had slid off the mound in the ashtray from time to time and founded a small colony in the shelter of a dust bunny the size of an overshoe. Each was no longer than half an inch, but he stripped them, spilled the tobacco out onto a page he'd ripped from the Bible in his own nightstand, and tore a square out of it to roll a cigarette. He licked the edge, smoothed it between his fingers, and twisted off the ends. He dug a book half full of matches out of a pair of pants hanging in the closet and smoked the handmade down to his lips, smoking part of Genesis. It tasted like shredded newspaper and burned like a fuse, but it settled his nerves.

He returned to the other room and reached for the phone, just in case Borodino pinch-hit for either of the two cab companies he hadn't tried, but withdrew his hand in case the gypsy called and found the line busy. He felt like a teenage girl sitting at home Friday night. A shop-damaged teenage girl with a lungful of scripture and the taste of burned newspaper on her tongue.

When the ring came, an hour and a half after he'd spoken to the dispatcher at Hollywood Taxi, he almost fell off the stripped bed stabbing for the receiver. He'd wallowed into a stale doze and had dreamt several times of a key rattling in the door and Clare charging in, as if the room were his, flushed to the roots of her hair and yelling at him for calling her all over town and violating her sanctuary down the street.

"Palmer, this is Detective Boyle."

"Yes."

"The man at the desk gave me this number."

"Yes."

"I think you better come down."

"Yes."

He replaced the receiver, gently as crystal. He wondered, with a last dim glitter of hope, if he was still dreaming.

Chapter Twenty-six

Francis X. Russell stood at the window facing City Hall. The sun was hitting the window on the other side of the courtyard, turning it into bright metal, and he couldn't see what Irene Garvey was doing. Not that he couldn't guess. If he saw the mayor's secretary on the street with a telephone receiver bolted to the side of her head and her fingers grafted to a typewriter keyboard, it wouldn't have surprised him as much as if she'd been carrying an umbrella and a handbag like everyone else. For all he knew she slept at her desk and took her nourishment from fluorescents, like some species of cultured plant.

He turned away. "I understand this kind of killer rarely alters his method. Are we certain it's Black Bag and not some imitator?"

"Print man and the ME says no," Prokanik said. "The prints on the bag were the same as all the others and it was Pearl Arno's torso. The ME got suspicious when the other parts in the bag showed few signs of decomposition, whereas the torso was weeks old. Also when he totaled it all up with the parts recovered before, she would've had four arms and three legs."

The detective partners, Prokanik and Boyle, stood in the center of the office, the man with his thumbs in his pockets, spreading his coat, the woman more or less at military attention. The chief disapproved of her short hair and loose blazer. A woman who tried to conceal the fact of her gender—particularly an attractive woman with some poise—aroused his distrust. Nevertheless she seemed the more composed of the two. Her partner looked bloated with his collar unbuttoned behind his necktie and Russell could smell the licorice on his breath from the other side of his desk. Only drinkers and diabetics ate candy in quantity on the job, and both were material for dismissal.

"We're positive the other victim is the Sayer woman?"

Boyle spoke up. "Yes, sir, from the prints on the hands. We had them on file. She was booked four years ago for soliciting in the Triangle Bar."

"Foolish of her in an election year. Still, that was fast work. Congratulations."

"We caught a break," said Boyle. "The security man at the Railroad Arms, a man named Palmer, was a friend of hers. When she didn't show up this morning he called me and asked me to issue a BOLO on her and the cab she was last seen riding in."

"And he called Homicide? Wait. Palmer, is he the man who reported that Vernon Goshawk was staying at the Railroad Arms?"

The woman nodded, a brisk tip of her chin. "Yes, sir. We met over a suicide there a month ago. He had my card. He's downstairs if you want to see him."

"Crying like a little baby," put in Prokanik.

"That's when we learn how to do it, Detective." Russell kept his tone flat. He glanced at the typewritten report on his desk. "We have an officer in the hotel room waiting for this man Borodino to call?"

They said, "Yes, sir," in unison.

"BOLO's out, and we have officers canvassing the Circle for a maroon ten-year-old Chevy with a bad paint job and yellow reflectors on the body," Boyle added. "We sent a radio team to Hollywood Taxi to get a description of Ivan Borodino. He may be an illegal; DMV has no record of a driver's license issued under that name and he's not on the tax rolls. We're looking for a bank account, but my guess is the company paid him in cash and didn't report it to state or federal."

"Disgraceful. We'll look into that situation next term. Just now I'm more concerned with a butcher so bold he'd deposit his offal on our doorstep. You can imagine what Mrs. Rice-Hippert will do with that."

Boyle said, "He wants to be caught, sir. That's why he combined his two most recent victims in one bag and took the risk of being spotted with the evidence right outside headquarters. The cycle of shame has come all the way around."

"Well said, Detective. I doubt your helpful Dr. Aguilar could have put it better."

She colored. "You have to agree it makes sense."

"Inasmuch as the reasoning of a diseased mind ever does. Excellent work, detectives, but let's not think small. This is the strongest lead we've had, and the first head start. Raise the BOLO to an all-points: Find this gypsy cab driver, and by the end of day. He may have seen Black Bag take delivery of his prey."

"What about Palmer?" Boyle asked.

"Send him home, with our thanks and condolences. It's a sad thing to lose a friend so young and in such a way. It's sad enough even without those features."

Prokanik started toward the door. Boyle hesitated. Russell raised his humorous eyebrows.

"There's nothing new on Goshawk, sir," she said. "We think the publicity may have driven him out of town. For sure whoever sent him would think twice about replacing him. There's too much attention."

"I'd nearly forgotten about him. Well, let's hope that's the case. I'd like to put that cruiser outside my house back in the rotation."

When they left, Russell filled his pipe from the leather humidor on his desk and turned his attention from City Hall to the window that looked out on Commercial Street, where Civic Center Drive crossed and became Cathedral. The steeple of Our Lady of Perpetual

Misery rose to the west, and to the south he could see the corner of Volcanic Wholesale Plumbing Supplies against the homely box of *The Derrick*. Volcanic's big red *V* was just visible. It looked less like the victory symbol of World War II than like the trademark on a common brand of wooden mousetrap. All the houses of God and government and greed were within five minutes' walking distance of one another. It really was a small town, and hardly worth the fuss.

"Well, I'm off."

Anthony Zeno looked up from his survey of the books and record albums arranged on the shelf opposite his chair and saw Deanne standing in the open doorway of his study. She had a carry-on slung by its strap over her shoulder and her wheeled bag on the floor at her side. She looked like a flight attendant with her dark blonde hair pinned back and no visible jewelry. She was dressed for battle in the streets of New York City.

"So soon?" He drank from his glass and returned it to the orangewood table by his chair. "I thought you might get ten minutes' more wear out of what you bought last month."

"Cab's waiting. You going to help me with my bags or what?"

"Since you overtip the drivers, let's not withhold that opportunity."

"You're drunk."

"Mildly."

She hoisted the strap up farther and grasped the wheeled bag's extended handle.

"When you come back, you'll need to make other housing arrangements," he said. "I'm putting this white elephant on the market and our lawyers can argue over how to split the sale price."

Her eyes went from pale blue to twilight. He'd always found them more reliable than mood rings in gauging where he stood with Deanne. "You're throwing me out?"

"I'm throwing us both out. Why should we make each other miserable when there's a whole population out there that's too happy for its own good?"

"I can't talk to you when you're drinking. That's when the cheap gangster comes out."

"Certainly not cheap. I was doing some figures this morning. I'd be ten million ahead if you and I had never met. If I'd spent that much on a mistress I'd have expected a good deal more from her than I ever got from you."

"You're a flabby old man. It's worth more than that just to try and get a rise out of that limp old dick."

"Thank you. I mean that. I was afraid this conversation would make me feel guilty."

"You won't think ten million's so much when I get through with you. I'll take you for everything."

"You'll find it all in this house and the opera box and in the inventory at Volcanic. I'm not drawing any income at present."

"Fuck you, you son of a bitch."

"Not since I can remember."

After the front door banged, shuddering the walls, he finished his bourbon and soda, got up, rinsed out his glass, and poured brandy into it from the bottle of Napoleon from the case he'd bought at auction last Christmas and had shared with Hugh Dungannon. The bishop was the only man in his circle who appreciated such things as much as he did. Zeno wondered what Dungannon had wanted to talk to him about that morning. He hadn't left a message at Volcanic, just his name. Zeno made a mental note to call him later. With chilly youth out of the house he felt drawn to acquaintances of long standing.

The telephone rang, and seemed to go on ringing a long time before he thought to answer. It sawed a little at the inside of his skull. He'd been drinking steadily most of the day—not enough to get sopping, just enough to remain afloat—and wondered if it was possible to be inebriated and hungover at the same time. He started to call out to Toby, then remembered he'd given his bodyguard the day off, as he'd decided to stay in. He lifted the receiver and put it to his ear. He spoke no greeting.

"Mr. Zeno?"

It was the lathed, androgynous voice he'd heard off and on for ten years without ever having met its owner face to face. He associated it with the hot damp hand and balloon-tight features of Nicholas Bianco, its employer. "Yes."

"Please hold for Mr. White."

He waited. The pleasant fog he'd been working on since morning began to burn off, leaving behind a dull humming headache. It was like coming out of novocaine.

"Hello, Anthony. I tried to reach you at your office, but they said you haven't been in. Does this mean you've gotten over your little bout with the Puritan ethic?"

"I had some work to do that's better doing at home."

"No boss worse than yourself, am I right?" That hollow chuckle came tumbling down the line. "Listen, I'm sending over a visitor. I wanted to make sure you'd be alone. He's shy just now."

"Who is he?"

"I think you can guess. Given the changed circumstances he needs to confer with you on strategy. You know the town better than anyone."

"He's still here?"

"Leaving him there posed fewer challenges than getting him out. Expect him after dark."

"My advice to him is to stay in his hole. If he does what he came here to do, it won't change anything. It'll just make things worse."

"An example must be made. Perception is everything in our business. If our competitors get the idea you can cheat the concern without consequences, we'll all be in early retirement. Or worse."

"Tell him to park on Seventh and come in the back. I'm pretty sure the police are watching the front."

"Parking won't be necessary. He gets around by cab."

"What if the driver recognizes him from his picture?"

"He's an ordinary-looking fellow, Anthony. That's one of the reasons he's lasted as long as he has." The line plopped and went dead.

Zeno had four hours to wait. He hadn't slept a night through for more than a week. He tried napping in his chair, black leather on a steel frame with a base shaped like a steering wheel. He'd let the chair go with the house, along with everything else Deanne had brought in to turn a comfortable masculine retreat into a modern-art gallery, only without a decent smear on the walls to take one's mind off the cold showcase furniture; at the time it had seemed important not to protest and be thought old-fashioned. But when he closed his eyes, the chair reeled like a single-engine plane flying through turbulence. He was drunker than he'd thought. You knew old age had you by the balls when you lost your tolerance.

He took a shower—steaming hot, then needle cold—put on a silk sport shirt and poplin slacks, stuck his bare feet into a pair of soft loafers, and raided the Sub-Zero refrigerator of leftover caviar, which he ate between whole-wheat slices in the red leather-upholstered dining room with a glass of skim milk. He hadn't been hungry, but he felt a little better afterward and caught the end of a baseball game on the big screen in the TV room. It was a soporific pitchers' duel that went into extra innings and had him struggling to keep his eyes open to see how it came out. Dimly he reflected that someone would have money riding on it, but not in The Circle or Little Brazil. He fell asleep on the sofa. When he woke up, the room was dark except for the television, which was playing a hospital drama.

The back doorbell rang, a hollow double-chime in an empty house. He switched off the set and went to answer it, flipping on lights as he passed through the house. He left them off in the kitchen and opened the back door three inches. Light from the dining room left pools of shadow in the cheeks and facial lines of the man standing on the covered porch.

"Goshawk." Zeno wasn't sure. They'd met only once, and the man's features were difficult to carry in one's memory.

"Yeah."

He stepped back, pulling the door open wider, and the visitor slid in around the edge. He wore tennis shoes, mottled jeans, and a sport shirt whose spread collar rolled over the lapels of his cotton Windbreaker, a style of wearing it that Zeno always associated with low-level hoods. "Wife in?" Goshawk asked.

"She's away. We'll talk in the study."

"Study?" A smile tugged at the corners of the man's lips. "Sure. Okay. Let's go in the study."

Zeno led the way. Inside the smallish room, Goshawk circled the floor with his hands in his pockets, looking at the titles stamped in gold on the spines of the books. His shoulders fell off abruptly from his collarbone and he moved with a lanky, awkward-looking stride, like a stray dog with a hitch in one leg. He took a hand out once to slide an album off a shelf. "Opera, huh? I heard you went, but I never knew nobody who sat home and listened to it."

"Brandy?" Zeno had the mahogany cabinet open.

"Scotch, if you got it."

"I've got bourbon."

"Sure." Goshawk slid the album back in place.

"Club soda or water? I can get you some ice."

"Neat. I like to travel light."

He poured two inches into a cut-crystal glass, hesitated over the squat bottle of Napoleon, then selected an identical glass instead of a snifter and mixed a bourbon and soda for himself. "That was a bonehead play you made on Russell at his house," he said. "You brought down the wrath of God."

"I hit where I aim."

Zeno turned toward his guest with a glass in each hand. The one in his left exploded and something struck him hard in the abdomen. The second bullet hit his throat. He dropped the other glass, backpedaled into a shelf, spilling books off it, and fell on top of the pile. He lay on one hip with his torn and bleeding hand supporting him on the floor. Goshawk hadn't moved from his spot. The barrel of his revolver tilted down unnecessarily. Zeno's throat was filling and he could feel himself draining away.

"You were the target, not Russell," Goshawk said. "I slung one his way to keep him busy. You should've listened to Mr. White. You don't make friends with the hired help."

His arm buckled and he sprawled onto his back. He'd never really looked at his ceiling before. The tiny holes drilled in the panels grew sharp as it descended. He thought if he put his palms together and stretched his arms over his head he might fit through one and escape. He pictured the look on Goshawk's face and then Bianco's, started to laugh, and choked on the bubbles in his throat.

A squad car team from the Third Precinct spotted a maroon ten-year-old Chevy cab with yellow reflectors all over it parked outside Riley's and found the owner inside, eating a plate of Polish sausage at the bar and washing it down with beer. They took him to police headquarters.

Ivan Borodino sat at the steel table bolted to the floor in the interview room with his big black-knuckled hands making damp prints on the top. He was round all over, head and shoulders and belly, combed his hair in music-sheet strands across his scalp, and wore a smudge of moustache and a flannel shirt over a gray sweatshirt. He had no driver's license, no Social Security card, no green card, and almost no English. A sergeant named Radachev was brought in from the Ninth Precinct to interpret.

Through him, Prokanik and Boyle took turns questioning the witness. Borodino, terrified of deportation, spoke rapidly and had to be told to slow down several times for Radachev to translate. He had a standing appointment to take on the same woman passenger on Depot Street at the same time every third Wednesday of the month and bring her to an address on South Terrace, then come back later—the time varied—and return her to where he'd picked her up. The arrangement had been in place since January. He identified Clare Sayer as the passenger from a mug shot taken at the time of her arrest for solicitation. No, the man never gave his name. No, he always paid in cash. Yes, Borodino knew the address and gave it, but he didn't think the man lived there because he was always standing in front when the cab stopped, dressed for the weather, and Borodino had never seen the pair actually enter the house.

"Can you describe the man?" Prokanik asked.

When the question was translated, the cab driver nodded and spoke slowly.

"Big man," Radachev reported. "Tall, heavy build, short white hair, fifty or older. Spoke with some kind of accent."

"What kind?"

Borodino shrugged.

Boyle said, "How did he dress?"

He shrugged again and spoke.

"Nothing special. Just—"

The driver interrupted the interpreter. Radachev lifted his eyebrows.

"Not like in his pictures, he says."

Borodino lunged back in his seat as both detectives stepped toward him.

"What pictures?" said Prokanik.

"TV, the papers."

Boyle said, "You said you didn't know his name."

Radachev listened to the answer.

"No, he said the man never gave it. He's heard it, but he can't remember it. He says he's no good with Western names."

Borodino gestured, slashing a finger across his throat.

"What's he doing?" Prokanik said. "Is he saying he saw Black Bag kill the Sayer woman?"

The sergeant spoke. Borodino shook his head, made the gesture again, and replied.

"A collar," Radachev said. "He says in his pictures the man wears a white collar."

CHAPTER TWENTY-SEVEN

Joe Cicero pushed himself back from the glossy slab of his desk and folded his hands on his stomach, pleasantly exhausted and grateful for once for the solitude of his ice palace high above the hurly-burly of the city room. The first copy off the presses of the extra edition lay atop the desk, its thick headline smudged at one edge where the ink had come off on the heel of his hand:

MOB CHIEF SLAIN AT HOME
Police Seek Goshawk in Inter-Gang Killing

Centered beneath, flanked by images of Anthony Zeno at ages eighteen and fifty-eight, was a two-column print of the picture Quentin O'Meara had managed to snap at Zeno's house just before the lieutenant in charge realized he wasn't a police photographer and threw him out. The racketeer lay on top of a jumble of books on the floor of his study with a plainclothesman's suit coat draped over his upper body. Goshawk's mug ran in the lower left corner, with a file photo of Angela Rice-Hippert balancing it out on the right, mouth open above a caption quoting her expression of shock and outrage that nothing seemed to have changed in Gas City since the dark days of Prohibition. Cicero had pondered whether to bury the statement inside, then at the last minute had decided to be generous, as nothing short of a meteor crushing Francis X. Russell and Jerry Wilding to death on live television would return her to public office. The publisher of *The Derrick* had signed off only five minutes ago on an editorial ghosted by Sid Burton, pointing out that Russell's relentless attack on vice in the city had driven the mob to panic and destruction from within. It would run in every edition tomorrow, along with a biographical feature on Russell's rapid upward motion through every rank of the department, researched and written by the reliable Charles Rynearson, whose history of the local underworld continued, with a new chapter in composition.

On an easel in a corner rested a cartoon by Andy Wynant of Tony Z.'s sleek white head and upraised arms whirling down a Volcanic Wholesale Plumbing Supplies toilet, flushed by a generic broken-nosed thug in a tweed cap and a pinstripe suit. It looked old-fashioned, but Cicero's stubborn resistance to the trend toward color and runaway white space had earned his composition crew three consecutive Best Layout awards from the National Association of Newspapers. Everything came back around, just like a sheet through a cylinder press.

The trucks were thundering away from the loading dock bearing the extra edition in bales when his telephone burred. It was Burton, calling from the city room. "Are you watching?"

"Watching what, my step or my weight?" He felt impish whenever his managing editor sounded tense. Sid always took a while to wind down.

"Turn on the TV."

That was rare advice from a newspaperman who considered even owning a set a conflict of interest.

"What channel?"

"Doesn't matter."

After Burton hung up, Cicero found the remote and flicked on the screen across from him. It happened to be tuned to WGAS.

Dave McCormick, his hair glossed a step past perfection, sat at a woodgrain-print desk with a graphic projected behind him of Hugh Dungannon, dressed in vestments with a pair of reading glasses astraddle his bent and twisted nose. He appeared to be following the text of McCormick's report over his shoulder.

". . . in his confession, the bishop stated that he and the victim had had a personal relationship for some years in an apartment he maintained outside Our Lady of Perpetual Misery, but that of late the affair had been conducted on a businesslike basis."

What do you think being a mistress is? Cicero's scorn was automatic.

"Police believe Sayer was slain in the bedroom of the rectory and the body dissected in the church basement. They would not confirm reports of evidence that some of the other murders and dismemberments took place there as well."

He stared at footage he'd seen before of bodies in black plastic bags being dragged from ditches and scooped from Dumpsters and lifted with grapnels from the Boggen Drain. A jumpy unedited tag shot showed Dungannon in street clothes being escorted through portable floodlights by detectives and uniforms from the rectory at Perpetual Misery to a black-and-white. His hands were behind his back and his mouth hung open like an idiot's. ARREST IN BLACK BAG MURDERS read a legend in yellow at the bottom of the screen.

McCormick's face replaced the bishop's. The over-the-shoulder graphic now was the serpent-and-stick caduceus of the medical profession. "When a prominent clergyman stands accused of violent crime, 'Why' is the question uppermost on everyone's mind. We've invited Dr. Feliz Aguilar, psychiatrist with the Gas City Police Department, into the studio. . . ."

Cicero turned off the set as the well-barbered Hispanic was smoothing his necktie. He got Harvey Stone on the line at the print shop and told him to wait for a new front page.

Palmer left his room with the TV playing, running its endless loop of body parts in garbage bags, sound bites of Chief Russell, Jerry Wilding, Angela Rice-Hippert, and the police shrink who looked like a professional gigolo, Hugh Dungannon stumbling down the walk to the squad car, and photographic portraits of all the murder victims, including a picture Palmer had never seen of Clare smiling with a silk scarf tied around her neck. When the door didn't close, he looked down, kicked away the empty Ancient Age bottle, and pulled the door shut with a bang.

He caromed off both walls in the stairwell and missed the two bottom steps, landing hard on his feet with spurs of pain shooting up both ankles. Turnbull called out to him on his way through the lobby, but everything was coming through his ears with the same sound quality and whatever the desk man said was lost in the skidding of Palmer's heels on the tiles and the wheezing of the pneumatic door closer and the boom and shudder of a stake truck carrying bundles of newspapers down the street. The newsprint banner stapled to the sideboards read: BISHOP BEAVER CLEAVER: SHE WAS GOING TO LEAVE ME.

The hotel detective tripped on the threshold entering a pawnshop at Commercial and Boiler Row, caught his balance against a gumball machine on a cast iron stand, and spoke to the man behind the counter, who watched him from under amphibian lids until Palmer scooped a wad of bills out of his pants pocket and dumped them on the glass top. The man counted the bills, smoothed some out and put them in a green metal cash box, and climbed a ladder. Palmer left the shop three minutes later with a camera slung over one shoulder by a leather strap.

He'd started early, but the weather was warm and he'd sweated through his sport coat by the time he got to the civic center, where a crowd was boiling around the gate to the courthouse grounds, which looked like a prison exercise yard, trodden bare by defendants and bailiffs and bailbondsmen and bottom-feeding lawyers and the jury pool under the meshed and barred windows. Dungannon was scheduled for arraignment that morning, and the word had spread like a virus. The walk and Turkish-bath treatment had sobered Palmer somewhat and he was more steady on his feet, but he'd slept in his clothes and he hadn't shaved or combed his hair. The sergeant at the gate, a pear-shaped county officer with just enough chin to keep the strap of his Smokey the Bear hat from riding up to his nose, gave him the same look he'd gotten from the clerk in the pawnshop as Palmer wriggled toward him through the press of bodies, gripping his camera strap tight.

"How's chances of getting a shot from inside the gate?" Palmer asked him.

"Shot of what?" The deputy had an out-of-town accent. Visitors always seemed stopped-up once they got a whiff of the gasworks.

"Of Dungannon. I'm with *The Derrick*."

"Where's your pass?"

Palmer gave him a card.

"Who's Patricia Boyle?"

"Read the rest. She's with Homicide."

"This isn't a pass."

"Help me out, Deputy. They got me out of bed. I didn't have a chance to stop at headquarters. Call Boyle's extension. They can patch you through from your radio." He knew on this morning of all mornings she'd be hard to reach.

The deputy smacked the boxy Motorola on his belt. "That's for official business. Let's see the camera."

Palmer unslung it and gave it to him. The deputy hefted it. "What is it, lead?"

"Steel, and it's a good thing. I drop it a lot. There's the catch." He pointed out a small lever on the back.

The deputy opened the compartment, looked at the film inside, and closed it and handed back the camera. "What's your name?"

"O'Meara."

"Nobody goes through the gate without a pass, O'Meara. But I can't stop you from taking pictures outside."

"What of, the back of some jerk's head?"

"When the prisoner comes I'll tell him to turn your way and smile, how's that?"

Palmer worked his way back through the crowd and walked around the other side of the grounds. The gate to the parking lot was

chained and padlocked. He poked his camera through the gap and set
it on the ground and tried to squeeze through sideways, ducking under the chain, but stopped when his chest seemed about to collapse.
Coils of razor wire topped the chain link. He returned to the front of
the building. The crowd was even thicker than before, with a spark
of new anticipation coursing through it. Palmer shoved and jostled,
but could get no closer to the gate than three tightly packed rows
back. He started to cry, big snotty tears that made his closest neighbors shrink away as far as the pressure of people would let them. He
should've stayed where he was. In the privacy of his confinement he
unscrewed the lens from the camera, reached inside, and drew out
the little silver .25 pistol he'd bought at the pawnshop.

It was hot in the crowd. He was sweating again and thought he'd
pass out. His system had grown unaccustomed to alcohol and he
hadn't eaten since breakfast yesterday at Shangri-Larry's. His eyes
were stung and swollen and his blood roared in his ears.

He felt the electric charge again, passing from body to body,
stronger than before. The air throbbed with the pulse of an engine
approaching up Civic Center Drive from the direction of police
headquarters.

In earlier days, before the attempt on Big Mike Wilding's life at
the old Elks Hall, cars could drive right up to the courthouse entrance, where security began and ended. Shysters had leaned against
the porch posts in their straw boaters, smoking and spitting and pok-
ing their business cards down the front of county jumpsuits, and
folded bills into the hands of the officers who escorted the men
wearing them with their wrists manacled behind their backs. Now
the Cyclone fence and gate decreased the pistol range and homely
concrete abutments were sunken three feet down just inside to prevent vehicles from ramming through. The unmarked police unit,
Chief Russell's own, turned in from the drive and drifted to a stop
short of the open gate, between tight galleries of spectators shoving
themselves up against the barricades on either side. Officers of the
county and city stood one to a sawhorse, feet spread and facing the
crowd, the ends of their batons tapping the tops of their boots.

Russell got out first, followed by the uniform behind the wheel and Detective Stan Prokanik from the backseat. Hugh Dungannon emerged next, with Prokanik's hand under his arm to help him find his balance in his steel cuffs. The bishop had on the same clothes he'd worn when he was arrested, a loose twill jacket over an open-neck shirt, tan slacks, and black shoes with tassels, softly gleaming. His big dented face bore no expression, his eyes like stained glass. They gave the impression of being able to see clear through to the back of his skull.

Patsy Boyle slid out of the backseat to take Dungannon's other arm. Her blazer swung open as she stood, showing the butt of a handgun strapped to her belt. As the walk started, Palmer felt the temperature change. A woman began sobbing loudly. A snatch of the Lord's Prayer floated Palmer's way. A deep, braised voice, accustomed to shouting, called the man in cuffs a rotten fucking bastard. Something, a crumple of paper or a plastic drinking cup, made a long trajectory and bounced off the bishop's shoulder. Gun arms bent, but Dungannon didn't react. The party picked up its pace. Someone yelled when a baton struck his hand pushing at the top of a sawhorse. "Get back there!" barked a voice with a badge in it. The crowd compacted. Palmer's arms were pinned to his sides, the little pistol lying along the seam of his trousers with his hand covering it. The procession, with Russell in front and uniformed officers bringing up the rear, drew abreast of where he stood.

Palmer twisted his body and flexed his elbows, making room to bring up the pistol. The camera strap slid down his other arm; he let it go. Someone gasped and cursed close to his ear. The camera was heavy enough to break a foot. Palmer shoved himself forward off the balls of his feet. His elbows encountered ribs and kidneys, and when the bodies around him shifted in pained and indignant reaction, he plunged through the gap, pushing for the barricade with the pistol above his head. A woman screamed, an eardrum-shredding shriek like tearing tires. He saw the faces of Prokanik and Boyle turning his direction, other unfamiliar eyes under shining black visors. Guns came out of holsters. Dungannon stared straight ahead, his battered-pug's profile three feet from the muzzle. The trigger pushed against Palmer's finger.

A light came on in his head and flew apart, scarlet and green and gold. He felt scorching heat, a crest of nausea, and a gush of cool rain that put out the heat as it slid between him and the light. His bones and flesh dissolved and he drained away through the gravel at his feet.

Moe Shiel stood over the body in the center of a rapidly expanding circle as the crowd broke away from the source. It lay in a twisted pile on both knees and one shoulder, with blood and black cranial fluid sliding into a pool from the broken skull. The pistol had hit the ground first without discharging. Shiel's pipe wrench dangled from his hand, clotted with blood and hair.

"Police! Drop it!"

It was a chorus. Immediately, the former unofficial mayor and police chief of The Circle let fall the wrench with a clunk and clasped his hands on top of his head. He let himself be seized and hurled up against the fence while the rest of Dungannon's escort hastened the bishop through the gate and up the steps to the courthouse.

Close of Day

A rch Killian's son Earl found him in a drainage ditch off West Riverside, just before the land began its relentless climb toward the top of Factory Hill. The old man was never gone longer than two hours on his morning walk, and when he hadn't returned home by eight o'clock, Earl had gone looking along the usual route. At first he thought Arch had been struck by a car or slain for whatever he'd had on him, by someone with humanity enough to lay him out gently on his back with his hands folded on his sternum, but after Arch's heart specialist diagnosed coronary thrombosis, he knew his father had realized he wasn't coming back out of the ditch and had made himself as comfortable as possible to wait. He'd celebrated his seventy-ninth birthday three days earlier at a family dinner.

Alone with him before the visitation at the Stillwell Brothers Mortuary, Earl placed his hand on Arch's. "Well, Dad, there's no one left now who remembers Morse the First."

As the old man had predicted, all the friends of his youth who might have carried him to the cemetery were dead. Chief Russell, wearing a black armband to mourn his late wife and another band across his shield to note the solemn occasion of the passing of a longtime resident and relative on Marty's side, led a pallbearing party recruited from among family and Earl's own friends, some of whom remembered Arch in his worn rugged surveyor's clothes popping bottles and cans off the low stone wall in Roosevelt Park, a favorite spot, with his old broom-handled Mauser; the park patrol had always managed to be somewhere else to avoid citing a cousin or something of Russell's, who was then chief of detectives. The funeral was Russell's last public appearance in uniform, having announced his retirement shortly after ex-Bishop Dungannon was convicted on his confession of seven counts of homicide.

Crews from WGAS and WCRV captured the chief's arrival on tape, then packed up their equipment and left. The funeral of an obscure citizen was no story, and the city attorney was convening a press conference that morning to announce a new investigation to search for a copycat Black Bag killer. Dungannon had denied any association with an eighth victim, a female impersonator who'd entertained at the Club Sahara, and technicians had acknowledged that the bags containing the transvestite's body parts were the only ones that didn't bear the former bishop's fingerprints. Meanwhile Dungannon was in the Carbon County Jail awaiting removal to the state penitentiary to begin serving seven consecutive life sentences and was under twenty-four-hour surveillance to prevent suicide or another attempt on his life like the one that had taken place the day he was arraigned.

His assailant, James Palmer, a security officer at the Railroad Arms and part-time pimp, had played out as a story of interest weeks earlier. Beaver Cleaver's final victim had been a prostitute in his association, and Palmer had acted out of proprietary interest. When no one came forward to claim his body, it was interred at city expense in Strangers' Field. Palmer's slayer, Morris Shiel, a former dock foreman at Volcanic Wholesale Plumbing Supplies, had also disappeared from public view after a manslaughter charge against him was dropped for his action to protect the life of a prisoner in custody.

The city council had appointed Lieutenant William Casey to finish Russell's term of office. After the swearing-in ceremony, with Mayor Wilding at his side, Casey had declared his intention to run for his own term in November. There simply wasn't time enough in the news day to cover yet another burial in a city whose below-ground population was triple the one above.

Father Emiliano Rojas of St. Anne's led the Killian mass at Our Lady of Perpetual Misery, where he'd been assigned until the arch-diocese could select a pastor to replace Dungannon. The mandolin plunks and plinks of drips from the roof contrapunted the singing of the choir.

The cathedral was filled for the first time since the mass for Martha Rose Russell, with tarpaulins slung from the ceiling to shelter those seated directly beneath the leaks. Standees crowded the back. Archibald Vail Killian had entered Gas City alone as a young man, but like a pebble cast into a quiet pool had sent forth ripples without end in the form of grandchildren, great-grandchildren, nieces, nephews, and their children and grandchildren. Most of them followed the casket, local fir with stainless-steel handles as the plain old man had requested, to Mount Ararat Cemetery along the wandering path Arch had walked through the city every morning for ten years as the sun lifted itself from the wallow of the Boggen Drain. Hearse, limousine, sedans, compacts, station wagons, vans, two-seater convertibles, and pickups with trade names painted on the doors of the cabs crawled east on Cathedral past the Knights of Columbus Hall, south on Commercial between Volcanic Wholesale Plumbing Supplies (closed, awaiting new ownership) and *The Derrick*; east again on Boiler Row, where merchants sold auto parts and hardware and storm windows from barrackslike buildings erected on the sites of peeling Victorian mansions once cut up into rental rooms where Arch had lived as a bachelor. Around the Circle then and north on Seventh to the river, with the obelisks of the convention center shining like sheet metal one block over. On East Riverside, in a gusty wind seasoned with water and cut grass and effluvia made harmless by the precise balance of lethal chemicals released by the refinery, the casket was lowered into the ground beside Elizabeth Noonan Killian's before a red marble double marker whose final date had waited to be chiseled for seventeen years.

The casket held a secret, known only to Earl and his wife and kept from their two children, who had reached the magpie stage of long memory and promiscuous repetition: Arch's ashes, cremated according to his wishes and in secrecy, to prevent bickering in a family evenly divided between orthodoxy and casual faith. More controversy still would have erupted over the fact that Arch's son had withheld a few ounces of his father's mortal remains from the casket and placed them in an empty peanut butter jar in his wife's kitchen until after the services. Its destination was illegal according to a city ordinance, but that had meant little to a man who'd been accustomed to discharging an unregistered pistol in a public park.

At supper hour the next day, alone as directed, Earl Killian set out with the peanut butter jar along the same route, on foot. It was late autumn, chilly, and his breath came out in silver jets, but very soon he was sweating. As a middle-aged man in fair condition, he could not fathom how the old man had made that trek daily. Glaciers had plowed deep furrows into the townsite, shoving up the earth on either side, and when he wasn't laboring up a hill he was trying to brake himself to avoid tumbling like a snowball down to the base of the next. The distance was three miles from point to point but easily ten in terms of surface. He fell once, dropping the jar, and spent five anxious minutes spreading clumps of tall razor grass with swiveling motions of his feet before he found it, unbroken with its lid in place, against a fist-size rock that reminded him a little of the old man, weathered and mottled, with a sharp spine. He picked it up, intending it as a keepsake, then discarded it when it grew too heavy in his hand. The surveyor's tough constitution had died with his father.

At last he crossed FDR Parkway, sprinting across six lanes in a brief lull caused by staggered stoplights, and clambered up one more hill to stand at the northeast corner of the park. A half century of beer bottles, newspapers, orange skins, coffee filters, toenails, broken chairs, mattresses, hair snarls, and disposable diapers had found the bottom finally of acres of swamp once owned by the McGrath family and been frosted over with earth and sod, with swings and slides and bridle paths and a softball diamond placed on top.

Here, approximately, was where Arch had come fact to face with Morse I, been called a kneeler and shanty Irish and threatened, and saved the old industrialist from swallowing his tongue in an epileptic fit and been thrown off, to take his reward later in the form of a job that saw him through thirty-nine years to retirement. He'd never seen Morse again in person, but the picture he drew from memory had been more vivid than any his son had seen in books and newsreels. Earl knew the story by heart. He'd repeated it to his children, with all his father's pauses and chuckles and timely throat-clearings intact, like an itinerant poet singing his verses throughout the ancient world for his crust of bread; but whenever Arch had been in earshot he'd found something to correct, the model of McGrath's museum-piece touring car or what Lou Pupkin had said about the old man being rabid or the size of the uprooted tree that had stalled his vehicle and forced him to continue his journey on foot through muck and water and venomous snakes. (The snakes were a one-time feature, never repeated.) He'd suspected Arch of changing the details on purpose to maintain proprietorship, like Grandma withholding a key ingredient from a recipe to keep anyone from duplicating it. Now he could tell it without interruption, but it would always be Arch Killian's story.

Earl sat on the low stone wall, pocked all over where the Mauser had missed its targets, to catch his breath and slow his heartbeat while traffic swished and clicked along the parkway, ten miles over the limit but still well within the commonlaw margin of grace observed outside holiday weekends. In his father's time, all this had been malarial marsh and worked-over fields, with only the burnished copper domes of the McGrath tanks and arrogantly upraised finger of the burning stack to mark how far industry had managed to penetrate the wilderness.

His son could not picture it. But he remembered when the parkway was two lanes of narrow bleached-out concrete with the tracks of the extinct interurban separating them before they were torn up and Big Mike's yellow bulldozers ground the clapboard stores on either side into the dirt to widen the street and cut the travel time between the eastern and western city boundaries from forty minutes to fifteen, provided you went ten over the limit. In those days there were still some entrenched citizens who persisted in giving their address as Garden Grove. He remembered when City Hall had a clock tower and the year all the one-room school-teachers throughout the district were rounded up like snarling dingoes to bully six-year-olds in the new elementary school. He remembered—but had he incinerated his father only to take his place as the family raconteur? It was no great feat to have been present at something and outlived all the witnesses who could correct your account. Poor Lou Pupkin, slumbering somewhere in Europe alongside his companions in fatigues and dog tags, would remember what he'd said on this spot better than anyone; people remembered their own words spoken scores of years ago, even if they couldn't recall what they'd said that had started the argument they were involved in right now. Earl's own children would tell their kids how old Chief Russell carried their grandfather's casket and crime was contained to the Circle and Little Brazil. Everyone was an old-timer.

The wind came up, swelling west from Blacksnake Lane with its olfactory memory of animal entrails from the vanished tanneries; the city, too, had its store of anecdotes to share. The sun hung just above West Riverside. He rose, stepped over the wall, whispered a verse from Psalm 1—*And he shall be like a tree planted by the rivers of water, that bringeth forth his fruit in his season*—Arch's favorite; unscrewed the lid, and cast the jar's gray-and-white contents in a sweeping upward loop. They separated in a cloud that dusted the grass and caught a swirling pocket that sent them across FDR Parkway, past Our Lady of Perpetual Misery, and on toward Gas City's tallest hill, where Morse McGrath's flame burned and burned without consuming.

About the Author

Loren D. Estleman has written more than sixty novels. His work has been awarded four Shamus Awards for detective fiction, five Golden Spur Awards for Western fiction, and three Western Heritage Awards, among many professional honors. His most recent book is *American Detective*, the nineteenth novel featuring Amos Walker. He is currently working on *Frames*, the first novel in a new series of mysteries. He lives with his wife, author Deborah Morgan, in Michigan.

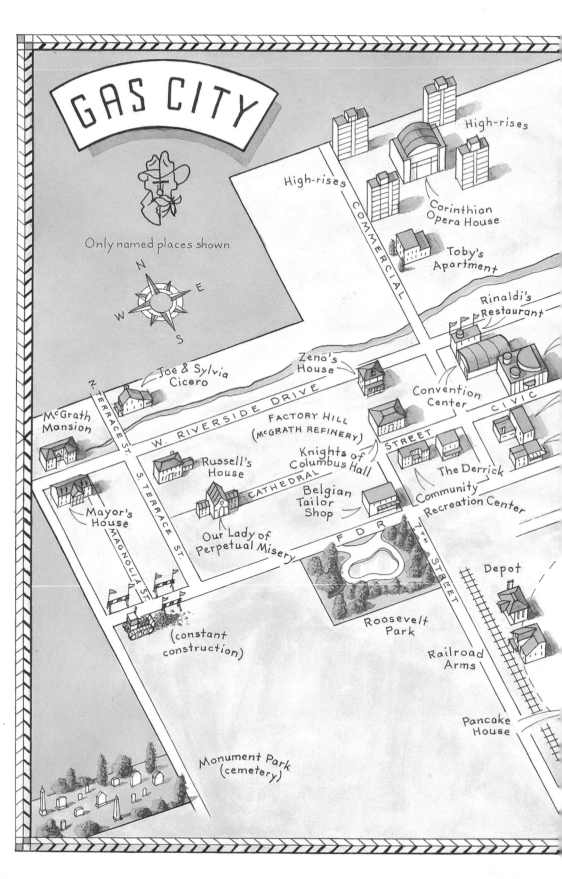